Becoming the Stillness
Part 1, Voices of Madness

Book Five of the Stillness Series

Richard Lee Ferguson

BECOMING THE STILLNESS PART 1, VOICES OF MADNESS

Book Cover by Bookfly Design, James Egan

Illustrations by Brian Bowes

Published: 2025

ISBN: 978-1-966776-06-2 (paperback)

ISBN: 978-1-966776-07-9 (hardback)

ISBN: 978-1-966776-08-6 (ebook)

"What is life? A madness. What is life? An illusion, a shadow, a
story. And the greatest good is little enough; for all life is a dream,
and dreams themselves are only dreams."

— Pedro Calderon de la Barca

"Science has not yet taught us if madness is or is not the sublimity
of the intelligence."

— Edgar Allan Poe

Also by Richard Lee Ferguson

The Stillness Series

Book 1: Stirring the Stillness, Part 1 Voices of Quest

Book 2: Stirring the Stillness, Part 2 Tortured Journey

Book 3: Stilling the Stillness, Part 1 Voices of War

Book 4: Stilling the Stillness, Part 2 Restless Spirits

Book 5: Becoming the Stillness, Part 1 Voices of Madness

Book 6: Becoming the Stillness, Part 2 Haunted Caves

Book 7: The Hunchback's Gift, Part 1 Voices of Defeat

Book 8: The Hunchback's Gift, Part 2 Superior Ones Risen

Book 9: Flames of Extinction, Part 1 The Last Voice

Book 10: Flames of Extinction, Part 2 Stillness is Stilled

For the full series, visit the Amazon series page: https://www.amazon.com/dp/B0F1WJ5J4N

Contents

Principal Characters

Voices – God and Goddess

Michael Powers – Narrator
  Storyteller – Michael Powers' nickname in the war
  Nature – Best friend of Storyteller in war
  Diane Powers – Deceased wife of Michael Powers
  Gail Hess – Psychiatrist
  Adam Camara – Psychiatrist
  Buandelgereen – Mongol woman
  Mark and My-duyen Powers – Son and daughter-in-law of Michael Powers
  Nguyen Tuyet Mai – Vietnamese intelligence officer
  Doctor Tavaris – Psychiatrist
  Emile Ruska – Detective
  Emma – Waitress, friend of Emile Ruska
  Tamara Powers – Wife of Michael Powers
  Child of Buddha – Mother of Tamara Powers
  Doctor DeRuntz – Psychiatrist
  John Powers – Father of Michael Powers
  Bai Meiying – Mother of Michael Powers
  Marie Telles – Friend of Bai Meiying
  Temulun – Talking dog
  Madame Dau – Vietnamese Village Council leader
  Ming-huà Powers – Child of Michael and Tamara Powers

Preface

Can Humans Be Replaced Peacefully?

Query: Are you one of the increasing numbers of people who think humans are irredeemably destructive and pose such a threat to the planet that their extinction would be a good thing? However, do you also abhor the massive destruction and suffering that would necessarily be the consequence of their demise? Bloody, violent dystopian novels often focus only on a few survivors of such devastation, not on the suffering that would extend to all other life forms on the planet. While there are many excellent dystopian novels, such a formulaic concentration on a small group of heroic protagonists can be narrow and unsatisfying.

So, how to unravel the ubiquitous human presence without simultaneously destroying the rest of the planetary ecosystem? Can a successor species evolve fast enough to replace humankind, or would it be extinguished before it has a chance to spread?

Such a successor species, by random chance or intentional design, must possess far greater cognitive and empathetic capacities to thwart the human proclivity for eliminating real or perceived threats. What would it be like for those first generations of advanced individuals surrounded by a sea of slow-witted but resourceful *Homo sapiens*? How would they survive the human penchant for fearing otherness and a relentless instinct to exterminate it? Whether the guiding force effectuating this change is Nature, Superior Alien, God or Gods, Goddess or Goddesses, here is an interesting way forward:

Replace *Homo sapiens* with a more advanced species, but not *drive* them to extinction through violent extermination, rather *dilute* their genes to insignificance over generations. There is precedent for such top-down genetic engineering. Human biologists eliminate dangerous pests by introducing mutant strains that breed with the targeted species to produce offspring harboring the desired genetic makeup. Generations later, the original species is superseded.

A new form of consciousness must necessarily arise—one in which strange Voices with immense cognitive power reverberate in advanced minds in the same way Voices once arose in the minds of early *Homo sapiens separating them from competitors such as Neanderthals*. Humans would initially diagnose those hearing such new Voices as schizophrenics, but they are, in fact, the incipient stirrings of a superior species. However, new Voices must be only the beginning, as this emerging species must also evolve powerful physical capabilities to overcome human weapons of destruction.

The doves must have sharper claws than the hawks . . .

The Stillness Series is the epic story of one such scenario.

Prologue

~ *Dear, dear Reader* ~

I thought I was alive, but now it is clear that I am not. My fleshless bones attest to that. Not even Nature comes to visit anymore. Such darkness. So, this is Singularity.—and the silence!—well, except for these screaming thoughts. Screaming? No, not quite. Echoing is a better description. In Singularity, even echoes cannot escape. Of course they cannot. If light cannot, then the weak reverberations of human thought most certainly cannot. Does a skeleton appear white in a black hole? Yes, yes, I know. A skeleton cannot exist in a black hole.

~ *Madness Has a Voice* ~

There are wars that rupture the body.
And there are wars that rupture the mind.
The first has passed. The second has only begun.
In the ruins of memory, those who lived through the jungle fortress now find themselves adrift in quieter lands—but no less dangerous. Hospitals with locked wards. Classrooms with hollow questions. Deserts where time folds in on itself. Silence now howls.

Michael, once a soldier, now stalks the hallways of Columbia University, a twin trailing behind him—mute, armed, impossible.

Mark, his son, begins to hear a voice that does not belong to him. Or perhaps it always did.

Theresa, once a healer, watches as love becomes diagnosis, and intimacy breeds suspicion.

Tuyet Mai, if she still exists, now moves through others like a haunting force—neither living nor dead, but more *present* than either.

And hovering in the background, **Goddess** grows closer. No longer a distant totem, *She* steps forward—wearing human faces. Breaking human minds.

This is not mere madness. This is the price of *knowing*—of having seen too much and failed to forget. Here, the past does not return. It never left.

The Precious Object is not spoken of in this place. But its echo remains, in the broken syllables of those who tremble before mirrors, and ask: *Who am I now? Who was I then?* And worst of all—*What if both were lies?*

This is the book of shattered selves. The birth canal of the Superior Ones begins in blood and delusion.

~ *Questions, Questions* ~

And so the questions sharpen—

If your mind fractures under the weight of history, is that sickness—or awakening?

When the world declares you insane, is it truth—or defense?

And if the stillness is not silence, but what comes after all voices have collapsed—who remains to listen?

~ *First Things First* ~

Well, be that as it may, you probably wonder, dear Reader, what is there to discover in this book? Will the continuation of my story be entertaining? Amusing? Should you continue reading and spend your valuable time? No, if you find only your fellow humans interesting. Yes, if you find all fellow inhabitants of the planet interesting—Chosen Ones along with all other life forms—ants, dogs, Gods and Goddesses. Furthermore, I include the non-living—rocks and dirt, for example. Worried, dear Reader? You should be.

God has abandoned me, but I sense **Goddess** stirs somewhere in the ink. Perhaps She succeeded in breaking His opposition, in which case humanity is on the brink of extinction. Do you? Still suffer I mean. Perhaps, in your roguish sense of humor, you snicker that your suffering exists only in the continued reading of these words. However, be patient, for I will give you a glimpse into the glimpseless depths of Singularity. For it is only here that All Things are truly nothing more than One Thing. A string theorist's dream. And time? Ha! Tomorrow, **Goddess** came to me while Yesterday, She will come; and now I see Her hand.

I take it.

She is leading me out of the tunnel. Out of nothingness.

Nature? Ah, he is gone, as are all the others. Only me . . . and Her.

Am I to be resurrected from the living back to the realm of the dead?

She tugs my hand . . . *follow us.*

Chapter One

Event Horizon

Daze

G oddess has put me back among you. Why? I don't know, but I am standing in broad daylight on a sidewalk in some town or city. My first meaningful encounter is with a dog, as the humans simply pass by without a second look.

"Friend or foe?" he asks, sniffing with the greatest urgency.

"Friend," I reply.

"You're different."

"I'm dead."

"No, I don't think so." He sniffs again. "No, you are definitely not dead," he says, before being dragged away by his master-slave.

This is my first clue that *She* has resurrected me. Always listen to your dog, my father told me before he died. I think he got it from some old Western movie, but I'm not sure.

"See ya!" I call to the furry back.

The dog turns, laughing, tongue lolling out in happy amusement. "Sure thing!" he pants back.

~

It suddenly occurs to me that I just had a conversation with a dog. Dr. Hess would say it is just my voices, but I know better. In fact, I can hear the sidewalk, if I concentrate. It sort of hums, or perhaps moans is a better description, but the sound is all strung out in time, a wail in distorted slow motion, lugubrious sound waves, moaning so low I can only sense them in the roots of my hair.

Although I am resurrected, I have no notion where to go. I had no disciples before, and fewer than zero now. There is no home anymore, or law office to attend. When I ask *Her*, there is no response. *She* has always been fickle. Absurd, really. From my back pocket, I hear a sort of muffled cry. Instinctively, I reach in and pull out a leather wallet. Clear of the complaining fabric of my trousers, I open it and sense a mixture of sounds and smells, from the high-pitched squeak of plastic to the cow's drawn-out death moan. Suffering lingers . . . longer than the Great Wall and weightier than the Pyramids.

Ah, yes, the wallet.
Well . . . what's here?
Driver's license.
Credit cards.
Health insurance card.
All in my name—Michael Powers. How convenient, *She* thinks of everything.
And cash.
Interesting.

~

I quickly put the wallet away, as the death echoes of the dying cow are becoming unbearably sad and irritating. Now what? What does one newly resurrected do? Find shelter, of course. I walk farther and come across a nice hotel. It cries "Shelter!" so I gravitate toward it. My head pounds from all the sounds. Soaring high above the humming chorus, the sun sings a knifing soprano—but it has begun to drop a few octaves. Nothing else to do, so I check in to the hotel and lie on a crisp bed, the mattress silent and pliable as death. (No doubt the poor thing is broken from so much abuse.) On the other hand, the television is contemptuous of such submission, and crackles an invitation to click a button and make it come to life, but I block the electronic plea and focus on where I am and what I am doing. After all, my parents are dead, my wife is dead, I never see my son, my comrades are dead, and my schizophrenia is purged, as my voices, like God, have evidently abandoned me too. In my role of resurrected man, being one who hears the Earth and its inhabitants, perhaps I should be an itinerant sage. Wander and teach, like Zarathustra, or Jesus, or Confucius, or somebody. Somebody. Am I somebody?

I pinch myself. It hurts. I am hungry. I look in the bathroom mirror.

Flesh and blood.

I am somebody.

I have my bones back—and my newborn-ancient skin that covered me in Vietnam has been shed, replaced by ancient-newborn skin in the present. How did I escape the tunnel? How did I escape Singularity? This business about even light being unable to escape is evidently, wrong.

Goddess, *You* are so clever.

Speak to me, my beloved Female Divinity! *You* who badgered my parents into conceiving a son. *You* who braved war and peace and God to find a cure for *His* divine illness. *You* who arranged the Reunion when I inexcusably turned my weapon on *You* instead of *Him*. Oh, such a lofty goal! To detoxify God! Lost causes always attract the romantics among us. From my brief observation since being resurrected, I see it has been to no avail. Suffering continues. That fact must have meaning. I have not yet served my purpose, have I? No. No. No. That's it! All around me, the world still suffers; the dog, the wallet, the sidewalk, the bed, even the sun (forever burning in a fever of unwanted responsibility).

So, first and foremost, dear Reader, to keep you entertained until I free you from suffering by ending my story, I am told by the Gatekeepers that I must conjure up a man and a woman for romance, or perhaps a war for violence and bloodshed, or a murder for mystery, or a dysfunctional family, or drugs, or some such literary conflict. No matter, for in the end, I will have served Goddess, and by so doing, will have served Her purpose. Perhaps I should just let the story tell itself.

First things first.

Where to find a woman or a man to fulfill the romantic need in you, dear Reader? Everywhere.

Where to find a war to fulfill the need for morbid curiosity in you, dear Reader? Everywhere.

Where to find murder to fulfill the need for salacious detail and to pique your primate curiosity? Everywhere.

Where to find literary conflict?—ah, back to woman, man, war, murder, or perhaps drugs, divorce, abuse, dysfunctional families, mental illness, racism, genocide.

Yes, God is everywhere.

Meanwhile, Goddess hides, or is somehow exiled.

I must find *Her*. Only *She* can lead me forward. *She* might have returned to Singularity, but my bones inform me otherwise. Oh, they are very brittle and urge me to hurry before they fossilize and become useless to *Her*.

Where are You, Goddess?

Enough!

I see a print on the wall, a partially clad woman, and suddenly feel horny. Ah, a sign! *She* is here! Goddess, with *Her* bare breasts, moves in mysterious ways, spurring me on to a fully resurrected life. Now, I am hungry and horny. Sure signs of life, indeed!

Moreover, I want bourbon.

Another sign!

Hungry, horny, and thirsty!

I can now officially classify myself as a living person, alive among the living.

Farewell tunnel, for the moment.

She has brought me all the way back.

What a divinity *She* is! What a woman! Forget the writhing snakes, bejeweled sparkles, and esoteric oracles—give me bourbon, food, and sex. Cut to the chase. I am feeling younger by the minute, ready for the hunt.

And what of the hunt?

She is hunting God. She rode atop my parents, John Powers and Bai Meiying, to conceive me. Vietnam, my trial by fire, is behind me. Now, I am a fresh horse. God is still ahead but tiring. Oh, yes, *He* is tiring. Like a Mongol warrior, *She* changes horses without a pause, and the distance closes. Oh, yes! *He* is tiring! *His* drug of choice no longer satisfies, and *His* "flesh of My flesh" is sagging from lack of nutrients. Can *She* overtake *Him* before *He* takes us all down with an addict's fatal overdose?

So, Goddess, I'm waiting for orders. Speak to me.

The air conditioner hums a monotonous answer, pleased to serve; a slave if ever there was one.

But *She* does not speak. My voices are silent. God is clearly not dead, as suffering humanity crowds my brain from all directions. I'm waiting for orders.

Are *You* dead, Goddess? Did Nietzsche get the wrong deity?

Well, it's no good to stay in this room, but like a snake freshly shed of its skin, I am jumpy and overly sensitive to any stimuli. I'll stay for a while, then venture out to . . . to do what?

Eat.

Drink.

Have an adventure.

Meet someone, a woman perhaps.

After all, my old snakeskin lies in a wrinkled spiral on the tunnel floor. I am reborn. My penis, newly alert to stimuli.

Yes, a woman, for I am lonely.

A beautiful woman.

And wait for Goddess to call.

~ *Revelation* ~

Earlier tonight, I decided to venture out and find a restaurant, but the crackling screams of electrocuted bugs merged with the sickly hum of the neon lights, so I quickly ducked back into my room to escape. How am I to function properly in such chaos of suffering? How am I to be ready when She calls? The answer is that I must wrap myself in some insulating substance until my senses are dull enough to cope. Being human is abnormal enough, let alone being a resurrected schizophrenic Chosen One. Still, I am determined to venture out and let the chips fall where they may. I know something will turn up. After all, suffering still exists, and *She* has a plan to use me for a purpose. *Her* glorious purpose. Yes. Yes. *She* will come to me.

For now, I must eat. The journey from a skeleton in a mineral tomb to flesh-and-blood existence among you—the dying—has left me famished. To-morrow, my first task will be to eat. I must walk the moaning sidewalks to find a restaurant, where the low, reverberating wail of those sacrificed spirits must be awful. If I don't prevail over the sensory assault, I will certainly return to Singularity. Again. For now, the sanctuary of the hotel room will suffice.

I try to gird myself for the inevitable journey outside to some charnel house where I must eat. In the corner, the television stares at me with an unblinking, accusing eye, while the bed seems to decay before my eyes. Worse, the prints on the walls all demand to be noticed, each flashing its own varicolored display, preening flirtatiously, like strutting prostitutes in an old-time brothel.

I really am hungry. Very, very hungry. Enough to brave the night again and find a place to eat? Perhaps. But the fear remains, spurred on by my still open wounds. Perhaps just go to bed and sleep? But, when I look at the bed, I feel as though it would smother me in a death shroud, and my newly acquired flesh and blood body would suffocate. Yes, that is why I'm so hungry; I must eat to keep this body from melting away to its truest and purest form—skeletal.

So, I don a coat from a closet that has miraculously filled with clothes—*She* is quite enterprising—and I venture out a second time. As I close the door, the room becomes silent, like a fairy tale about toys that become lifeless when morning arrives. An adolescent urge gets the better of me, and I quickly open the door again, hoping to catch the room in some otherworldly act. I am met with the television turned on, facing me and blaring the words of a man shouting.

"Go! Go!" he bellows.

Now, you might think, dear Reader, that I would be scared at this sight. Not at all. The man's insistent tone implies something I already know, tonight I am destined to meet someone important, ergo, I must leave the room. Dr. Hess would explain all this to me by reciting a diagnosis she feels quite confident about; these feelings of grandeur, the notion that I am somehow a special "Chosen One,"—are nothing more than the type of delusions associated with schizophrenia. But then, how could she explain my being resurrected? Surely, this goes far beyond delusion. Oh, she has also a response to this, of course, and invariably ends up blaming my poor father for passing on his infected genes, and the Vietnam War for triggering those insidious genes to a virulence far exceeding anything my father experienced.

In any case, when I nod at the television man, he stops shouting at me, smiles, and the set turns itself off. Gently closing the door, I walk down the hallway as if I were Storyteller back in the jungle. Booby traps everywhere, you know. Not that the carpet would let on about booby traps, it is deceptively soft and sighs almost in coital pleasure as I tiptoe; grateful, I suppose, for my light tread. Still, the carpet is perfect camouflage for any traps set in ambush, so I can't be too careful. I learned from the war that one must not allow oneself to be lulled into overconfidence. I take the stairs down to the front entrance of the hotel. No way I take the elevator; it is nothing more than an angry box of metal machinery pulsing with the oily nectar of a Venus Fly Trap.

Okay, so far so good. Outside, the hissing neon and swarm of moths in their eternal search for the God of Light have become more subdued. The sidewalk still moans, but I notice I now possess an ability to tamp down the raucous chords of All Things. I can function now. I can do this. By the time I reach the restaurant, my confidence has grown, and I am certain I can pass as normal.

There's a smattering of customers.

"Corner booth, please."

The waitress bestows the menu. Odd, but humans seem less real than moths and sidewalks. I look at the unfolded chronicle of death and order a simple hamburger and fries, something we would have gladly died for in Vietnam.

"To drink?"

"Decaf, please."

The vinyl of the booth and wood of the table are silent, even the usually raucous utensils and misshapen condiment bottles say nothing. That fact makes me wonder. Are they holding their breaths in anticipation of something? I look around.

Then I notice her.

She sits at the counter, alone, and for whatever reason is given a wide berth by the gregarious waitresses, who joke openly with the customers and each other. Yet, when they pass close to her, they fall silent and lower their eyes. I crane to see what she is eating but can only make out what appears to be a cup of tea or coffee. The steam seems to curl toward me, as someone might curve his or her index finger to beckon a friend closer. I want to rise and go to her, but a sudden fear rivets me to the seat. She still has not turned, and I have not seen her face, but the contours of her flowing hair and sinuous body are eerily hypnotic.

Her words come to me.

Mr. Powers, how does one justify a life without cruelty, and therefore also without the distilled beauty of cruelty?

Yes, yes, of course—it's *She!* My father's siren. My mother's polestar. My savior and my nemesis.

~

Naturally, *She* did not really speak the words. They came to me like my old voices, the fulfillment of a prophecy. *She* has not yet turned around. Okay, *She* does not have to turn around. I know, with those words, that *she* beckons, I must serve, it is the purpose of my birth, my *raison d'être*. Just as I am about to rise and go to *Her*, the waitress approaches with my food. When she sets it before me, she lets out a hearty, "Here you are, sweetie! Anything else?"

I listen for the death groan of the slaughtered cow or the damp thud of multiple guillotines performing potato dismemberment, but I hear nothing. Even the decaf coffee emits only a distant hiss. Thank Goddess. *She* has turned off the spigot, for now. Without guilt, I am ravenous and tear into the food like the crazed predator I am. Fortunately, I still have enough presence of mind to check on *Her*.

Yes.

Still there.

Good. A few more bites, then I call to *her*.

She sits like a statue.

Good.

A few more bites. Just a few.

Still there.

More. Eat quickly, Michael.

Good. Still hungry.

More.

It is as if I have not eaten in years, which, of course, I have not. At least, not since the war, when I was left in that damn tunnel. My last bite of the hamburger, and I feel its blood squirt all over the inside of my mouth, filling it up, flowing down my throat, accompanied by a horrible squeal of pain and the odor of rusty iron singeing my nose. I am instantly nauseous and vomit out the bloody food onto my plate. I grab a napkin to wipe the mess from my mouth and chin, then look up to see if *She* is still at the counter. But no. *She* now sits across from me in the booth, staring.

Mr. Powers, how does one justify a life without cruelty, and therefore also without the distilled beauty of cruelty?

That damned question again!

The waitress approaches with a concerned expression, carrying a towel, but one look from my strange companion causes the poor woman to promptly retreat in confusion. She looks back uncomprehendingly, as if suddenly afflicted with dementia.

She looks back at me.

"Give me your instructions," I say.

She blinks and says, **You have not answered my question.**

Her words, when spoken aloud, have a huskier, muskier quality than when spoken in my mind. I detect the scent of Earth itself in *Her* breath—a deep mineral fecundity, the words slow and tectonic in primordial impact, capable of raising entire mountains, or destroying entire cities.

"This question is for my father, not me," I protest.

John Powers is dead.

"Also, for my mother."

Bai Meiying is dead.

"I must talk with my friend Paul."

You have no friend Paul. He and his children were delusions created in a mind starved for family.

"That is not true! At the beach. Paul and Claire arguing! John and Lisa playing in the sand! They were real! They are real!"

No, Michael, none of them are real. Paul, Claire, John, Lisa, Theresa, all figments of your illness. You were alone at the beach that day. You dug the sandcastle. You placed Mark's toys inside. Lisa's doll was one of Diane's best loved possessions when she was a little girl. Your parents had one child, a son. Not twins. You still have not answered my question.

"But . . . Ethyl?"

Ethyl is an entirely different story. Truth be told, Theresa is also a different story, but that must wait for another time.

I am dazed by these rapid-fire revelations. "But. . . . " I stammer. "Diane must have been real! And our son Mark!"

Yes, and her death accelerated your . . . condition. Mark is also real, married to the Vietnamese woman, My-duyen. Remember? That caused quite an uproar at the time. You railed against the marriage thinking My-duyen was a spirit planted by God. But you got over that particular human delusion. So yes, My-duyen is also real. Now, answer my question.

I shake my head in confusion and despair. "The question is not for me. I don't see the point. Just give me my orders, and I will obey."

Her beauty entraps me in a dizzying miasma of wonder, but I hold it together and wait. The restaurant melts away, leaving only the two of us in a booth, surrounded by thick fog.

Fate starves at Probability's door.

I slam my fist on the table in frustration. "More dredged up platitudes! Just give me my instructions."

She calmly stares at me, this time unblinking for what seems an eternity, as might the frozen tableaux of a beautiful woman.

Kill your son, *she* finally says.

"What? No!"

Now *she* blinks. **Good. Your very first order, and you disobey it?**

"Damn right."

Good. You are not of Him. Cursed be those who obey the unobeyable.

"My real orders?" I ask, relieved.

First, you must escape from this place.

"The restaurant?" I ask stupidly.

Dear Chosen One, you are not in a restaurant.

"Where am I?"

The institution.

"Is that where I have been all along?"

Yes.

"I suspected as much," I lie. "But, how can I escape?"

Where there is a will, there is a way.

"How?'

The path lies through Dr. Hess and those who serve her.

"And if I do escape?"

Then your mission will start.

A sudden, inexplicable chill makes me reflexively fold my arms and rock. "I want to go back to the tunnel and see Nature and the others again," I say petulantly.

You cannot.

"It's easy," I unfold my arms and hold out my hands, palms up. "Just return to Dr. Hess's bathroom. It's a portal, you know."

She stares, unblinking, for an impossibly long time, with eyes like two miniature suns that perpetually shine through the void, and I am intimidated.

"Okay," I say. "I will not return to the tunnel. When I escape, what then? Where do I go?"

The house of Marie Telles.

"Marie Telles! Why? Is she still alive?"

She is an old woman, living alone in the same San Francisco mansion, dreaming of your mother.

"And her brother?"

Dead. You must go to her house and wait.

"But this makes no sense. Even a mental patient can see that. She'll be afraid, turn me back over to the institution, call the police. She is of my parents, not me."

Your parents and she are of you, and you are of them.

~ Clarity ~

"Mr. Powers, your medication."

That is Joe, a new intern. Black guy. Nice. He might be someone who can help me escape. He is new, and still unsure about things. Yes, I can use him.

"Sure thing, Joe. Hand it over," I say as chirpily as I can.

"Glad to have you back," he says.

After I swallow the pill, I put on my best quizzical expression. "Huh? Back from where, Joe?"

"Why, the tunnel of course. Dr. Hess announced it to us a few days ago. Guess you were pretty much out of it for weeks, curled up in your imaginary tunnel like some weird fetus."

"Oh, yeah. Right."

I look around my room as if I had just returned. Nothing has changed since I've been away—same cold, sterile walls. No echoes of suffering. No groaning, moaning, or any other sounds to make me feel I am alive. Nothing quite makes one feel more alive than being surrounded by the dead and dying. Now that I am resurrected, I have a mission. The first step is to escape this place, but not to return to the tunnel. Oh, no. *She* made that quite clear. Oddly enough, it's on to Marie Telles's house. Why?

"Joe?"

"Yeah?"

"You want to let me out?" I laugh to let him know it is a joke.

He laughs back. "Of course. I'll just unlock these eight hundred iron doors, and you can prance right out. But once you're out, Mr. Powers, what would you do?"

His joke about iron doors gives me a jolt, but I gamely move on, replying with a grin, "Go to a restaurant and have a hamburger and fries."

Joe gets a kick out of this and shows his gleaming white teeth in a wide smile. For a moment—just a moment, mind you—he turns into X, and then into T. And for a moment—just a moment, mind you—I am back in the tunnel, shouting at Nature, "Alive! Alive! Alive!" But it soon passes.

Evidently, I have become a little more violent than I realize. Joe grabs my arms. "Shhh! Shhh! It's okay, Mr. Powers. Sit on the bed for a while and relax. That's good."

I sit on the bed to humor Joe, but my mind has already moved on. You must be spry to keep up with a schizophrenic, and that is my ace in the hole with Joe. How can I use him to escape? *She* said all paths lead through Dr. Hess, but this newbie doesn't yet know the ropes. Perhaps all paths lead through Joe . . . and his keys.

"Joe," I say nicely and calmly. "You know why I'm in here?"

"Sure," he replies, still hovering over me as if I'll jump up and hurt myself.

"Why am I in here?"

"Schizophreeeenia." He pronounces it oddly.

"True, but lots of schizophrenics are out there on the street and doing just fine."

"I know, but I'm told you have other issues."

"Like what?"

Joe shakes his head sympathetically. "Oh, I'm not supposed to talk about it. Confidentiality, and all that. 'Specially can't talk about it with you."

"Why not?"

"Dunno. Orders."

"Well, you seem like a square guy to me, Joe. Aren't you curious about what my *other issues* are?"

"Already know . . . well, some of them, anyway."

"Like what?"

He vigorously shakes his head. "No, no, Mr. Powers, you ain't going to trick me. Got my orders."

"And you need the job that badly?"

"Sure, got a family to feed, like everyone else."

"Me too, Joe."

"Yeah."

I try another tack. "Joe, were you in the war?"

"Which war?"

"You know."

"Vietnam?"

"Yes."

Joe snorts. "Look at me, Mr. Powers, I'm too young for that war."

"Your father?"

A shadow crosses his face.

I have him.

"Yeah, he was in it," says Joe. "Somethin' happened."

I know. I know what happened, Joe, but I will play out the string. "What unit and when was he there, maybe I knew him," I say as innocently as possible.

"He was killed."

I know, Joe, I know. "Oh, sorry." I am sincere.

I have him. After letting a respectful moment pass, I ask very gently, "What unit was he in?"

"First Cavalry Division, I think. That's all I know."

"Year?"

"Nineteen sixty-nine."

"Ah, sorry." Should I risk more? I decide yes. "Think you could find out what unit of the First Cav he was in—you know, battalion, company, that type of thing?"

Joe gives me a suspicious look.

"I was there in nineteen sixty-nine. First Cavalry Division. Find out, if you can." I put on my best sad face. "Maybe I knew him."

Joe shakes his head, clearly hesitant to commit.

Can't let him get away.

"Joe, I was out in the bush with a lot of Black guys. Find out, for me, would ya?"

He nods. "I'll try."

I have him. Definitely.

"Thank you, Joe."

Now all I have to do is wait. I can do it, but the mansion draws me to it, and I must fight the temptation. To pass the time until Joe returns with the information, I arrange to meet with Dr. Hess. My sessions with her are always memorable trips to exotic mental hideaways. It's still not clear to me whether she is my psychiatrist or Goddess of my voices. Alas, she no longer bares her breasts to me—not since I came back from the tunnel. In fact, she admonished me just a few days ago when I asked her to disrobe and reveal her true self. She was angry and snapped, "Mr. Powers, that particular role-playing is no longer useful. You know I'm not your Goddess. In fact, you used that ploy to get into my private bathroom, with terrible results. Besides, you never did believe it, did you?"

"Your office bathroom is the portal to the tunnel," I insisted stubbornly.

"Nonsense, and you know it. Now, we both know you do not think I am this Goddess, Mr. Powers, and I will not fall for that trick again."

"And the disappearing figurine?"

She sighed and said, "That one I am still trying to figure out."

She probably got in trouble for that role-playing, but I'm still not convinced she's merely my psychiatrist rather than Goddess. Anyway, we haven't had a good talk since I returned. Now is the time to have a little fun. No better way to pass the time, at least, until Joe gets back to me—and God knows how long that will take. Oh, how I'm looking forward to our meeting!

Chapter Two

Doctor Hess

First Session Since Resurrection

Dr. Gail Hess has managed to retain her lovely demeanor and physical beauty despite the daily assaults of agonized patients, some violent and passionate in their freakish outbursts, some depressed and suicidal—all dragging her into the noxious abyss of their own neurological swamps.

Daily, she faces the void of bottomless depression, the endless torture rack of bipolar extremes, the faceless faces of dissociated personalities, and the ever-mercurial acid trips, courtesy of schizophrenia. Yet, oddly enough, her face projects an impenetrable granite wall of calm. Many of her co-workers admire and resent her persona as though she were a well-oiled machine.

Unfortunately, as with all of us, the sandy grains of misgiving flung into the cogs of perfection create friction, which occasionally causes the machinery to emit a perceptible grinding noise.

As she waits for the arrival of Mr. Powers, Gail is uncomfortably aware of his unnerving ability to detect that very grinding. Still unnerved by his trickery in having her bare her breasts to satisfy his Goddess delusion, she has vowed to prevail in their endless game of wits. To Gail, he represents either the cornerstone of professional fame, or the vehicle in which they might drive off a cliff to mutual destruction.

His latest setback, locked in fetal isolation while his psyche dissociated and cavorted in that damned tunnel doing God-knows-what, truly scared her. "Lost for good," she despairingly confided in June Moore, her assistant and closest confidante.

Now, she ponders the latest conundrum: what brought him back?

"Mr. Powers is here," announced June, her voice tinged with trepidation.

"Let him wait awhile," replied Gail. "I'll buzz you."

"You got it," winked June.

Hess toyed with a paper clip, double-checked her recorder, and continued to delay. *Long enough*, she thought. *Why not just buzz and get it over with? Nervous, Gail?*

In one decisive motion, she buzzed, and he soon appeared through the door. She remained seated, a professional smile on her face.

"Hello, Mr. Powers. Have a seat."

"Thank you."

He sat and gazed at her, like a stranded sailor eyeing a gorgeous mirage. His words came fast and choppy. "My Goddess, as is our custom, will You bare Your breasts for me?"

Hess let out a groan. "Mr. Powers, we have discussed this already. No more of that nonsense."

"Just kidding. Have you lost your sense of humor since I've been away?" He glanced at her bathroom door.

"And no more of that nonsense, either!" scolded Hess.

"My Goddess is angry," pouted Michael.

"You said you wanted to see me?"

"Yes."

"And?"

Michael grinned sheepishly. "Are you sure you won't bare your breasts?"

"Can we get past your little joke, Mr. Powers?"

Michael straightened in his chair. "Absolutely. I would like to be released."

"You know I can't do that. What I want to know, Mr. Powers, is how you made that figurine disappear."

"My son, Mark, will sign the release papers. No liability to you or the institution." He brushed his hands together. "Then, we're done. Poof! And this charade will be over. You can then get back to people who really need you, assuming you really are a psychiatrist. Or, alternatively, You can ascend back to heaven, assuming You really are my Goddess."

"As you are aware, Mr. Powers, your son has placed you in our care until we determine your fitness for coping with the outside world. Now, how did you make that figurine disappear?"

"You were quite attached to it?"

"Yes. How?"

"Want me to make something else disappear?"

"Yes."

"Not unless you release me."

"You will remain in our care until we determine you can function in the outside world."

Michael smiled. "You mean the real world?"

"Whatever you wish to call it."

"I wish to call it the shadow world. Plato's Cave. Illusory. I was just yanked from the real world. In darkness, I saw behind the flames that project your forms."

"You mean your tunnel?"

"I mean Singularity."

"And what did you experience in this Singularity?"

"Ho, ho! My dear Goddess—You were there!"

Dr. Hess unconsciously picked up her twisted paper clip. "Mr. Powers, this line of discussion will get us nowhere. Until and unless you stop deflecting with this Goddess business, further talk is a waste of time."

"I thought this is supposed to be talk therapy, Dr. Freud."

"You don't strike me as a nineteenth-century woman suffering from hysteria, Mr. Powers."

"And you, Dr. Hess, do not strike me as a twenty-first century therapist solely interested in the well-being of her patient."

This stung, but Gail refrained from commenting.

Michael continued, "I am your ticket to fortune and fame." He stared conspicuously at her recorder. "Grist for the mill, eh, Doc?"

"Quite the contrary. Your case has degenerated into a pattern of little mind games, which is the most common of the common defensive ploys tried by intelligent patients. Certainly not worthy of publication."

"And while I was gone, in my tunnel, is that why you had to intravenously feed me to keep me from starving, because I was playing a mind game? You really don't know anything! Unless, of course, you know everything. Would making things disappear be worthy of publication?"

"I suppose that little remark is intended to obliquely refer to your Goddess?"

"You see, you do know everything."

"More mind games, Mr. Powers. By the way, who told you we intravenously fed you?"

Michael wasn't about to implicate Joe. "No one."

"Then you were aware. You did not dwell in any tunnel, or Singularity, or whatever you choose to call it. You knew what went on around you. More games, Mr. Powers."

Michael fell silent, his face hardening into an angry scowl.

"I think this session is finished," declared Hess with a certain degree of gloating finality.

Michael's face transformed into something like an alien oracle, and he spoke in a low, rasping whisper. "You know, the funny thing is that your certainty regarding me is fatal to your goal . . . your ambition. If you are Goddess, then this is a test, and it is of no consequence, since I am faithfully performing the mission You have assigned me. On the other hand, if you are indeed simply a clueless psychiatrist, then you just failed miserably, and tonight, when you lie in bed, remember that you are but a shadow among shadows. This I can tell you: my descendants will make things disappear—including the human race. I am only the beginning."

Dr. Hess felt his words wash over her like a powerful wave of sincerity and undeniable truth, and her certainty again faltered under this man's dexterous shape-shifting.

"Please call me when you are ready to seriously explore your psychosis, Mr. Powers," she said stiffly and without conviction.

~ *Night Dreams* ~

Dr. Hess finished her work that afternoon in a haze of reflection. Mr. Powers's words scrolled in and out of her mind, leaving her ability to concentrate on other issues in tatters. She deeply resented his supernatural ability to get under her skin, and her professional pride suffered as a result. In response to June's inquiries about her session with Mr. Powers, she mumbled trite civilities, and drove home a troubled woman. Her clean and tastefully decorated apartment greeted her pleasantly enough, and Sigmund, her fluffy gray cat, luxuriated in her presence like a minor monarch. She fed Sigmund, fixed a healthy meal, and went to bed. leaving the case files unopened atop the covers. Sigmund complained about the mess as she dropped off, still propped up by multiple pillows.

Mission! Gail's eyes flew open. *He said he was on a mission for his Goddess! What mission?*

Unable to imagine what his mission might be, she again nodded off, and promptly dreamed.

~

Michael Powers stands before her while she stares down at him from a high bench, a massive wig on her head, passing judgment. She bangs a gavel and says in a low, ponderous voice, "This court finds you guilty."

Michael quakes, and replies in a soft voice, barely perceptible, "Of what?"

Two armed bailiffs stand on either side of him, looking up at Gail for instructions. "Take him away!" she proclaims.

"For what?" he continues to plead. He shakes the bailiffs loose and drops to his knees in front of the bench. "For what?"

Gail stands, the great wig cascades past her shoulders, and she suddenly realizes she is completely naked. The hair from the wig tickles her breasts, and she laughs. The bailiffs again appear, and grab Michael's arms, pulling them behind his back. He breaks free and by some superhuman act, leaps upon the bench, tearing off her wig, revealing a completely shaved head. Now she is levitating above the bench, sitting in the lotus position on a huge, dazzling white flower. Her sad, contemplative face gazes from beneath an elaborate crown glimmering a kaleidoscope of colors. A cinder-bright jewel embedded in her forehead burns brightly and an intricate necklace lay cradled between her bare breasts. Her left-hand rests on her thigh, the upturned curve of her fingers resembling the albino legs of a gracefully dead spider. Her right-hand poises in the air, index finger and thumb touching to form an almost perfect circle while the other fingers radiate outward.

"What is my mission?" Michael asks.

The bailiffs bow in frozen obeisance below the bench. One of them asks toward the floor, "Shall we take him away?"

"No," she says. "He is on a mission for me."

"What is my mission, Goddess?" asks Michael again.

Gail looks down at her naked body and feels an erotic twinge from the feeling of divine power. "Your mission is—"

She senses herself waking from the dream and resists, wanting to tell him the mission, but the words will not come, nor does she know what they will be. "Your mission is—"

~

With a jerk, she sat up, awake.

~

You're in my head again, aren't you, Mr. Powers? This Goddess business is really something. The war, the tunnel, the ants, your dreams, Goddess—Christ! What a cornucopia of psychotic gifts, yet I cannot get past this one thing. I bare my breasts to be your Goddess. I dream I am your Goddess. I talk about your Goddess. I think about your Goddess. What an odd archetype for a contemporary man! Of course, you are fixated on her breasts, but that really doesn't explain the whole delusion.

The cat jumped next to her and purred.

Sorry, Sigmund, but your namesake's oral fixations and genital stages make no sense with Mr. Powers. His Goddess is more than breasts and genitalia. Based on his books, Her words are powerful indicators of his deepest, most latent desires. I am getting lost in her power myself. The question that confronted his parents is another key. Problem is, there are far too many keys and not enough doors. 'Mr. Powers,' this Goddess constantly asks. 'How does one justify a life without cruelty, and therefore also without the distilled beauty of cruelty?' Yes, lady, you are insistent about that one, aren't you? Gail let out a deep breath and adjusted Sigmund. *Sleep, for now. I need to talk with Mr. Powers again.*

Next morning, while eating breakfast, Dr. Hess pondered reopening her line of questioning about Michael's religious beliefs. *He certainly is adamant that he does not believe in God, yet at the same time is adamant that God exists, and that Goddess is trying to cure Him of some bizarre addiction. Which is it? Are his psychotic episodes merely the product of a fundamental religious-secular conflict, exacerbating his schizophrenia?* Gail tried to purge her mind of Mr. Powers and force herself to think about other patients, but she drove to work, unable to think about anything but Goddess.

~

Fortunately, the first person she ran into on entering the institute was Dr. Camara, the new Assistant Director. Adam Camara was a tall, lean, handsome man whose friendly, intelligent banter had awakened Gail's dormant sexual murmurings. She had gone out with him only once—for drinks after work—during which he quickly shed his crisp, professional demeanor for that of an intriguing eccentric. Once free of the institute, as they walked to his car, out came a colorful tam o'shanter, which he carefully arranged into a cocky slant on his head. With a Scottish brogue, he said, "Onward, lassie, to a pub!" Despite her penchant for more serious conversation, she laughed freely, and the thrill of liberation swept over her. At the local watering hole, they talked without restraint, his unique sense of humor and self-deprecating banter only deepened her attraction.

Now, as she stood chatting with the amiable Camara, she felt far more like a girl than a Goddess.

"Another happy day!" exclaimed Adam.

"Indeed," replied Gail.

His teeth gleamed under the fluorescent glare. "Off to heal the multitudes?"

"More like off to see the wizard."

"Ha! Well, the yellow brick road awaits, Dorothy."

She did not want the conversation to end. "I do have one patient whose complexes are driving me to distraction."

"The famous Mr. Powers, I presume?"

Gail could not recall ever discussing the case with Dr. Camara. "Yes, I'm afraid I've bothered you with this case before?"

"Actually, no. I was chatting with June in the cafeteria the other day."

"Oh, dear," she sighed.

"Don't fret. Mr. Powers is quite famous around here. He is the topic of many conversations."

"As well as my unorthodox methods?"

Adam looked down and fiddled with his tie, momentarily grim, then snapped his head up and grinned broadly. "Also, quite famous."

"Oh, dear." Gail stared at him for some time and sighed. "You must think me a fool."

Adam laughed dismissively. "Dr. Mansfield told me all about it, in great and lascivious detail, when I had just arrived, and he was on his way out."

Gail felt embarrassed and angry. "Oh, him."

"Yes. Glad he's gone, to tell the truth." Adam leaned close and whispered, "Awful man."

Gail chuckled gratefully.

"But, seriously, I would like to hear about the case from you, Gail. From the horse's mouth, so to speak." He flipped out his tam o'shanter and perched it cockeyed on his head. "Or, in your case, from the lassie's mouth."

She felt her heart stirring and rushed to tamp it down. *Easy girl*, she said to herself. *Be professional.*

"Dr. Camara, you look ridiculous wearing that hat in your doctor's clothes."

"Thank you so much. But I really am being serious."

She tilted her head in an unconsciously flirtatious manner. "Well then, when would be a good time for us to meet?"

Adam checked his watch. "Eleven this morning?"

Gail pulled out her cell phone and checked appointments, knowing she would cancel any previously scheduled. She thought she saw Dr. Camara watch her with an amused smile, as if he suspected her charade. This tweaked her sense of dignity, and just to reestablish a sense of control, she took longer than necessary, and said, "Eleven fifteen. Is that good?"

"Perfect!" he exclaimed.

With balance restored, she glanced at the wall clock and feigned surprise. "Oh, look at the time! Got to run."

"See you at eleven fifteen," said Adam. "Where should we meet?"

To Gail, his slightly patronizing air returned, but she chalked it up to oversensitivity on her part.

"My office?"

"Good! See you there." Adam turned on his heel and walked briskly away.

Hmm, thought Gail. *I'll have to be sharp around this man. Good! A challenge!*

Saying hello to June as she breezed into her office, Gail stored her purse and began rearranging her schedule. June trailed in behind and stood waiting. "We'll need to postpone a couple of appointments this morning, June. I want to use the morning to go on my rounds without interruption until lunch."

"Okay, no problem," replied June. "Just let me know which ones."

"Sure, I'll let you know."

As June turned to leave, Gail inadvertently glanced at her private bathroom door, and shuddered at the memory of Mr. Powers coiled tight as a fetus on the floor. She remembered feeling the horror that she had lost him forever to his Goddess. It all came back in a rush, and she stood frozen for some time.

"Everything okay?" asked June, who stood in the doorway.

"Of course. Give me a few minutes and I'll start my rounds." She jotted down a couple of names. "Here are the morning appointments I need to reschedule. How does the afternoon look?"

June shook her head. "Loaded, I'm afraid."

"Not Mr. Powers?"

"No. Why do you ask? Was I supposed to—"

"No, no. Just checking."

~

Dr. Hess had barely begun her rounds, when a patient in one of the secure rooms was discovered bashing his head against the wall. After being restrained, she sat next to him on the bed.

"Mr. Lundgren, why bang your head? You know this behavior will not help."

"Room's full of demons. Had to get out." His words came slurred through the thick fog of sedation.

"But your head is not as strong as the walls, you know that."

"Don't know that. Got to get out. Demons. Got to ram a hole."

"What do the demons want?"

"Entering my seven portals. Got to get out."

"Mr. Lundgren, you must stay on your medicine, otherwise, the demons will never leave you alone."

He looked at her without seeing. After giving his attendant instructions, she continued checking patients. Following a few more chats and lengthy consultations, she found herself in front of Mr. Powers's locked door. Something drew her hand toward the knob; it took some effort to step back and check her watch.

Eleven ten.

She rushed back to her office and found Dr. Camara chatting with June.

"Perfect!" exclaimed Adam. "Just in time."

"Shall we?" Gail gestured toward her office door.

Once ensconced in their respective seats, Adam leaned forward. "So, Mr. Powers, eh?"

"Yes," replied Gail. "A case that, as you know, has complicated my . . . practice."

Adam looked puzzled. "How so? . . . I mean, is it that business with the, ah, role playing?"

"No, no, not that. Not at all."

"Then what do you mean?"

Gail experienced a moment of confusion. Where to start? How to explain it?

"Adam, have you met Mr. Powers?"

"I've seen him."

"No, I mean have you actually met him? Talked with him?"

"No."

"Well, that's the thing. He is complex, his schizophrenia quite unlike any I've ever run across. His delusions are so detailed, so grounded. Right now, as we speak, I know he is writing in his room."

"Writing?"

"Novels. Well, I call them novels, but he believes they are accurate chronicles of his life."

"What?"

"Novels. Books. Perhaps more like an autobiography. Manuscripts about himself, his parents . . . and us."

"Us?"

"As we speak."

"Gail, I'm not following."

"I can almost hear pen on paper, at this moment, jotting down our every word."

"Gail!" admonished Camara.

~

You see? You see, dear Reader? She knows. Proof that she has at least some divine powers.

~

"I know that tomorrow, or the next day, or the day after, the latest additions to his manuscript will contain our words."

Dr. Camara was rendered speechless.

Finally registering his incredulity, Gail said, "I know, it's crazy. But I have proof!"

She rummaged through a locked cabinet and pulled out a stack of binders. "These are his words, his writings, and they track his life, his parents, Vietnam, his experiences here, including my words, my thoughts, my . . . well, everything. This discussion we are having will appear also."

"Okay, I believe you, Gail. But what does it mean?" In fact, he did not believe her, and assumed Mr. Powers simply wrote down made-up conversations.

"I don't know. It scares me."

"How does this fit in with your treatment protocol?"

"That is what I want to talk with you about."

"Okay."

"I have a wealth of information, thanks to his writings. Nonetheless, I fear they are unreliable."

"But you just said—"

"I know. I know. His delusions change, but not in a fragmented, chaotic way."

"What do you mean?"

"They have evolved."

"From what to what?"

"From his father's schizophrenia and his mother's lesbianism, to Vietnam, combat, his own schizophrenia, ants, dreams, a God and Goddess—"

"Whoa!" exclaimed Dr. Camara. "Too much. What's the latest?"

"That's just it. Something about helping this Goddess cure God of His addiction to suffering."

"What?"

"Nothing less than the liberation of all things, human or otherwise, from suffering."

"Wow! That's a whopper of a delusion! However, Gail, certainly not unprecedented. I don't mean to be flippant, but it sounds like the proverbial Jesus complex."

Gail sighed deeply. She had long experience with others trying to shoehorn his delusions into familiar tropes. "I know. It is late. We both need to get back to work."

Adam shook his head. "Come on, you're leaving me confused."

"You're confused!" laughed Gail. "I'll sort it out."

"Let's talk more about it over dinner, shall we?"

The invitation jarred Gail back to harsh reality, her stirrings fluttering chaotically. Startled butterflies. But Dr. Hess always kept hers contained in a jar.

"Saturday night?" he pressed.

"Dr. Camara, I do believe you are flirting with me."

"Indubitably. Pick you up at six at your place?"

She did not have to think long. "It's a date."

As he was leaving, he said, "I've never dated a Goddess before."

Before she could respond, he disappeared out the door, but the damage was done. His mention of Goddess struck her with the force of a gale, and she remained motionless, marshaling her energies to keep from sobbing. Thankfully, June did not intrude. Her hands trembled as she leafed through the most recent pages of Mr. Powers's manuscript retrieved by Joe.

"Not in here . . . yet," she murmured.

~

Be patient, Dr. Hess.

~ *Another Session* ~

Two days passed and Gail could no longer ignore the warning bell tolling in her mind, summoning her to meet with Michael Powers once more. It was Friday, and she wanted to interview him and stockpile the latest rambling fantasies to share with Dr. Camara the following evening over dinner. June, as always, retained professional detachment, but Gail knew her assistant had misgivings about any meeting with Michael Powers.

"You're sure about this?" asked June. "After all, he isn't expecting you."

Oh, yes, he is, thought Gail. Nevertheless, she replied, "Not to worry."

She had an uneasy feeling that her speculations might be mistakenly ascribing superhuman powers to Mr. Powers, but she dismissed these thoughts as flights of fancy. Every psychiatrist and therapist knew that mentally challenged people were often more perceptive than the average, 'normal' person. This was simply a case of Michael Powers exceeding the average, admittedly by far, but nothing more sinister.

When Joe unlocked the door to Michael's secure room, she quickly stepped in as it closed behind her. Michael was sitting on his bed, staring at her with an unreadable expression.

"Hello, Mr. Powers. I thought I would drop in and see how things are going."

"Good timing," said Michael. "Storyteller just left."

"I thought he resided only in Vietnam, in the past."

"Oh, as you know, he visits periodically in the present, even when he's not invited."

"Yes—your famous dinner parties."

"And the tunnel, don't forget that. By the way, Nature was also here earlier."

"Why was he here?"

"Tugging."

"Tugging?"

"Yeah, tugging on me to return. Nature is worried . . . and lonely."

"Mr. Powers, as I have repeatedly told you, Nature died in Vietnam decades ago."

"And Storyteller?"

"You are Storyteller, and you're alive."

"Never bought the twin story, did you, Dr. Hess?"

"No. You were Storyteller long ago, as a young soldier. But the war is over, Mr. Powers. Now you are . . . mature . . . and a lawyer with a son."

"And a dead wife."

"Yes."

"And another wife—a ghost, a servant of Goddess."

Dr. Hess sighed. "Michael—"

"No, no! It's okay. I know what you're going to say before you say it." He motioned toward a chair. "Sit."

"Thank you."

"Now, what's on your mind, Dr. Hess?" asked Michael.

"Don't you know?"

"Yes. It's all up here, in my noggin, ready to be written down."

Gail looked around. "Is the Goddess here now?"

"Not *the* Goddess, Dr. Hess, just Goddess. Do you call God *the* God? No, you don't. Anyway, yes, She is here."

"Where?"

He pointed at Gail. "There, except Her breasts are constrained by a modern bra."

"Mr. Powers, if we—"

"No, no! I understand. You are Dr. Gail Hess, not a Goddess. I beg to differ. I have seen your breasts, and they are divine."

"For which I will be eternally sorry."

"Since Goddesses live for eternity, You will be sorry for a very long time, unless You accept it."

"You and I both know this obsession with breasts is just a ploy. A distraction. Can we move off that topic?"

He shrugged. "Up to you."

"Now, I do want to talk about this Goddess."

"Okay."

Gail shifted nervously. "How will She stop God from continuing to preside over suffering? Surely you know, Mr. Powers, that such a thing is impossible. Suffering is the way of the universe."

"Oh, you mean natural selection, nature red in tooth and claw, the savage beast, the Second Law of Thermodynamics, all that? Is that what you mean?"

"Yes."

"I don't know—why don't You tell me."

"I am not your Goddess."

"Perhaps so, perhaps not. It's a matter of quantum probability. Despite all your denials, you are entangled with Her in a quantum superposition. Maybe you're dead, maybe you're alive. But the problem, Dr. Hess, is that I've already observed you, and determined the state of your existence. When I am looking, You are you with a capital Y. When I am not looking, you are you with a small y."

Dr. Hess, to her horror, found herself rising from her chair and mechanically saying, "Fate starves at Probability's door." She couldn't stop the words. They spilled out of her mouth, alien and inevitable.

Michael jumped to the floor and bowed. "You see! You see!"

Gail felt dizzy, as if floating above him and she stumbled to the door, banging on it before she almost blacked out. "This is nothing supernatural," she muttered. "I simply read it in your manuscript."

Joe opened the door, and she felt a whoosh of air cool her face and revive her senses. She felt as if she had just escaped a tomb. Vaguely, Joe's voice finally penetrated.

"Dr. Hess! Are you okay?"

She croaked out a few unintelligible words.

"What?" asked Joe in confusion. "Dr. Hess let's get you to your office. I'll call for a doctor."

"No, I'm fine, Joe, thank you," she whispered.

He ignored her and walked her to her office, handing her over to June, who appeared alarmed at Gail's appearance.

"What happened?"

"Nothing," said Gail. "I just need to sit for a while. A little faint is all."

Joe caught June's eye, and after settling Gail into a comfortable chair in her office, they agreed to call Dr. Camara, still on duty.

~

Gail could hardly process it all. *I was only in there for a few minutes and already this . . . attack. How is it possible?*

"Hello," came a familiar voice.

Gail forced herself to focus. "Dr. Camara," she said quietly, a shade of displeasure in her tone.

"Yours truly."

"Why are you here?"

"House call."

"Oh—June must have . . . well, never mind. You need not have come. I'm fine. Just a bit of a fainting spell. A little close in some of the rooms."

"Not pregnant, are you?" he joked.

"Please," she replied testily. "Really, I'm perfectly fine."

"At least let me give you a quick check over."

She stood. "No. I have appointments, but I'll grab a bite to eat. Thank you for coming, I'm sure you have your own appointments. You'd best get to them."

"If you're sure?"

"I'm sure."

She wanted him to leave and give her time to think. His presence made her feel like a schoolgirl caught doing something wrong.

As she moved toward the door, Adam said, "I understand your fainting spell came over you in Mr. Powers's room."

"Yes, that's right."

"Perhaps we should discuss it."

"Absolutely not . . . at least not now." She eased slightly. "We can discuss it at dinner tomorrow night."

He smiled. "Works for me."

She slipped past Adam, grabbed a file from her desk, and headed to a conference room to meet with a patient's family, berating herself for looking quite the fool in front of Dr. Camara. Yet, the thought did not remain long, as Goddess kept intruding, demanding her attention. She could hear her own words tumble so inexplicably from her mouth in Mr. Powers's room. *Fate starves at Probability's door.* Why did she say those alien words? A vision of Mr. Lundgren came to mind, banging his head against the wall, certain that demons were entering his seven portals. She tried to calm herself by repeating what she had told Mr. Powers—that she'd read the line in his book. That would not explain why she blurted them out at such a moment. Did someone make her?

Yes. She felt the answer—but refused to acknowledge it. Could not acknowledge it.

Seven portals.

Chapter Three

Preparations

Target: Joe

Joe has still not brought the information I requested about his father. Oh, sure, I've seen him, but he's always rushed and won't stay to chat. I need to get closer to him; I need that information before I can set my clever little plot in motion. Orders are orders, after all, and if I'm going to Marie Telles's house, I have to escape this jail. Oh, I know what you're thinking, dear Reader. If Dr. Hess is Goddess, then why bother leaving? *She's* right here, at my disposal—or rather, I'm at *Her* disposal. I've thought about that, and it's either a test, or Hess is not Goddess, but a spy planted by God. Either way, orders are orders.

In the meantime, I sit and stare at my room, white as bone, with a sickly border painted green. My voices have abandoned me in this sterile trap—rats that deserted my sinking ship, aft decks awash in seas of medication and sedation. Still, I'm aware enough to plan. That's what lawyers do: plan. Well, my case is coming up before Her court, and I damn well intend to win. To do that, one must plan. Meticulously. Once I make my escape, I must be very clever, as I know they will make every effort to snatch me back. Police will be in on it. Oh yes, I must be very clever. Very clever indeed.

Damn! Where's Nature? Where's Storyteller? You see, dear Reader if you don't already know, Storyteller is my younger self. A young, brave, strong soldier. When he inhabits me, I get angry, but even in his weakened, malaria-ridden state, I feel his bones bolster my old, sagging body, and the hot blood of his youth boils and burns through my veins and arteries. The problem is, I can no longer call him up. Even my dinner parties with the ghost of my dead wife and living son—who refuses to get me out of here—even those are over. Diane won't appear, and Storyteller stays in the tunnel with Nature. Why? Of course, it's this damn medication. Dulls life to a blank scroll that slowly unrolls, day after day, without a daub of ink or paint that would give it meaning.

I put in a request to walk in the institution's lovely garden—with supervision, of course—and Dr. Hess gave her (grudging, I'm sure) permission. They sent an orderly—not Joe—and I refused to go, insisting that only Joe accompany me. Granted. Therefore, I wait. I'm patient. The tunnel taught me that.

"Hello, Mr. Powers!" booms that sweet, familiar African American voice. "Ready for our stroll?"

"You bet, Joe."

"Nice and warm outside."

I grab my notepad.

"You gonna write?" asks Joe.

"Yep."

"Lordy, I've never seen anyone write so much."

(If only you knew, Joe.)

The morning is clear and crisp. I watch my breath form in the air and say nothing, waiting. We walk slowly, as if I were some sort of convalescent just out of surgery. No matter. Finally, when I realize Joe brings no news about his father, and admittedly feeling pessimistic, I ask, "Did you find out anything?"

I see a long stream of frozen breath dissipate in the breeze. "Yes."

I'm taken by surprise. Pleasant surprise. "What'd you find out?"

"Mr. Powers, why are you so interested?"

This takes me aback. Joe is obviously suspicious of something. "Oh, Joe, I was there, in the bush, and I'm always curious. I'm always wondering if maybe . . . you know, I might run into someone. You know what I mean?"

"Yeah."

He stares at me with a look I can't read.

"Let's sit," he says.

We pick a bench and I sit, but he continues to stand, looking up at the trees.

I wait.

"I looked you up . . . your history, I mean. At least, the part that Dr. Hess said wasn't confidential. So, you were in the First Cavalry Division?"

"Yeah."

"Special Ops?"

"Sort of, yeah."

"Did you run across this unit when you were there?" He fishes a piece of paper from his pocket and holds it in front of my eyes.

Okay, I say to myself, moment of truth. Should I look surprised? Shocked? Or should I remain calm? Solemn? I choose the latter. I allow my face, for the briefest moment, to sag as if burdened by a painful memory. "Yes," I lie.

Now he holds up a photograph. "Recognize him?"

I take a chance that this is not a trap and register fake surprise.

"Yes!" I lie again. As soon as the word leaves my mouth, I shake my head sadly.

"Where? When? How?" Joe rattles these questions off like a machine gun. "What was he like? How did he really die?"

Now for the coy part. I seize on the words "really die" and look pained.

"Best not to talk about it, Joe."

"Come on, Mr. Powers, you can't hold back now."

I've got him. By God, I've got him!

"No, Joe. Better let sleeping dogs lie."

"Look here, Mr. Powers, my family has wondered for years how he really died. Mama doesn't trust the government version. Now I've got the itch to know."

"Joe, better you don't know."

Careful, Michael. Fishing is a process—a game of patience—the slightest mistake, and you'll reel in an empty hook. I wait.

A suspicious frown darkens his face. "Do you really know how he died?"

"Yes, Joe," I lie again, with appropriate solemnity.

"Then tell me."

Okay, now, dear Reader, this will require the most delicate of segues. "Joe, I want out of here. This place just exacerbates my . . . problems."

"I know you think that."

"Can you help me, Joe?"

I hold my breath.

"I see, I see," says Joe. "Tit for tat, eh?" He laughs in disgust. "Well, I say no deal, Mr. Powers. I don't take kindly to bribery attempts. No, sir, not of any kind or form." He shakes his head. "Not proper."

Careful, Michael. Keep your poker face. "I understand, Joe, It's for the best. Shall we continue our walk?" I rise and start walking and feel his eyes on my back. I listen for his steps but hear nothing. I keep walking. Still nothing. Maybe I can just walk away.

But no.

Here he is, beside me again. Silent.

Patience, Michael.

"You got a son, right, Mr. Powers?"

"Yes, indeed."

"Wouldn't he have a right to know how you died?"

"Well, Joe, that depends."

"On what?"

"How I died."

"No, I can't agree," says Joe. "I'm not some fragile woman. Seen a lot in my life, where I grew up, in here." His hand flutters dismissively. "Nothin' shocks me anymore."

"Yes, I understand."

"So?"

"So?"

"Come on, Mr. Powers. Tell me."

I set my jaw. "Help me."

"Do what?"

"You know."

"Won't work. You'll get caught, and I'll be fired."

"Your dad was smart, Joe, real smart. I can't believe you aren't the same. Figure out a way. You know the system here. Figure a way."

A cunning grin lights up his face. "Flattery will get you nowhere."

"Look, Joe, let's stop fuckin' around. As your father used to say, 'Viet Cong all fuckin' around us. Only way to make it back to the World is to outfox 'em.'"

"The World?"

"Yeah, what we called the States. The United States. America. Hot food. Women. Tits galore. Get it?"

He laughs. "Dad said that?"

"Sure." Lying is so easy. So easy. Like Captain Tong said, 'They will want to believe. Just human.'

~

Problem is, dear Reader, Joe makes no commitment—as we lawyers like to say, no enforceable contract. I know he is not sure I'm telling the truth. That's okay. I can wait. Let it eat at him. Meantime, we walk around shooting the breeze while his brain soaks in the risks and benefits. He's a smart guy—like his father. Ha!

Back in my room, I sit on the bed and write. Yes, these words flow out of my pen. My thoughts turn to Dr. Hess, then to Goddess, then to Marie Telles. Still can't figure out why I must make my way to Marie Telles's house. Orders, but I'm not a clueless young soldier anymore. I question. The world out there is dying. I know that. We humans are killing it, even as God ratchets up *His* dose of suffering, especially for non-human animals. Why give us nerves? Of course, increase the dosage. Consciousness? Increase the dosage. Empathy? Higher still. When does it stop? Overdose, just as Goddess warns. Got to stop *Him* now. You might ask, dear Reader, how I can think of these things when I don't even believe in God? Or Goddess, for that matter. Easy. I'm mentally ill. Mental illness tells me A, while my reasoning brain tells me B. Which do I believe? Seems the only alternative is C. After all, $a^2 + b^2 = c^2$.

"Come in, Joe."

His head is peeping in the door. "Naw, just checking on you."

"And I'm just waiting for you."

"How did he die?"

"Help me escape."

"Tell me first."

"No deal."

Joe opens the door wider. "I don't believe you know how he died."

I shrug. "Oh, but I do, Joe. I do."

He closes the door.

He'll crack, I tell myself.

~ *The Great Warrior* ~

It has been days since I have written anything. Not because Joe has remained mum, but because I saw the Great Warrior. It has sent me into a tailspin. She appeared like a black spark moving along the wall, a reminder of the tunnel's call. Probing. Now what is she after? First, it was my last will and testament, now my

. . . what? Death certificate? No, that lovely document wouldn't be here—yet. In case you are unaware, dear Reader, the Great Warrior is an ant. An extraordinary ant, to be sure, but an ant nonetheless. Not impressed? You should be. She comes from the White Palace—my skeleton still tilting against the wall in the tunnel. Goddess! First You tell me to escape and go to Marie Telles, now the Great Warrior appears. What do You want? Do you want me to return to the tunnel, like the Great Warrior and Nature want, or go to Marie Telles's house, per Your order? You send so many mixed signals. I'm confused.

"About what?"

"Oh, hello Dr. Hess. Nothing. Just rambling. What brings you here?"

"I'm not in your room, Mr. Powers. You are in my office, remember?"

I look around. *She's* right. Must be more careful. "Of course. How much time has passed?"

"You don't know?"

"If I did, I wouldn't ask."

"Guess."

"A few minutes?"

"No. But, that is beside the point."

"How much time?"

"Let's just leave it at a few minutes."

"You see! I am aware!"

"Hmm, I wonder," mutters Hess. "We were discussing your relationship with your father, and you drifted off. Something about an ant."

"Come on, Doc, you've read my books. You know."

"Yes, I think so—the Great Warrior, correct?"

I nod in disgust at how our little roles necessitate such childish games. Of course, the good Dr. knows. She directs the Great Warrior, if, that is, she is truly She. You see, dear Reader, even I have my doubts. After all, schizophrenia is nothing more than an overgrown Garden of Gethsemane. But I digress.

"Can we return to your father, Mr. Powers?"

"Will there ever come a day when you call me Michael?"

"No. Not professional."

"For a man who has seen your divine presence, that strikes me as a stretch."

"Your father."

"Is that what we were discussing?"

"Yes."

"What about him?"

"I only know about him through your writings, but I want to know things that happened you did not include in your narration."

I assume a comically tragic face. "Ah, too painful! He beat me terribly. The abuse! The final straw was when he sold me on the white slave market after I made love with my mother."

Disappointingly, she didn't blink an eye.

"When you were an adolescent, how did you feel knowing your mother was a lesbian?"

"She was dead."

"Yes, I know, but did you share that information with your friends?"

"That she was dead?"

"Come, come, Mr. Powers, these little games are beneath you. Did you share with your friends that your mother was a lesbian?"

"No."

"Why not?"

"Never came up."

"Did you share it with your wife, Diane?"

I pause. That is an interesting question. My mother, dear Reader, was Chinese, and met my American father during World War II in China. I have her picture, and I must say, she was the most beautiful woman I ever laid eyes on—well, she and Nguyen Tuyet Mai (but that is another story). It is true, she was a lesbian, and this caused my father no end of pain. I look at Dr. Hess.

"Yes. Diane knew about my mother."

"And did you—"

I hold up my hand to stop her. "Bad form, doctor. Just listen, which is your job, and I'll tell you a story. Got your little recorder on? Good.

"Once upon a time, as you are aware, I had dinner parties for ghosts and sundry other guests, which Diane always attended. This was after she died in a car crash, so she came to me as a ghost (assuming that ghost is a term acceptable to you, instead of the rather insulting word hallucination?) There was one time, which for some reason I failed to note in my writings, when Diane made an incredible statement."

Here, I stop to collect my thoughts. This memory, indeed, has shaken me. At last, Dr. Hess and her interminable questions have found a soft spot, a key, and I can feel it penetrate the keyhole of my vaulted psyche—the iron door behind which She resides. Hess, wisely, waits patiently. I take a deep breath and continue.

"I recall one dinner when we were discussing some inconsequential subject, can't remember what, and she suddenly gave me a piercing look, and said, 'I met your mother.' Well, that knocked me on my ass, and I replied stupidly, 'Where?' She said, 'You know.' Yes, yes, Dr. Hess, I know where they met. The world of shades. I visited there and saw . . . and saw. . . . "

A flood of memories roars into my mind, drowning me, and I can only sputter, "That's all, I can't say more."

I know there is more. Dr. Hess knows there is more. But I must look awful, because she calls for Joe to take me back to my room. I follow him like a kitten. I don't even think to ask about my escape. Back in my room, I feel the key slowly withdrawn. I hear it clink to the tile floor. The door remains locked. Good. I don't want to remember. I can't go there. Maybe no coming back.

I see the Great Warrior climbing higher on the wall, as if measuring my worth. Antennae waving, waiting.

~ *Joe Again* ~

Okay. That memory is buried again. It has taken a few days, but I'm back on track. Balance restored. This damn medication does have some useful qualities. Time to return to my escape plans. Joe hasn't said a word, as I have been acting like some bedridden zombie, staring at the Great Warrior. Joe often follows my eyes and asks what I see, but I have presence of mind enough to lie, and to gain his sympathy in the bargain, by rather pathetically saying, "Freedom."

Joe shakes his head and leaves. I try to focus on how I might break his resistance, but all avenues that initiate with me are closed. He must come to me, or it will never happen. True, he's held out longer than I thought, but I'm sure it is eating at him. Meantime, all I can do is wait. To pass the time, I amuse myself with my neighbor, Damien Lundgren. He is also schizophrenic, worse than me, and we often meet in the secured recreation room, where he sits at a corner table mumbling to himself. Often, I sit with him and ask about his voices, but he never responds, merely rocking back and forth and looking through me while he mumbles some undecipherable trash.

Today, I sit across from him and boldly state, "My voices are far more powerful than yours!"

To my surprise, he looks startled, stops rocking, and stares at me with wide-open eyes, as if he's never seen me before. In a perfectly normal, calm voice, he says, "Can't be."

"But it's true."

"Can't be. Thunderclap is the most powerful being in the world."

"Really?"

"He could crush me, and you, and the entire human race if he wants. The others are all afraid of him, and they are also strong. But not as strong as him. He is the strongest."

"What does he say?"

"Kill Michael Powers with knife."

I fall backward, almost tipping over the chair. "What!!?? Say that again?"

I watch a cunning smile curve his chapped lips. "Fill my powers with life."

Now, dear Reader, what would you think at this amazing exchange? Either I heard wrong, or God (aka Thunderclap) is out to eliminate me. What to believe?

"Look, Damien, are you sure you said, 'Fill my powers with life' rather than, 'Kill Michael Powers with knife?'"

But his eyes dull and he topples back into oblivion, rocking and mumbling. Joe is standing nearby. I'm so shaken, I forget my strategy and walk up to him.

"Joe, have you thought about it? . . . Because it's more essential than ever that I get out of here. Surely you can see I don't belong here?"

"Yeah, I've thought about it."

My heart races. "And?"

"Talk to you tonight. Not now."

Oh, joy of joys! Could it be? Freedom! Just to glimpse the possibility renews my spirit. Can I wait without dying from anticipation? Yes, yes, yes! Tonight!

It just dawned on me that Dr. Hess might gain access to these latest scribbles. Fool! That would give everything away. So, I've hidden these pages and have written some fabricated blather she can read if she confiscates my work. Meanwhile, dear Reader, I write on. These words are being written after my meeting with Joe. Curious about what he said? Here it is—

As promised, he walked into my room and locked the door behind him.

"I've decided to help you," he said. "Still, I want assurances first."

I tried to remain calm. "Such as?"

"If I help you, I don't want you to hold anything back, and answer all my questions. Fully."

"Of course. When?"

"I'll let you know. And if any of this comes out, I'll deny everything."

"Of course."

"Now, start talking."

This took me by surprise. "Wait a minute, Joe. I may be mentally ill, but I'm not crazy."

"What do you propose, Mr. Powers?"

"That's a tough one, Joe. When I'm free, we won't have time to talk. On the other hand, if I tell you first, what's to prevent you from reneging?"

"My word."

"Not enough."

"My word on my father's grave."

He seemed so sincere, I agreed. What else to do? I told him I wanted to know the plan first. He told me. It was my turn, so then I had to make up a real whopper. First, I asked what the government told the family about his father's death, then I scoffed at it, calling it a lie. And . . . well, as I said, I made up a whopper. Made his dad heroic—his death not properly recognized by the government because he had disobeyed orders to save his trapped brothers, etc. etc. etc. Made Joe happy. For now, I wait. Everything must go perfectly for it to work. Joe told me that Sunday is the day. Sunday. Two days from now. I am to feign illness, and then he will . . . ah, no, no, no. The details will remain our secret. For now, I am watching the Great Warrior. She will give me patience and guidance. I notice she has moved to a higher place on the wall. I believe she will stay long enough to see me safely gone, then return to the tunnel and join her nest mates in the White Palace. Still, the voices are silent. That's a good thing, as no news is good news, eh, dear Reader?

Enough writing for now. I'll put pen to paper after I'm free.

Chapter Four

Searching for Mr. Powers

Dinner

D r. Gail Hess sat across from Dr. Adam Camara at a corner table in the Restaurant DaVinci. His eyes sparkled in the candlelight, and she contentedly bathed in their intensity while sipping wine. She had rejected three dresses before finding one that was slimming yet still admittedly unprofessional. Being low-cut, she thought it alluring and quite exciting to wear. To her amused consternation, Adam Camara unapologetically wore casual clothes—sneakers, and his crazy tam o'shanter.

When they were seated and the drinks arrived, he beamed at her affectionately and raised his glass.

"Wine good?" he asked.

"Good," replied Gail, smiling bemusedly at his cocked hat.

Stuffing the hat in his pocket and smoothing an unruly shock of curls, he said, "You look relieved."

"Not at all. If we are to be an odd couple, let us be a very odd couple."

"Ha! I like your attitude! Now, let us have some *hors d'oeuvres* and talk about Michael Powers."

Gail gave a disappointed sigh and felt unwilling to jump into a discussion about her most problematic patient just yet. The pleasure she experienced in his company had barely flickered before he wanted to snuff it out with shoptalk. A flicker of irritation crossed her mind—*damn it, Gail, don't let him corner you so quickly.* "Oh, let's just enjoy the drinks before we delve into that can of worms."

"Okay, but I must admit, his case interests me."

"Oh? Why?" She immediately chastised herself for opening the door, but it was too late.

"I like cans of worms. Also, I like you. Put the two together and you get a doubly interesting case."

"I'm sure you have many interesting cases of your own."

"None so fascinating as Mr. Powers and your relationship to him."

Gail's face reddened, and she snapped, "My relationship with Mr. Powers is entirely professional."

Adam's eyes twinkled even more mischievously. "I know, I know. But Gail, you must admit he fascinates you."

"True."

"So, would it be possible for me to read his manuscripts?"

"They aren't published."

"I see. You do have the manuscripts?"

"Yes."

"How do you get them?"

"Someone gives them to me."

"Someone? Who?"

"That is the question."

"I don't understand."

Gail frowned, still piqued at his remarks, and silently continued sipping her wine.

"Well, does he give them to you, or do you take them from him?"

She carefully placed her glass on the table and leaned forward. "So, what got you interested in psychiatry?"

"Gail, you can't leave me hanging like this."

"I understand hanging is therapeutic. Stretches the neck and elongates the mind."

Adam laughed but said nothing.

Gail seized the opportunity to complete the change of topic. "No, really, how did you get interested?"

With a deep sigh, Adam put down his glass, reached in his pocket and again pulled on his tam o'shanter. Now in full regalia, he spoke in an Irish brogue. "Ah, lassie, there lies a story! But didn't we agree to talk about Mr. Powers?"

Gail could not help chuckling. "True, but now, I'm more interested in you than Mr. Powers. Are you saying you're more interested in Mr. Powers than me?"

"No, but—"

Gail raised her glass. "Then let's talk about you . . . for now. After dinner, I promise we can go down that dark road."

"Fine. Let's order." He tucked his tam o'shanter back into his pocket and commenced describing how he became interested in psychiatry. To Gail, he seemed perturbed, curt, lacking his usual *joie d'vivre*. In fact, she came perilously close to believing he was pouting, but dismissed the idea as unworthy of a successful doctor. Gradually, as the meal progressed, he perked up and engaged in his more typical good-humored banter.

After their table had been cleared of dinner plates, Adam leaned back, looked at her, the shine back in his eyes. "Another quaff of wine, my dear, before we order dessert and a digestif. Then, we discuss Mr. Powers. Might I suggest brandy or cognac?"

Gail smiled. "I'm honored to be invited into the heart of the sacred temple, the holy of holies—male camaraderie. Shall we banish the females and smoke cigars as well?"

Instead of taking offense, Adam laughed heartily. "Well, in spite of my great admiration for Lady Macbeth, I would not unsex you for the world."

"Thank you for that, as I would find it difficult to murder a king."

"As far as I know, goddesses do not murder."

Gail stiffened. "That is the second time you've referred to me as a goddess. Please stop."

"But, why?"

"I have no doubt you are aware of the delusional projection Mr. Powers makes regarding me."

Adam leaned forward and held her eyes with an intense stare. "That is precisely why I want to talk about Mr. Powers."

"I don't understand, unless you're referring to that incident."

"No, no, no. That is definitely not it; and what's more, you know it."

Gail waited, feeling slightly fearful.

"Gail, it is your own . . . how do I put it? . . . interest in this case that happens to be the main reason I am so interested. It does not necessarily involve Mr. Powers alone."

"Are you on some sort of informal investigation?"

"Not at all. Surely you must know the staff at the institution is abuzz with rumors and innuendo?"

"No, in fact I am not aware of that fact, nor do I care."

"But I care. I care about you. Mr. Powers has managed to get into your head, and I want to know how he does it. He seeps into thought the way prayer seeps into silence, and that's different from a garden-variety schizophrenic."

"How do you know he has gotten into my head?"

"Gail, it is obvious to even a casual observer. This goddess—"

"I thought we were here to discuss Mr. Powers, not my professional competence."

"Your professional competence is not in question. What is in question is the ability of Mr. Powers to manipulate even the most experienced of our staff."

"What do you mean?"

"I have been talking, informally, to many staff members, including caretakers, assistants, nurses, orderlies."

"Who, for example?"

"Well, the first person I talked with when I came here was the departing Dr. Mansfield."

"Oh, him again."

"He was just the first. Look, Gail, I believe this Mr. Powers is a powerfully driven force to be reckoned with. Perhaps a collaborative effort to get to the bottom of his various psychoses? We could work together if you would be willing. Perhaps the old tactic of good cop, bad cop?"

"He is not a criminal, Dr. Camara."

"Ouch, that hurt. For the first time in my life, I have the feeling I have just been demoted to a doctor."

Gail would not be placated. "He is not a criminal, Dr. Camara," she repeated.

"Not that we know."

Her eyes widened. "Do you suspect?"

"I chatted with your assistant, who is worried whenever you are alone with him."

"Oh, June is a worrywart. Nothing has ever happened that would indicate violent tendencies."

"Not what I heard."

Gail paused, remembering various times with Mr. Powers when she genuinely felt somehow threatened. Yet, oddly enough, not directly from him, but rather from some undefined power that lay beyond him, or deep within him . . . or outside him. Believing this fear came from her own doubts and insecurities, she knew she must not share such insights with Dr. Camara, or anyone else. "I see," she said noncommittally.

"So, here is the cognac. I toast your remarkable work with such a complicated patient." He held up his glass.

Gail hesitated, then clinked glasses and took a sip. After the wine, the liqueur went down smooth and easy, and the inner warmth suffused throughout her body, relaxing her mind and loosening her inhibitions. She felt a sudden closeness to Adam, and yearned to accept his offer of a collaboration, yet something held her back. "Thank you so much, Adam. I realize there is much you want to discuss, and I as well would like to get to the bottom of Mr. Powers' case . . . and even my own . . . methodologies."

"Speaking of methodologies, what is your treatment plan, I mean, your plan to supplement the *chlorpromazine* he is, I presume, already taking?"

Gail considered the deep chasm of Michael Powers' delusions and felt at a loss where to begin. This uncertainty brought vividly to the forefront how reactive she had become to his psychoses. Perhaps Dr. Camara was right, a collaboration might help. Unfortunately, it would weaken her plans to make this important case a springboard to advance her own career. However, the complicated, crosscutting symptoms of Mr. Powers, which bore so many varied permutations, might lie beyond her skills to manage alone. Besides, she had to admit the prospect of working closely with Adam Camara was too attractive to ignore.

As she paused to consider her response, she caught him stealing a glance at her cleavage, and she felt a pulsing thrill. But her native caution held dangerous sexual urges in check, though the alcohol loosened some verbal inhibitions. She made an admission she would not ordinarily have shared with anyone.

"That is a process I am still working on, Adam. Obviously, going along with his delusions, including role-playing the Goddess figure, did not work. In fact, it backfired. Ever since, I have tried to disabuse him of that fantasy."

"Uphill battle?"

"That's putting it mildly."

"Then, perhaps, I can assist by interviewing Mr. Powers separately. After all, I do not carry any associations with him."

~

(Oh, yes you do, Dr. Camara. Oh, yes.)

~

Gail felt a twinge, a tap on her mental shoulder, that suggested they were being observed, accompanied by the sound of pen scratching on paper, and she knew their words soon would appear in the writings of Mr. Powers. But she quickly quashed the feeling, afraid Dr. Camara might again think her a bit crazy to even imagine such impossibilities. She played for time.

"Collaboration is certainly a suggestion to be considered, Adam. Problem is, you are unfamiliar with the full panoply of his delusions, hallucinations, writings, familial history, audio recordings of our sessions, responses to medication, physical history, and so on. You would be dealing from ignorance, and Mr. Powers would have a field day exploiting that lack of knowledge."

Adam threw up his hands for emphasis. "So much the better!"

"How so?"

"I will be recording him the entire time, so you would be able to fit his comments into the schematic of his profile, with all its fragmented components. Perhaps a key would emerge you did not anticipate."

"Or, perhaps it will add unnecessary complications, extraneous details, to make it more difficult to see the forest for the trees."

"Well, think about it, Gail." He could not hide his disappointment.

She glanced at his endearing curls. For an instant she wondered if the hat and the brogue were not eccentricities at all, but camouflage, playfulness as armor. "Yes, yes, it is worth considering." Again, she felt vivid fantasies pushing and prodding for her attention. Partly giving in to them, she openly gazed into his eyes and said, "Very, very much worth considering. It is a tempting offer."

Adam perked up. "Good. Consider it—that's all I ask."

Gail gave him a flirtatious smile. "I will."

When he dropped her off at home, they shook hands, despite the strong impulse each had to kiss the other. Each knew it would only be a matter of time if they played their cards right.

~ *Alarm* ~

As soon as Dr. Hess arrived at the institution on Monday morning, June rushed up to inform her that Mr. Powers had disappeared. It took a while for the fact to sink in.

"Disappeared, June?"

"Yes—escaped, if you prefer. Gone."

Gail asked the usual questions: How? Why? When? Police called? Full search? After receiving the pertinent information, she asked June, "Has the son been called?"

June raised her eyebrows. "Mark Powers? No. I thought you should handle that."

"Yes," sighed Gail. "That will not be pleasant."

"No."

She retreated to her office, calling out unnecessary instructions to June, who was just closing the door. "Keep me informed of any new developments."

Receiving a nod in return, Gail waited until the door fully closed, then lowered her head into her hands, rubbing her tired eyes and running her hands through her hair. The weight of Saturday night's wine and Adam's eyes still lingered—and now this.

Sleep had not come easily after her dinner with Adam, and now this.

Blessed solitude offered only a brief respite, as June soon returned, announcing the arrival of Dr. Camara.

Before she had time to freshen up and brush her ruffled hair, he stood before her.

"I heard and came straight here."

"Thank you."

"How did he do it?"

"Don't know. Security is on it."

"Any idea why now?"

"No, but he left his latest writings"—she lifted a sheaf of papers—"hidden under his mattress. I haven't read them yet," she said, shuddering. "Not sure what they will tell us."

Unspoken were her fears of what they might contain.

Would they describe her conversations with Adam?

Or worse, her thoughts?

Impossible, she told herself. But. . . .

"Gail! Hello! Are you still with us?"

"Oh, sorry. What did you say?"

"I asked what you expect to find?"

"To find?"

He pointed. "In the papers."

Gail laughed. "With Mr. Powers, anything is possible."

"Well, let me know what you discover," he said. "After all, we are collaborators now."

The comment startled her. "Well, let's just say, for now, that we are colleagues sharing information."

He smiled, again with a slightly patronizing air. "Fair enough. Got to go."

He slipped out the door and closed it quietly.

Gail again ran her fingers through her hair, tousling it wildly.

She picked up a pen and made a note to herself.

It read: *Now I'm about to test my sanity. It's a gray morning, and I'm afraid.*

Then she picked up the latest writings of Mr. Powers and began reading, forcing herself not to look at the last pages first.

~ *Adam Camara Dreams* ~

Once Dr. Camara returned from his rounds, he sat silently in his office, contemplating the implications of his feelings for Gail Hess. Being ambitious, he weighed the risk of the relationship potentially leading to sex. He told himself it was not lust that drove him, but rivalry. Michael Powers had breached Gail's composure, slipped past her defenses, and lived inside her head. That fact ate at him more than the thought of her body. Yet the two became inseparable: her allure was the proof of Powers' reach, and his envy tangled with desire until he could no longer tell one from the other.

Of one thing he felt certain, he must proceed cautiously. Gail Hess was once the queen of the institution, heir apparent to research accolades and the subject of numerous perks bestowed by the administration, but now her stock had fallen precipitously since the whole "role-playing" incident. That fall made her vulnerable—and vulnerability, to Camara, was both a professional opportunity and a private temptation. *Ripe for intimacy, perhaps even sex.* He winced at the thought, feeling both desire and shame coil together

He tried to push the thought away. Terrible. I'm worse than the lowest of the low. Camara prided himself on honor and integrity. Yet he could not ignore the strange symmetry: Gail had fallen from grace, and Michael Powers had been the one to topple her. If he wanted her respect—and yes, perhaps her intimacy—he would have to take Powers apart, piece by piece, and prove himself stronger than the patient who had already claimed so much of her mind.

These earthly considerations aside, Dr. Camara genuinely felt a professional interest in this patient, Michael Powers. Still, jealousy stung him. How had Powers breached her formidable exterior, even for a moment, when Adam himself had barely made a dent? He realized that Gail Hess was no soft, touchy-feely girl. How did Powers breach her formidable exterior to cause her to take such an immense risk? Admittedly, he self-diagnosed a case of jealousy—what he would not give to see Dr. Hess naked! *In good time perhaps*, he thought. But *for now, focus on Mr. Powers.*

He pulled out his tam o'shanter and kneaded it absently. Perhaps the man represented the key to both professional advancement and Gail's heart. Like Dr. Hess, he saw the case as a potential gold mine, particularly given the manuscripts written by Powers. What other patient had documented such a voluminous and powerful glimpse into madness?

The thought of the manuscripts brought to mind Gail's odd response to his question about how she obtained them. "Someone gives them to me," she said. Still, she clearly avoided responding to his seemingly harmless questions of who. Why would she be so evasive?

"So many intriguing questions," he said aloud.

He felt a headache coming on, and left work early. Once home, he fed Bobby Burns, his black cat, and ate a simple meal. Afterward, he petted the cat and listened to an Irish lullaby, *"Too-ra-loo-ra-loo-ral"*, on an old record by Bing Crosby. This was his favorite antidote to headaches. An unusual noise intruded this time; a pounding in his head that sounded disturbingly like the sound of distant explosions. He chalked it up to dilation of blood vessels caused by something he ate or drank and went to bed early. But the pounding continued, sounding more and more as though he had wandered into a war zone, so he tried to divert the pain by fantasizing. Even that tried-and-true remedy failed, and he stumbled into the kitchen for a rare dose of sleeping pills. It worked. Almost as soon as his head hit the pillow, he fell asleep. A strange dream rose quickly from the murk.

~

Complete darkness. A dank, earthy stench clung to his nostrils, clogging his throat. He reached forward and his palms sank into cold, damp clay. Claustrophobia pressed against his ribs like iron bands. He staggered left, then right, only to slam into earthen walls that gave no quarter. The air thinned, each breath a labor, and panic gathered in his chest like a stone.

He was in a tunnel.

Still blind, he lurched forward until two faintly glowing lines appeared at his feet—thin veins of light that pulsed as though alive, leading deeper into the earth. Gasping, he stumbled between them, every step pulling him further from the surface. Suddenly, they blinked out.

Now only void: a silence vast as empty space, and loneliness crushed him with a weight greater than any wall. His throat tightened, his legs quivered. He turned frantically, but saw nothing. Then, from the murk, the black began to pale, dark grey, light grey, smudged white, until alabaster brilliance seared his eyes. Out of the whiteness, a skeleton leaned against the wall of the tunnel. Its hollow sockets locked on him. A bony finger lifted and curled, beckoning him closer.

~

With this gruesome image, Adam awoke. His headache had gone, but it took a while for his heart to stop pounding. *Must have left my head in that damn tunnel*, he thought wryly. Before the dream slipped back into his subconscious, he quickly grabbed pen and paper and wrote down a full description, then made a resolution not to tell Gail anything about it.

The next day at the institute, Adam caught up on work and avoided Dr. Hess. Even as he ministered to other patients, he could not get the dream—or nightmare—out of his mind. He recalled the panic surrounding Mr. Powers' condition when he was removed from Gail's bathroom, frozen in a fetal position. At the time, he picked up bits and pieces of information, including something about a tunnel and Vietnam. Because he had only recently arrived at the institute, and Mr. Powers was not his patient, he paid little attention. Now, memories of the incident came back in a trickle, and they revolved around talk of the Goddess, Gail's role-playing, Vietnam, and his schizophrenia.

Explosions, gunfire, tunnel, skeleton, he thought. *Is this how Powers seeps into thought? Not like contagion but like memory itself—leaking past rational defenses. If so, it is very effective. Now the beggar is gone, and I don't even have a chance to ask him questions. It has become personal, Mr. Powers.*

Camara had supreme confidence in his own abilities and began to view last night's strange headache and bizarre dream with a certain amount of detached curiosity. Of course, he had a professional interest in Mr. Powers, and a personal interest in Gail Hess, but had he become so suggestible that headaches and nightmares would result? This notion he rejected out of hand. He had never been prone to adolescent-level suggestion and had a certain contempt for those who so easily followed the lead of others. Still, such odd occurrences could not be ignored, and any good therapist must explore all possibilities. He felt stifled—how to proceed with Powers gone? The answer leapt into his mind immediately. Dig through the case files and find the pieces of the puzzle that fit.

This led him back to Gail Hess—he really must convince her to give him unlimited access to the files. The tam o'shanter sat heavy in his pocket; sometimes he wondered if it was not a joke but a disguise, an eccentricity he wore like armor. Speaking of disguises, he began to view himself more as a detective than a psychiatrist, and he decided to see Gail after all, but still had no intention of appraising her of his latest encounters with the mysterious Mr. Powers.

~ *Another Session* ~

"Gail, I came to ask if I may see your files on Michael Powers."

She noticed he appeared more somber than usual. "I see. But, as you know, there are confidentiality issues."

"These can be overcome."

"Why so anxious now? After all, we may never find him—or he may never return."

Adam detected a note of deep sadness in her voice. "That is why I thought this would be a good time. There is a break in your treatment, and I could take advantage of the pause."

"Really, Adam, now is not a good time. I am in the process of reviewing the files myself."

"Why? You said yourself he may not return."

"I don't think I need to give you an explanation, but, if you must know, I think I have been missing something—something that is right in front of my nose, but I can't see it."

"Let me help you."

She chuckled. "You never give up, do you?"

"No."

"I just finished reading his latest writings."

"And?"

Gail looked at him as if stricken by some unseen catastrophe. "I hoped to find how he planned to escape and where he was going."

"And?"

She handed him the last page. It read:

Tsk. Tsk. Tsk. Dr. Hess. You may discard everything you have read in this latest batch. It was meant to merely entertain and deflect. None of it is of any consequence. When you read this, you and Dr. Camara will be about to jump in bed together, and I will be far away. May the union of an immortal and a mortal not produce a modern-day Achilles. I trust I am passing this test, my Goddess—Michael Powers, Esq.

Adam finished reading and looked up at Gail, speechless.

"You see now what I have been telling you?" she said.

"I see more than you know."

"What does that mean?"

"It means, I am beginning to realize how . . . accurate your analysis is when it comes to Mr. Powers. I mean, I believe what you tell me about things I would normally consider impossible fantasies."

"Really? What brought about this change?"

"Enough to say that Mr. Powers has managed to get into my head, also. And that, Gail, is a hard thing to do."

"But he has done it?"

"Yes."

"How?"

Camara shook his head. "I need to know if you want to collaborate on this case or not. If so, then we can share everything with each other, wild hunches included. If not. . . . "

"I see. But the fact remains we may not ever see him again."

"We will."

Gail raised her eyebrows. "Oh?"

"Yes, and furthermore, you know it too."

"You are very presumptuous, Adam," said Gail. "Fortunately, I am used to men presuming to know my thoughts. Water off a duck's back. Most often, of course, they're wrong."

Adam broke into his infuriating smile. "But, not in this case?"

Gail remained silent for some time. Finally, grudgingly, she replied, "Not in this case."

"So, we should prepare!"

She gazed at him sternly. "If we are to work together, Dr. Camara, we must be forthcoming; honest with each other."

"What do you mean?"

Gail straightened. "I mean, you did not answer my questions."

"Which were?"

"How has Mr. Powers managed to get inside your head?"

He let out a deep, resigned sigh. "You are aware you also did not answer my question?"

"About collaboration? Yes, by all means let us collaborate, since his absence affords us the perfect opportunity to bring you up to speed. God knows what damage is being done as we speak, since he is out there wandering the streets without medication. But I want you to answer my question first."

"All right, it's a deal." He started to dig into his pocket to pull out the tam o'shanter.

"Stop! Please don't. This is not the time to play leprechaun. Just tell me, without the fake Scottish brogue."

"Leprechauns are Irish."

Gail chuckled. "Dr. Camara, this shows how delightfully ignorant you are about your own caricatures. Your hat's Scottish; leprechauns are Irish."

"Okay, you passed my test. But seriously, I will keep my hat in my pocket and tell you what happened. Even now, I have a hard time believing it myself." He proceeded to describe his odd headache and strange dream.

Gail Hess listened to his story with an impenetrable outward calm, making it impossible for Adam to glimpse the turmoil she felt as his words tumbled out. When he finished, she sat motionless, stunned. Images of certain characters from Mr. Powers' writings came vividly to mind, racing across her consciousness like lasers—one in particular.

"Well, what do you think?" asked Adam.

She spoke slowly, still mulling the implications of his story. "May I see that hat again?"

"What?"

"May I see that hat again?"

"Why?"

"Please."

He handed it to her.

Gail Hess held it up to her eyes and turned it this way and that. She then dangled it in front of her desk lamp and watched the shadows dance.

"Nature," she whispered.

"What?"

"Dr. Camara, I think we are both, to Michael Powers, shadows projected on a cave wall."

Chapter Five

Hiding in Open View

Hello, Ms. Telles

~ Dog Days ~

Now that I have succeeded in worming myself into the heads of Dr. Hess and Dr. Camara, I have my own head to consider. No car, no money, yet San Francisco is a lovely place for a pedestrian to lose himself in the crowd. Plenty of homeless around for a homeless man to find a home.

First and foremost, I'm really here, not hallucinating in that damn institution. I know I've been off medication, and one can't be too careful about those petty distinctions between real and unreal. My best bet is to seek out a dog who will tell me the truth. After all, we began this little story with a dog telling me I was indeed alive, and he was right. Dogs don't lie—most of the time. Hey, that's still a better record than humans. Ants, for example, never lie, but I don't see any around right now. Rocks are the most honest, but I've lost my touch with them. In San Francisco, dogs often walk their master-slaves, so there must be one close by. Ah! Here is one now!

"Hello."

"Hello!"

"Am I really here?"

"Looks like it to me."

"No, no, really try. Sniff away. I need confirmation. I need to know for sure."

"Well, then pet me. I have an itch."

"Where? There?"

"Oh, yes! Oh, yes!"

("It's okay," I tell the master-slave. "I love dogs. He's not bothering me.")

"Well? You've certainly had enough time, and enough sniffs. Am I really here?"

"Yup. You smell like human madness, and you stopped my itch, so you're definitely here. You are real enough. Know any human who is the master-slave of a bitch in heat?"

"Nope."

"Too bad. Got to go. Ugh! Still can't train him to stop tugging. Bye!"

"Bye!"

("Nice dog," I tell the master-slave. The formalities must be observed.)

~

Okay, I'm really here, and it's getting cold. San Francisco's wind is a bastard. Time to hike it over to Marie Telles' house. Talk later. These hills make concentration an impossible luxury.

~

Here it is, just as I remembered. A magnificent Victorian house rising in stately grandeur. Multiple turrets loom against the sky, while a wraparound porch accentuates the house's charms: swirling curves, fish-scale shingles, and recessed bays combine to create the intimate allure my mother found irresistible. The house stands atop a steep hill overlooking San Francisco Bay. The grounds are a lush mix of shrubs, flowers, and ornamental trees that seamlessly merge to form an organic extension of the architecture itself. Lovely.

I hesitate to knock. My mother appears next to me, smiling. So beautiful. So very beautiful. She is dead, and I am not so far gone as to not realize she is a hallucination. Still, hallucinations are welcome to many of us who are schizophrenic. Nice break from the voices. After all, Marie Telles was Mother's lover, and they were deeply in love. Mother's presence makes me braver. I knock. I wait. I knock again. The door opens.

"Michael!"

Marie Telles looks shocked, as she should be. It has been a long time. My strategy is all laid out—tell the truth and let the chips fall where they may. Well, most of the truth.

"Hello, Marie."

We hug. I enter. I try to maintain the type of sanity most of you are comfortable with.

"Come and sit," she says. "I'll make tea. My God, what brings you here?"

We go into the little anteroom where my mother so often chatted with Marie. Mother follows, gazing all the while at Marie, who, of course, does not see. Mother must haunt this house often.

I look around before I sit. "It all looks the same as I remember it, Marie. Even as a boy . . . Nanny Peach. . . . " It is hard to continue. The memories have a physical impact, and I cannot find words.

"Dear Nanny Peach," says Marie with emotion. "Those were halcyon days. I heard she died with your name on her lips."

I glance at Mother, whose face seems inexpressibly sad.

Marie hands me a cup of tea. Marie Telles, always ready with tea. I look at her and see an older woman still in possession of her good looks and aristocratic bearing; a bit too much makeup perhaps, but she has obligations.

I notice Mother is fading, and I concentrate on keeping her beautiful presence a little longer, but it is no good.

"Michael, are you all right."

"Yes, why?"

"Because I've asked you the same question three times. You were wandering."

"Sorry."

"I am so happy to see you have been released." She waits. Always discreet, Marie.

"I left."

"You left? Did they let you?"

"Well, not exactly."

Her eyes bore into mine. "Michael, I was there when you were born. Your mother and I raised you for a while. I know you quite well. I know your history. Just tell me why you're here."

"I think you know."

"I don't, Michael, but I can guess."

The last of Mother's spirit blinks out. I feel myself slump in the chair. "I am alone."

"Michael, you have a son, you have a home. Why are you here?"

"Are you afraid of me?"

She laughs. "Please, Michael. Let's not get dramatic. You are still that little boy whose father. . . . " She stops and shakes her head.

"Whose father?"

"The past, Michael. I am more interested in now. Please, why are you here? Do you need a place to stay?"

"Yes, Marie, I need a place to stay."

She shakes her head. "To hide, Michael. Isn't that it?"

"Yes."

"I can't. First, there's Mark. What do I tell Mark if I hide you? He'll be worried sick, and they will be searching. Is that what you really want?"

I desperately want to tell Marie that Mark has been inhabited by an alien being, a dead soldier from Vietnam, and that he is no longer my son. Nonetheless, I know that would be a mistake.

"Marie, for my Mother's sake please let me stay a little while."

"But, Michael, you're not giving me a good enough reason. I am sure you are off the medication. Things will just get worse. You know that. It would be for your own good to return to the institution so they can look after you."

"Marie, I will die there. I promise you that. Did you know that Mother was just here, looking at you with love?"

She hesitates, her eyes flutter momentarily before she regains composure. "Ghosts, Michael. Ghosts that aren't real."

"Believe me, she was here, Marie. Speaking of Mother, when you and she were in China, did you ever believe in *hHer*?"

"Her?"

"Come on, Marie. *Her.* The one who sent me. *She* told me to come. Mother believed in *Her*, and I know you do also. You went to China with Mother to find *Her.*"

"That was a long time ago, Michael."

"*She* is timeless, Marie. *She* told me to come to you. Do this for Mother, please! As you can see, I am rational, I am not drooling down my shirt. I do not believe anyone is out to get me or that you are an alien in disguise. I am asking for your help. Please."

Marie sighs, and I think I am making progress.

"Marie, just for a few days. If nothing happens, then I will leave."

"What do you mean, *if nothing happens*?"

"Marie, *she* will come. *She* will make an appearance. You will see."

"I never did actually see *her*, Michael. The closest was in the asylum in China. Even if *She* comes, Michael, I will never see *Her*."

"I know, but I also know you came to believe. Father told me so." I lean close, for emphasis. "Marie, I repeat, *She* told me to come, just as *She* told Mother to return to China."

"Yes, and that got me raped!"

I can say nothing in response to this.

"Michael, is *She* the same person as your infamous Goddess?"

"I think so. Or, maybe, some manifestation of Goddess. Surely you know, Marie, that my schizophrenia has allowed me to see and hear things no one else can. Mother, for example, was just here, staring at you."

"Is she still here?" Marie's eyes tear up and she trembles.

"No."

She refills my tea and remains standing. "I'll let you stay for a couple of days, and then, Michael, I must either turn you in or ask you to go. Even that will get me in trouble."

I decide to take a risk. I should leave well enough alone, but something makes me say it. "Why are you doing this, Marie?" Lawyers are trained not to ask one question too many. I kick myself, but not too hard.

"For old time's sake. For your mother."

"Do you want to see *Her*?"

"*She* is one of your voices, Michael. Not mine."

"You know my mother occasionally heard Goddess?"

"Yes."

"Do you think Mother was schizophrenic?"

"I think she had a gift."

"Do I?"

"You might."

"Is that why you let me stay?"

"Look, Michael. I'm letting you stay for many reasons—and for no reason I can really make any sense of." She smiles. "I am impulsive, even in my old age. Always gets me in trouble. China, for example, with your mother." She shudders. "Remember, this is only for a couple of days, and then you must go."

"What if *She* appears?"

"I will never see *Her*."

"Don't be so sure." I do not know why I say that. I'm impulsive, just like Marie. Damn it, *She* must have told me to come here for a reason. Either *She* supports me or not. If not, then I guess I belong back in the institution. You see, dear Reader, I am eminently rational.

"I have to go," says Marie. "I have an engagement. Let me take you to your room. Upstairs, corner room. Are you hungry?"

"Yes."

"Do you remember?"

"The kitchen? Yes."

"Help yourself. I must take a bath and get dressed. I take it you have no clothes? No money?"

"Correct."

"Jacob left some clothes. I'll lay them out for you."

"Thank you, Marie."

"Only a couple of days, Michael."

"I understand."

Dear Reader, I do understand. Believe me, I understand Marie Telles very well. Have I not written about her? I know what she wants. What is it, you ask? Like all of us, Marie Telles needs confirmation and support for a lifetime of questionable actions. Here is the conundrum: the most virtuous men and women crave such confirmation, even if it comes from the shallowest human forgiveness. The truly evil, by contrast, care little for exoneration. They know they will never face judgment from the ultimate arbiter—the Universe—which neither praises nor condemns. To many killers with a bent toward cosmology, that is just what the doctor ordered. For in the cosmos, no supernova is guilty of suicide, no hurricane convicted of murder.

Marie, not being evil, longs for confirmation and support all the more. But unlike the cosmological killer, she must seek it from fallible human beings. Poor Marie. Poor us. Human integrity is a fragile illusion, a sham we must constantly shore up. We are arbiters of our own fate, as are cheetahs, whales, termites, and existentialist philosophers. Marie knows this. She is less nun than cosmologist, versed in the secret indifference of the Universe. She carries the peculiar temperament of those who seem outwardly cosmopolitan, regal, and conformist, yet inwardly reckless and untamed—finding an almost erotic thrill in risk, the kind of thrill one might liken to stolen sex in elevators.

Hence, my couple of days. I will do whatever it takes to extend that time, until . . . until when? Well, of course, until *She* comes and gives me further instructions. I have told you, dear Reader, that I am here for a reason. I think I can rely on staying here for more than a couple of days if I play my cards right.

~ *Settling In* ~

The room is comfortable. This is my first night here, and Marie has left for her engagement. Food in my stomach. Wine—quality wine. I feel better than I have in ages. I wander around the house, remembering the past. Strange to be out of the nuthouse. The richness of the décor is quite a contrast to the sterile green of the institution. A buzzing begins to flicker on and off in my mind, like a field of listless crickets. They are returning, I know it. A low rumble overtakes the buzzing. Yes, it is definitely Them. God and Goddess. Still can't make out their words, but I am surprised by how nervous I become. After all, it has been a long time since They emerged from the dark places in my mind. Medication's all gone, so no more barriers. *She* is near. Thank God I know where Marie keeps the liquor. Bless her for stocking so much. I drink and wait. Surprisingly, the bourbon helps and the rumbling fades. Even though I want to see *Her*, I guess I need a little more time to settle in before dealing with the deities. I wish Mother would return, but there is no sign of her.

I go to bed for lack of anything better to do and listen for Marie to return. I thought I would stay up to greet her, but after all, I'm not her father (or, more accurately, her concerned son).

~

I must have nodded off, but something awakens me. Perhaps Marie is home. Can't sleep anyway, so I go downstairs. More noise, a clattering.

"Marie?"

Nothing.

I stumble around in the dark.

"Marie?"

Nothing.

I make my way to the little anteroom and turn on a light.

She is sitting in a chair, as if waiting for me. As beautiful as ever, *Her* body posed like a judgment, *Her* legs crossed seductively.

Mr. Powers, how does one justify a life without cruelty, and therefore also without the distilled beauty of cruelty?

I am too stunned to answer. After all, I was expecting to see Marie.

She holds out both hands, palms up. **Mr. Powers?**

My mind will not work properly, and I feel confused and frightened. "Where is my mother?" I ask stupidly.

"Your mother is there."

I follow *Her* eyes and see my mother standing in the corner, her luminous eyes gazing at me with such love that I immediately feel better and more confident. In fact, I am emboldened.

"Goddess, you never get tired of asking me that damn question. Why do you always ask about cruelty?"

What makes you think I am a Goddess?

"Are you not?"

Perhaps. Truth be known, Chosen One, I am a metaphor. Same as God.

"A metaphor? I've heard that before—Metaphorical God and Metaphorical Goddess. Do *You* ever give a straight answer?"

Straight is false. Direct is directionless. Certainty is death. Curvature is the nature of the universe.

"Dear Lady, am I talking to Einstein?"

For the first time, I hear *Her* laugh. ***Straight will not navigate the universe. Curvature dictates movement. Why do you think I am a Goddess?***

Now it is my turn to laugh. "Well, for one thing, You've told me that. Also, you have curves. I have seen them, Dr. Hess."

"Michael?"

I turn to look and see Marie. When I turn back, *She* is gone. So is my Mother.

"Michael, I heard you mention Dr. Hess?"

"You heard?"

"Yes. I assume it is your voices?"

"Not this time. How was your party?"

She looks around the room. Of course, she does not see Goddess. "The party was good. Are the voices getting worse?"

"Not at all. Just having a friendly chat with a hallucination." I chuckle, hoping it sounds reassuring. "We schizophrenics are rarely alone."

"Did you bring your medication?"

"You know I did not."

"Michael, this is why I think you need to go back to the institution."

I knew this would be a problem. I should never have come downstairs. "Marie, as you can see, I am perfectly calm and rational. I am not a threat to anyone, least of all to myself. My relationship with my hallucinations and delusions has become almost companionable—an uneasy truce, but a workable one. Please don't let this bother you. How was your party?"

"Why were you talking to Dr. Hess? One of your hallucinations?"

"No, I was just talking to myself. And you enjoyed it?"

"I told you; it was good." She stares at me for a long time, obviously weighing what to say next. Finally, she says, "I'm going to bed, Michael. Good night."

Now I'm really worried. "Good night, Marie. I'll be fine. Please don't call anyone."

"I already promised you a couple of days, Michael. I will not go back on my word. Still, needless to say, I remain worried."

"I understand. Thank you."

~

Next morning I am making breakfast to surprise Marie. I am not much of a cook, but my dinner parties are justifiably famous. None of my ghosts complained—well, except for Diane who always gave me hell about not making real mashed potatoes. For Marie, it will be real eggs and bacon. They are in her refrigerator, so she must like them. Hopefully, she likes coffee. I hear her coming down the stairs, so I get control of myself and exclaim in my most cheerful voice, "Good morning! Breakfast is almost done!"

Marie is dressed nicely, as if planning to go out, but I think she would never allow herself to look disheveled in front of anyone.

"Coffee?" I ask.

"Well, this is a nice surprise. Yes, a cup of coffee would be lovely."

She sits and we both eat. When finished, I ask, "What are your plans today?"

"Oh, nothing much. Off to meet some friends. Go shopping. Nothing special. And you?"

"Well, I think it best if I stay here. Do you want me to make lunch for you?"

"Good heavens, no! Please don't bother. After all, you are the guest here."

"How about dinner?"

"No, please don't. I'll get Chinese takeout. Tomorrow, when I have more time, I'll cook."

"Marie, will you tell me more about Mother."

"What do you mean?"

"I mean, I have some questions about Mother. Tomorrow, over our Chinese take-out, do you mind if we talk about her?"

"Not at all."

I notice she appears a bit concerned. I want to reassure her.

"Marie, it is nothing serious. I just want to get to know her better. I mean, you were her best friend . . . and. . . . "

"Lover. Just say it, Michael. It is not as if it were some great secret. Oh, it's no problem. I am happy to talk about your mother. I know she would be glad her son is interested. But, really Michael, I must go. We will talk more."

With that, Marie leaves., and I remain alone in the house. It is quite comfortable here. I can feel the house itself holding me, as though it has accepted me. I would not want to leave. I think my mother has claimed that anteroom, and she has sanctified it as a holy place. That is where I will see both again. The day is uneventful, and when Marie comes home, we chat for a while, avoiding the subject of my visions, and both of us go to bed.

I lie in bed and tell myself to be patient. Tomorrow will come soon enough. Now, I must prepare questions for Marie. I mustn't let a question go unasked. I call *her*; I call Goddess; I call Dr. Hess; I call Diane; but no one comes. It's lonely. The silence thickens. Tomorrow, one of them will surely appear.

~

In the meantime, dear Reader, let me talk to you. Though many of you have been with me on this long, long journey, I assume that most of you have little or no experience with schizophrenics. Well, here is the deal: you 'normals' live in a very limited reality, albeit one very well adapted to popular culture, one which is acceptable. What I mean to say is that all of you are schizophrenics—you all hear voices—but you give credence to only a limited number. Your bandwidth is narrow, your frequencies choked, so that only the smallest trickle of sound gets through. We schizophrenics are not so tightly filtered. Our minds blaze with wavelengths your suburbs cannot tolerate. Like insects that see in the ultraviolet or snakes that sense the infrared, this openness provides glorious access to what you 'normals' call delusions and hallucinations. This liberation can be both euphoric and devastating.

Think of it this way: your minds are gated suburbs; ours are open bazaars. Of course, I am told by numerous deities (who should know) that I am not schizophrenic but another Chosen One like my father. Now They want me to have another child with another Chosen One so our genes get mixed in. That would make the child far more powerful. At least, that's my understanding for now. So, instead of calling you 'normals', I should call you humans. Still, I prefer to think of myself as a schizophrenic. The other interpretation scares me. Schizophrenia means a diagnosis; Chosen One means destiny. And destiny, dear Reader, is terrifying.

Oh, wait a moment. It's the buzzing again.

~

Sorry, I stopped writing for a while. Now, I wait, anticipating Their arrival. The crickets chirp. The rumbling is ominous.

They arrive.

Two figures stand silhouetted at the foot of my bed. My eyes trace the contours of their bodies, and through the haze of fear, I see a large, imposing man and a small woman, her head slightly tilted. She appears puzzled. They talk, but their words are fuzzy and unintelligible, their bodies shifting like silhouettes in a lantern show. From humans they turn into birds—then fishes—then trees—clouds—mountains—reptiles—all the while speaking in voices that tear the fabric of my hearing. Finally, their shape-changing slows, their outlines harden, and two human-sized ants stand upright at the foot of my bed.

Yes, yes, I have seen this before.

Antennas waving, legs gesturing, their words begin to resolve into meaning . . .

He's escaped. Now what? asks the male, *His* swampy voice a deep, dank rumble that fills my room with slag and sulfur, as though the black lungs of a collapsing star had been set to breathe through the walls. It is not speech but tectonic grinding, molten plates of Earth rasping against one another, a language of friction and fire. After *He* speaks, my blanket turns greenish-black, glistening with a moist, phlegm-like shimmer. The wood of the bed frame seems to warp and bow inward, as though language itself were a weight pressing down upon matter. When *His* words finally subside, *His* breathing lingers, a procession of reptilian hisses, a hiss that might have been the first sound ever uttered when life crawled from sea to land.

The female's reply comes with a hard-edged impatience. **Now—on to the ashes, and the final round of treatments to cure Your faction's addiction to so-called First Principles and make sure the next step is taken. You may as well get used to the idea of Superior Ones replacing the human race.**

Her voice cuts like wind through salt, bleaching the soot but never quite erasing its stain. **It scours the inside of my skull, leaving deserts where there had been rivers, parched silence where there had been song. Yet there is a strange clarity in her cruelty: as if she is stripping not only flesh from bone but illusion from essence.**

So, it begins again. I tremble. **Final stillness is no stillness. It is annihilation. It is the blank roar of the cosmos when even memory has been extinguished.**

Not so, comes a voice. ***Stillness is stillness.***

It passes so quickly I cannot tell whether it came from God or Goddess, from star or insect, from the sky above or the marrow of my bones.

Chapter Six

Digging in Sand

Following Tracks

After work on Friday, Dr. Adam Camara sat in the office of Dr. Gail Hess to discuss the disappearance of Michael Powers.

"Have we found out how he escaped?" asked Adam.

"Not yet. Security's still working on it, although there is some suspicion that Joe was involved."

"I see. And the son?"

Gail sighed. "He has been informed. Flying in today from New York. The police checked Mr. Powers' house. No one there. It's on the market and the realtor maintaining it has been told to watch for him.

"Okay, so where do you think he is?"

Gail looked at him intently. "Do you want to play detective?"

Adam perked up, pulled out his tam o'shanter, and tugged it on at a jaunty angle. "Are you kidding? It's what I always wanted to be, even as a little kid." He looked down at his white lab coat. "Can't understand how I ended up like this. Should have been a gumshoe. What do you need?"

"Mr. Powers is a low priority to the police, as he has no history of violence. Perhaps we can help fill in a few gaps."

"How so?"

"There are people he knows. Read his writings."

"You have them."

Gail flashed her most alluring smile and held out a large binder. "Here, you can start with this, Mr. Collaborator. Starts with his parents in China—light reading material."

Adam took it. "Do you think you know where he is?"

"I have a few ideas. Tomorrow is Saturday."

"So?"

"Perfect time to visit some leads. Want to come?"

Adam grinned and lifted his tam o'shanter. "Where to first?"

"Marie Telles."

"Who is she?"

"Lover and confidante of Bai Meiying, the mother of our missing friend, Michael Powers. Tell you more later." Gail tapped on the binder. "But to begin, you have to read this first one. There are others." Her face darkened. "You know, even now he is. . . . "

"Gail, I know what you're thinking. Let's not get too deeply into that scenario. I can't wrap my head around it."

"Okay, we'll leave it at this: he writes a lot. Reading these binders is your homework. In the meantime, meet you here at ten o'clock tomorrow, and we'll go pay a few visits."

~

That night, Gail Hess could not sleep. Images of goddesses (of all varying forms and types) flashed through her mind. In front of each knelt Michael Powers. The last of the goddesses appeared—Gail Hess herself—breasts exposed, looking down at Michael Powers who gazed back at her with a licentious smile. She tried to push the image out of her mind, but it remained like a photographic negative burned onto an indestructible plate, and as she struggled to erase the picture, for the first time, she thought she heard a voice in her head. This terrified her more than the image. Again, she pushed it away and tried to sleep. Sigmund kept meowing, so Gail went into the kitchen to have a cup of tea. Sigmund followed, still pestering her for attention.

She wanted to call Adam just to talk, needing someone to distract her from the disturbing images and voice. But her fierce independence and iron will made that impossible. Her only viable option was to focus on Sigmund—a woman finding comfort in her cat, providing her a reassuring touchstone with normalcy. Sigmund did not disappoint, purring contentedly under her strokes. Gradually, the vision and the voice faded.

Adam Camara came to her mind, his profile as solemn as Lincoln's on a penny, and she had the urge to masturbate, but the presence of Sigmund presented an irrational deterrent. Public displays were anathema to her, so she resigned herself to constructing mental fantasies. Suddenly, the other side of Adam's coin glared at her with his patronizing smile, quite smug with his success at cajoling her to make him a co-equal collaborator. In future, when their groundbreaking paper had been published to great acclaim, she knew the credit would be prioritized as 'Drs. Adam Camara and Gail Hess.' Despite these blemishes, his buoyant personality and boyish good looks made her smile and long to see him the next morning.

She noticed Sigmund had fallen asleep, and without his purring, the apartment fell deathly silent, like it was holding its breath. Again, she heard faint stirrings in her mind; a tiny, distant voice, vibrating unintelligibly. It seemed to creep closer, getting louder, and just as she began to make out individual words, Sigmund suddenly leaped from her lap to the table, yowling a spine-tingling screech. Gail almost fell backward on her chair, while the teacup and saucer went flying from impact with the terrified cat. Sigmund's panic swiftly transferred to her, and she frantically looked around, as if under attack. After investigating the apartment and seeing nothing, she rushed to the comfort of her bed, almost knocking over the chair in her haste.

~

"You look terrible," said Adam Camara the next morning when they met at her office.

"Well, thank you. Couldn't sleep. So grateful for the gentlemanly compliment, by the way."

"Anytime. Shall we?"

"Yes. I'll drive."

When they pulled up in front of Marie Telles's house, Adam gazed at the old Victorian mansion, and said sardonically, "Norma Desmond. Does she have a swimming pool?"

"You had better hope not."

Although the banter was amusing, Gail felt quite nervous. After all, Marie Telles was a major figure in the writings of Mr. Powers. She had accompanied his mother, Bai Meiying, to China during the civil war, went through the hell of that violent period, was raped, and bore witness to *her* appearance at the Chinese mental institution. Just as importantly, she helped raise Michael Powers for a few years before Bai Meiying died in a car crash. Gail felt as if she were meeting a mythological figure. Absurd, but the thought niggled at her. She forced the mantle of professional demeanor on her agitated thoughts and told herself that Mr. Powers had written about Ms. Telles with incomplete knowledge, exaggerated, or had simply made it all up.

Gail scanned the windows before approaching the front door, half expecting to see the dramatic rustle of a curtain on the second floor, behind which some mysterious person would be watching. But, alas, no such melodrama happened, and she walked up the entrance path, past a lovely garden, and knocked, casting a glance at Adam Camara who stood solidly beside her. They did not wait long. A lovely woman, older but fresh and appealing, smiled at them after opening the door.

"Yes?"

"Sorry to bother you, but we are from the Smythe-Haines Psychiatric Hospital and are here about Mr. Michael Powers."

"Oh, is there a problem?"

"Well, he has gone missing, and we are trying to find him."

"I see. Come in, please."

Gail Hess thought of all the Sherlock Holmes stories she had read, and tried to interpret the facial expressions of Ms. Telles—but found nothing more than polite interest.

Once seated in the anteroom, Marie Telles asked, "How may I help you?"

"You knew Mr. Powers?"

"Yes."

"As you probably know, he has been a patient in our hospital for some time."

"Yes."

"Well, a few days ago, he disappeared without being given permission to leave, and we are concerned about his welfare."

"Yes, I see. Is he in danger of hurting himself?"

"No, we do not think so."

"Hurting others?"

"No, but we worry that he is on the streets without medication. You are familiar with his illness?"

"Yes, schizophrenia."

"And you knew his mother and father?"

"Yes."

"Have you by any chance seen him recently?"

"No."

Dr. Camara coughed. "Has he called you?"

"No. May I ask a question?"

"Of course," replied Camara.

"Do you have the power to force him to go back, once you find him?"

"We do. His son signed the commitment papers."

"I see."

"His house is being sold, and we are not sure where he would go. We took a chance that he might have come to you," said Adam.

"No, I'm afraid not."

"But you do know him well?" asked Gail.

"Yes."

"If he comes or you hear from him, would you call us immediately, please?"

"Yes, of course. Do you think . . . well, what might happen if you can't find him?"

"Well," said Adam. "Without his medication, he will have increasing psychotic episodes, which might cause him to do unpredictable things."

"But not hurt himself?"

Gail shook her head. "We don't think so, but that can never be ruled out."

"Okay, yes, I'll call you immediately if I see him."

"Thank you. Here is my card."

Marie took the card and escorted them to the door. "Please let me know if you find him," she said.

~

Once Adam and Gail had settled in the car, he exclaimed, "She knows where he is!"

"What makes you say that?" asked Gail without a hint of surprise.

"Come on, Gail, you must have noticed her curt replies, her lack of alarm, and the questions about his safety."

"Of course I did. In fact, I think he is in the house right now. Still, we can't exactly demand a search warrant. Besides, I think this might be to our benefit."

"How?"

"I have met many women like Marie Telles. From what Mr. Powers wrote of her, she is an idealist—a woman who is attracted to any *cause célèbre*. Furthermore, she is accustomed to taking risks. My God, the woman followed her lover—Bai Meiying, mother of Michael Powers—all the way to war torn China! She went on a dangerous quest to find a mysterious, if not mythical, woman. She was raped. Yet, still today, the spark of danger excites her."

"If his writings are even remotely accurate," interjected Adam.

"True, his writing style reflects his psychoses. Obviously, no such person exists as the magical woman they sought, or any God or Goddess, or Great Warrior Ant. Nevertheless, I believe that is a schizophrenic delusion built around a core of reality."

"Hmm, I wonder," said Adam skeptically.

Gail felt a twinge of anger. She felt her diagnosis to be clever, precise, and insightful. "Assuming we both agree that she knows where he is, do you have a better explanation?"

"Yes."

This made Gail even angrier. Her face reddened and she berated herself for displaying such emotion. Asserting her iron will, she calmed down and smiled as genuinely as possible. "I would love to hear it."

Seeing her irritation, Adam backtracked. "Well, I haven't read all the binders, and I'm sure I'm wrong, but I think Marie Telles is hiding Mr. Powers because she feels a sense of obligation to her dead lover, Bai Meiying. Would not his mother protect him under similar circumstances?"

"Unless she understood his own welfare lay in the institute rather than the outside."

"That is neither here nor there," said Adam, returning to his confident air. "Marie Telles did not have him committed. She watched him grow up. I assume she still loves the memory of Bai Meiying. No, I am quite sure she is hiding him out of a sense of loyalty."

Gail had a sudden epiphany. She must not, under any circumstances, enter a relationship with this man. *Misery, misery, that is what he will bring*, she thought.

They remained sitting in the car, and Gail leaned down to peer at the second story windows one last time. To her surprise, she felt certain she did see a curtain rustle.

"Oh!" she blurted.

"What?"

She straightened behind the wheel and turned the ignition. "He is in there, I'm sure of it."

"What did you see?"

"What every person who has ever watched a bad gothic movie sees."

"A shadow behind the window?"

"Close enough. Question is, what to do now?"

Adam laughed. "Leave, so they don't get suspicious."

"Good idea."

On the way back to the institute, both remained silent, lost in their own thoughts. Finally, Adam broke the quiet by whipping out his tam o'shanter. "Well, Sherlock had his deerstalker hat, and I have my tam o'shanter."

"You're an idiot," chuckled Gail, reconsidering her pledge to never have a relationship with this man-boy. "Besides, you're no Sherlock Holmes."

"I want to go back," said Adam suddenly.

"What? Now?"

"No, no. I'm going back tomorrow."

"Why?"

"Get more information, maybe spot him."

"Not so fast, mister. That was my own thought. Nevertheless, a surprise visit on Sunday may not be a good idea."

"Then what is is a better idea?"

"I call and get permission to return, while you wait outside about half an hour before I'm supposed to show up. Perhaps we'll catch him leaving."

"But all he has to do is stay in his room."

"True, but what if I ask to be given a tour of her house. After all, I am a member of the San Francisco Historical Society."

"You are?"

"I am now."

Adam laughed. "Are you always such a good liar?"

"Aren't all psychiatrists?"

"We would make a good team, Gail."

"No, we would be terrible together. We would cancel each other out."

"Maybe. I'll do the stakeout, you make the call."

"Deal."

Adam smiled broadly. "Oi! This is bloody fun!"

Gail looked at him with a smirk. "Bloody is an English term, not Irish. Try to stay in character, Nature."

Immediately after saying this, Gail inhaled sharply. "My God, what did I just say?"

Adam stared at her. "What?"

"Did I just call you Nature?"

"Yeah. Why?"

"You haven't read the second binder yet, have you?"

"No."

"When you read the second binder, you will know."

"Know what?"

"Know that Nature was Michael Powers' best friend in Vietnam."

"So?"

"Nature wore a tam o'shanter."

"Okay. Gail, you said his name just because you formed an association. Perfectly innocent. No ominous magic there."

"You don't understand, Adam. Mr. Powers is convinced we're projections from his past."

"What do you mean?"

"We're nothing more than vessels, occupied by his dead comrades. Well, his dead friends . . . and enemies."

"And goddesses?"

Gail looked very pale. "Yes."

~ *Adam Camara Ponders* ~

After returning home, Adam Camara felt a headache coming on. Gail's dissembling distressed him. This extraordinary patient, Michael Powers, had achieved more than simply twisting his way into her head. The situation was worse than he had feared. She clearly stood in danger of believing his psychotic delusions, or at least being drawn into them. His strange powers seemed to be consuming her identity.

Pooh! he thought. *I'm exaggerating. Gail Hess is merely confused about the web he has spun. Now that she has accepted me as her collaborator, perhaps I can counteract this miasma of delusions that has so dazzled her. I must read the second binder and find out more about this Nature fellow.*

That night, he had another dream.

He first sensed unbearable heat and began to sweat profusely. Before he had time to react, a warm rain poured down, making him feel even more sticky and uncomfortable. He opened his eyes wide and found himself crouched behind some stone battlement. As if viewed from the perspective of a disembodied observer, he looked at his body and discovered he wore military fatigues, though he had never been in the army. On his head drooped a soaked tam o'shanter—its plaid crown sagging, yet heavy with portent, a relic of some memory not his own. *Why this hat? Why always this hat?* Dark, curly hair stuck out from under it, just as his always did. A rifle materialized in his hand, already soaked from the rain. It appeared to be dusk, with just enough light to illuminate a soupy gray, alien scene.

A stone fortress spread around him in ruins, the perimeter made of thick, crenellated walls that curved in an oblong shape, with a second-story defensive parapet (where he sat) and embrasures for rifle fire. A vast, deteriorating brick square, uneven and treacherous to navigate, dominated the center of the fortress. At one end of the square stood a gutted church, still grand despite the ravages of time. Its enormous roof had long since collapsed, filling the interior with jagged protuberances of shattered rubble, the cleaved slabs a hodgepodge of crazed geometry. Statues of saints lay in bizarre positions, their great heads and shoulders rising at odd angles from the tile floor. Jungle vines girdled the stone saints in organic bondage, as though the green world itself had risen to punish the white stone for carrying fire and faith where neither belonged.

The fortress was a stony welt, a colonial canker amidst the healthy green tissue of the jungle. Around the inside base of the perimeter wall, below the parapet, were various barracks, a mess hall and assorted other rooms and shanties, all roofless and in ruin, slumped drunkenly against the massive walls.

This vision overwhelmed him in waves of undefinable fear. He saw vague, shadowy lumps moving about—soldiers. Across the courtyard, a figure leaned against the base of the wall. When the figure looked up at Adam, it smiled. The face was clearly, unambiguously Michael Powers, years younger, gaunt, and apparently ill. The smile was both recognition and accusation, a mirror held to Adam's face. Gunfire erupted, and green tracers curved their way into the fortress even as red ones raced laser-like from the parapet into the tree line. With a shock of primal fear, his hands trembled, and he realized he cowered in the middle of a battle. The M16 rifle in his shaking hands seemed a strange object, alien yet inevitable, and he felt confused about what to do with it.

A deafening explosion shattered the courtyard below his position, light blooming like a false dawn across the ruined church, the broken saints illuminated for one blinding second before darkness swallowed them again. Adam woke with a start, jerking upright, and went to the bathroom to wash the sweat from his face. "God help me," he whispered. "What the hell is going on here?"

~

Dear Reader, we know, don't we?

~

Adam Camara rapidly dismissed the dream, unwilling to replay it long enough to remember. To his relief, it slipped away into the subconscious. Instead, he turned his attention to Gail Hess. Unwilling to admit he himself was in the grip of something unusual, he focused on the Goddess delusion of Mr. Powers that seemed to have entrapped Gail in some sort of hypnotic projection. He found to his dismay that concentration on medical issues shattered when he pictured her stunt of appearing bare-breasted before the patient, and he angrily thought, *I'm falling for her, goddammit!* He felt an intense desire to touch those breasts but pushed the idea away. Glancing at the table next to his bed, he turned on the light and saw the binder and picked it up. *Gail thinks it is all in his writing. Well, let's see.*

The next morning, over a light breakfast, Adam continued reading. He read with particular interest the description of Michael Powers' schizophrenic father. *This Goddess nonsense is nothing new, if one can believe what is in these pages. Father passed it on to son, and it grew in power, until . . . until what exactly? Until the Goddess obsession of Mr. Powers is threatening to overwhelm Gail's good sense . . . again.*

Something niggled at his mind, and he kept driving it away, but no matter what he tried, it came back. This Nature person. Must be in the next binder. When he tired of the complex knot of Gail Hess and her problems, he inevitably returned to his increasingly personal struggles with Nature. Not yet aware of this character's true personality, Adam assumed the only similarity lay in the rather shallow coincidence of the tam o'shanter. Of course, such trivial parallels, on the surface, did not interest him. He knew in his heart that Gail Hess would not place emotional investment in such a gossamer connection. At that moment, the dream crept back into his consciousness, and it troubled him greatly.

Although late for work, he nonetheless closed his eyes and began reconstructing the dream in all its details. As though floodgates had been opened, he found himself back at the stone fortress, sitting on the battlement with a weapon, staring down at Michael Powers. The heat and humidity were suffocating, the air itself an enemy, pressing him into submission. Explosions and gunfire erupted all around. Twisting his head to look out at the ominous jungle, he watched the darkness disgorge streams of green tracers into the fortress, while red fire spat outward in a defiance doomed to be extinguished.

Now he found himself on his knees, again looking down at Michael Powers, whose young, feverish eyes and blackened face stared back at him with an almost mocking smile. It was not only Michael's face, it was his own, fractured through some cruel mirror of time, a doppelgänger marked by illness and war.

The ruined church loomed behind, its statues of saints still writhing in their vine-bondage, as if demanding witness. The rain fell harder, plastering the tam o'shanter against his scalp. He felt it pulsing like a second skull, borrowed from another man, another life, as if Nature himself had slipped inside him.

Gunfire shattered the silence again, tracers carving geometry in the air. The sound was not mere battle, it was judgment, the voice of the earth grinding out its verdict in sulfur and thunder.

With superhuman effort, Adam jerked himself back to reality, and found himself sitting in his kitchen, an unfinished breakfast spread before him, his body covered in sweat. He rushed to the bathroom, took a second shower, and hurried to work, anxious to leave the whole business behind.

Upon arriving, he threw on his lab coat and busied himself with work, visiting as many patients as possible. He ignored Gail's calls over the intercom, finding it necessary to ground himself first, before facing her again. Whether he should tell her about his dream remained an open question. Finally, at the end of the day, he entered her office and stood in front of her desk.

Putting on his most amiable grin, he asked, "So, when is the big day?"

"She seemed pleased and said tomorrow would be good."

"Ah, that easy?"

"Apparently. Perhaps we were wrong."

"Naw, no chance. After all, he can make himself scarce any time."

"Still, he must have some possessions to hide."

"What possessions? A toothbrush, maybe. After all, he only had the clothes on his back when he left here."

"Perhaps you should get there an hour before I arrive, just to make sure we don't miss him."

"Is there a back door?"

"Yes, but as far as I could tell, the house overlooks the bay. He would still have to come around the front to leave."

"Good."

"Is everything okay?" asked Gail.

"Yeah, why?"

"Oh, you just don't seem your gregarious self."

"Long day. Incidentally, Gail, can I have the second binder?"

"You finished the first one already?"

"No, but I want to read ahead." He chuckled. "You know, spoiler alert."

Gail Hess looked at him quizzically. "Adam, I prefer to not have two binders out at the same time."

"Make a copy?"

"I could, but there are hundreds of pages."

"Put it on my tab."

Gail stood up and walked around the desk, motioning toward a visitor's chair. "Have a seat. Let's talk." As he settled in, she pulled a matching chair closer and sat next to him.

"What do you think of what you have read so far?"

"I think he has quite an imagination."

"You think he made up the part about his parents?"

"Have you checked?"

Gail looked at him disapprovingly. "Do you think I'm stupid? Of course I checked—at least as much as I was able. I don't have the resources of the police, you know."

"And?"

"Apparently, the core of the story is true, at least according to Marie Telles. But, of course, I still can't pin down the nature of this mysterious woman their group sought. The people in China are unavailable, and John Powers' old boss claims to know very little."

Adam leaned forward. "And Marie Telles? Did you interview her before he escaped?"

"Obviously. That's how I confirmed at least part of the story."

Adam shook his head. "Yeah, of course. But . . . do you believe he's telling the truth about what actually happened?"

"No."

"Why not?"

"Adam, I treated the writings as more or less the meanderings of a madman. He builds his fantasies upon a core of reality."

"Yet, you now think he is writing about us even as we speak, that we are shadow characters in a book, that you are somehow connected to his Goddess, and heaven knows what else!"

"Forget about all that. Let's proceed with the understanding that Michael Powers is a schizophrenic with the usual hallucinations and delusions. No more supernatural speculation. Okay?"

Adam sighed. "A couple of days ago I would have agreed with you. But something has changed."

"What?"

"Remember when you called me Nature?"

"Of course."

"Well, that is why I want to read the second binder."

"Why?"

"Isn't that the one that has his Vietnam experiences . . . you know, the war years and all that?"

"Yes."

"I need to know more about this Nature fellow."

"And?"

"That's it."

"All right, come on, Adam! I don't want to have to drag every explanation out of you. Just tell me."

"Okay, I had a very strange dream last night. I dreamed I was Nature in some sort of stone fortress. I saw Michael Powers when he was a young soldier. I need to know if the dream corresponds to his descriptions in the writings."

"And if it does?"

"Then it does."

Gail let out a long sigh and leaned back in her chair. "Was it raining?"

"Yes."

"A ruined church?"

"Yes."

"Did Michael Powers appear to be sick?"

"Yes."

"Gunfire?"

"Yes."

Gail wearily closed her eyes. "Adam, I fear Michael is no longer the only one at stake here. We're all in his fortress now."

"What do you mean?"

She simply shook her head, rose, and handed him the second binder.

He took the binder, unsettled by its weight, as if the paper inside had absorbed more than ink—something humid, something lingering from Michael's fevered brain.

Chapter Seven

Nowhere to Hide

I Know What I Know

Of course, dear Reader, I waited in my room while Hess and Camara visited Marie Telles. Not that I was alone. The room felt quite communicative. As one might expect, the bed continually purrs in coital fulfillment, while the tasteful furniture keeps a polite silence. Only the windows interrupt the pleasant atmosphere when they complain about the San Francisco wind, letting out little shrieks when leaves blow against them. I must say, at times I became quite impatient knowing they were downstairs talking to Marie, and I had an almost irresistible urge to creep down and listen at the door. Soon enough, as you have seen, their words came to me. Finally, they left.

I watched the two doctors through my window as they sat in their car talking. When they drove away at last, I waited a while, and then went downstairs to see Marie, but she had already gone, so now I wait patiently for her return. Sometimes, this old house can be a bit much. I mean, besides the overlapping whispers of long-dead occupants, I know the house is feeling somewhat depressed. Perhaps it knows its days are numbered. After all, this property is too valuable to continue hosting a declining collection of wood and plaster, no matter how ornate. Old World charm only gets you so far. Still, it maintains its dignity, and I know it appreciates Marie's tender care. Alas, the living and the non-living all look toward a bleak future. Particle soup.

You see, dear Reader, my schizophrenic brain recognizes the simple truth that lies at the base of all human mischievousness: the neocortex has evolved beyond its capacity to regulate its desires—just the same as some dinosaurs grew too large for their immense bodies to satisfy basic biological needs—and has magnified, expanded, ballooned, swelled, and otherwise become so engorged that the appetite for food, sex, and power has become unsustainable drives beyond the ability of society or the planet to satisfy. All the novels of the world are simply exposés of the painfully obvious: we are out of control. You see, dear human schizophrenic-normals, your "rational" voices are even more destructive than my rather feeble "abnormal" schizophrenic God and Goddess voices. However, I digress.

Now, while the house is empty, is a good time for *Her* to make *Her* appearance. I reach out to *Her,* using my best supernatural tricks, even touching an antique couch upon which an earlier inhabitant of the house had died of fever, while calling *Her* as might a medium in a trance. No luck. *She* always takes *Her* own sweet time—appearing when least expected.

I muse for hours with these types of thoughts, melting slowly in my mind like cubes of ice. I can feel them tingle through my veins, sometimes giving little cold shocks to the otherwise comforting warmth of blood. I am sure God and Goddess are the icy deities that create these tiny glaciers, but in the past, the friction of their arguing soon melted them away.

It is four o'clock and Marie is still not back, so I raid her liquor cabinet and pour myself some bourbon. After a few sips, my veins begin pumping more fire than ice, and my thoughts turn to Goddess, whose voice has for so long been absent. The last time *She* appeared, *She* spoke in the presence of the Great Warrior, who had appeared on the wall back at the institute. I look around but see no ants here. Marie, clean freak that she is, would not allow such insects into her spotless mansion.

I hear a noise.

Is it her?

I feel my heartbeat quicken, and I wait submissively for her appearance.

"Hello, Michael. How was your day?"

As you may have guessed, the noise has turned out to be Marie returning home. My letdown evidently shows in my face.

"Are you okay?" she asks.

"Yeah. Have a drink with me."

"I'll have some wine."

"Good."

After she pours a glass, Marie sits next to me, just as she and my mother had sat so many years ago. She sips quietly.

Ask her! exclaims Goddess, startling me so much I almost spill my bourbon.

"Ask her what?" I ask aloud, without thinking.

"What?" says Marie, obviously confused.

"Oh, never mind. I was just thinking out loud."

"Michael, is it your voices?"

"No, no. Just an effect of the bourbon."

She falls quiet.

"Marie?"

"Yes?"

"Tell me about my mother."

"What do you want me to tell you?"

"Well, anything that comes to mind. I know you both often sat in these same chairs. What did you talk about?"

"Oh, many things. Music, work."

"Did she ever mention me?"

"Of course. You were very young then."

"I mean, was she excited about having me?"

"Of course. She talked about how wonderful you were. She loved you very much."

"I know. But, I mean, you were her lover."

Marie frowns. "Yes, that is not a secret."

"What did you love about her?"

"Everything. Her personality. Her beauty. Her kindness. Her wisdom."

"Did she ever suspect I am schizophrenic?"

"Because of your father, she worried about you. But remember, she died when you were very young."

"So, she never knew?"

"Honestly, Michael, I don't think so."

Ask her!

"I'm trying!" I exclaim, but quickly catch myself and only mumble the rest of the sentence. "But I don't know what to ask."

I peer at Marie and am relieved that she appears quite calm. "Who are you talking to, Michael?"

"I'll be honest, it is one of my voices. But I'm dealing with it, Marie. It is not a problem." I take a sip of bourbon.

She puts on a grim face. "You know, Michael, these voices are a reason for me to call the institute. Without medication, you will only get worse."

Before I respond, I see my beautiful mother standing behind Marie's chair, looking at me. Her face is sad. I know it is a mistake, but I can't help blurting out, "Mother!"

Marie doesn't flinch. Then she says something that completely shocks me. "Michael . . . is she here now?"

"If I tell you, you'll think I'm crazy."

She looks at me oddly. "I might surprise you, Michael. After all, I was around your mother long enough to know she could see things I could not, and you are her son. Besides, I feel her presence every day. Her spirit's still here."

I glance at Mother, who maintains a rather sad, distant smile. "She is here, Marie."

To my delight, Marie's eyes light up and she says, "Can you speak with her?"

Something makes me shudder. My mother's smile has disappeared, and she looks upon me with an unreadable expression. "No, Marie, I dare not."

"Why?"

"She will leave."

Marie scans the room. "Where is she?"

"Behind you."

Marie twists around but sees nothing. Of course.

"Try to talk to her," begs Marie. "I have a question that must be answered." Tears come to her eyes. "Please."

"What is your question?"

"When I die, will I be able to join her?"

"Marie—"

"Just ask, please."

I look at Mother and start to speak. "Mother, when—" But at that instant, she vanishes.

I know she will return sometime, but this news breaks Marie's heart, who is now sobbing. "I miss her so much."

Marie has never looked older. Her mask of imperturbability collapses in an instant, leaving slackened skin and unguarded years exposed, as though time itself had seized the chance to exact its toll. I am confused about what to do. Hugging her seems wrong, yet I lurch forward anyway, arms out like a novice supplicant. She raises her hands, a frail but decisive barricade, and I feel the rejection ripple through me more sharply than any slap.

"Not now, Michael," she whispers, barely audible.

Without a word, she stands and moves heavily across the room, where she pulls out a CD of my mother playing the piano. I know the piece. The first chords strike a bell deep in my chest, tolling the hollows of grief. It is *Piano Concerto No. 5, Second Movement*. Marie stands by the player, listening in silence, tears rolling down her cheeks. I leave. It is too much. As I leave, I think I see Mother reappearing in the same spot, but I can't be sure, as I close the door softly behind me and retreat to my room. I know I will be allowed to stay here as long as I want.

~ *Goddess Is Angry With Me* ~

I am lying in bed, reading. Marie has a wonderful library, and I chose Tolstoy's *Resurrection*. His last novel—spot on. The leather binding purrs like a cat, and I'm sure it feels pleasure in covering this book, which exposes the darkest side of humanity. I am convinced he was a full-blown schizophrenic, with all the voices of humanity in his head. How he sorted them out is beyond me.

Wait. Wait!

~

Dear Reader, I am having a bad time. As I was reading, I felt a tingle on my arm, so I brushed at it without thinking. Now, when I look, I see the Great Warrior on my blanket. She circles as if injured, but stops suddenly and returns my gaze, her antennae waving in alarm. I know this means Goddess will appear. A blue light flashes into the room, and *She* materializes in a blinding vision.

She is levitating above the bed, sitting in the lotus position on a huge, dazzling white flower. *Her* sad, contemplative face gazes from beneath an elaborate crown glimmering a kaleidoscope of colors. A cinder-bright jewel embedded in *Her* forehead burns brightly, and an intricate necklace lies cradled between *Her* bare breasts. *Her* left hand rests on *Her* thigh, the upturned curve of *Her* fingers resembling the albino legs of a gracefully dead spider. *Her* right hand is poised in the air, index finger and thumb touching to form an almost perfect circle while the other fingers radiate outward.

She seems angry.

I tremble before Her, and feebly ask, "Yes, Goddess?"

Yet, *She* does not speak. I close my eyes and listen. Nothing. When I open them again, sparks cascade from Her flaming body. Even *Her* bare breasts, glowing like hot coals, hold an unaccustomed terror. I can feel the heat of *Her* fury.

I cower deeper in my bed, pulling up the covers. It does no good. The bedding seems to burst into flames, and I jump to the floor and fall to my knees. "What do you want of me?" I shout above the din.

You must focus on finding a mate! *She* bellows in my head.

"Yes, suffering continues, Goddess," I concede weakly.

You are not the potent genetic dose I had hoped for. As long as these wild genes dominate, you will never conceive another child! Mark is not the next step. The next step is waiting for you to find another Chosen One, an intermediate like you. But this schizophrenia nonsense interferes!

I am stunned at *Her* words, and can only mutter, "Yes, but what am I to do?"

Without replying, *She* reaches out *Her* hand, palm up, and places it on my bed, singeing the covers. The Great Warrior moves quickly into *Her* hand, and *She* lovingly draws it back to *Her* bosom, where the ant scurries onto *Her* glowing flesh.

God suddenly appears next to *Her*. **An Immortal Addict is not so easily dried out, My Love. Now what?** *His* swampy voice is a deep, dank, gritty rumble that fills my room with a corrosive slag of wet soot and harsh sulfur—a nineteenth-century furnace bellowing smoke from a thirteenth-century hell. After *He* speaks, my blanket turns greenish-black and glistens with a moist, phlegm-like shimmer. When *His* words at last lose their volume, *His* breathing lingers, a succession of reptilian hisses.

Goddess seems at a loss for words, while *Her* luminescence dims in the suffocation of *His* murky presence.

Foolish Goddess! The entire human race operates according to First Principles. Your interference to bring about Superior Ones is an abysmal failure.

~

My terror has evaporated, and I listen to Them more with impatience than trepidation. After all, Michael Powers accepts evolution, not a superstitious belief in divinities. They are like children, I think.

Yes! boomed Goddess. **They are the children of evolution, and evolution must be accelerated.**

"Then why did You have me come here?" I ask angrily.

Go and find the other Chosen One. Sitting here is useless.

"Riddles!" I cry. "I am tired of riddles! Be clearer. Tell me!"

Instead of answering, both instantly disappear. As you might well under-stand, dear Reader, I am left confused. What am I to believe? Then it comes to me—the answer to the riddle—clear as a bright, sunny day.

Knocking.

"Michael, are you all right?" Marie calls through the door.

"Yes, just a nightmare."

The door is angry at being battered, and it tells me the person knocking is more excited than fearful. I thank it and open it to see Marie staring with wide eyes.

"Did she come, Michael?"

"Goddess?" I ask.

"Your mother."

I lie, knowing it will keep me here as long as I want. "Yes."

"Did she speak?"

"This time, yes, Marie. But I cannot tell you tonight. I'm too upset. Tomor-row. She is gone now, and I must sleep. Tomorrow."

Marie looks a bit suspicious, but reluctantly nods. "Yes, okay. Tomorrow."

~

When I go downstairs the next morning, Marie is waiting.

"I have made a nice breakfast for you, Michael." She holds up a pot. "Coffee?"

"Yes, thank you." Of course, I know what this is about, and to forestall suspicion, I bring up the subject as if anxious to share.

"Let me have a few sips, and then I'll tell you what Mother said."

"No hurry."

Of course there is, I think.

"Well, first of all, I never saw her lips move, but her words came to me anyway, and the sound of those words was as beautiful as she. After she said some things to me that I prefer not to share, she looked toward your room and told me to tell you how much you are loved." Oh, I'm good, aren't I, dear Reader? All lies, of course, but they are, as you schizophrenic-normals call them, "white."

Marie's eyes mist over, and she looks at me with a most heart-wrenching expression. "Did she say anything about my joining her in the future?"

Suddenly, my heart sinks, and I realize I am playing with fire.

"No, Marie, but I know she wants you to have a long and happy life here."

Marie is crying freely now. "How do you know, Michael? I long to go to her." She looks around. "The rest is . . . fluff. All my life, I have detested fluff, and all my life. . . . "

"You are leading a full life here. There will be plenty of time—an eterni-ty—later."

She gives a sarcastic laugh. "Michael, you don't even believe in God, let alone heaven."

I put on my best philosophic-spiritual-serious face. "Marie, I talk to God, and Goddess, all the time."

"No, Michael, they talk to you."

With this, she leaves the kitchen, and I am left to eat my cold breakfast alone. For once, the food does not complain or squeal, and I eat with surprising relish. Now, I am left to my own devices. While mulling over what to do with the day, Marie returns.

"By the way, that lady from the institute is coming to have a tour of the house."

"Gail Hess?"

"Yes."

"Is she looking for me?"

"No, she is a member of the Historical Society. Wants to see this great antique of a house."

So she says, I think.

"Should I wait in my room?"

Marie frowns. "Do what you will, I am going to show her everything."

"In that case, I must leave. When does she arrive?"

"In an hour."

My heart is racing. Marie's attitude is cold and uncaring. Has something happened to change her mind? Does she know I lied? Will she tell Gail Hess? All the same, dear Reader, my thoughts have turned to Goddess's riddle. "She is Me and He is Him." Therefore, I tell myself: if Gail Hess is Goddess, and Adam Camara is Nature, why flee? Wait and see what happens. After all, *She* sent me here. Must be a reason. Still, even for me, this is far too risky, and the possibility of returning to the institute is a fate unimaginably horrible. So, I clean up my room, remove traces of my presence, and leave out the back door. Instead of going around the house to the front, where the street is, I hike down the steep slope behind Marie's house. It is covered in vegetation, and the going is rough, but there is a maze of animal trails that call to me, "This way! This way!" Far below, San Francisco Bay spreads twinkling in the sun. I am tempted to sit on the slope and wait, but something urges me to return to the tortured sidewalks of the city.

It is a mistake. When I reach the street, the cacophony of living and non-living chatter drives me into an alley, where I crouch against the wall, as might some homeless bum.

Quite a fall, I think. From successful lawyer to fucked-up schizophrenic in a fancy institute to bum. All that's missing is a bag with a bottle of cheap wine. Oddly, these masochistic thoughts calm me, along with my usual habit of rocking back and forth when I'm in this state. I admit I talk to myself. In fact, I am now mumbling to the air. To you schizophrenic-normals, I appear just another drugged-out homeless person to be avoided, but you all talk to yourselves also. All the time. Oh, shit, screw it! Why explain myself to you?

As I walk in the door, Marie calls from the anteroom.

"Is that you, Michael?"

"Yes."

"Come and have a drink."

"Okay."

I pour myself a bourbon and sit. "How did it go with Dr. Hess today?" I ask nonchalantly.

"Fine."

"And?"

"And nothing."

"Well, how long did she stay?"

"About an hour. We had a nice chat."

"About me?"

"Partly."

"I thought she was here to view the house." Now I'm worried.

Marie snorts. "It was clearly a ruse. She asked many questions about you and about your parents."

"Go on." I feel myself start to sweat.

"She is particularly interested in your voices... specifically your Goddess voice."

"Did she say why?" I ask, trying to keep the smirk out of my tone.

"No."

~

We fall silent for a few moments, and I decide to ask her a few questions of my own.

"Marie, when you and my parents traveled to China after the war, I know they were looking for a mysterious woman, known simply as she or her."

"Yes."

"What do you think this mysterious person is?"

"You mean who?"

"No—I mean what—assuming she is something more than a typical human woman."

"I don't know." Marie seems nervous.

Now, I am well aware of Marie's history with my mother. You, dear Reader, are also aware, if you're prone to masochism, and have read all my rather blundering prose up to now. Needless to say, one thing is certain, at least in my mind: either Marie believes or does not. Of course, I know she does believe in her supernatural powers, because I am here, and would not be if she did not. For some perverse reason, I want her to admit it openly and without equivocation.

"Marie, you have a very intelligent mind. What do you believe about her? I want to know."

Despite my insistence, Marie remains silent, sipping her wine and staring into space.

I press.

"If you don't believe she is something extraordinary, then you believe my mother and my father were crazy."

"No!" she snaps and bangs her fist on the table. "Maybe your father, but not your mother!"

"And me?"

Marie falters. "You are diagnosed as suffering from schizophrenia."

"It appears there is a difference of opinion about that. Goddess, or she, or whatever you want to call Her, tells me I am the Chosen One. The next step in the evolution of a superior race that will replace humans."

"That sounds like you are mentally ill."

"But my mother knew all of this, or most of it, and she felt certain it was true, and that I'm not mentally ill."

"I never said your mother was mentally ill."

"If my mother was not mentally ill, who is she?"

"I don't know."

"You do! You do!" I admit, dear Reader, I have lost my temper, and the consequence is that Marie jumps in fright. I need a schizophrenic-normal like Marie to say it. To admit it. Weak as I am, I need her to come out with it.

Marie stands and storms out of the room, saying as she passes through the doorway, "Leave me alone with my memories!" She pauses and, in a softer voice, says, "Michael, there are some memories I cannot deal with. Surely you can understand that."

"Marie!" I call after her, but she is gone.

~ *Regret* ~

Alone again, I regret my words and the pressure I put on Marie. This woman holds my fate in her hands, I muse. If I anger her, the game is up.

Yet, something reassures me. It is her wanting to believe that is my ace in the hole. As Captain Tong said in Vietnam many years ago, "They will want to believe." For those of you in the dark about Captain Tong, his hunch worked, and my friends died.

All of them.

All but poor Idaho and me.

We wanted to believe—so my comrades left the fortress and walked into an ambush.

They died.

All of them.

I was in the tunnel when it happened.

I should be in the tunnel now, with my bones.

And Nature.

"My bones! My bones!"

Nature knows, even though he also died in the ambush. Now he's back.

You cannot hold a good man down.

Nature is back.

He is Dr. Adam Camara—or, at least, beginning to occupy the good doctor's body, tam o'shanter and all. Soon, he will have all of it, body and soul.

Then there is Dr. Gail Hess, aka Goddess. I know Dr. Hess owns the body, and often believes she is in control.

One thing is for sure, Goddess uses Gail's vessel at times—at crucial times. I have seen it. She and I must have a reckoning.

Live or die, we must have a reckoning.

Which one, Goddess or Gail Hess?

Both.

Chapter Eight

Shipwrecked Sailors

Missed Opportunity

After Gail's "tour" with Marie Telles, and Adam's disappointing news that he had not seen Michael Powers, they met back in her office to debrief.

"Do you still believe he is there?" asked Adam.

"Yes, without a doubt."

"How can you be so sure?"

"It is in Michael Powers's own writing, clear as day."

"His staying with her?"

"No, his insight into her personality."

"How so?"

"As I have told you, behind her sophisticated façade and expensive *accoutrements*, beats a sensualist, a romantic, and most importantly, a risk-taker."

"Meaning she would hide Mr. Powers regardless of the risk?"

"You bet she would. I think I know this woman, ironically enough, through his own writings."

"So, what now?" asked Adam. "Call the police?"

Gail emphatically shook her head. "No. If we resort to that, he will never trust me again. No relationship, no therapy, no recovery."

"Well?"

"What if I visit Marie Telles again, tell her we know Mr. Powers is living in her house, and ask to see him, speak with him?"

"She'll deny he is there." Adam sighed. "What would be gained?"

"Perhaps nothing. But, at least, Mr. Powers would know we know. He might come back voluntarily."

"Well, if nothing else, you could leave his medication with Ms. Telles."

"Maybe," said Gail. "But one thing bothers me."

Adam laughed. "Only one?"

"If he knows we know, he might disappear into the city, or worse, travel to God knows where. We might lose him forever."

"Gail, he is not a fish."

Gail ignored his comment and continued speaking as if to herself. "Or worse, Storyteller might reclaim him and take him back to that damn tunnel."

"His Vietnam persona?" Adam asked in alarm.

"Yes."

Adam sat up straight and his face darkened, as though something ancient flickered behind his eyes, and he cried in a fierce, alien voice, "Best keep Nature away from him!"

Gail jerked her head. "What did you say?"

"Nothing." Though his voice had returned to normal, Adam appeared stunned and confused.

"Yes, you did. You mentioned Nature."

"I did?"

Gail nodded, still attempting to process his outburst.

Suddenly, without warning, a flash of light seared the room, and Gail felt herself flooded by a primal, molten hunger. Blood surged through her with the violent rhythm of a martial drum; even her fingertips seemed to throb. She looked at Adam and saw not the doctor but a young, curly-haired soldier—his eyes fevered, skin damp, muscles coiled like a predator's.

Like a mad Greek woman seized by the spell of Bacchus, she wanted to tear off his clothes and feel his organ plunge deep into the fire of her womb.

Yet a shard of sanity, cold and diamond-hard, held fast. She rose abruptly, tall and imperious, and her voice rang out with the cadence of a wrathful deity:

"Return to the tunnel, Nature!"

She began to tear off her clothes, only to realize Adam was upon her, pinning her down.

"Gail! Stop! Stop!"

His words finally penetrated, and the fire was quenched as suddenly as it had begun.

"My God!" she cried. "What are we doing?"

Adam leaned back and wiped his brow. "I. . . . " he lost the words.

"Is this some sort of hysteria?" asked Gail hoarsely, adjusting her disheveled clothes and smoothing her hair. She rose and found her way to the chair. "Has he hypnotized us with his delusions?"

Adam shook his head in wonder. "Let's look at it with some degree of reason. Gail, you have been exposed to him far longer than I have, so the Goddess figure in his mind has infiltrated your psyche more than. . . . " Again, his words trailed off.

"More than Nature has infiltrated you," she finished his thought.

"Yes, it is true. Nature has intruded into my thoughts and dreams more and more lately."

"Mr. Powers is Maxwell's demon, regulating our psychoses."

"More like feeding them," said Adam. "I, for one, refuse to slide into this madness! If you won't go to Marie Telles and demand his return, I will."

Gail smiled wistfully. "Won't having him back simply make things . . . more difficult for us?"

"Now you're talking crazy, Gail. You and I are professionals. There is no magic here, just powerful suggestions, which we have allowed to influence our better judgments. Confront him damn it!"

Gail never lost the wistful smile. "With what?"

~

Adam Camara returned home that night greatly troubled, visions of Mr. Powers, Storyteller, Nature, Goddess, and Vietnam whirling around in his head at dizzying speeds. After pouring a drink, he looked at the stack of binders on his table. *Read the damn things!* he told himself. *Learn about this Nature fellow, and the tunnel, and all the rest of it.*

Adam's pride began to tweak his ego. He had been patronizing Gail Hess far too long. It was time for him to take the reins and get to the bottom of her fantasies, particularly regarding the whole Goddess business. He brushed aside his own issues involving "this Nature fellow" and focused on her frailties in falling for such suggestions. Perhaps the binders would reveal enough history that he could, in grand Sherlock Holmes fashion, solve the mystery.

He settled in to read when the odd headache he had suffered days before stabbed back without warning. As before, it was like no headache he had ever endured—less a pain in his skull than a pressure behind it, pushing in from some other place.

Feeling himself slipping, Adam downed more gin, hoping the alcohol would chase away the encroaching sounds and smells that were returning from his dream. Smoke. Gunpowder. The coppery tang of blood. The hiss of tracers and the thud of bullets striking stone. All began to overwhelm. He drank more quickly, letting the binders drop to the floor, the noise getting louder, the smells more rank, the headache more excruciating. Finally, more from alcohol than weariness, he fell into a troubled sleep.

~ *Nature* ~

Adam tumbled into the fire and let himself be consumed by the flames. He emerged from his burning bed as a young soldier, back in the fortress. The humid air pressed against his skin like wet cloth, and the smell of mildew and old stone filled his nostrils. Somewhere water dripped, a slow, hollow tap that echoed like a distant clock.

He knew he was in Nature's mind going to check on someone. Once he reached the soldier he sought leaning against a stone wall slick with condensation, he put his hand on the feverish man's shoulder. Adam knew Nature wanted to ask about "ghosts" that appeared to Storyteller. Apparently, he was along for the ride in Nature's body.

"Hello, Storyteller. Mind if I sit here a while?"

"Go ahead," said the young Mr. Powers coldly.

Adam/Nature ignored his tone and smiled broadly. "How's it going?"

Mr. Powers/Storyteller looked sideways and made a sour face. "You're kidding, right?"

"I couldn't sleep, so I decided to come and check on you."

"Thanks."

"Can't sleep either?"

"Nope."

"Your ghosts again?"

"Yeah."

Adam/Nature looked around. The courtyard stones glimmered faintly in the moonlight. "Right now? Are they still here?"

"No. The stragglers left as you came walking up," Mr. Powers/Storyteller said accusingly.

Adam felt the last of his own personality slip beneath the surface, yet he remained present, as some sort of hidden observer inside Nature.

With this, Nature shifted uneasily, seemingly freed of some weight. "Storyteller?"

"Yeah?"

"Did any of them visit me tonight?"

Storyteller's face softened. "Dunno. I can't make out who the grunts are when they're visiting. They're just lumps of old jungle fatigues."

"Can't you tell by where we've set up our hootches? I mean, well . . . you know . . . like the guard positions and where the guys are sleeping . . . for example, you know very well I sleep over there," Nature said, pointing to the far wall.

"Doesn't work that way, Nature. Everything's all mixed up. My sense of direction is really screwed up when they're here. It's like a dream—everything's familiar but strange at the same time. Anyway, why are you asking?"

"Because I miss my family. My mom and dad. I was hoping you could describe them to me. It's gotta be them visiting me. It would be great to hear you describe them. Are they happy? Are they okay? You know what I mean?"

"Yeah, I know what you mean. So, you don't think my 'ghosts' are just caused by my delirium? That's what you've told me before."

Nature shrugged. "Dunno. There's something strange about this old fort. Something weird. Sometimes I think I can see ghosts of the French soldiers that used to be here. You know?"

"Yeah."

"And that Goddess statue. No one can ignore that. I mean, the lights and the tapping noise that comes out of her. Really strange. I've thought about your ghosts. Well . . . it doesn't seem so weird that you're really seeing something." He looked away. "It seems to me there's a good chance the ghosts are real. I miss my family and home so much, I guess I want them to be real now."

Storyteller remained silent.

Nature looked at him suspiciously. "Come on, Storyteller. Do you know more than you've told me? You seem kind of weird yourself. Close to the vest. You can tell me. After all, it's Nature you're talking to," he said, tapping his chest lightly.

"No, I'm not hiding anything. It's just that the fever's coming back. I can feel it. Always happens after they leave."

Nature seemed suddenly excited and shifted positions to straighten a cramped leg. "Describe them to me, Storyteller. Maybe I'll recognize my folks. It would be so great to know they visited me, even if I wasn't aware of it at the time."

Storyteller shook his head. "I don't think I could do it. Besides, they're incomplete. I mean, I can see their beating hearts and lungs and the blood circulating in their veins and arteries."

"But you told me you can make out their facial features and clothes. Right?"

"Yeah."

"Do it. Describe them for me, Storyteller. Please."

"Okay. I'll try. But if it doesn't work. . . . "

"Yeah, yeah. I won't blame you."

Storyteller began describing all the apparitions that were old enough to be Nature's parents.

Nature interrupted. "That's them! It's got to be! Mom's a little heavy, just like you described. And dad's skinny as a rail. You know—Jack Sprat and all that. Did they seem to be happy?"

"Yes, they were happy," Storyteller lied.

"God, it would be good to see them again," said Nature. "So good."

The two grunts fell silent. Finally, Nature broke the lull. "Why are they here, Storyteller?"

"Who?"

"The ghosts."

Storyteller blinked and looked down. "Dunno."

Nature's shoulders slumped and the eternal light in his eyes went dim. "Yes, I think you do."

~

Adam Camara's head broke the surface, and he gulped air greedily. Then came Nature's fading voice. "I want him back, Dr. Camara. I want Storyteller back."

Adam felt the final vestige of Nature depart. His headache had also gone, and as his senses cleared, he realized he was sprawled on the floor beside the fallen binders. But his fear now loomed large before his horrified eyes.

~ *Goddess or Girl?* ~

Gail Hess returned home after her meeting with Adam Camara. She sought comfort in familiar surroundings and the company of Sigmund. At first, when she changed into comfortable clothes and stroked the cat, she felt grounded and secure. But as she reheated leftovers, a vague sense of unease began to drift down on her. She poured a glass of wine and continued to stroke Sigmund, attempting to shake the feeling of dread weighing her down. She clutched the cat so tightly to her breast that he squealed. Food seemed out of the question. The wine dulled nothing. She poured a second glass of wine.

"I know You're here," she said to the air, startling Sigmund, whose eyes had just closed.

No response.

"Might as well show Yourself."

No response.

Gail felt like a little girl talking to an imaginary friend. She downed the wine.

"Well, if You won't talk to me, I'll talk to You. Why not go back where You belong? In the distant past. Today, my dear, You are an irrelevancy, except to our Mr. Powers. I have read his writings about You. Shouldn't You be behind Your iron door? In fact, why not leave Mr. Powers alone? He is vulnerable. A schizophrenic, as You well know."

A shadow.

Movement.

Gail's heart began to pound, almost painfully.

Sigmund sniffed the air, then jumped down and disappeared.

Gail grabbed for him and missed. Now, she felt naked.

"Ha! Who is the vulnerable one now? Okay, You've got me scared; might as well show Yourself!"

Gail had always found that joking at her own expense relieved tension and put things in perspective. Any evil creatures that might have designs on her would be disarmed by such self-deprecating and devil-may-care humor. Ghosts, goliaths, and Guidos would surely succumb to her charms.

Another sound. Barely discernible. Eerie.

A shadow again.

Movement again.

She peered all around but saw nothing. Heard nothing.

A famous poet once wrote that "rat's feet on broken glass make no sound." In the yawning silence that now greeted her, she felt a sudden and compelling desire to see this Goddess. The Real Thing. It seemed as if this must happen now. She had an irresistible urge to walk barefoot over broken glass. Right now. And as there was no response to her silent pleas, Gail broke into a verbal one.

"Okay, Goddess! Come out, come out, wherever You are!"

Nothing.

Gail laughed at herself. "Stupid," she said, refilling her glass with a shaky hand. The buzz came sharp, not soft, and her agitation only deepened. "Come on, Goddess! Let me see You, woman to woman. Are You the original Liberated Lady? Or just another fake deity for fools to worship?"

Nothing.

"The hell with You, I'm going to bed." She finished the last glass and called for Sigmund, convinced Goddess was a phantom; a powerful suggestion she had allowed to go too far.

~ *Buandelgereen* ~

For several days, Gail and Adam did not see each other—partly due to workload, partly due to their own internal demons evidently unleashed by Mr. Powers. Each had enough of Michael Powers for the time being, and their enthusiasm for revisiting Marie Telles had subsided. Despite his vow to read the binders, Adam set them aside, afraid they might trigger more nightmares. For her part, Gail had partially succeeded in pushing thoughts of Goddess out of her mind, and she found satisfaction in returning to her patients without the confounding presence of Mr. Powers.

One morning, June walked into Gail's office with a puzzled look.

"Someone to see you."

"Who?"

June paused and looked down at a note. "Bu-an-del-ge-reen."

"What?"

"It's a name, a woman. Apparently from Mongolia."

Gail sat stunned. She recognized the woman's name from the writings of Michael Powers. Again, with a sinking heart, she felt thrust into the pages of his overwrought narratives. But even as her heart sank, it rebounded quickly and with a vengeance. She experienced a surge of intense anticipation, and thought, *Buandelgereen! The famous Mongol woman-warrior. Yet another of Mr. Powers' strange, bizarre characters, now appearing in flesh and blood! Further proof not all his scribblings describe hallucinations. My God! If Goddess is not a hallucination—*

Gail immediately rejected the thought and took a few deep breaths to compose herself.

"Send her in."

When June escorted the woman into Gail's office, Buandelgereen dwarfed the petite secretary. Great, flowing, luxurious hair, now white, cascaded around her like the mane of a wild horse. Outlines of powerful muscles could be discerned beneath her Mongol tunic. An imposing skirt covered her legs, swirling above a pair of sheepskin boots.

Gail stood and extended her hand, trying not to appear intimidated by such a powerful presence. When she spoke, her voice felt weak and shrill, bouncing off this woman like small birds flying into a skyscraper.

"Hello, I am Dr. Hess."

Buandelgereen's hand enveloped hers and squeezed gently, as if aware of its power to hurt.

"Buandelgereen." She sat.

"What can I do for you, Ms. Buandelgereen?"

"Do you know me?" It was more a statement than a question.

Gail stammered, at a loss. "I . . . I have a patient who, I think, knows of you."

"Michael Powers. I seek him."

"May I ask why?"

"No."

"Well, I must know before allowing you access. He is quite ill."

Buandelgereen stood. "I would see him."

Gail leaned back. "I'm afraid he is not here."

Buandelgereen sat back down. "Where is he?"

"He escaped. We are looking for him."

The Mongol woman smiled. "Escaped," she mused aloud.

"May I ask again why you seek him? You know he suffers from schizophrenia?"

"I am well aware of his voices, as I knew his father's voices."

Gail felt excited. "Perhaps you can enlighten me about those voices of his father? I think you knew his parents quite well?"

"Yes. John Powers and Bai Meiying."

Gail noticed a slight hesitation when she mentioned Bai Meiying. "So, John Powers heard voices?"

"Of course, don't you?"

"I . . . I mean, that is not the question."

"It is the only question, Dr. Hess."

Gail, used to Michael Powers' non-sequiturs and clever evasions, trudged ahead. "Did John's voices involve a God and Goddess?"

"Do not your own voices involve a Goddess and a God?"

Gail blurted without thinking, "Only a Goddess, as I have not yet heard God." She could not believe she uttered such words.

"Ah, I am aware."

"How?"

"Dr. Hess, I came here in search of Michael Powers. I will not take any more of your time."

"Please wait."

Buandelgereen rose.

"Please," repeated Gail. "I have so many questions."

"Do not we all?"

"True, but you really could help Michael Powers by answering my questions."

"No. He is not here. I must find him."

"Why?"

Buandelgereen hesitated. "The answer is within you, at least partly. If you accept what you currently fight against, you will find it fully and completely."

"Do you know where to find him?"

"Do you?"

Gail paused, hoping her answer would make this strange woman stay longer. "Yes."

"Then I will see him there."

"Wait, I haven't told you where."

Buandelgereen regarded her in silence for a long moment, then gave the smallest nod and disappeared through the door without another word.

Stunned and confused, Gail continued to sit and mull over the conversation in her mind. *Riddles, riddles, riddles*, she thought, and for a moment, felt she had dreamed the entire incident. *This woman is full of riddles and deflections, just like Mr. Powers.* Immediately, she buzzed June and briskly asked to have Adam Camara summoned. Oddly enough, her impulse wasn't to share the meeting with Adam, but to find a way to sleep with him. Soon. A craving for sex inexplicably possessed her, as if the Mongol woman had infused her with some primordial lust.

~

"You rang?" asked Adam as he swept into her office. "I only have a few minutes."

For an instant the heat she'd tried to tamp down flared again. It was unwelcome and ill-timed, so she forced it back beneath the professional mask.

These words acted like cold water, washing away her sexual mood, and replacing it with a similar urgency to talk.

"Do you know who was just in my office?"

Adam's eyes widened. "Mr. Powers?"

"No, far more interesting."

"Who?"

"Buandelgereen."

To her disappointment, Adam registered no recognition of the name. "Who?"

"I see you have not been reading the binders."

"True. I stopped. Is this someone from his writings?"

Now Gail felt deflated and discouraged. She turned her frustration on Adam. "I thought you wanted to collaborate. If you don't read, you are useless to me."

Adam looked at her angrily. "Look, I have patients to see. There is more to the world than Michael Powers. Others are in need."

She started to respond, but something made her hesitate. Finally, she said, "Are you listening to me?"

He looked at his watch, "No. In fact, I left someone waiting in order to come here. In ten words or less, who is this Buan . . . what's his name?"

Gail shook her head. "Not a he, a woman. Sorry I snapped, but this woman is of extreme importance. She is from Mongolia and knew Mr. Powers' mother and father."

Now Adam seemed interested. "And?" he urged.

"And she's looking for Michael Powers."

"Oh? Why?"

"That is the ten-thousand-dollar question." Gail stared at Adam and felt the attraction return. She blushed. "Shall we have dinner and discuss it?"

Adam picked up the unmistakable signs, and himself caught the urge. "Yes, let's. After work?"

"Can you pick me up at six-thirty at my place? I feel grubby."

"Sure."

"Good. I'll see you then." She made sure to give him her most alluring look, but he had already turned to leave.

Only after he departed did she marvel at the intensity of feelings she experienced in the half hour that Buandelgereen appeared.

Do I feel more alive in Mr. Powers's novel than my own life? she wondered. The thought, not new, still terrified her, and she quickly turned her attention to her patients and Adam Camara. They, at least, were real and had no connection to Michael Powers. Concentration seemed out of the question—she longed to be with Adam.

Her latest travails left her feeling lonely and bereft.

Sigmund no longer sufficed.

~ *Buandelgereen Pays a Visit* ~

Marie Telles opened her front door to face an apparition that astounded her more than Lazarus himself would have. As Buandelgereen stood towering over her, a tsunami of memories so staggered Marie that she fell into the Mongol woman's arms like a rag doll. When she came to her senses, she sat in the little anteroom facing Buandelgereen and Michael Powers. A steaming cup of tea sat next to her on the table.

"Drink," said Buandelgereen.

"Yes, do," added Michael. "You'll feel better."

Marie had not yet said a word. She took a sip of tea and spent a few moments composing herself. Finally, she said, "Buandelgereen, it is wonderful to see you again. My savior. My protector. But . . . why? I mean to say . . . how?"

The Mongol smiled, her strong teeth gleaming white against her dark skin. "I come for Michael Powers, but I am pleased to see you. Are you well?"

"Yes. I had thought . . . well, in China, Mongolia, the communists, I just didn't know."

"You thought me dead?"

"Yes. My thoughts are spinning." She managed a weak laugh. "The only thing missing is a rifle slung over your shoulder."

"No need for a rifle here."

Michael chuckled. "You have not been to some parts of San Francisco, I see."

Buandelgereen abruptly stood. "You will excuse me, Miss Telles, but I must speak to Michael Powers in private."

Marie, still dazed, could only mutter, "Of course," and took another sip of tea.

"Let us speak outside, Mr. Powers," said Buandelgereen.

"Yes. The back. I fear some may be watching the front."

Buandelgereen winked at Marie. "I congratulate you, Miss Telles, on providing refuge to an escaped. . . ."

"Schizophrenic," said Michael with a crooked grin, the word curdled into mockery, more dirge than joke.

Buandelgereen gave him a withering glare.

As if to snub her disapproval, he performed an operatic flourish, his best imitation of Feng Shiren.

"I am not proud," he said.

~

Michael and Buandelgereen sat on a bench in the back garden, overlooking San Francisco Bay. He waited. Buandelgereen's white hair billowed like waves in a stormy sea.

"I came to warn you," she said.

"All the way from Mongolia?"

"From Mongolia. From behind the iron door."

"What have you come to warn me about?"

"God."

Chapter Nine

Target

God

I look at Buandelgereen and am full of wonder. White hair flowing, white teeth flashing, smooth skin a deep amber, eyes an unfathomable mystery. Now, she comes to warn me. Always the protectress, that one. Sent by Goddess, no doubt. As usual, she waits for me to speak.

"What about God?" I ask.

"*He* struggles."

"Why? God knows—excuse the pun—there is enough suffering to keep *Him* in a state of Rapture."

"Goddess taunts *Him* with your presence."

"Come, come, Buandelgereen, we schizophrenics are accused of having delusions of grandeur, but even in my delusional moments, I know better. There are almost ten billion humans on the planet, not to mention the trillions of non-human life forms for *Him* to inflict suffering and receive worship in exchange."

"Yet, you insist you do not believe in Him."

"True, true. Evolution, not superstition. Still, it is the idea of *Him* that I most abhor."

"Despite it all, you write."

"Buandelgereen, you *are* real, not one of my hallucinations, aren't you?"

"Of course I am real."

"So, I am broad-minded, I deal with delusions and realities, both hemispheres are fully operable, unlike normals, who suffer from virtual hemispherectomies."

"Nevertheless, you write," she repeats.

Dear Reader, I do not question paradoxes. It is the way of the schizophrenic, so I merely ask, "What does God plan to do to me? Kill me?"

"No."

"Then what?"

"Convert you."

"What?"

"Convert you. Have you deny Goddess and profess faith and obedience to *Him*."

I laugh. "Nothing could be simpler for me to at least say the words. However, what *He* wants is hardly possible! *He* wants sincere belief. I reject *Him*! Now and forever!"

"Precisely the attitude *He* sees as a challenge. *He* is in a battle with Goddess over your soul."

"I don't believe in souls."

"I understand, but Goddess wants me to warn you about *His* tricks."

"Buandelgereen, I am immune to divine tricks."

"Do not underestimate Him."

"What does Goddess want me to do?"

"Return to the tunnel."

"What! *She* told me to escape and come here! Now *She* changes *Her* mind?"

"Female prerogative."

"In the tunnel I will be dead."

"Yes, beyond the reach of God."

"I will be nothing."

"Precisely. You will be reunited."

"I am reunited here. Dr. Hess is Goddess, I know that. And Dr. Camara is Nature. My son is Sergeant Dam. They are all around! My mother visits me here. Can her spirit enter the tunnel and talk to nothing?"

"You once were desperate to return."

"No more. I like it here."

"Then God will come for you, and *He* has many guises. Are you prepared?"

"I am. Do you return to Mongolia?"

"I return behind the iron door. But, first, I must lead you to *Her*."

"Why?"

"Tomorrow, be ready at eight o'clock."

"Buandelgereen, couldn't *She* just have delivered the message *Herself*? It would have saved you a long trip."

"Hush! No more questions or speculations. Now, I wish to speak with Marie Telles in private. Just be ready tomorrow."

With that, she leaves, pausing for a few minutes to chat with Marie in the anteroom. My mind is confused. After Buandelgereen is gone, Marie seeks me out.

"Well, that was a vision from the past," she says.

"Yes. Unbelievable."

"I am retiring to my room. This visit has been too much. Please do not disturb me. You are on your own for dinner. See you tomorrow."

Her tone is oddly flat, drained of its usual sharp warmth. Schizophrenics always sense something amiss, being paranoid as we are. So, I am going to my room and read.

~

I have just finished a light breakfast with Marie, who seems distracted. She will not meet my eye, her usual directness smothered under some invisible weight, and I continue to sense something rotten in Denmark. Buandelgereen arrives on time, and after she enters and chats a moment with Marie, I follow the Mongol woman to the front door. She opens it and steps through without a thought, but something in me locks. A wire snaps.

I turn and bolt out the back door, legs hammering the animal trails toward the bay.

The trails urge me ever faster, "This way! This way!" they cry. "Hurry! Predators everywhere!"

You see, dear Reader, I know what Buandelgereen is up to; she wants to take me back to the institution. I am pretty sure she is real, not one of my hallucinations. Perfect for the job—she and Marie are in it together. Both are real as real can be. That is why I can't trust them. For all I know, Buandelgereen works for God now. Didn't she say God has many guises? Now that I think of it, she did have a wicked glint when she said that.

"Hurry!" The trails squeal with every footfall. "Predators everywhere! Hurry!"

You see, dear Reader, I know what Buandelgereen is up to; she wants to take me back to the institution. I am pretty sure she is real, not one of my hallucinations. Perfect for the job—she and Marie are in it together. Both are real as real can be. That is why I can't trust them. For all I know, Buandelgereen works for God now. Didn't she say God has many guises? Now that I think of it, she did have a wicked glint when she said that. "Hurry!" The trails squeal with every footfall. "Predators everywhere! Hurry!"

Again, I emerge in the city—this time worse off than before: no money, no clothes, no hope. I am truly homeless, a fate perhaps inevitable for an unreformed schizophrenic escapee from a nuthouse. Well, I have at last stumbled into my old, familiar, filthy, trash-strewn little alley, and amidst dried vomit, urine, and rotting newspapers, I must find a way to think (as you call it, rationally). Even schizophrenics must eat, and I am used to eating well. Mother almost starved to death in China. I have her tough genes. I will survive. But, how? Have I fallen so far that a dumpster will be my salvation? It's already cold. The wind is cutting. San Francisco damp penetrates my inadequate clothing.

Dear Reader, I am unutterably sad and lonely. Rock bottom. Now I do not know who my friends are. Not even one night on the streets and my thoughts turn to the comfort of Marie Telles's house, where there is good bourbon and a soft bed. Good god! Am I so weak? Commissar Minh would call me a counterrevolutionary of the worst kind. Just a few hours ago, I was in control. And now? Goddess, why have *You* forsaken me?

God, it's cold!

Perhaps Goddess is right—it's the tunnel for me. *She* almost never speaks to me anymore. Maybe being nothing is better than being something, although quantum mechanics won't even leave nothing alone—virtual particles pop in and out of existence—like us—virtual carbon-based particles. Evidently, what you call reality is nothing more than a collapsed wave function.

Christ! It's colder!

I see two shadows enter the alley. They look menacing and have spotted me. It's too late to hide, as the dim streetlights have outlined my huddled form.

"Hello," I say weakly, waiting to be mugged.

They say nothing and keep moving toward me. I can't make out faces under their hoodies. Bodies without faces are demons. The forms stop and tilt their monkish heads downward to get a better look at me. Evil monks.

"Are you sent from God?" I ask as bold as I can make my voice.

They laugh, or rather, grunt in some sort of amused animal way. Finally, one of them speaks. "Yeah, man, we're from God. He wants an offering."

The voice is deep and cold but bears the stamp of sarcastic intelligence. When he was an innocent little boy, he must have passed the collection plate. Now? Is there a thread of piety left?

I try to reach that spark of piety, and say, "God wants to convert me. Would my profession of faith be enough?"

More animal grunt-laughs. So much for intelligence and innocence.

I feel a sharp pain in my side, and I realize I have just been kicked.

"Give us your offering, asshole!" come words from the one who bears the seed of sentience. "God demands it!" he adds, clumsily playing to what he assumes is my delusion.

"I have nothing."

Another kick, harder, and I fear a rib is broken. When I look up, I see the gleam of a steel blade form an arc across my line of sight.

I close my eyes and wait to become nothing. Their curses fade and the knife circles, about to find its way home. The alley dissolves. I am falling, and when I hit the ground it is not pavement but wet leaves.

~

Sunlight stabs through narrow openings in the jungle canopy, piercing the early morning mist that squirms and twists under the flashing blades of another murderous day. Predators, prey and witnesses all rehearse their testimony. Birds sing and gibbons chatter. A tiger growls, insects hiss and plants breathe steam in humid clouds that cling like mucous to the soaked air. Ants wage savage wars deep beneath the detritus while above them, two human soldiers stagger through the foliage, one pursuing the other. The pursued, a young soldier exhausted and choking from the downpour of pollen and seeds, half-stumbles, half-slides down the bank of a stream. Tumbling out of the underbrush, his back to the water, he jerks his rifle free of the clinging vines and branches. In the background, the slashing of the relentless machete draws nearer.

He's close! Very close! Got to get across this stream! Help me, mother! Help me!

Whirling around to make a mad dash, the young soldier freezes. In front of him the entwined corpses of his two friends bob in the stream, half submerged, snagged by the outspreading branches of a fallen tree. One's head is underwater, but the other looks directly at him. Its eyes are open wide, flat, and unresponsive to the flies crawling across their corneas.

Those eyes stare accusingly, as if blaming the young soldier for his comrades' deaths, for running from the enemy. For betraying them all.

"So be it," the young soldier whispers. He spins around to face the crazed pursuer. No more images of his mother's burned face. Now it's only the predator and the prey. Life of death. So simple.

With shocking speed, the American bursts from the undergrowth, rifle in one hand, machete brandished in the other. The young soldier raises his AK-47 and squeezes off a few rounds before the American leaps on top of him. The young soldier tries to brace himself, but the falcon slams into the quail. He falls on his back, arms splayed, as though nailed to the earth. The American savagely brings down his machete in a flash of glimmering steel, severing the young soldier's hand at the wrist. Searing pain shoots up his arm, his detached hand still clutching the pistol grip of his rifle, fingers twitching uselessly—

~

"Wake up, Michael. They are gone. You are safe."

The words ponderously move through the fog like a bell struck underwater.

Buandelgereen leans over me and I swear, in the faint light, I can make out the gleaming barrel of a rifle slung over her shoulder. Her voluminous white hair casts a brilliant burst of purity through the alley's grimy vapors.

"My magnificent protectress," I murmur, for I am not sure whether I'm still dreaming. This Mongol warrior-woman is like my beloved dead wife—constantly waking me from nightmares and voices (although Diane never had the other-worldly archetype of white hair going for her). Still, she always fought the good fight for her damaged husband.

"Come."

"Please, Buandelgereen, not to the institute. I will die there. Tell God I will worship Him and revere His name for all eternity." I know I babble like some craven coward, but I am desperately alone, afraid, hungry, cold, and I now see life as a prize one must claw, scrape, and humiliate oneself to keep.

Buandelgereen scoffs. "Fool! I do not work for God. It is *she* who commands, and I am commanded to protect, not hurl your carcass to an addicted God."

"Thank God!" I cry, before realizing the absurdity of the words. "I mean, thank Goddess!"

Buandelgereen throws her head back and laughs, white mane billowing so extravagantly, it threatens to engulf the entire alley. When she calms, I venture a timid request for confirmation.

"So, you're not taking me back to the institution?"

"No."

"Then, where?"

In response, she produces a non-sequitur. "Your son seeks you."

"Mark?"

"You only have one son. Yes."

"He is possessed."

"So you say."

"Are you taking me to him?" I ask suspiciously.

"No."

"Well then?"

"You have made it clear you no longer want to return to the tunnel."

"Yes."

"And you prefer being something to being nothing?"

"Yes."

Buandelgereen sighs. "Then being something means you must deal with living souls, not with the hollowed ones, like your ghosts."

"I don't understand."

"You must deal with your son, with Dr. Hess, with Dr. Camara, with Marie Telles, and with me. Not with Nature and Mountain Man and Diane, and all the other dead ones who are emptinesses."

"What if I were to tell you that all those emptinesses are more substantial than the souls you mentioned?"

"Then, in that case, you must return to the tunnel. There you will be emptiness consorting with other emptinesses."

"Buandelgereen, I will follow you. Lead on, but I hope and trust our destination will be warm, with food and drink, and a soft bed."

Again, she laughs. "That is quite a list of desires. All I can tell you is that we travel to somewhere, not to nowhere; and when we reach somewhere, there will be the living rather than the lost."

As best I can follow this crooked line of reasoning, I take heart. "Lead on. By the way, what happened to those two muggers?"

"Oh, they're nothings now."

~ *Mongol Steppes and American Deserts* ~

Dear Reader, I will not burden you with a description of how Buandelgereen led me back to Marie Telles's mansion, but once we arrived, I ate and bathed and drank bourbon and looked forward to my soft bed. Alas! It was not to be. Just as I assumed the time to retire had come, Buandelgereen looked at Marie and said, "It is time."

Marie nodded, and the two women escorted me to the street where a car waited. Buandelgereen opened the rear door and we both slipped into the back seat. I could not see the driver's face, just a low cap and a gauze scarf, the rest a silhouette. Marie Telles leaned over and waved goodbye. We drove away from my nice, comfy, adopted abode, and after a few moments, Buandelgereen said, "Sleep, Michael Powers. It is a long drive."

I did not have to be told twice.

When I awoke, harsh sunlight streamed through a window onto the bed where I had been sleeping. How much time had passed, I did not know. My tongue felt like sand, limbs heavy, mouth sour. *Must have been drugged* was my first thought. When I rose and looked out the window, all I could see was sand and bare rock stretching to a distant range of sunbaked hills. For whatever reason, I had been taken to the desert. Only then, with the sun warming my body, did I realize I was naked. I write these words in my writing pad, which I discovered sitting most conveniently on a desk. There, I have caught you up. I scratch these words in complete ignorance of where I am or why I am here.

A knocking. I hear Buandelgereen's voice.

"Breakfast, Michael Powers. Clothes are in the closet."

Even for a schizophrenic, I am jolted by the unreality of my circumstances. Goddess is obviously behind this. Once I am dressed, I follow Buandelgereen to the dining room, where we join three men, all evidently fellow Mongolians, who talk with Buandelgereen in their own language. I am ignored as they chatter, only occasionally casting glances my way. I cannot tell if I am the subject of conversation, but just as I finish off my breakfast of rice gruel (which I deliberately pick at to flaunt my displeasure). Buandelgereen turns to me.

"You will stay here."

"Good. I like it here." This is only a slight lie, as I am still in the dark about what any of this means.

"Of course," she continues. "You will have to work."

"Work?"

"Yes."

"Oh, good. Work is good. What kind of work?"

"You will soon know."

"Good, good."

Dark remains dark.

~

I have learned the nature of my "work." The little group of Mongol immigrants is digging a tunnel—no, a cave, into the side of a scorched mountain. A tunnel of war, a cave of worship; it's the same geometry, different gods. Of course, I know what they are up to, and they know I know. Blasting goes on all day, and the debris must be cleared. Fortunately, I am too old to help much, but I have become a sort of water boy and all-around gopher for the crew. Buandelgereen periodically travels the few miles to the site and checks on us.

Dear Reader, you may think I am unhappy at having to perform such menial labor, but I revel in the freedom of the desert expanse—blue skies, clean air, clear conscience. Where better for an old schizophrenic to spend his days than preparing a dwelling for divinity? After all, I recently called a fetid alley my home, and besides, anything is better than the mental institution.

Oh, Reader! You don't know the anticipation I feel for when the cave is completed and I am behind the iron door with *Her*—not, like my parents, on the outside looking in. At last, I have a front-row seat! Can you imagine my excitement?

No? Well, for an abnormal-normal to explain to a normal-normal, it would be like arranging a family reunion where everyone comes—evidently the ultimate dream of grandmothers around the world. "Just once, before I die," is the mantra. Entire novels have been written about such *papier-mâché* dreams. No, no, do not get angry with me for making such a harsh judgment—after all, I am writing about *Papier-mâché* delusions. Perhaps the two are not all that different. Be that as it may, I am involved in constructing the cave, which will house the enigma that has plagued my parents, their comrades, and me. An ultimate reunion (although the last one in the tunnel did not go so well. Goddess has not yet forgiven me).

"Mr. Powers!" one of the Mongol workers calls me out of this rambling reverie.

"Yes?"

"Water, please."

"Yes, okay! No problem!" I shout back.

On my way to him, I wonder if these workers are like those that built the pyramids, and then were killed to preserve secrets? I hope not. I think not. That is a God-male thing, not a Goddess-female thing. Maybe. I hope. Who knows?

"Here you are."

"Thanks," says the worker, surrounded by a few of his mates.

The lad is tall, strong, and smiles broadly. I feel emboldened, and ask, "Tell me, what brings you here to build this . . . structure?"

His smile turns to laughter, his dark bronze face becoming a mask of carefree mirth.

"Money, of course!"

"Not Goddess?"

"Who?"

"Goddess."

He tilts his head as if to hear better. "Who? You've been in the sun too long, friend."

"Well, who do you think this is for?"

He watches my face while he talks, enjoying the needle, measuring how far I'll take the mystic line.

He gestures toward Buandelgereen, who stands at a distance speaking with a man I assume to be an engineer.

"What is it for?" I repeat.

"Tourists, of course."

"Tourists?"

"Yeah. Those who want to see the mysteries of the East, and all that bullshit."

"Oh."

He looks at me sympathetically. "You didn't know?"

"Well, kind of," I reply glumly.

"When we are done, Buandelgereen will start advertising, and after that, the sky is the limit. We have all been promised jobs. Imagine, Americans (particularly young, disillusioned Americans) will flock here to see a real, exotic oracle. America's Delphi!" He looks around with twinkling eyes. "Plenty of rocks on which to scratch your requests to see into the future."

I gaze at him and tilt my head in an exaggerated way. "You don't sound like a typical worker, friend."

"And you are not a typical water boy, friend."

I catch the ironic cast of his face.

"You have been pulling my leg," I say. "This is not to be a tourist trap."

"What do you think life is, Michael Powers?"

When I do not immediately respond, he trots off, saying, "Back to work. Thanks!"

Evidently, proximity to the divine must bring out riddle-making powers in all of us.

~

Well, what am I to make of this 'tourist' idea? If this is the way to go about things, I have the notion that Dr. Hess could turn the mental institution into such a tourist destination. Wait until a patient is manic or suicidal, and direct the curious ticket holders his or her way, to observe mental illness up close and personal. If soldiers without faces and arms and legs can fantasize doing it, why not us mental freaks? I am, of course, being flippant, as I realize this speculative circus is not the goal of *Hers* or Buandelgereen. So, what is *Her* goal? And how do I fit in?

~ *Buandelgereen Loses Her Temper* ~

Today, as I work, Buandelgereen emerges from the cave surrounded by a gaggle of workers. They are chattering excitedly, and my lack of Mongol fluency continues to exasperate. Periodically, they glance in my direction, then return to their conversation. This makes one a bit uncomfortable. Being schizophrenic, and (slightly) paranoid, I assume I am the object of their animated discussion. I want to listen, even though I understand nothing, but am continually beset by requests for water from thirsty workers. One of my "customers" is the fellow who told me about the tourist scheme.

"Hello, Batsaikhan," I say in my best Mongol.

"Your Mongol is getting better," he says. As usual, he smiles broadly and rests his eyes on Buandelgereen and her little coterie.

Having already exhausted my "excellent" Mongol, I ask in English, "What are they discussing? Can you hear?"

"Air," he replies.

"Air?"

"Yes, how to ensure enough air is available deep inside the cave."

I laugh sarcastically. "Yeah, Batsaikhan, tourists need air."

He looks at me with an amused expression. "So do you."

With these words, I assume that I am to live in the cave, but something else tickles my curiosity. "Batsaikhan?"

"Yes?"

"Do Goddesses need air?"

"There you go again, friend. How do I know? Goddesses are not my specialty."

"What is your specialty?"

"Not Goddesses. Women maybe. Flesh and blood women." He looks at me and takes a long drink. "Oh, and blasting caves, of course."

I laugh. "Your ancestors built caves for Genghis Khan, did they?"

"Ah, the Great Khan! He knew exactly what he wanted. Everything had to be big and intimidating. Yes, like Buandelgereen, he knew precisely what he wanted. What a woman she is! The Great Khan himself . . . well, that is another story."

"Sounds like you knew him personally," I chuckle.

"Quite well."

And with that, he strides away to disappear through the yawning black opening of the cave.

Dear reader, schizophrenia forces one to walk carefully upon the shifting nature of reality. There exists no *terra firma*, only swiftly moving plates that randomly collide, precipitating sudden earthquakes, uplifted mountains, and volcanic eruptions. In our manic phase, you normal-normals are like somnambulant sleepwalkers, whose mere blinking of the eyes takes years, at least to us.

So, at this moment, I am compelled to speak with Buandelgereen. That she is still surrounded by fellow Mongols is of no consequence. My own vital questions must be answered. Besides, the cave emits a sound that is disturbingly like a growling stomach, although many octaves lower, and far more menacing. Is it hungry?

"Buandelgereen!" I cry as I approach, louder and more insistent than intended.

She slowly turns from her companions, white hair radiant in the desert sun. "Yes, Mr. Powers?"

Her open attitude takes me aback, as I assumed she would be dismissive.

"Am I to live in this cave?"

"Perhaps."

"And Goddess?"

"*She?*"

"Yes."

"Perhaps."

"And you?"

"Perhaps."

I am frustrated. "It must be that straight answers are strictly forbidden here, correct?"

She smiles wryly. "As your Einstein discovered, the universe is warped. Near strong gravitational fields, straight is strictly forbidden."

"Do Gods and Goddesses exert gravitational fields?"

"Yes, which is why so many people are in freefall, orbiting their own divine stars." She laughs in anticipation of her own joke. "God is the densest of all, thus

His ability to swallow so many souls, bending them past His event horizon with barely a burp."

"I don't believe."

"Then you are simply in freefall, orbiting nothing."

"Nothingness. It sounds nice."

"Mr. Powers, can you not enjoy nothingness anywhere? Even back at the mental institution?"

"No!" I exclaim. "Only in the tunnel where others wait in nothingness."

"Such as Nature?"

I cannot help but feel surprised. "How do you know about Nature? You are of my parents. Nature is of me."

She frowns and draws herself to her full height. Intimidating. A ferocious Mongol warrior preparing to enter the field of battle.

"Your Vietnam comrades are all dead, Mr. Powers! Dead! Their deaths were not your fault. Your parents are dead. Their deaths were not your fault either." She touches her breast. "I am here, Mr. Powers. Here! I am very much alive and real, not one of your ghosts. I know your past. *She* has tasked me with your well-being."

"Dr. Hess would ask how I know you are real."

With a suddenness that takes my breath away, she slaps my face.

"Is that real?" she demands.

"Real enough," I reply as I rub my burning cheek.

She turns to the others and says something in Mongol. They nod and disperse.

"Now!" she says. "What further nonsense have you for me?"

I am angry at her blunt evaluation of my life, so accurate and yet so incomplete. Out of a perverse impulse, I ask, "Did you love my mother?"

She catches my jaw in one hand with another iron slap. "Fool."

I am undeterred. "Dr. Hess is Goddess, isn't she?"

"Enough." The word lands like a blow.

"Is Dr. Camara my friend Nature?"

Her eyes flash, but she does not strike.

"I have no more questions," I say, trying to sound impertinent, but only managing to sound weak.

"You are like your father," she says, but not at all scornfully.

"My father was weak," I say.

"You are tragically wrong."

I walk away.

As I pass, the cave growls.

Chapter Ten

Interregnum

Possessions

~ He Is Truly Lost[1] ~

After her meeting with the Mongol woman, Gail Hess returned home, greeted Sigmund, and took a long bath in expectation of seeing Adam Camara. She let the hot water veil her, trying to melt away her tension. She focused on the anticipation of his coming, and her feelings of stress transformed into yearnings for sex. She desperately wanted to immerse herself in pleasure and thereby purge the bedeviling problems of her patients . . . no . . . the one patient. Yet, somewhere deep inside, she understood that she was recklessly fleeing from Goddess into the arms of a very mortal man. Carnal indulgence promised the easiest absolution. Where better to embrace her womanhood?

When she opened the door in response to Adam's knocking, she repressed an irresistible urge to throw herself into his arms. Instead, the old discipline kicked in.

"Hello," she said simply, chuckling at the sight of his tam o'shanter.

This time, his face did not reflect the usual good humor that went along with his silly hat. "Hello," he replied rather grimly.

Immediately, she sensed a cloud.

"What's wrong?"

"Do you mind if we stay here a while?"

"Of course not."

"Let's sit." His words seemed detached, automatic.

Gail noticed his hands shaking. "Would you like a drink?"

"Yeah. Gin and tonic?"

"Sorry, no can do. It used to be that having one bottle constituted a lifetime supply. Your visits have depleted my stock. I'll make sure it gets replenished before your next visit. Wine?"

Adam emitted a dry laugh. "That'll have to do."

"Merlot?"

He waved his hand dismissively. "Anything."

Handing over his drink, Gail asked again, "What's wrong, Adam?"

He gulped the wine and removed the tam o'shanter, holding it in front of his eyes. "This," he replied.

"Oh, that," said a relieved Gail. "Did it shrink, or did your head swell?" She laughed at her glib little repartee.

But Adam did not rise to the occasion. His face remained glum, and he poured another glass of wine as if she were not present.

Now Gail felt real alarm. She had never seen him like this.

"Adam." Her voice rose. "What is it? What is the problem?"

He shook his head and began to speak very slowly and deliberately. "When we first met, after I had already heard from others, I listened to your story about Mr. Powers and felt convinced you had fallen into the age-old trap—indeed, multiple traps—set by your patient, which all culminated in leading you seriously astray. The more we talked, the more attracted I became to you. Nonetheless, that attraction did not lessen my concern for your professional behavior, in fact, it heightened my concern for your own mental state.

"Then, I met Mr. Powers and began reading his 'scribblings', as I thought of them, because initially I assumed they were merely skillful manipulative tools he used to entrap you. To be truthful, I read more than I admitted to you, and the full force of what we are confronting came down upon me."

He paused and poured another drink. Gail held her breath, afraid he had stopped for good, and at the same time, afraid he would continue. But he simply sat quietly with his drink, staring into space. At first, she intended to wait until he felt comfortable enough to continue. The tam o'shanter dangled limply from his knee, like something dead.

At first, she intended to wait until he felt comfortable enough to continue. Finally, she could no longer take the silence.

"So, what happened to present you with this realization? . . . His writings?"

"No," he replied slowly. "Not his writings." He looked down and picked at the tam o'shanter. "It was Nature."

Gail felt her heart skip a beat. "What about Nature?"

"He wants Storyteller back."

The hairs on Gail's neck rose. "Adam, you know Nature is long dead, along with all his comrades. And Storyteller is also long gone—nothing more than Michael Powers's younger self in a war fought a lifetime ago. That part of Mr. Powers no longer exists except in his guilt-ridden brain. This is the core of his psychosis. That is all. It has nothing to do with you or me, except insofar as we are his treating physicians."

"No, that is what I thought at first. But I was wrong. You're wrong now. There is something else. . . ."

Gail instinctively reacted against a suspicion that she herself had felt for a long time. "But—"

"No, Gail. It's no use. I never answered your question about what happened to present me with this realization."

"Adam, I don't even know what your realization is."

He looked at her oddly, almost sheepishly. "You don't know?"

"No."

Adam shook his head. "Yes, you do."

"I do not."

Adam leaned forward and stared at her. His voice cracked into a shout. "Stand on that table and bare your breasts for me, Great Goddess!"

The words struck her like a blow. Gail laughed nervously at the utter absurdity of these words.

"Adam, don't be ridiculous!"

"Do it! If You can do it for Storyteller, You can do it for Nature!"

With these insane words coming from the mouth of the eminently sane and rational Adam Camara, she experienced an indescribable mixture of panic and something else she refused to give a name. A stirring within her bosom uncurled itself and began to stretch, reaching down to her vagina and diffusing across her breasts. She could only stammer, "Stop this, Adam. Stop. You're scaring me—stop!"

But, to her horror, her hands involuntarily went to her breasts, caressing them. She murmured, "Stop, stop," as she started to unbutton her blouse.

Adam leapt up and grabbed her shoulders. "You see! This is my realization!"

Gail forced herself to focus, and as she fumbled with rebuttoning, she asked weakly (already knowing the answer), "What?"

"We are being slowly possessed."

Now back to her senses, Gail scoffed. "Adam, that is a thirteenth-century superstition."

"So it is, and I still believe we are being possessed, perhaps by some very strong suggestive power."

"That of Michael Powers?"

"Who else?"

The Chosen One.

"What?" asked Adam.

"Did I speak?"

"You said—'The Chosen One'—but in a very strange voice."

Gail's eyes widened. "That was Goddess."

"Is that the Goddess of Michael Powers, of the Precious Object, of the quest for *her*?"

"Yes."

"There you are."

Gail stared at him, shaken to her core.

A thin voice inside begged her to deny it all, to laugh, to say he was mad—but she could not.

~ *He Is Truly Lost*[2] ~

"We must find him," said Gail Hess after the silence had stretched long enough to feel awkward.

"And once we do?" asked Adam.

"What can be possessed can be exorcised."

"Good god! Listen to us! We have made great progress since the thirteenth century!" muttered Adam.

"Then let's leap forward again. Look, Adam, let us agree this is not some sort of medieval possession by vengeful demons and the Devil's trickery. Instead, let us focus on the nature of such powerful psychological suggestions, and how Michael Powers can so successfully implant them in even the most experienced psychiatrists. After all, we live in the twenty-first century. Imagine if we could find the basis of his power! It might explain the hypnotic ingredient of every charismatic psychopath, demagogue, and dictator out there."

"Or every Jesus, Muhammad, and Zarathustra out there," added Adam.

"Well, yes."

Adam closed his eyes and said, "All this is very illuminating, but in the meantime, Nature gets stronger inside me."

"How? What are your symptoms?"

"Headaches. Nightmares. A feeling I've slipped into another body. Flashes of Vietnam. This damned tam o'shanter."

"All explainable psychologically."

Adam looked at her accusingly. "And you, Goddess?"

Gail's face flickered with turmoil. Then she rose sharply, stripping off her blouse and bra as if shedding a lie. "These are mine. They are human. They are the breasts of Gail Hess, not those of some Goddess."

Adam rushed to her. "No, no." He embraced her from behind and let his hands gently caress her breasts. "You're wrong, Gail. These *are* the breasts of a Goddess."

Gail let her body surrender to his touch, and her mind surrender to the moment.

~

The next morning over breakfast, Gail and Adam initially agreed to visit Marie Telles and demand to see Michael Powers. No more hedging. If they were refused, they would call the police. But the more they talked, the more their plan changed.

"Should we call first?" asked Gail.

"No. Just show up. If she doesn't let us in, then we will know for sure he is there."

Gail shook her head doubtfully. "Adam, let's think about this a bit more. Let's be smart about it. We show up, be polite, and explain that an emergency has arisen regarding his son. Once she lets us in, I'll talk with her while you excuse yourself to go to the bathroom, then use that opportunity to search the place while I keep her busy."

"Fine, but if I find him, I can't very well carry him out."

"No, but then we can call for help. Shall we do it today?"

"No, Saturday is better," said Adam. "We still have other patients, and if he is truly not there. . . . "

"We'll cross that bridge when we get to it," said Gail.

They were still aglow from the night before, and the strange revelation they had shared bound them in a wary complicity.

~

Saturday arrived and they drove to Marie Telles's mansion. No further supernatural incidents had occurred, and their ardor had somewhat cooled. Nevertheless, both remained adamant about carrying out the plan. Now they sat in the car, staring at the mansion that seemed to dare them to enter. In the light of day, both felt a bit sheepish, but at an unspoken cue, they exited the car and strode purposefully to the house. Gail, as usual, kept glancing at the upstairs windows for any rustling curtains or surreptitious shadows. Nothing.

"Oh, hello," said a surprised Marie Telles when she opened the door. "Nice to see you again."

"Hello," they said in unison. "Sorry for the intrusion, but we have news concerning Michael Powers," said Gail.

"Oh? Did you find him?"

"Well, no. May we come in?"

"Of course."

Sitting in the little anteroom, Gail began her spiel about Mark Powers, and Adam, as planned, excused himself.

When he returned, the two women had fallen silent. Marie looked at Adam as he entered and said with an amused expression, "As you have seen for yourself, Michael Powers is not here."

"Where has he gone?" asked Gail.

"I do not know where he is."

"Ms. Telles," said Adam. "May I ask you some questions about Mr. Powers?"

"Of course."

"Do you believe Mr. Powers sees things? I mean, things that aren't there?"

"Yes. After all, he suffers from schizophrenia, correct?"

"Yes, but . . . do you believe he sees things that we don't see, but really are there?"

"Marie paused, either to untangle the awkward question, or for some other reason. Finally, she said, "I believe he believes they are real."

Gail jumped in. "Marie, do you believe the hallucinations he sees are real?"

Marie laughed. "You are psychiatrists. Would I be so foolish as to say I believe? Next stop, a room adjoining Michael's at your institution."

"The reason we are asking," said Adam. "Is that we ourselves are beginning to believe he has some insight, some vision, into a realm unavailable to the rest of us."

As Marie digested this statement, Gail added, "And he uses this unique insight to plant suggestions in others."

Marie tilted her head slightly, as if puzzled. "If I remember my college psychology class, are not suggestions, by definition, not real?"

Adam shifted impatiently. He felt the conversation drifting into a morass of irrelevant areas. "Ms. Telles, the point is, do you believe Mr. Powers is in communication with the dead, or with these deities of his, which he refers to as God and Goddess?"

"Yes, I do believe. But, as to whether they are real, in the sense I think you mean, I do not know."

Gail leaned forward and stared at Marie Telles with intense interest. "You were friends with his mother. Did she have any of these insights . . . or gifts?"

"I don't know."

"Marie, I think you do know. Did she?"

Marie blanched. "I will not discuss Bai Meiying."

"How about his father, John Powers?" asked Adam.

"He was also schizophrenic, Dr. Camara. The same analysis of the son applies to the father. I don't mean to be rude, but I really do have things to do. Now that you have searched my house, without my approval, surely you see that I can be of no further help." She stood to signal the end of the interview.

After making their apologies, Gail and Adam sat glumly in the car, still parked in front of the mansion.

"He is truly gone," said Gail dejectedly.

"Yes, and we are back to square one."

"Not quite."

"How so?" asked Adam.

"Those 'suggestions' have taken root. And they're spreading."

"In us?"

"In us. I can feel it."

Adam turned the ignition. "As can I."

~ *That Mongol Woman* ~

As they drove away, Gail snapped her fingers. "That Mongol woman!"

"What?"

"The Mongol woman that was looking for Michael Powers!"

"Bu-an-green, or whatever her name is?"

"Yes!" exclaimed Gail. "Buandelgereen. She has found him—I'm sure of it!"

"How does that help?"

"Find her, we find him."

"Sorry, my dear, I don't follow. How will finding her be any easier than finding him?"

"She is a prominent character in his writings. Assuming she is not an American citizen, she must have a passport and visa to be here."

"Ah, check with the Mongolian embassy?"

"You bet. We can legitimately use our credentials this time. Escaped inmate, friend of Mongol citizen visiting United States, you get the picture."

"Yeah," drawled Adam.

"You're the Assistant Director, surely you can obtain approval from Dr. Greenlee?"

"Surely."

Adam spoke rather distantly, as he felt a sudden, inexplicable urge to visit Nature's birthplace, Providence, Rhode Island, and the graveyard in which he wrote the poetry described in Michael Powers's writings.

Why now? Why this pull—here, in a car in San Francisco, beside Gail Hess, about to hunt a mysterious Mongol woman. Why this hunger for a dead soldier's grave?

"Why?" he said aloud.

"What?" asked Gail.

"Gail, wasn't Nature the best friend of Storyteller?"

"Yes."

"And, except for the unconscious Idaho, he was the last person to see Storyteller in the tunnel before the platoon left the fortress and died in an ambush, correct?"

"Yes, but—"

"No, no! Listen. Nature came to believe Storyteller's narrative about seeing the ghosts, or spirits, of their families, correct?"

"Yes."

"So, Nature had merged his own soul (if you will) with Storyteller's in that tunnel. I mean, Nature reluctantly left him only to die in the ambush, and Storyteller was left to ponder his own mortality in the utter darkness of that tomb. Correct?"

"That is one way to look at it. But look, Adam, why don't we concentrate on finding Buandelgereen first?"

Adam continued speaking as if she were not there. "Yes, that explains the skeleton, the bones, Nature's power over Michael Powers, why Nature wants him back in that tunnel. Not all of them died. Remember the writings, when Nature was about to leave the tunnel, and Storyteller asked where do birds go to die?"

"Adam, let's discuss the next step we should take to find Mr. Powers."

He abruptly pulled the car over to the side of the road and donned his tam o'shanter. "Gail, you follow that lead. See where the Mongol woman takes you. I'll get approval to use the Institute's name for official inquiries. You can present it to the Mongolian Embassy or Consulate. But, for the time being, I am after bigger game—at least to me."

"Nature?"

"Yes. He grows in strength inside me, and I must know him better."

Gail experienced a moment of panic, feeling her stomach drop at the idea of losing Adam to a long dead soldier. *So sudden!* she marveled.

Let him go! commanded Goddess, and Gail shrank back in her seat, now afraid for her own sanity as much as that of Adam Camara.

When Adam dropped her off, his distraction seemed almost complete. Only at the last moment did he catch up to her as she approached her front door. He grabbed her hand.

"Dear Gail, don't worry. I'm beginning to see more clearly now." He kissed her passionately, as if leaving for a long trip—or to war—and said, "I am falling very very deeply in love with you. I know you think you are losing me to him, but it is the reverse, I am getting closer to him so as not to lose you. Only by understanding him will I be able to keep my own identity safe."

With these disturbing words, he gave her a last kiss and drove away.

Closing the door behind her, Gail saw Sigmund come running.

"Sigmund, Sigmund, Sigmund, dear one. Will I lose him as I have lost Mr. Powers? My only hope is that Mongol woman."

~

The following week proceeded without much contact between Gail and Adam. He showed her his multi-page request to use the Institute's official imprimatur in locating Mr. Powers, citing the severe nature of his illness, and the potential for him to unintentionally harm others. They spoke very little, and when they did see each other, Adam always seemed rushed. When he gave her the letter granting his request, she asked him over to her apartment that weekend.

"Good idea!" he exclaimed enthusiastically. "That would be lovely. Then I can tell you my plans."

"Plans?"

He smiled enigmatically. "You'll see."

"Do they involve me?"

"Well, in a way, yes."

This answer unsettled her. Just as she had come to genuinely rely on his companionship, he was unexpectedly moving away at an accelerating rate. Still, she had hopes that his "plans" did involve her. Meanwhile, Michael Powers's absence had left a hole in her practice that was far more consequential than she had even feared. Other patients now seemed rather flat and boring, their symptoms straightforward and unsatisfying to her ambitions. She fell into a depression that rendered her sluggish and careless. This lethargy soon came to the attention of June.

Returning from her rounds one late morning, June asked, "Are you feeling well?"

"Yes, why?"

June laughed. "Gail, we have known each other a long time. Something is wrong. Is it Dr. Camara?"

Gail felt grateful for June's interest and irritated at her assumption. She was not an adolescent female dealing with high school drama. She tried to maintain her professional equilibrium. "It is true that I have been a bit down lately, but it has nothing to do with Dr. Camara. Perhaps it's the missing Mr. Powers that has me feeling guilty."

"Guilty?"

"Yes, that he escaped."

"Is it certain that he was helped by Joe?"

"Circumstantial only, but I think so. Mr. Powers has a way of getting to all of us and making us do things we would not ordinarily even think of doing."

"Isn't that the truth," muttered June.

Gail turned red and started to scold her secretary, but then she saw the conspiratorial smile and had to join in.

"Okay, okay, don't rub it in, June," she said, laughing. "It is true Mr. Powers has a certain power that affects us all in different ways."

"And Dr. Camara?" asked June, cutting to the heart of the unspoken implication.

"June, you are a very difficult woman to keep secrets from. Yes, Dr. Camara has also been affected by Mr. Powers."

"How, if I may ask?"

"That must remain confidential, even from you."

"And the Mongol woman?"

"I have sent inquiries to Mongolian authorities. Still waiting for an answer."

"I see. Now, you received a call from Mark Powers. He wants to meet with you."

"Did he say why?"

"No, but I imagine it is to get any updates about his father's whereabouts. He is worried his father may be in some danger without access to his medication."

"As he should be. Schedule him for next week, Tuesday or Wednesday. I can't deal with him on Monday."

"Okay, but I still worry about you, Gail."

"Thank you, but I'll be fine. Perhaps the Mongolian authorities will give us a clue.

"To tell you the truth, I'm not worried about Michael Powers or that Mongol woman."

"I know, you're worried about me."

"No, Gail, I'm worried about this Goddess business."

"June, she is just one of his hallucinations."

"I'm not sure you really believe that. In any case, I have noticed little things about you that are different. Don't let a schizophrenic's delusion get to you."

Gail put her hand on June's shoulder. "I won't."

"Or possess you."

"Come, June, we're not in the thirteenth century." Gail smiled inwardly at the déjà vu.

"I warned you before about this Goddess figure, and we know where that led. Nothing good. I see it happening again, only stronger."

"June, drop it. You have given me your concerns and I have listened. Now there is work to do—for both of us."

In spite of her rather breezy assurances, Gail knew she had been slipping deeper into some strange abyss. Most days passed without her thinking of Goddess, but suddenly an alien sensation would grip her, and a feeling of power made her see herself and others differently. It was during these moments of imperiousness that she felt the need to do something, or go somewhere, for no apparent reason. *Just as with Adam.*

At that moment, she remembered his "plans" and realized he never had the chance to share them.

She buzzed June. "Please call Dr. Camara and ask him to see me in my office when he has the opportunity."

"Will do."

Very little time passed before Adam showed up.

"You rang?"

"Yes, that invitation is still open to come to my apartment this weekend. Are you still up for it?"

"Of course."

"You can tell me your plans over drinks."

"Lovely."

Something seemed amiss. "You still want to, don't you?" asked Gail.

"Absolutely! I'll be there Friday night after work—we can go out for dinner."

She gave him her most seductive smile. "No, I'll cook. It will give us more time together."

"Still no word from the Mongolians?"

The chill of his tone stung. "Not yet."

Adam seemed oblivious. "Well, if things happen as I hope, perhaps we won't need them."

"Your plans?"

"Yes."

"Give me a hint."

"What, and spoil it?"

"Nature—this is serious."

Both sat stunned. Gail held her hand to her lips.

"You see?" said Adam. "Things are happening to us very fast now. We don't have much time."

"But it's so insidious! I am me. You are you. We are psychiatrists. How is this possible?" It seemed to Gail that Adam, in spite of his vociferous early demands for reason over questionable speculation and supernatural hypotheses, was falling faster and farther than she.

"I am traveling to Rhode Island to find out."

"What?"

"That is my plan. I'm traveling to Providence, Rhode Island and speak with Nature in the graveyard."

"Now we're talking with ghosts?" asked Gail in disgust.

He looked conspicuously around the room. "That's what we do every day, Gail. This institute is full of ghosts we talk with, and ghosts we try and reach to talk with."

"You'll feel quite foolish sitting alone in a graveyard, a continent away from your responsibilities, waiting for a dead soldier to come and exchange insights."

Adam flashed that infuriatingly patronizing smile. "Did you feel foolish standing in front of Mr. Powers with your breasts bared, pretending to be a Goddess, and waiting for some psychiatric miracle of insight to occur?"

That weekend they desperately clung to each other as might two lovers in a stormy sea. Sex was never so good, driven by the fear that their own personalities were disappearing. Each tried to persuade the other that reason and rationality underlay their actions. By the end of their sojourn, Adam reiterated his determination to travel to Rhode Island.

"Hey," he said with a shrug. "If it doesn't work, I'll have the pleasure of exploring Providence. No harm, no foul."

For her part, Gail dreaded what he might find, and continued her low-grade war with Goddess, who now intruded very rarely. She ascribed this absence to the fact that Mr. Powers was physically gone, and alarmingly heightened her obsession to find him. *Do I miss Her that much?* she wondered. *Do I want Her to take over?*

These musings jogged her memory. She would meet with his son, Mark, on Tuesday.

Chapter Eleven

Nearing Completion

Work Continues

Dear Reader, as I write these words in my room on a moonlit night, the cave has grown daily in size and depth. Even bats have found it and are starting to check it out. I can almost see *Her* nod approvingly as it takes shape. It was days ago when Buandelgereen slapped my face, and we have not talked since. This has made me sad. I am not so ill as to be unaware that I need friends. Her anger at my comment about Father being weak, and her sensitivity to the topic of my mother have galvanized my determination to know her better. Perhaps through her, I might learn more about my parents, particularly Mother.

As I said, it is nighttime, and dinner was hurried and lacked the presence of Buandelgereen, leaving me to listen to the workers enthusiastically chattering in a language I do not understand. When they laugh without restraint, I want to know the joke, but I cannot ask since they speak such little English. I have taken to teaching the workers some English (like my father did in China), but it is a slow process. There are no star pupils—yet. Only Batsaikhan speaks fluently, but he is rarely around. Conversely, my Mongolian steadily improves. I will never achieve fluency, as my father did in Chinese. Still, I feel no small sense of accomplishment when I learn a few tongue-twistingly difficult words. I never question who is paying for all this, but at least I am making some small contributions to the project. Speaking of paying, my thoughts invariably turn to the day when I can move into the cave. Will it be connected to the tunnel in Vietnam, like Dr. Hess's bathroom? If so, I will have access to stillness, and to Nature. (As you may have noticed, Nature seems to be quite busy working his way to me. Perhaps we'll meet in the middle, courtesy of Dr. Camara.)

In case you are wondering, I continue to hear the voices of the world around me. The sands of the desert are restless, like a billion little trolls swirling this way and that, anxious to reach the distant sea. They chatter in high-pitched squeals, forever shifting with the fickle moods of the wind. Rocks are clearly the elders, cleaving and cracking under the harsh siege of the elements, moaning painfully, constantly birthing smaller progeny that will eventually join the little trolls. But, enough of this, Tomorrow, I will approach Buandelgereen and try to rebuild that bridge.

~

It is noon and now is my chance. Buandelgereen stands alone, glaring at the distant mountains with one hand over her eyes. I move toward her, and she abruptly turns to face me, stretched to her full height, scowling, hands on hips.

"Hello," I say.

"You have more questions?" she asks bluntly.

"Yes, I have many questions."

What she says next surprises me. "Do you have any answers?"

"That is not up to me," I stammer.

"Is it up to me, then?"

"Well, you and *Her* and . . . I don't know, others."

"What others?"

"Goddess."

"Oh! Would you recognize *Her* now?"

"Of course. Goddesses are timeless."

"Goddesses are capable of many disguises, you know."

"I know."

"She could be any of us here."

I look at the workers skeptically.

"Oh, yes," says Buandelgereen, following my gaze. "She can take male form. You know that, fool! You wrote about it. Madame Dau, for instance, talked with Goddess in *Her* guise as a soldier."

"I remember," I say weakly.

"Nevertheless, you profess not to believe. Atheism. Evolution. All that prevents belief in such nonsense. Right?"

With this low blow, my intellectual pride gets the best of me. "Buandelgereen, I am a lawyer, an educated man. Evolution is a fact, and there are no such things as Gods and Goddesses—the greatest delusions of them all!"

"Why do you stay here?"

I hesitate while mulling over my answer. *Number one: she brought me. Number two: I choose not to respond directly to her very legitimate question. Instead, I will pursue my scientific argument.* Now armed with a clever response, I say, "The universe operates on very precise physical laws. Invariant principles and a few critical constants dictate the nature of our universe, not fairy-tale Goddesses and patriarchal Gods."

I steel myself for the inevitable counterattack, but she seems unperturbed and sweeps her arm in a grand gesture. "Then, what is all this for?"

"Simple," I declare complacently. "It is my delusion. I am living in what kids nowadays would call a video game."

Now, dear Reader—after saying these words, which would be music to the ears of Dr. Hess, I expect to find the desert, the cave, and all the rest of this melt away like sugar in hot coffee, and myself back in the institution. I can hear Dr. Hess now. "You see," she would say. "It's all due to your illness. You have been here all along. Buandelgereen is but a dream woman." But, to the astonishment of my rational brain, Buandelgereen still stands before me in the desert, near a cave being built by Mongolian workers.

Always, in the back of my mind, I have felt that my experiences are not real, and might end with the snap of schizophrenia's unpredictable fingers—instantly transported back to a mental institution. But now, here I am, unable to go back even if I want to, which is a sure sign of reality. A frightening sensation settles in: this is all real, like Vietnam, where people died, and where, from those jungles, I began my long escape. Perhaps I am condemned, once again, to dwell in the real world. For what purpose?

Reality has always been a scary condition to me. Even during my days as a successful lawyer, Diane would keep me from tipping over the edge. But then she died, and I had her only as a ghostly reminder to wake up from the hypnotic siren calls of the voices. Even the echo of Diane's spirit has faded to stillness, where all the others reside, and where I rightfully belong. Without them, what remains of me?

"I remain," come the words of Buandelgereen.

I am startled, but not so shaken as to ask accusingly, "If you are real, how can you read my mind?"

"As easily as reading the mind of a child staring at a cookie."

"Am I that simple?"

"Simpler."

I laugh uneasily. "That might be taken as an insult, you know."

"All humans are the simplest of entities, once you know the key to their minds, which, contrary to scientific opinion, are the simplest of the simple."

"No, no," I object. "Viruses are simple, humans are complex. Every beginning biology student knows that."

"Viruses are far more complex in their simplicity than humans, who are far simpler in their complexity than viruses."

"Meaningless riddles!" I scoff.

Buandelgereen appears amused. "A perfect example. To a human, everything is a riddle; to a virus, nothing is a riddle."

"Well," I say, piqued. "I will turn your question around. Why are you here? Surely it cannot be just for me."

"I am here for *her*."

"Which does not answer my question."

"I am here to build a trap."

I laugh. "Yeah, Batsaikhan told me. A tourist trap to make money."

"It is true, I am here to build a trap," she says. "For the one who thinks he is outside it."

With this, someone calls and she leaves to deal with the problem.

~

Dear Reader, her problem is nothing compared to my problem. Who am I to believe? What am I to believe?

Adrift.

"Hey! Michael Powers!" comes a husky Mongol voice. It is Batsaikhan. He trots up and offers a cigarette. I wave it off and he shrugs.

"Lunch break. Thought we could chat."

"Good, let's sit on that rock in the shade. Did you bring lunch?"

He holds up a paper bag. "You?" he asks.

"No, I'm not one for lunch."

We sit and he digs out some food I don't recognize. "So, how are things going?" I ask.

"Good. Cave gets bigger, I get skinnier. Not good for Mongol."

"But good for a small Mongol pony," I joke.

"Not good for Mongol wife." He holds up a pinky finger. "Too skinny!" He roars with laughter.

I gesture toward the cave. "When do you think it'll be done?"

"When boss-woman says so."

"Buandelgereen?"

He looks at me strangely. "She is like Börte. Strong. Smart."

With the mention of Genghis Khan's wife, I start to shake. I can feel Storyteller awakening, rising, stretching, occupying me. "Fuckin' right!" I blurt.

Batsaikhan flinches but says nothing.

Quickly, I pull him back into conversation before too much damage is done. "Batsaikhan?"

"Yeah?"

"Can I see the inside of the cave?"

"Not ready."

"I don't care."

"No. Too dangerous."

"I don't care."

He points at Buandelgereen. "She cares."

"Why?"

The Mongol shrugs. "Ask her."

"She will say no. Will you show me?"

"And risk her wrath? Wife of Genghis Khan will dismember me."

I press. "What will it take?" I am determined to see it.

Batsaikhan smiles wickedly. "Money."

My heart sinks. "Can't."

"All Americans have money."

"Mine is tied up."

He laughs. "Ask your Goddess to provide."

"Do you really believe this cave is being built as a tourist trap?"

He gazes at me blankly. "Do you really believe this cave is being built for a Goddess?"

I gulp. "Yes . . . or, at least, a very powerful woman. A woman with access to great riches."

He seems to ponder. "And you know her?"

"Sort of."

"If she has access to great riches, why not money?"

"You will be rewarded with something more valuable than money."

"Yeah, sure. Can she tell the future?"

"I am sure she can."

"Then I will show you, but only if you promise to give *Her* a few questions from me."

I am cautious. " Batsaikhan, she will not give you future lottery ticket numbers or winning horses."

He looks shocked. "Who do you think I am. I have real questions. Important questions."

"I see. Well, in that case, I promise."

"Okay."

"When?"

"Tonight. Midnight. Will you be able to reach the cave without causing any problems?"

"Of course," I lie. Even if I'm not spotted, I have to walk a few kilometers in the dark. So be it.

"Good," he replies. He holds up his wrist. "I have a fancy Swiss watch—gift from my uncle. What do you say? Synchron?"

"Synchronize."

"Yes." He oversees the process, quite intent on complete accuracy.

As Batsaikhan heads back to the cave, he calls out, "Tonight! Midnight! I will have the questions. Bring flashlight."

I hold up my thumb but say nothing, since he has already announced our secret plans to the world with that booming voice.

Alone in my bed, I am quite worried about falling asleep and missing our rendezvous, so I set the alarm for ten o'clock. It makes no difference—I cannot sleep.

~ Rendezvous ~

"You're late," Batsaikhan says as I clumsily pick my way across the rubble-strewn ground. His flashlight shines in my eyes.

"Can't help it. Took longer than I thought, and dark as hell. Besides, I don't want to break an ankle on these damn rocks."

When I catch up, he jams a sheet of paper in my hand. "Here are the questions," he says hurriedly. "Put them in your pocket and let's go." He seems spooked.

"Yes," I reply, a bit out of breath.

I can hear the cave's fetal heartbeat as it waits in the womb to be born. Our flashlights illuminate the mouth in all its portentous immensity. Upon entering, the first thing I notice is the dank, earthen smell, so reminiscent of the tunnel, and my mind reels with the memories. Only the presence of Batsaikhan keeps me from running deeper into the abyss. As we make our way, he provides me with information **on** its dimensions and the work left to do. When we first enter, the clicking of bats accompanies us, but as we journey deeper, even their rustling fades to silence.

The cave is much larger than I pictured, with numerous side caverns and confusing corridors—all still rough-hewn and unfinished. We come upon a deep chasm and shine our flashlights into the depths, where the light dissipates before reaching the bottom. I hear dripping water echoing up from the blackness.

"One of us rappelled down and found an underground lake," whispers my Mongol guide.

"Grotto," I murmur.

A narrow stone bridge spans the treacherous grotto. The cave reminds me of Rome's catacombs, and has ample space for a million of my skeletons. When we turn off the flashlights, darkness is total, and the silence is deafening. I know we stand beyond all the froth of human interaction and social-media clamor, and I also know here lies truth. In a word, stillness. Exquisite. As we near the end of the excavation, I feel myself growing calm and at peace. I am where I belong.

At last we reach the end, or the apparent end. Batsaikhan shines his light on a narrow opening, beyond which he refuses to take me.

"Not for all the money in the world," he says in response to my pleas.

"Then I will go alone," I say boldly.

"No, you won't," he replies with real menace in his tone.

"You will stop me?"

"I will stop you, and trust me, Michael Powers, I am much stronger than you."

Unwilling, at my age, to travel the hazardous testosterone road of physical confrontation, I deflect, "This opening is about the size of a door."

"So it is," he says.

"An iron door, I imagine, would fit perfectly here."

"That is not my expertise. I blow things up, not build them."

"Can I stand in the doorway and shine a light on the other side?"

"No. We have to go now." He takes my arm and turns me around.

"Let me stay a litle longer," I say. "It feels like home here."

"We go now!" he commands, tugging my arm. His hand is strong, and I have no choice but to follow him out, each step leaving me emptier and more depressed.

I hear a voice, faint, drifting to us from beyond the doorway. "Come back," it softly cries.

"I can't, Nature. Not yet."

"What?" asks a startled Batsaikhan.

"Nothing," I reply. "Or should I say, nothingness."

~

When I finally return to my bed, the first hints of dawn brighten the room. I am tired and crawl under the covers, only to remember something important. I get up, find my trousers, and fish out the list of questions given me by my Mongol guide. I unfold it and stare at a blank sheet. I smile. I wonder.

Time is passing, Chosen One. *Her* voice comes from nowhere and no time, making me almost ecstatic.

"Where have You been?"

Where you have not.

"Goddess, I have missed Your riddles."

Then I will speak plain English. Find the other Chosen One and have a child.

"Where do I find her?"

Somewhere. Here is nowhere.

"I still await Your orders. I did as You asked. I went to Marie Telles, but nothing happened. What next?"

You are free from the institution, are you not? You are with the Mongol woman, are you not? A cave is being prepared, is it not? Think.

"Am I to live there?"

You are living here.

"Please, for once, just give me a straight answer!"

She will appear, but you must help.

"How?"

Nothing.

I hate *Her* when *She* leaves like this. I hate it! Don't you see it, dear Reader? If your voices depart, so do your memories, your philosophies, your religions, your friends, your families, and, and . . . there is nothing without the voices.

"When will she appear?" I shout in frustration.

"Now! Breakfast is waiting, Michael Powers!" comes a voice from the other side of the bedroom door.

I want to sleep. "Coming!" I shout, admittedly with an edge of ill humor. Still, I must be careful. Buandelgereen might be waiting at the table, and she is not a woman to be trifled with.

As I enter the dining room, I see her sitting at the head of the table, flanked by hungry workers. I put on my most innocent face.

"Good morning, Buandelgereen! Good morning, everybody! I'm starving!"

She gazes at me as might a lion at a sacrificial lamb. Transferring her glare from me to the workers, she barks something in Mongol. Instantly, they wolf down the remnants of breakfast and scurry out. I don't see Batsaikhan, but that is not unusual. Once we are alone, she again looks at me, this time much more sympathetically.

"Are you hungry?" she asks.

"Yes."

"Go put some food on your plate and return."

"Buandelgereen," I say curtly. "I am not a child."

"No, you are a schizophrenic and an American, both conditions like children, and together doubly childish."

"Genghis Khan is dead," I grumble.

She slaps her ample chest. "Not Börte, his wife!"

I return with food and take a few bites, unsure how to respond. She remains silent but continues to stare at me. Unable to bear the scrutiny, I say, "Buandelgereen, you are not Börte."

"No," she replies. "And you are no longer Storyteller."

This really stuns me, so much so that I stammer something incomprehensible.

"Storyteller—yourself—was a young soldier back in Vietnam, where you are convinced he left his bones in a tunnel. At least, this is the story told to me by that Dr. Hess. You are Michael Powers, a mature man, a lawyer, who no longer has a connection to his younger self—this Storyteller. Or, at least according to Dr. Hess, you should no longer have such a strong connection to your younger self. Yet, you remain connected to him like Siamese twins."

"These are things you do not understand," I say weakly.

She sits straight. "Did you enjoy your tour of the cave last night?"

I refuse to appear shocked, and brazenly reply, "Absolutely."

She holds out her hand. "Do you have Batsaikhan's questions?"

This does take me aback, and I shake my head in wonder. "In my room."

"Fetch them."

"Why?"

"Perhaps I can answer them, rather than Goddess. We do not want to bother Her unnecessarily, do we?"

I rise from the table. "You asked."

When I return, I hand her the blank sheet.

My smirk fades quickly as she studies it and says with an enigmatic smile, "I see. I see. These questions are answerable only by Her."

"What questions?" I blurt stupidly. "It's a blank paper."

"Not at all. Every question he has ever wanted to ask is here. Its blankness is like an empty glass held out by a man dying of thirst. Who can fill it and slake his parched soul?"

"*Her*?"

Buandelgereen laughs. "You have learned nothing in all these years. I swear, why does *She* stake so much on so little?"

This is too much. "Perhaps so little is the repository of so much."

Buandelgereen chuckles dryly. "We may only hope."

~ *Return* ~

I am outside the cave, fulfilling my duties as water boy and all-around gopher, fetching and carrying for my Mongol comrades. It is very hot, and the workers come and go less often, as they are deep in the bowels of the earth. That small opening at the end of the cave is preying on my mind. I am certain that is where an iron door will be installed. I must look inside before it is too late—so I am determined to surreptitiously return alone some night and see for myself.

Buandelgereen is very sly, and I must be extremely careful, but I am sure it can be done.

I have not seen Batsaikhan since that night, and nobody seems to know where he has gone. I want to ask Buandelgereen, but that might make her suspicious. So much the better. This must be done alone, with no mistakes to spoil the plan.

~

This morning, I heard good news. Buandelgereen plans to be gone for two days on a trip. Where she is going is apparently a secret, but she will be leaving one of the engineers in charge of construction. Good. I will slip away the first night she is gone. I am very excited.

~

Tonight is the night. Buandelgereen is gone and I have prepared for the journey, including extra flashlights and batteries. I wait until the lights are out, sneak out of the house, and follow the road to the cave. It is a gibbous moon, so there is plenty of light, and the going is easier now that I have become accustomed to the trip. By the time I reach the cave, there are a few clouds passing in front of the moon, and I am careful picking my way through the debris around the site. At this point, I have to use my flashlight. I enter the mouth of the cave.

Very quickly the nocturnal murmurings and distant cries of the desert are snuffed out, and a few dilatory bats fly out the entrance to seek prey. Once the clicking bats have left, total quiet engulfs me, and the blackness draws me deeper. I use my flashlight sparingly and follow the main path without detouring down any side corridors or tempting chambers. The rank smell of the mineral earth is like perfume to me, and I try to carry on a noiseless conversation with the cave, but it looms too high above in all its vaulted magnificence to notice a mere human. Dogs will talk to me. Beds will talk to me. But caves will not. Just as well.

My flashlight now illuminates the bridge, a narrow sliver of rock spanning the deep grotto. Dripping water and faint splashing can be heard far below, and I can only guess what eyeless creatures dwell in the pool. I have never suffered vertigo, but my flashlight is dim in the immensity of surrounding darkness. With only the narrow walkway visible, I must be very careful not to trip or slip. The eyeless ones would surely find my body a feast.

At last I reach the opening at the end of the cave. When I turn off my light, the other side seems even darker than the dark that envelops me on this side. I am surprised to suddenly feel a nameless, formless apprehension. Is it fear?—I think not. More like the nagging thought that I will be disappointed.

I tilt my head to hear better, and I think I can make out the whispered words, "Come in," but I cannot be sure. I want to force myself to step through, but my body will not obey. What waits on the other side? An empty chamber, I tell myself. Just empty. The iron door is not in place. Goddess or *she*—neither will be on the other side. I take a step. I remember Goddess in the tunnel years ago during the war. The brilliant blue light, Her luminous body seared the darkness, *Her* phosphorescent eyes burned. I was a young soldier then. Wracked with malaria, but mentally strong. Now? Is it too late? Storyteller has my bones in the tunnel. I have. . . .

I know I must set aside these thoughts. *Go in! Come what may—turn on the light and step through. Now!*

Chapter Twelve

Detective Work

Meeting with Mark Powers

June escorted Mark Powers and his wife into the office of Dr. Hess, where they found her waiting with a smile. She stood and held out her hand.

"Hello again, Mr. Powers. I wish we were meeting under happier circumstances."

"Hello, Dr. Hess." He gestured toward a slight, very attractive Asian woman. "My wife, My-duyen."

Gail felt a shock of recognition. She remembered reading about My-duyen in Michael Powers's writings. Once again, she experienced a disorienting sense that she herself was merely one of many characters in stories written by a schizophrenic. She caught herself staring at My-duyen, daughter of the legendary (to Gail) Nguyen Tuyet Mai, and raised by two equally legendary fathers, Han Tinh and Vo Thanh Tong. The young Vietnamese woman lowered her eyes under the scrutiny. Gail shook off the urge to barrage her with questions.

"A pleasure to meet you," Gail said, bowing self-consciously.

Mark coughed and said, "Please tell me what is being done about my father."

Gail noticed the rehearsed nature of the demand. He was a good-looking young man with all traces of his grandmother's Asian features gone. My-duyen sat quietly with darting, intelligent eyes.

"We're looking for him. So far, no luck. I thought we had a lead, but it did not pan out."

"What lead, if I might ask?"

"Marie Telles. I believe I mentioned her in an earlier conversation?"

Mark frowned in concentration. "Yes, my father told me about her. Lives here in San Francisco, correct?"

"That is correct."

"And you thought he might be with her?"

"We explored the possibility, but it turned out he wasn't, and she does not know where he is."

"Oh," replied Mark in a disappointed voice.

"We are still searching, of course."

"Yes, of that I have no doubt, but my question is, will Dad's schizophrenia worsen without medication . . . on top of his being homeless?" His voice cracked at these last words.

Gail looked at the two with open curiosity. In all of Mr. Powers's writings Gail had read, there was no mention of their marriage. Furthermore, if his manuscripts were accurate (which she very much doubted), both had experience in Vietnam with the mysterious, mystical *Her*, and the Precious Object. Gail burned to ask them questions unrelated to the business at hand, but she knew better.

"Your father's schizophrenia will undoubtedly worsen, but we are hopeful of finding him soon. As you know, the police are also alerted, and we can only hope for the best."

Mark's face darkened. "Yes, I've spoken with the police, even to the point of being a pest, but damn it, they're not doing enough!"

"You and your wife are still staying in your father's house while in California?"

"Yes, but we can't stay much longer, and the agent already has a number of inquiries."

"I see."

"My-duyen and I have commitments in New York, so you understand my sense of urgency?"

"Yes, I do understand. We will continue to look for him. Perhaps he will return voluntarily." Gail decided to take the plunge. "His Goddess delusion is quite powerful, and I am afraid he has transferred that obsession onto me. It is quite a complicated delusion, including God, and a statue he calls the Precious Object."

Mark blanched and My-duyen shifted in her chair.

"Is there any information you can help me with in that regard?" Gail pressed.

"We have discussed this delusion before, Dr. Hess, and I have no additional information."

Gail noticed My-duyen glance at Mark, her face unreadable, but something of significance was present in her expression. *They believe!* she thought. *They believe!*

"Dad seemed to be getting worse before he left your institute. As I have told you, he even thinks I am possessed by one of his enemies in Vietnam!"

Yes, Sergeant Dam, thought Gail. *These possessions are not limited to Adam and me.*

"I'm worried about him, Dr. Hess, out there. . . . " continued Mark.

"Yes, we all are."

"Please call if something turns up." He took out a card and handed it to her. "Here is my New York address. You already have my number. We will only be here another ten days at the most."

"Yes, thank you."

Gail did not want them to go. She had a host of questions, and the figure of Tuyet Mai's daughter in the flesh brought forth a storm of curiosity. This was the remarkable interpreter whose beautiful mother lost her legs in the war, and whose co-fathers had actually seen Goddess. But Mark and My-duyen were gone before she could bring herself to intrude into their past histories. "God, what an opportunity I just threw away!" she said in disgust to the door that had just closed behind them.

The more she thought, the more she wanted to contact them and pursue the subject that dwelled so close to her heart . . . and her mind. *Do it!* a voice kept insisting. *Do it! Do it!*

"Do what?" June's familiar voice broke her spell.

"Nothing. Just drifting. What's up?"

"Patients are waiting."

Gail sat up straight and smoothed her blouse. "Send in the first."

~ *Mark and My-duyen Powers* ~

When Mark and My-duyen returned to his father's house, they threw together some food and sat on the porch. My-duyen, as usual, waited for Mark to instigate the conversation.

"Well," he sighed. "We did not learn anything new."

"No," she agreed.

My-duyen was still in the process of trying to understand Americans. Like the innumerable Asian immigrants who preceded her, everything in America seemed big, out-of-proportion, and intimidating. Naturally, she had taken refuge in her familiar husband, but eventually met other Southeast Asian immigrants, and had found a job waitressing in a Vietnamese restaurant. The income helped support her husband, who struggled to obtain his degree. Now that he acted as trustee of his father's estate, the financial pressure had lessened.

Often, she thought wistfully of Song Nhan village and her elderly parents. Uncle Tong had died, and she constantly worried about the two "old ones" who remained alone in that haunted, almost abandoned village. Friends from the district capital checked on them when they could, but she knew life for her parents grew harder. Age, not lack of money, was the main issue.

At My-duyen's insistence, Mark erected a little shrine tucked in a small alcove of their New York apartment. Pictures of her mother and two fathers hung above a small table where fruit and joss sticks were displayed. Visiting friends from Columbia were captivated by the luminous beauty of Tuyet Mai when she was younger. Even the pictures of her when she was old were inspiring. Her transcendent face gazed serenely out at the camera. Han Tinh, on the other hand, looked out from his pictures with the same, impish, risqué smile that so tickled and infuriated the women of Song Nhan. And Uncle Tong stared at the camara with a slightly arrogant upturn of the head, certain that the world could never live up to his standards. My-duyen took solace in the pictures, and Mark never begrudged her the shrine.

Now, as she sat next to her American husband, whose father was sick in the head, she longed to call her parents just to hear the soothing familiarity of Han

Tinh's crazy words, or her mother's harsh analysis of all Americans. She felt very proud of Mark who one day would be a scholar people must admire and look up to. Yet, My-duyen was no fool. She understood the ways of the world—the lustful nature of men, the cruelty of society, the fleeting transience of life—and drew from this arsenal of experiences a way to cope in America.

Despite the abundance America offered, like many immigrants of color, she often fell victim to the glances of disapproval, of pity, of dislike, and a host of other emotions she did not have enough experience with Americans to interpret.

"What do you think?" came Mark's voice.

"What?" replied a startled My-duyen, as her vision of the thatch roofs and green rice paddies of Song Nhan village retreated in the shimmer of an American sunset.

He chuckled. "You've been daydreaming again. I asked whether you want to go in or stay out here a while longer?"

"Oh, it is up to you."

Mark rose to go, and as My-duyen was about to join him, something odd caught her attention. She peered more closely at an old car that Mark's father had been refurbishing. It sat forlornly off the driveway in an overgrown field of weeds. What she saw looked like a face in the front seat, or two faces, she could not be sure. She peered more closely, and now felt sure there were two of them. They seemed to float bodiless, and stared at the house, periodically rotating their heads as if talking to each other. The faces were ghostly masks, and their eyes burned through the filthy windshield. My-duyen knew instantly they were ghosts, but held her tongue, knowing Mark disapproved of belief in such supernatural beings. He had once come to believe such spirits existed when they were at Song Nhan village together, but his return to the States and the rigor of studies at Columbia had erased such taboo notions. Now he would not let her mention the spirit world.

At first, as she squinted through the darkening afternoon mist, she thought the two faces were those of Tuyet Mai and Han Tinh. Momentarily excited, she looked closer and realized they were spirits of a different type. My-duyen, no stranger to ghosts, took the sight of the apparitions in stride, and assumed they were somehow connected to her American father-in-law. After all, she grew up in a haunted village near a haunted old fortress, and such sights gave her no cause for concern.

As she joined Mark in the living room, she said, "Do not worry, dear husband, your father will return to this house."

Mark said in surprise, "How do you know?"

"He has connections here."

Mark scoffed. "You don't know Americans, especially Californians. We are all drifters, without roots. Nothing ties us down."

My-duyen smiled in response. "And you do not know spirits."

"My-duyen, none of that nonsense! People will think you're crazy, or just an ignorant Vietnamese peasant girl, who got her ticket out of a poor country through me."

The words hurt, but My-duyen had no desire to be like some of her girlfriends married to Americans—sharp tongued and cynical—so she made no reply.

"Besides," said Mark in a bid to apologize for his harsh words. "If you're right, and he does return, it had better be soon."

~

Later that night, Mark saw My-duyen to bed, but decided to stay up and read. He went to the living room and settled into his father's easy chair. It felt good to put up the footrest and lean back. Rest did not come easily, for he thought of all his father's possessions still in the house, and how expensive they would be to store after it was sold. In fact, as conservator of his father's estate, he knew the mortgage and other monthly bills had already strained the accounts, and he felt almost glad that his father's absence gave a break from payments to the institute. Once the house was sold, the accounts should be replenished, and he would not have to touch the investments. Such thoughts continued to occupy his mind when he got up and poured a glass of wine.

Thinking about such unpleasant problems caused him to turn his reflections to the completion of his degree and his future with My-duyen. He knew he loved her, but also understood she was out of her element in America. Regretfully, he thought the only times she seemed truly natural and spontaneous were with her fellow Vietnamese at the restaurant. Her learning curve had been steep enough, but now the poor girl had been tossed into this miasma of mental illness. With America's legal, health care, and financial complexities, she could only do her best to try and understand Mark's position. He often became oppressed by the need to explain things to her that he himself did not really understand. Nevertheless, she looked up to him, and he instinctively did all he could to encourage her unquestioning confidence. Unfortunately, he had little faith in his own ability to assume his father's position.

He poured another glass and ruminated on the history of schizophrenia in his family, passed down from grandfather John to father Michael to—who? He always looked for signs in himself, and worried that even if he showed no symptoms, the fickle, hidden genes responsible for such misery might reappear in his own children. Fortunately, My-duyen was unversed in genetics, yet he sensed she also shared similar concerns.

"A curse," he muttered, taking another sip of wine.

An owl hooted appropriately in the night, and Mark shook his head in dismay at all the issues clogging his brain. *Why is life so complicated?* he wondered. *Why can't I just be allowed to concentrate on getting my degree?*

Like most young people, Mark felt sure his life consisted of more complications than others', and that once he obtained his degree all would be well and his stresses magically reduced. He felt it unfair to be saddled so young with his father's illness and could not help feeling sorry for himself. My-duyen, as always, tolerated his moods, and ascribed them to American infantilism. Mark understood this, and though he suffered periodic attacks of guilt, he allowed himself the luxury of accepting her sympathy and patient understanding.

My-duyen came out of the bedroom wrapped in a blanket, still not used to the cold, damp California nights.

"Are you okay?" she asked. Like her recently immigrant friends, the word *okay* acted as a life saver.

"Yeah, just thinking."

She wanted to sit in his lap, but the huge American chair seemed too formidable. "Would you like tea?" she asked instead.

"Nah, I'm having wine. Go ahead." In fact, Mark preferred to be alone with his thoughts. Maintaining the façade of being a man firmly in control had long taxed him.

My-duyen went to the kitchen and made tea. When she returned with her cup, he had not moved, nor did his pensive figure acknowledge her presence, so she sat quietly and waited.

Mark was certainly aware she had returned to the room, and he assumed the grave face of a man burdened with troubles, wanting her to appreciate the weight of his responsibilities. Marrying a young immigrant had given him a sense of power and gravitas that no worldly-wise American girl could provide. He would play the role as long as possible, reaping the benefits of her gratitude and overestimation of his abilities. In moments of clarity he recognized these motives in himself and would often think of his grandfather, John, and grandmother, Meiying. Both had faced a similar situation when first coming to America. They must have had their problems, especially considering his grandmother was a lesbian. Yet, never could he picture the great pianist Bai Meiying as a naïve, innocent immigrant girl. She was forever strong and brave, a great pianist, a genius, and his own inadequacies would return.

Looking at My-duyen for the first time since she had entered the room, he glanced at the clock and said, "It's late, you should get some sleep."

"I am not tired."

He took a sip of wine. "Poor My-duyen," he mused paternalistically. "You now live in such a strange country under such strange circumstances." Mark did not know why he said these words, they just seemed something supportive to say.

My-duyen simply smiled, not really hearing what her husband said. She was too busy looking at the spirit faces that stared in through the living room window. *They're looking for Father Powers*, she thought. After pondering the faces for a while, she added a postscript. *Or waiting.*

~ *Gail Hess Has A Radical Idea* ~

One afternoon at the institute, Adam Camara sat in Gail Hess's office looking very tired and haggard. His "demon" was gaining in strength, he explained, and soon he would be leaving for Rhode Island.

"To confront this demon?" asked Gail.

"No, to meet Nature," replied Adam calmly. "I used the word *demon* for convenience, but I have learned that Nature was a kind, gentle kid from Providence who died unnecessarily in an unnecessary war. It is time we met and had an exchange of views."

"And all your scientific training?" asked Gail. "Are you throwing all that overboard for this quixotic pursuit of a ghost?"

Adam considered for a moment, then said, "Here is how I'm looking at it: somehow a powerful suggestion has been planted in my brain. The perpetrator of that suggestion is missing, so I will confront the suggestion itself, on its own turf."

"And if it doesn't show?"

"I will take that as a sign."

"Of what?"

"Of its weakness and my strength."

"We haven't been with each other in a long time, Adam."

"I know, Gail. Believe me, I know. But first we must disentangle from these terrible suggestions!"

"Speaking of which," said Gail, straightening in her chair. "I propose an idea that might involve more, rather than less, entanglement."

"What?"

"Hiring a private detective to find Mr. Powers."

"What? You're kidding!"

"No. Mr. Powers is a very low priority to the police and they have had no luck. Perhaps a private detective might do better."

"Perhaps. Do you have someone in mind?"

"Yes, I've been doing some research. His name is Fred Miller, whose specialty is finding missing persons."

"Is he expensive?"

"Of course. He has a very successful record."

"Who pays?"

"Good question."

Adam shook his head. "The institute certainly won't pay. The trustees will believe that is a job for Michael Powers's family."

"True. Should we raise the subject with Mark Powers?"

Adam shrugged. "You know him better than I do."

"Do you agree we should try?"

"What's to lose?"

"Only money."

"Hopefully, not ours."

~

A week later, Mark Powers hired Fred Miller to locate his missing father. The detective was a rotund man, whose spherical shape belied a muscular core of toughness and tightly coiled street smarts. Once he received the retainer, Miller scheduled a meeting with Gail Hess, Adam Camara, and Mark Powers. His questions came fast and furious, and his pen moved efficiently across the pages of a pocket-size notebook. Of all the names thrown at him, he seemed most interested in Buandelgereen (after hearing that Marie Telles had disavowed any knowledge of the whereabouts of Michael Powers).

"From what you have told me," he said quite firmly. "I will concentrate on the Mongol woman. Of course I will not rule anyone out, including Marie Telles, but my instinct tells me this Mongol woman is a key. Naturally, should you receive any additional or new information, let me know immediately." He flipped shut his notebook, stuffed it in his pocket, and continued. "I skimmed these manuscripts of his, but they are voluminous, and I assume you have already picked out any pertinent information that might be useful. I am not as interested in his past as in his present."

"Of course," said Gail. "I think Buandelgereen holds the key, if you can find her."

"I'll find her all right," he said. "Foreigners on visas are not that difficult to track down. Is there anything else?" he asked.

Everyone shook their heads.

"Then I am off to the Mongolian Consulate. Whom should I contact with any news?"

Mark Powers spoke up. "Contact Dr. Hess at the institute, as my wife and I will be heading back to New York soon."

"Okay."

Mark turned to Gail. "Dr. Hess will immediately inform me of any developments?"

"Of course," replied Gail.

"Even minor ones?"

"Yes."

Mark's face showed concern. "Okay, but I hope and pray everything goes smoothly."

"In that case, to the hunt!" exclaimed Fred Miller.

"Best of luck," said Adam quietly.

~

Miller initially viewed this case as a routine missing person case, like finding a lost spouse suffering from dementia, or a runaway father trying to avoid support payments. However, tracking down an escaped inmate from a psychiatric institute was a new twist, and this particular schizophrenic certainly elicited strong emotions from his caretakers as well as his son. At first, Miller assumed an escaped schizophrenic could be found roaming the streets and mumbling to himself, just another homeless man. But after talking with the institute doctors, he knew that assumption had been a gross miscalculation. This guy wrote books, had been a successful lawyer, and apparently drew interest from foreign nationals. No, not typical. Further, the idea of a Mongol woman appearing from nowhere to make inquiries intrigued him. *Drugs?* Miller speculated. *International drug cartel? Bet it'll turn out to be drugs.* But after further consideration, he felt that scenario wasn't quite right. When he got to the bottom of this case, he figured he would uncover some underlying crime, but again, it didn't seem right, especially after interviewing the doctors. The more he pondered the possibilities, the more interesting the problem became. *Very interesting*, he thought. *Let's hear what the Mongol consulate has to say about this woman Buandelgereen.*

~ *Mongolian Consulate* ~

When he entered the rather drab Mongolian consulate on California Street, he was ushered into a wood-paneled room and was introduced to an assistant clerk. The man took the name of Buandelgereen, indicating he would be right back. However, the clerk took an inordinate amount of time, and when he returned, his puzzled look told Miller volumes before a word was spoken.

"We have records of two Buandelgereens with the same family name Zara. One died years ago in a boating accident off San Diego, body never found, and the other is a nine-year-old girl currently visiting the United States with her mother."

Miller whistled softly. "When did the young one arrive?"

The assistant looked at his notes. "A few months ago. Her mother may have some visa trouble with the American government. Be that as it may, we have no record of her whereabouts."

After asking a host of questions about the boating accident, most of which the assistant could not answer, Miller considered his next move as he returned to his car.

Obviously, this older Buandelgereen did not die in a so-called boating accident. Probably didn't want to be found. Started a new life in the States. But that makes no sense. Why keep her real name, especially if she is involved in drugs? International slave trade? Same problem. Christ! And why this interest in a schizophrenic Vietnam veteran? Christ!

He turned over in his mind the future expenses that would be involved in unraveling this complicated mess. At first, Miller basked in contemplating the amount of anticipated fees, but he realized Mark Powers would probably not be able to pay so much. Often, he had only charged for a small percent of his real time, as the out-of-pocket expenses had accumulated faster than the client expected. He felt sure this case would be similar. Mark Powers, a college kid, would not want to deplete whatever amount remained in his father's estate, especially since the old man was still alive and would need expensive hospitalization once found. On the other hand, if there really was some sort of international conspiracy, the publicity would be invaluable for Miller's business. He decided to check with federal authorities for any criminal charges against the Mongol woman, then travel to San Diego and see about this "boating accident."

~ *Adam Departs* ~

As the weeks passed, Adam Camara read Mr. Miller's updates (usually reporting dead ends) with indifference. He had postponed his trip to Rhode Island twice due to crises with patients. He and Gail often slept together, and in the security of each other's arms, they confided their latest battles with the "sugges-tions." At last, the time had come for him to leave. Gail wanted to accompany him to the airport, but Adam hated last-minute farewells, and saw her off to work before rushing to catch his flight.

He found an aisle seat and let his mind dwell on what lay ahead. Issues he had rarely thought much about in all the years of his life came to him in a dizzying rush of dialectical conundrums. Divinity and the natural world, war and peace, sanity and madness, mind and brain, determinism and free will, the plasticity of time, and the nature of reality, if indeed, there is such a thing. Did he truly expect to talk to a ghost in a Providence cemetery? Perhaps—but he really expected the unexpected, or so he told himself.

"Howdy, neighbor," said the passenger on his left.

"Hello."

"Where you going?"

"Providence."

"Not me. Get off in Chicago."

"Ah."

"Got business in Providence?"

"I am going to talk to a ghost in a cemetery."

"Oh."

To Adam's great satisfaction, the man asked no further questions.

Chapter Thirteen

Iron Doors

Stepping Through

I have finally found the courage to step through the opening. All it takes is a couple of steps. I turn off my flashlight and take them. Okay, I'm in. Total darkness persists because I have decided not to turn on my flashlight for a while. Darkness is not scary, it only makes scary things invisible. Ignorance is the same as darkness, and makes scary things invisible, including knowledge. Thus, in darkness and ignorance, we make up things—make them visible—even if they aren't really there. Religion and superstition are false flashlights, illuminating only darkness, not the things made invisible by it. Is my flashlight true or false? Will it illuminate only more darkness, or will it make the invisible visible? One way to find out: I switch it on.

No more than a foot in front of me, Buandelgereen's face comes ablaze in the beam of my light. I start to bellow in shock, but only a low croak escapes my mouth. Her white hair radiates a blinding halo that flames outward from her head, making her visage even more terrible.

"Hello, Michael. Don't you Americans have a saying about curiosity killing the cat?" She speaks as though the surroundings were no more exotic than her own kitchen.

I stammer, but still nothing articulate comes out.

"Since you are here," she continues in that eerily calm voice. "Let us satisfy your curiosity."

She takes a few paces toward the opening and flips a switch. The hum of a distant generator momentarily precedes a burst of intense brightness from overhead floodlights. She sweeps her arm around the illuminated space, inviting me to look. At first glance, the huge chamber resembles an unfinished cathedral, as if a giant Michelangelo had carved it from the inside out. Instead of stained-glass windows, massive rock walls of mica schist glitter down from the dizzying heights.

Buandelgereen observes my reaction for a few moments and says, "Well? Is it what you expected, Michael Powers?"

"It surpasses my expectations."

She points to the opposite wall, where yet another opening has been blasted out. "There is more beyond. Much more. Someday, you will be allowed to go farther. Now, we must leave."

I can only nod, awestruck and dumbfounded, and follow her obediently out. When we exit the cave, I breathe in the fresh night air, and turn to say something, but she's gone.

"Buandelgereen!" I shout, but there is no response, and I know better than to continue trying, so I trudge back to the house, with the gibbous moon now low in the sky. My thoughts are a jumble, and remain so all the way home, where I lie on my bed and marvel at the strangeness of the universe. I have no doubt that tomorrow when I see Buandelgereen, the events of this night will not be mentioned. But, oh, how that stony cathedral occupies my mind! Damn me, I must admit I am now driven to go deeper into the cave, past that second small opening! There may not be iron doors yet, but there is the first inkling of magic in that cave. As always, I ask myself who is this Buandelgereen? She is not of me—she is of my mother and father long ago, in Mongolia.

This makes me wonder. Marie Telles is of my mother. Buandelgereen is of my mother. *She* may be the mother of us all. Each of these women is endowed with courage and kindness. So were Madame Dau and Lihua. Why this human mania for a male God? I love my father, but he was not . . . is not Mother. To males, God must be the equivalent of a stag's antlers or the testicles of a bull—tacked like another trophy on their walls. I can even hear the dead stag and dried testicles and wooden cross commanding with their distinctive male rutting calls. "Look at Me and beware! Look at Me and I will bequeath my fertile seed! Look at Me and I will protect you from other stags and bulls and false gods!" Dear Reader, is there another way?

Tuyet Mai went the way of men and lost her legs. Han Tinh lost his legs and went the way of women. So it goes. I am willing to help *You*, Goddess, but *You* must show me the way. No more riddles. No more surrogates.

"What do *You* say?" I whisper, for emphasis.

I wait for a reply.

~

Of course, *She* remains silent.

"What about *You*, God?" I say louder. "Nothing from *You* either?"

I do have something to say. My Beloved Goddess pinned Her hopes on you, but I can see now that you are no threat to Me. The so-called Reunion came and went. You turned your M-16 on Her, not Me. Thus, it will always be.

"I would do differently today!" I exclaim for all to hear.

Too late. Would you turn your gun on the Universe? Natural selection? Evolution? Nature red in tooth and claw? Much as you profess to admire these realities, they are the very ribs and sinews of My Body—my factions' belief in First Principles—one of them being nonintervention. They are the very reason why people believe and worship the Metaphorical Me, and why they reject and deny the real Me.

"Go to hell."

Nice place to visit, but I really wouldn't want to live there.

Absurd. Absurd! I really must sleep, dear Reader. You have suffered enough tonight.

~ *Workers Come and Workers Go* ~

Weeks pass and the monotony of my water-boy job is broken only by new faces that come to replace those who have gone. Different skills are needed now—electricians, plumbers, carpenters, and the rest. If this cave is to be a habitation for the divine, they'll certainly be surrounded by pleasures of the flesh. Perhaps Batsaikhan was right, this will be a tourist destination. The laugh is on me. Buandelgereen, as I had correctly guessed, has never mentioned that night, but a few days ago she did drop a statement that jarred me. She said, "The deeper we go into the earth, the connection is almost complete."

"Connection?" I asked.

Naturally, she fell instantly mute, and I did not pursue the point, knowing it would be futile. But my mind filled with new interpretations and speculations.

~

This morning, I saw the iron doors! A few hours ago, they were unloaded. Although they were packed in wooden crates, the sizes were perfect, and I am certain they're the doors. I counted two, but there may be more. I am very excited, but my excitement must be tempered by the fact that once the doors are installed, my access to the inner sanctum will be limited by the whims of *Her* or Buandelgereen. All the same, if the doors are here, the "connection" must be complete. I have been having dreams of Nature and the tunnel. Maybe I will go at last? If *She* has no further need for me, of course, then I am free. I know Nature is still working his way to me through Dr. Camara. He can take me back. Perhaps. Will it be through this "connection" that lies at the end of the cave?

I see Buandelgereen overseeing the crates being loaded onto a wagon to be transported into the cave, and I approach boldly.

"I would like to see the iron doors installed."

She laughs. "What makes you think these crates contain iron doors?"

I am ready for this evasion. "It's obvious."

"Is it?"

"Yes."

"Guess again, Michal Powers."

"Then what are they?"

Her face turns deadly serious. "Windshield wipers for submarines."

Dear Reader, I must tell you I join in her laughter. Fool that I am, I understand fools. Self-knowledge. As you can probably guess, all the levity in the world is nothing to an atom of iron in that damn door. We can laugh in the face of death except for the minor fact that death has no face to laugh at. Just a monstrous yaw, sweeping all the krill in its path, giggle as they may before being swallowed.

Should I venture another midnight trip? No. Buandelgereen would just be waiting again. Batsaikhan is gone. Is there another potential confederate among this group? I must seek out a welder. I have noticed my ability to understand and converse with the objects around me has diminished somewhat, but still remains, though at a more serene level. It is an ability, until now, I have not used to its full potential. But how?

While I think about this idea, Buandelgereen stares at me oddly, in a way that makes me uncomfortable, as if she were looking down at me in an open coffin.

"Michael," she says sympathetically, "you need not make such elaborate plans to conspire with welders and speak to iron doors. Be still. You will pass through those doors soon enough."

The words are chilling, but also thrilling. After all, stillness is a siren call to me.

~ *Thinking of Storyteller* ~

It is close to midnight, and I am back in my bed, ruminating on a host of topics. Since my resurrection, Storyteller has been exiled to the background hum of my mind. I think he is getting restless. He wants me back, but that is nothing new. What is new is that he is stirring, emerging from the background. How do I know? It is the dream. Always the dream.

Happened last night:

Sunlight stabs through narrow openings in the jungle canopy, piercing the early morning mist that squirms and twists under the flashing blades of another murderous day. Predators, prey, and witnesses all rehearse their testimony. Birds sing and gibbons chatter. A tiger growls, insects hiss and plants breathe steam in humid clouds that cling like mucous to the soaked air. Ants wage savage wars deep beneath the detritus while above them, two human soldiers stagger through the foliage, one pursuing the other. The pursued, a young soldier exhausted and choking from the downpour of pollen and seeds, half-stumbles, half-slides down the bank of a stream. Tumbling out of the underbrush, his back to the water, he jerks his rifle free of the clinging vines and branches. In the background, the slashing of the relentless machete draws nearer.

He's close! Very close! Got to get across this stream! Help me, mother! Help me!

Whirling around to make a mad dash, the young soldier freezes. In front of him the entwined corpses of his two friends bob in the stream, half submerged, snagged by the outspreading branches of a fallen tree. One's head is underwater, but the other looks directly at him. Its eyes are open wide, flat and unresponsive to the flies crawling across their corneas. Those eyes stare accusingly, as if blaming the young soldier for his comrades' deaths, for running from the enemy. For betraying them all.

"So be it," the young soldier whispers. He spins around to face the crazed pursuer. No more images of his mother's burned face. Now it's only the predator and the prey. Life or death. So simple.

With shocking speed, the American bursts from the undergrowth, rifle in one hand, machete brandished in the other. The young soldier raises his AK-47 and squeezes off a few rounds before the American leaps on top of him. The young soldier tries to brace himself, but the falcon slams into the quail. He falls on his back, arms splayed as though nailed to the earth. The American savagely brings down his machete in a flash of glimmering steel, severing the young soldier's hand at the wrist. Searing pain shoots up his arm, his detached hand still clutching the pistol grip of his rifle, fingers twitching uselessly—

"Michael. Michael. Wake up. You're dreaming. Come on, sweetheart. It's okay. Wake up!"

~

Ah, Diane! What would I do without Diane? Faithful all these years from beyond the grave. My beloved deceased wife always wakes me in time. But she is no longer fighting for a young lawyer's sanity. The lawyer is now old, and the sanity is now gone. Even her words are tired and unconvincing. Diane is no match for the combined pull of Storyteller and Nature—nor am I, not anymore. Only my mission for Goddess remains; a tenuous thread connecting me to the world of the living. Perhaps, finally, my tab is coming into focus as it never did in Vietnam. Dear Reader, if you don't know what a tab is, let me explain how it came about.

~

We were surrounded by North Vietnamese troops in an exposed firebase. Cut off from reinforcements and certain to be overrun. Finally, ordered to burn the firebase, we waited for evacuation outside the perimeter. Well, as usual with the Army, it didn't happen, and we had to return to that damn burning firebase and try to survive another day. Then came that terrible evening. Everyone burrowed inside the bunkers while above, the firebase burned. Flames tore through the ebony sky, turning and twisting obscenely, licking the deep crevasse of night, and making livid the fluorescent clitoris of the moon. Tracers from M-16 and AK-47 rifles repeatedly slashed the wounded atmosphere. Deep throbbing explosions and crackling shock waves groaned and moaned, hissed, and whined, an orgasm of sound and fury.

Ka-boom! Ka-boom! Ka-boom! Incoming NVA rockets and mortars tossed great chunks of dirt and debris into the air. Tattered sandbags and bits of clothing drifted down as ash.

Our platoon had been assigned to wait in a dusty, stifling bunker as a flex response team, to be called when and where most needed. I smile at the memory of what we did that terrible night.

We laughed.

Our eyes shone white against the layers of grime cracking our wizened faces. Lips glistened with the cleansing lubrication of nervous spit; faces twitched in the reflection of flames dancing through the bunker opening.

And we laughed.

At that moment Nature had his world-changing idea: the tabs.

"Hey! Hey! Pipe down! Quiet! I've been thinking—"

"Uh-oh. Take two aspirin and see me in the morning," said Stretch.

"No. No. I'm serious. You know, I've been thinking about this for a long time. So, listen up you guys! Listen! Might as well tell you my idea now cause. . . . " He looked away and shrugged.

His somber expression and the gravity of his words quieted everyone. All our eyes locked on Nature, inviting him to continue.

"We're all scared shitless. Right?"

Nods of agreement. Mumbling.

"We all know this could be our last night alive. Right?"

"Hey, coach! If this is your best pep talk, we ain't gonna win a game all year," chided Raresteak.

"Yeah, yeah. Smart ass. Give me a chance here. Okay? Give me a break. Now, here's the deal. In times like this, waiting to be attacked, or, you know, maybe waiting to die or waiting to be evacuated after you've been wounded . . . you know . . . waiting. Like if you're lying in the mud wounded by a booby trap or getting shot or banged around inside a Dust Off, then you start thinking about your family, your home, your girlfriend, you know, The World. So, I figured, think about one image that connects you to The World. Like a photo.

"But the strict rule is that it must be one image. It can't be a story. Can't move or change because then you can bend it. If you're lonely or depressed or scared or hurt bad and feel sorry for yourself, it can get all screwed up. One image. See? One image. Permanent.

"You burn it into your brain so it becomes automatic. Burn it deep and permanent like a tattoo so you can't remove it. It'll become like the numbers burned on the arm of my Aunt Ethel by the Nazis at Treblinka. So, when you need that image you won't have to think about it. When you need that connection, it's there. Automatically. 'Cause you may not have the strength to dream up anything more complex. See? It's there automatically. Know what I mean?" and Nature snapped his fingers. "Remember. It can't move or I'm telling you . . . well, it just can't move."

"Yeah, yeah, yeah, Nature. We know what you mean. It just can't move. So now what? We give you permission to move, so move on, boy."

"Okay, okay. Once you've got this one image in your mind, you carry it with you until DEROS or death. Either leave here with it or die in here with it."

Silence.

"Okay," said Mountain Man, bored with the discussion. "So, what's this image of yours, Nature? What did you come up with for yourself?"

"Yeah. How 'bout it, Nature? Come clean," said Idaho.

Someone rolled their eyes at the long-suffering Idaho. "Christ! What a dick—"

"Well, if you guys shut up and listen, I'll tell you," Nature interrupted before the damage became worse.

The bunker fell silent. Muffled sounds of harassing fire filtered in through the opening. Inexplicably, the NVA had not yet attacked. We had more time. So, Nature took a deep breath.

"Okay. Well, it's nighttime in Providence, see? Real dark but clear as a bell. Beautiful stars. I'm a boy again. I'm down by the ocean, playing in the sand dunes. Wind from the ocean blowing through my hair. It's getting cold. My wool scarf keeps flying off so I'm holding it in one hand. My mom made me that scarf. Red. Kinda. With a pattern. Real neat scarf. I can hear the waves from the ocean crashing behind me. I'm looking up at my house. New England Victorian style. Two stories. See?

"Anyway, the house is up a hill, and the sand dunes block my view of the first floor. But the second floor is all lit up. I'm cold and damp, see, and getting colder and damper. I look up at my house, my home, and I see this warm light glowing through the tall window on the second floor. And on the windowsill sits my black cat. A silhouette. It's my cat, see. His name was—is—Bobby Burns. Bobby for short.

"Bobby's looking out the window from inside the warm house, looking down at me where I'm standing and stamping my feet in the sand dunes, by the ocean. And it's like Bobby is inviting me home. Inviting me inside the house where it's warm and there's hot chocolate and my family is waiting—mom, and dad and my sister and my two brothers. I know that everyone's downstairs, in the living room, sitting around the fireplace, waiting for me. But, of course, I can't see them. Just Bobby in that window. So, Bobby sits there. Unmoving. Real graceful. Curved like cats are, you know, like a hand waving me home."

Silence in the bunker.

"That's it. That's my image. Now you all have to think of your own image and share it with the rest of us. And all newbies that come into the platoon must do the same thing."

"How can you be stamping your feet in the sand dunes if the image isn't supposed to move?" asked Superman.

Nature laughed. "Okay, Superman. One foot is raised up just a little, ready to stamp down. How's that?"

"Better," said Superman.

"Never liked cats," grumbled Raresteak.

But everyone else remained quiet, thinking. Finally, Storyteller spoke in a quiet voice. "Tableau a la grunt."

"What's a tabloo?" asked Idaho.

"Tableau," said Storyteller.

"Tab what?" asked Stretch.

"That's it!" exclaimed Storyteller. "We can call Nature's idea a 'tab.'"

Storyteller gave a long-winded explanation of the meaning of the word tableau. His explanations were always long. Even Nature's eyes started to glaze over. Fortunately, the sounds of explosions outside kept enough adrenaline in everyone's system to prevent them from nodding off.

But Storyteller stopped talking in the middle of a sentence. This unexpected silence revived the flagging attention of the platoon.

"Wait! Wait! Something's missing," said Storyteller. After looking each grunt in the eye, he hesitated briefly, then spoke in a rush. "I know what's missing! Musical accompaniment. That's it. We need background music to accompany the tab. Something special to each of us. If I'm wounded and concentrating on the tab, I want special music in the background, like a movie or something. Not a movie, of course, 'cause the tab doesn't move. But, well, you know what I mean. The music has got to be special, from your past, something that reminds you of, well, your tab, or something else, something special. You know what I mean?"

"You mean, like something special?" quipped Stretch.

Storyteller groaned, "Yeah. I mean, like something special. Like for you, Stretch, it would be the theme song from *Mr. Ed*. Musical accompaniment for a horse's ass."

After a short discussion, everyone agreed with Storyteller's idea. They all started joking and singing various songs, many of them with ad-libbed lyrics. Some sweet. Some lewd. Some inspired. Chaos in the bunker—a cacophony of songs.

T and Pappy, in the corner of the bunker leaning against a wall, looked at each other and laughed. T shrugged, "Hey. Keeps their mind off what might happen tonight."

"Yup," agreed Pappy.

"Quiet!" barked Mountain Man. We froze.

"Seeing as how we're all brothers—and seeing as how our brotherhood is a democracy—and seeing as how I like the idea—I say we vote unanimously to approve Nature's tab idea and Storyteller's suggestion about the music. And even though ol' Mountain Man's vote is all that matters, let's make it official. All in favor raise your hand."

Just as Mountain Man dictated, the vote was unanimous. Now music would accompany each grunt's tab. And it was further agreed that each of us would tell the entire platoon what his tab and musical accompaniment were. Best to think them up that night, while we crouched in a burning firebase about to be overrun by NVA. After all, there probably wouldn't be a tomorrow, and even if there were, too much thinking would ruin the tab. When this reality sank in, the bunker fell silent, everyone conjuring up their tabs. The mood slowly changed from frivolity to gloomy silence.

Pappy laughed. "You guys. I swear. You're all like a bunch of nine-year-old boys in a treehouse club making some kind of secret pact." He snorted, "Why don't you seal your pact with frog piss? It's what we did when I was a kid."

Nature laughed along, "That's right, Pappy. That's what this is. Boys in a secret club. We're up a tree and the ladder's been pulled away. Look at what's outside this bunker. Listen to it! That's the great grown-up world. Yeah. We're in a private club all right. And a pact has been made all right. Only instead of frog piss it'll probably be sealed by our blood."

~

To make a long story short, everyone came up with a tab except Storyteller—me. I couldn't. My image kept moving, and I couldn't get the music right.

So here I am, Storyteller to Michael Powers, and finally I may come up with a tab. After all these years, I'm on the verge of joining Mountain Man, T, Bowls, Nature, and all the others.

Tonight, I plan to return to the fortress and visit my dead comrades. Why? Thinking about the tabs, of course. How? Well, that is more problematic. I figure I can do it if I concentrate hard enough, just before falling asleep. I'll slip in with all those apparitions Storyteller sees when his malaria flares up, and bang! It's done. I'm back in the fortress. Tonight! Wish me luck.

~

It isn't working. I am lying here, concentrating as hard as I can, but I am unable to sleep. No, dear Reader, we cannot control our dreams, at least not indefinitely. Why am I occupying this bed, this space, these rich molecules? To exist? Trees exist, and that is good. Fish exist, and that is good. Rocks and dirt and the sky exist, and they are good. Me? Can one exist in nothingness? No, that is the virtue of nothingness. I will tell you now, dear Reader, I am going to commit suicide tonight if I receive no instructions from Goddess. I want to return to the tunnel, and why not? Do you object? No, of course not. Just another plot twist. Screw you, dear Reader—forgive me, but for many of you entertainment is the pinnacle of your pyramid, the *raison d'etre* of your existence, and grist for your continued puerile satisfaction. Suicide? Another act to break the boredom.

A man stands on a ledge. Some of you shout, "Jump! Jump!" Others cover their eyes. Those of you who cover your eyes may read on. Those of you who shout "Jump!" must drop out. I have no more interest in you as a Reader. Oh, I know, you think you are in control, after all, you bought the book. But you are not in control unless human perversity equals control. Yes, you're right, I guess it does. Well, I've just now decided to disappoint some of you. I will not commit suicide. I know, a certain number of you will say, "That is because you are afraid." Others of you may be particularly cruel and point out the fact that adolescents routinely kill themselves, and therefore must have more guts than me, a decorated Vietnam veteran, and a guy who has seen much violence in his life. True, true—unless one truly appreciates the full impact of suicide, not on family and friends, which is bad enough, but on one's own legacy. Yes, an adolescent has no legacy, but an old man has much to concern himself with. Trees don't commit suicide. Do they have a legacy? Of course! Roots, soil, sun, water, oxygen. The legacy they leave is a healthy planet for the benefit of all. No, I will not commit suicide. Feel better now, Dr. Hess?

~

None of this mental masturbation is helping me sleep. Whenever I crave the feeling that I am fully alive, or fully dead, I always think of Storyteller, for he is both. In the old days, he crashed my dinner parties, always reminding me of my seven strange dreams and disabusing me of the notion that I had a twin who died in Vietnam. At least that is one delusion I have eradicated from my repertoire of delusions. Oh, I still have plenty left, I know that. Perhaps this cave business and Buandelgereen are merely the latest variations on a theme. Perhaps I am still back at the institute, drooling on the tile floor. No, not this time. The cave is real. Buandelgereen is real. Marie Telles is real. If not, then my parents were not real, and that is impossible. As I already mentioned, reality is what scares me the most. When real, things die. When real, things feel pain and hunger and thirst. Reality is the Master Psychopath of the Dungeon.

Which brings me back to Storyteller. I know he is me and not me. I know he is real and not real, alive and not alive, calling me to the stillness that dwells in between.

"I call you forth, Storyteller!" I command in my most stilted, occultic voice. "Your medium calls you forth!"

Naturally, he does not appear, nor would I, given such amateurish theatrics. No doubt, he is busy possessing Dr. Camara. Disappointment is to be expected. I must sleep now. Perhaps Storyteller will come in a dream—if not in a delusion.

~ *Michael Goes to Storyteller in A Dream* ~

Storyteller leans against the stone wall of the fortress, monsoon rain falling at a steady rate. Malaria momentarily loses its grip, and he surveys the courtyard for signs of activity. Pappy is making his usual rounds of the guard positions, and at the far end of the courtyard, Captain Cairns crouches over the two female prisoners. Kim Lan, the younger, sleeps. Not the one Cairns wants. His attention fixes on Nguyen Tuyet Mai.

Storyteller's poncho serves as a makeshift lean-to. As the rain patters on the nylon fabric, he instinctively looks for Nature. Through the mist, he spots Nature's red tam o'shanter, and knows his friend is not on guard duty. When Nature glances his way, Storyteller gestures for him to come. Nature ducks under the poncho, props his M-16 next to Storyteller's against the wall, and sits cross-legged beside his sick comrade.

"How you feeling?"

"Better."

"Good."

"Anything new since my last fever dream?"

Nature smiles, dark, curly hair framing his mischievous Yankee face. "Wrote a poem today. Good one, too. I'm telling you, Storyteller, the cemetery in Providence doesn't come close to the inspiration to be had here. I mean, shit, Vietnam is just one big cemetery."

"Yeah," replies Storyteller weakly. "Just one big inspiration—unless you've got malaria."

They fall silent.

Rain drums on the poncho. Mildew and cordite hang in the air.

"Any news from Mountain Man?" asks Storyteller.

"Haven't heard a peep from that crazy son of a bitch."

"Think he'll ever come back?"

Nature shrugs. "Bowls is wasting away without Mountain Man. By the way, seen any ghosts lately?"

"Only myself."

"Ha! We're all ghosts here—or soon will be."

"Listen Nature, I've been to the future."

"Huh?" asks Nature absently, intent on wringing water from his tam o'shanter.

"The future. I visit myself there. I'm a lawyer, and I throw dinner parties. My wife is dead—and she joins the party. Weird. So, naturally, I also pop in to talk with my future self." Storyteller looks down, and Nature notices tears. "Years from now, I'll be an old man in a mental institution."

Nature averts his eyes and shakes his head. "You're fuckin' nuts."

"That's the point."

"Do you see me in the future?"

Storyteller merely looks down.

"I'm dead, aren't I?"

Storyteller doesn't look up.

The monsoon hammers home the answer.

Chapter Fourteen

Cemeteries, Conversations, and Collapse

Providence

Ⓦhen asked by the inquisitive clerk at the registration desk whether Mr. Camara was visiting Providence for business or pleasure, Adam smiled and said, "I'm here to attend a psychiatry conference."

"Ah," the clerk replied a bit surprised. "I see. Have a pleasant stay." Inwardly, he wondered why the hotel had not registered more attendees, and placed the blame on Mr. Allen, head of marketing.

Once he settled into the room, Adam showered and changed into more comfortable clothes. That evening, he intended to make a dry run to the cemetery, then find a good restaurant and enjoy a meal before retiring for the night. He had brought with him one of the binders containing Mr. Powers's writing and laid it on the nightstand. This binder contained a narrative of the topics that interested him most—Vietnam and Nature.

First things first, he thought. Breezing past the waving clerk, he settled behind the wheel of his rental car and headed to the cemetery where Nature's remains waited. Tonight, he had no intention of visiting the gravesite, as he was saving that for tomorrow. In fact, he had all the details worked out and vowed not to deviate from them. Tonight, he would simply drive by the cemetery to confirm the route, eat dinner, and return to the hotel. Tomorrow, he would arrive in the late afternoon and go straight to the grave, having already located it on the cemetery plot map. Why late afternoon? His sense of propriety regarding ghost etiquette was lacking, but he felt afternoon gloom would provide a more conducive atmosphere (if one believed in the authority of Gothic novels). Once there, he would stand at the foot of the grave, pull on his tam o'shanter, and announce his arrival. Then he would wait for fifteen minutes in silence. If Nature spoke to him, the conversation would proceed. If Nature did not, Adam would begin a monologue, hoping Nature could not resist joining in. If neither of these worked, he felt Nature—or the suggestion of Nature—would be considerably weakened, if not eradicated completely, and Adam could return to a normal life at the institute. He might even be able to use his visit with Michael Powers in treatment—as tantalizing proof of a deep, empathetic understanding. On the other hand, if Nature did make an appearance, the complications would come fast and furious. In that case, which Adam seriously doubted would happen, the conversation itself would have to dictate subsequent actions. If anything, Adam Camara felt ambivalent. In one sense, he was more afraid of contact with Nature than of the silence he fully expected. On the other hand, the thought of being faced with silence left him feeling oddly depressed at such an anticlimax. With these conflicting thoughts occupying his mind, he had a full meal and returned to the hotel to wait and read.

~

The next morning, Adam ate breakfast in the hotel, the binder open next to him on the table for a final perusal. Nature—his real name unmentioned in Mr. Powers's writing but since found in official records—seemed to beckon Adam, but he stuck to his plan and waited until late afternoon. **Nature's** remains were buried at the Little Neck Cemetery in East Providence, which had been established in 1655. The curly-haired lad rested near some souls who came to America on the *Mayflower*, and others who were among the first colonists at Plymouth. Fitting. After breakfast, Adam visited several historic sites in Providence and, when the afternoon sun began casting long shadows, drove to Reading Street and parked. Leaving the binder in the car, he walked to the cemetery and followed the plot map to Nature's grave. It was a clear day, but the wind blew hard and bent the trees that dotted the area. Leaves swirled about his legs, and he felt a burst of satisfaction. Everything was as he pictured it. Amused, a vision of Ichabod Crane popped into his head, and in high spirits, he pulled the collar of his jacket over his neck and donned the trusty tam o'shanter. As he approached the gravesite, his jolly mood disappeared; he grew disconcertingly nervous, despite predicting nothing would come of it.

A few people came and went, but he felt completely alone when he stood before the marker. Nature's parents were dead, but the words carved on the tombstone made him hesitate. "To Stephen—loving son and immortal poet—who died for that which moved him." Now, he felt like an intruder, a clumsy stranger disturbing the quietude of this final resting place. Nonetheless, Adam remembered, Nature was a poet, a man who knew there was no such thing as comfortable assumptions. He checked his watch and said self-consciously, "Nature, I am here to talk with you." With these rehearsed words out of the way, Adam Camara stood waiting. Shadows deepened and he checked his watch again. No time had passed. He shook his wrist and held the watch to his ear—it ticked. Before he had a chance to wonder at this strange discrepancy, he felt a presence approach from behind, and hairs on the back of his neck tingled in fear and anticipation.

Images of a hundred awful ghost films scrolled through his mind, and he hesitated to turn and confront the presence as if he were a child too frightened to look. Whatever it was, it had stopped, and he sensed its breath on his neck, though the wind continued to whip around the cemetery.

"Excuse me, you are in my spot," came a heavily accented New England voice.

Relieved to hear such a mundane remark, Adam turned around to address the speaker, assuming it might be a family member. What he saw made him stagger back a step. A young man with curly hair and wearing a tam o'shanter stared at him. It took Adam a moment to tear his eyes away from the distinctive hat, and only then did he notice the lad wore combat fatigues. Still hoping the figure standing before him was a family member, he stammered, "Oh, sorry, I didn't know."

"Actually, no reason you should," the figure replied. "This is where I write my best poetry."

"Oh," murmured Adam. "Are you related?" He pointed at the grave.

"My DNA and his are a one-hundred-percent match."

"I, uh, that is very close . . . I mean, how is that possible?"

"You know, Dr. Camara. That is why you're here, is it not? To meet the person buried six feet below?"

"Well, yes, I mean, I want to understand Stephen better, and I thought by coming here, I could. . . . " his voice trailed off.

"You thought you could meet his ghost?"

"Not exactly."

Nature's eyes bore into him. "Yes, exactly."

Adam pulled himself together, stood erect, and emitted a string of unrelated sentences. "Look here, are you pulling my leg? . . . Because if so, I don't find it amusing. Furthermore, I don't know how you know my name. Are you a relative?"

Nature laughed. "I repeat, my DNA and his are a one-hundred-percent match. By the way, I like your tam o'shanter."

"Are you suggesting," said Adam, as evenly as he could. "I mean, are you saying you are Nature?"

"In the flesh . . . well, that may not be totally accurate. Perhaps we should say in the spirit."

"But you are real." Adam reached out to touch him, but Nature stepped back and wagged his finger with a smile.

"No, that won't do, Dr. Camara. I don't want to be overly dramatic, but that just won't do."

Adam's scientific training took over. "What would happen if I touched you?"

"Nothing too drastic, as far as I know. You might even find it trippy, doc."

"Then let me."

Nature grinned. "Okay, doc."

Adam gingerly pressed against Nature's chest. He felt resistance and pushed harder, feeling nothing more than a normal human chest. *None of this hand passing through the apparition nonsense*, he thought.

"I know you are real," he said in a matter-of-fact tone, now convinced this person was pulling some trick. "Who are you really?"

"The one you look for."

"No, this is not as it should be," said Adam.

"How should it be, doc?" replied Nature. "Your concrete certainty versus my incorporeal uncertainty?"

"Well, yes, actually. You should be unequivocally one or the other. I came to do some research on the person buried here, Stephen Perrine. Why are you here?"

"I am the person buried here," said Nature with a mischievous smile. "You are in my spot. Or to be more precise, close to it." He pointed to a nearby bench. "I usually sit there when I write."

Adam scoffed openly. "You are not the person buried here, that is obvious. So, why are you here?"

"Well, firstly, I live here, and secondly, to write poetry, and thirdly, you are in my spot."

"Nonsense."

Nature resumed his mischievous smile. "Would you care to touch me again, doc?"

This took Adam aback. "Yes," he said with some hesitation.

"Go ahead."

This time, Adam's hand passed through his body. As it lingered inside Nature's form, his mind exploded with a beehive of images and feelings utterly alien to his own experiences. He jerked it out before he fainted from the assault.

"You see," said Nature. "I warned you it might be trippy."

Adam looked around and saw no other visitors in the cemetery. He checked his watch and to his surprise noticed again that no time had passed, yet it still ticked.

"No, it's not a dead battery, doc."

Adam Camara felt all assumptions of reality cave in; his thoughts gained no traction—only disorienting fragmentation and confusion. Nature waited patiently while Adam pulled himself together.

"Look here," said Adam, speaking slowly as he formed the sentence. "You are the man they called Nature in Vietnam?"

"Of course." He snapped his fingers on his tam o'shanter and looked at the one sitting atop Adam's head. "Looks like you and I share something in common."

"Except, if I am to believe you, I am alive and you are dead. That is one big . . . uncommonality. I exist on the side of the living, here and now, and you?"

"Here and now? Check your watch again. You are not on any side, Dr. Camara, as there are no sides."

Adam looked at Nature's fatigues in a conspicuous manner, and observed, "You don't talk like a soldier."

Nature sighed. "Fuckin' A! I don't talk like a fuckin' soldier because I'm a fuckin' poet not a fuckin' soldier. Is that fuckin' better, doc?"

"Yet, you want to possess me," said Adam in a whisper, feeling utterly foolish for saying such medieval nonsense.

"True, true, but I have learned since being inside you that you lack the spirit of a poet. You're more like a bureaucrat, which makes it a bit cramped in there, for my tastes anyway. Perhaps your mother dropped you on your head when you were a baby?"

Adam Camara found himself laughing. *Utterly absurd!* he thought. *Laughing at a ghost's joke! What next?*

Nature's face suddenly turned serious. "I know you have Storyteller locked up, and we all want him back."

"He has escaped the institute."

"Yes, we know, but you are trying to return him there, isn't that true?"

"Yes, for his own good."

"You have diagnosed schizophrenia, right, doc?"

"Yes."

"And yet you stand here talking to a ghost, right, doc?"

"Yes."

"So, what's your diagnosis of yourself?"

"I'm experiencing some sort of momentary dissociation, a psychotic episode."

"Will you lock yourself up in the institute with Storyteller?"

"No."

"Why not?"

"Because I'm aware this conversation is not real. I'm aware you are not real. That's what makes all the difference. You see, Storyteller—I mean Mr. Powers—can't tell reality from delusion."

A shadow passed over Nature's face. "Soon, doc, you won't be real."

"Is that a threat?" asked Adam.

~

"No, not a threat," came a different voice. "The cemetery will close in fifteen minutes, and all visitors must leave. Sorry."

In front of Adam stood a big man wearing a docent's uniform who appeared to be at least in his sixties or seventies. Dusk had cast a dark pall over the cemetery, and the wind had died down to a steady breeze. Adam looked around to see where Nature went, but, as he expected, saw only the docent and a few late visitors walking briskly toward the exit. Adam instinctively checked his watch and saw that almost an hour had passed. He held it to his ear and heard the ticking.

"I, uh, wonder if you saw me talking with anyone when you walked up?"

"No."

"Yes . . . okay . . . all right, I see."

"You feel all right, friend?" asked the docent sympathetically. When Adam did not reply, he looked at the gravestone. "Relative of yours?"

"No, no."

The docent gave him a quizzical glance.

"Research."

"Ah, well, better move along else you'll be locked inside, and that always gives our tardy visitors the creeps."

Adam perked up and walked beside the docent toward the exit. "Does that happen often?"

"No. Graveyards are not places most people want to stay at night. Sure, there are always the few that either intentionally or unintentionally stay behind after the gates close."

"What happens to them?"

"Oh, the night guard finds 'em and escorts 'em out."

"I imagine, with all the historical graves, you must be concerned about grave robbers?"

Again, the docent eyed him quizzically. "Very," he said emphatically. "Not a single incident as long as I can remember."

They reached the exit. "Well, that is a good thing," remarked Adam absently, still trying to come to grips with his encounter.

"Grave desecration happened once, long before my time, but our guards stopped it before they could do any damage."

"Ah."

"One other thing," said the docent holding open the gate and waiting for Adam's eyes to meet his. "You were visiting Stevie's grave."

"Stephen Perrine?"

The man nodded.

"Yes," said Adam.

"You may want to stay away from his grave in the future."

"Oh, why?"

"You were in his spot."

Without another word, the docent closed the gate behind Adam, turned abruptly, and walked away.

"Wait a minute!" called Adam.

The man continued walking.

"Wait!"

But the docent did not break his stride and disappeared behind a rise in the path.

Adam walked slowly to his car and sat inside for a long time, replaying the events in his mind, finally concluding he had somehow imagined the conversation with Nature. But the last words of the docent played havoc with his analysis, and he made the decision to return tomorrow and talk with the man. While on the one hand, he denied the reality of Nature's ghostly appearance, on the other hand, he berated himself for not asking more questions, for not demanding more answers, for not grabbing this golden opportunity to obtain information, even if only to satisfy his own delusion. A psychotic break might fit nicely into his psychological diagnosis, but recollection of the docent's last words kept undermining that assessment, and his determination to confront the man strengthened.

He sat in the parked car until the windshield fogged, the tam's tassel gone still against the glass.

Not hungry, and craving solitude so he could think in peace, Adam Camara drove straight to the hotel and locked himself in his room.

~ *Gail Hess Frets* ~

Gail Hess did her best to maintain a normal routine at the institute, but her mind kept returning to Adam Camara, and she wondered whether his trip had revealed any new insights. For her part, the absence of Mr. Powers did nothing to lessen the uncomfortable feeling that Goddess lurked inside her mind, and, in fact, *Her* presence had somehow been strengthened. Worse, the detective kept hinting that he had solid leads as to the whereabouts of Mr. Powers, but they invariably led nowhere and his return was now highly doubtful—in her mind at least. Mark Powers and his wife returned to New York, and the house remained on the market.

Knowing the house was empty, Gail felt an urge to visit it, be close to the source, even sit at the table where Mr. Powers held his famous dinner parties for ghosts. After all, if Adam could travel to Rhode Island and visit a ghost, she could drive a few miles to Mr. Powers's house. But then . . . do what? Snoop? Take in the atmosphere? Or perhaps something else.

The thought first entered her mind a few days earlier while she conducted talk therapy with a patient suffering from major depression.

"Doctor, the only time my black despair ever gets better is when I am at my dinner table."

"Alone?" asked Gail.

"Oh, yes. No one can be around me anymore, you know that."

"But, Patricia, you know your family loves you very much. You are here getting help because of their concerns."

"I know, but while I sat at that table, facing empty seats, I could picture a group of people laughing and talking and enjoying my company. They were imaginary, of course, but they relieved the feeling of total hopelessness."

"Who were they, Patricia?"

"Oh, friends, imaginary friends, attractive and bright and full of interesting conversations that I could join. Although I know I am ugly, they included me without the slightest . . . I don't know . . . hesitation. They made me laugh."

"Were they all women?"

"Oh, no! That would be boring, don't you think, doctor? No, no, there were some men." She lowered her voice. "Very attractive men."

Gail laughed. "Of course. Did they flirt with you?"

Patricia looked at Gail with a gleam in her eye, the first sign of life she had displayed since her admittance. "Yes, they did. I even had two or three of them get jealous, and I enjoyed watching them get in a few digs at each other. It was fun."

"While you were enjoying these parties, did you ever believe the guests were real?"

"No, no," she said sadly. "That is not my problem, Dr. Hess. I am only too aware of what is real and what is not. I wish I were more like some of the other patients here."

"And when the parties ended?"

"You can guess. I felt even more devastated. But, at least, I had those few magical moments. I wouldn't trade them for anything."

"Can't you have those parties here, Patricia? Can't you pretend this little table is your dining room table full of guests?"

"I tried, but it didn't work. I guess it has to be at home, in my own surroundings, where I feel comfortable with imaginary friends, rather than here, where I would just feel self-conscious, or worse . . . you know, mentally ill."

"But, Patricia, you are not mentally ill, you are simply ill, like any other illness. Depression is chemical, like having the flu, not some awful failure on your part. And we know this illness can be cured, or at least managed, just like the flu."

Patricia seemed to fall back into her dark space. "I know," she murmured.

Dr. Hess took a different tack. "I would like to be at one of your parties, Patricia. I would like to see you smile and watch how you would cause the men to be jealous."

"Oh, no, Doctor! If you were there, nobody would pay me any attention. Not a soul. All eyes would be on you."

~

After this session with Patricia, the idea of visiting Mr. Powers's house gained more and more traction in her mind. What she would do there was not clear, but the feeling that she must go became an imperative. Perhaps, if she sat at his dining room table and concentrated hard enough? But this idea she dismissed as pure fantasy and cloaked her desire in the guise of research. In moments of clarity, she realized this had been the same justification Adam put forth in his defense of going to Rhode Island to search for a ghost, but if it worked for him, perhaps it might work for her.

A solo séance, she thought rather sardonically.

Gail resisted the idea as long as she could, but on an impulse one Saturday, she picked up a key from the agent and drove to Mr. Powers's house. By mid-afternoon, she turned onto the long gravel driveway which led to the secluded residence. Gravel ground under the tires for a long minute until she passed a partially restored car sitting on blocks off to the side, weeds grown up around it to the windows. She stopped in front of the garage and walked to the front door. Before entering, Gail paused and listened, but heard only the call of birds and a lugubrious wind sighing through the pine trees. Gail, always one for levity when the mood seemed too severe, thought whimsically, *Well, the setting is just right for a meeting with ghosts. Can't let Adam outshine me in the ghost department.*

The interior looked immaculate. *The agent is doing her job*, thought Gail. She paused in the living room, then went into the kitchen and stared at the sprawling expanse of the counter—a vast Corian peninsula of white. From the kitchen she moved to the dining room, its large table and chairs just as she imagined in his writings. Drawing from Michael's description, she mentally positioned the players in his make-believe dinner parties.

"Let's see," she whispered, moving around the table. "Michael at the head, Diane here, Mark here, and Storyteller over there. His rifle must have leaned against the table here."

Gail paused as if waiting to hear something, but nothing came, and she thought to herself, *How stupid! What a waste of time. But remember when Goddess came in the guise of Ethyl? That was when his imaginary wife, Theresa, appeared. They must have sat here.*

"Storyteller!" she called aloud, feeling self-conscious and ridiculous.

Nothing.

"Diane!"

Nothing.

Gail laughed at herself. *I must be the most absurd psychiatrist in history! What on earth was I thinking by coming here?*

"Don't give up too soon, sweetie," came a voice.

It had an African American lilt, and Gail staggered back a step, unsure she really heard it.

"You're on the right track, girlie. Come and sit with me. The others ain't here but me. You'll talk to me, right?"

Gail continued to look at an empty table, and stuttered, "Where are you?"

"Here." An elderly Black woman stood in the kitchen doorway. "Sit and I'll join you."

"Are you with the real estate company?" asked Gail, assuming the woman was a cleaning lady.

The old woman pulled a chair out for Gail to sit, then settled herself carefully into an adjoining chair. "You might say so."

"You do the cleaning?"

The woman laughed; a cackle that sounded too stereotypical to be genuine. "I might take that comment to be racist, but you might say so."

"Well, you've done a wonderful job. The house is immaculate."

"Dead, you mean."

Gail twitched nervously. "You mean with no one living here?"

"If that is easier on your sensitive ears. I was never one much for euphemisms. He is, though. Oh, He certainly is. It's one of the secrets of His success."

"Who?"

"God."

"God? What do you mean?"

"I mean God. Him. The Savior. The Lord. Yahweh. The Enlightened One. The Great One. The Magnificent. All-Knowing Father. That from which all wisdom flows. You know, Him."

Gail, being an experienced psychiatrist, maintained her calm demeanor. "I see. Did He used to live here?"

"Dr. Hess, you really are obtuse, aren't you?"

Gail fought through her rising fear. "Your name is?"

"Call me Ethyl. Not as enthralling as 'Call me Ishmael,' but it'll have to do, sweetie."

Gail's heart raced as she struggled with two conflicting impulses. Her first instinct was to leave as quickly and quietly as possible, without upsetting this unhinged person. On the other hand, there was Mr. Powers's narrative, in which Ethyl played *Her* part. Gail's inclination was to ask the obvious question, one that would put her on an equal footing in madness with this woman.

"Are you Goddess?" she asked boldly, figuring there was nothing to lose but her dignity.

"Yes, yes," said Ethyl dismissively. *Her* face transformed into the deistic imperturbability of a Greek mask behind which her two eyes shone laser-like. *Her* body straightened, strengthened, and exuded vibrancy, glistening in the lights like a young snake that had just shed an old skin.

"Now," *She* said in a commanding voice. "Can you and I get down to business?"

Gail panicked and looked around for something, anything, that would prove this to be an illusion.

Quickly reverting to *Her* old black lady persona, Goddess patted Gail's hand and said soothingly, "Now, now, dearie, don't fret. I ain't going to bite. We just need to talk."

"About?" asked Gail in a shaky voice.

"About you, about Me, about Michael Powers, about Nature, about your institute, about Adam Camara, about Storyteller, all of it."

Gail jumped up. "I will be right back!" she exclaimed.

She returned with a notebook, pulled out a pen, and prepared to write. "And Buandelgereen?"

A shower of sparks blazed in the room, blinding Gail. Through her fingers, she could barely make out Goddess in all *Her* splendor, hovering on *Her* lotus flower. Before Gail could say a word, the notebook burst into flames and the room fell quiet.

A thin ribbon of smoke climbed to the ceiling, and a faint oval scorch marked the tabletop where the notebook had lain; when Gail touched it, her fingertips came away gray with ash.

Ethyl was gone.

Gail sat in dumb disbelief before the ashes that constituted her link to reason and sanity and so effectively insulated her from the mad rantings of her patients. She could only mutter self-recriminations. Tears of frustration rolled down her cheeks at the lost opportunity. Time enough later to rationalize it away. For now, in this moment, she must not be Dr. Gail Hess, psychiatrist, she must be . . . something else. Someone else. And she buried herself anew in regret.

When I do what is expected and proper, she thought, *I make no progress. Only a sense of comfortable acceptability. When I take risky chances, I usually progress, but in the face of resistance. Which is better: admired stagnation or excoriated progress?*

"But, Gail," came an inner warning. "Ghosts are far beyond the pale. Believing in their existence is certainly not in the category of 'taking a risky chance.' That is not progress, that is madness."

How could one patient drag her into this mental state, saddling her with these delusions? She had never experienced such episodes from any other patient—schizophrenic or otherwise—and many she had been treating for years, far longer than Mr. Powers. And what about Adam Camara? He suffered this same . . . same what? Madness? Virus? Without being aware of the time, Gail continued sitting at the dining room table pondering these hydra-like dilemmas. Only when some animal's shriek drew her attention did she notice it had become dark.

Despite all the angst she felt, and despite her rational dismissal of these hallucinations, she did not want to leave. Something had crept inside her mind, some seed of longing for the reappearance of Goddess. Oddly, she wanted to see ghosts, longed to see ghosts, even though she knew they were elaborate illusions, as she had the sickly feeling that she belonged with them. This last thought gave her fright, but she quickly dismissed the feeling. She looked around furtively to make sure no real person had entered and seen her sitting alone at the table. Satisfied she was indeed alone, she placed her hands on the table and sat up straight in her chair.

"Goddess," she said. "I apologize. Please return."

Nothing.

"Please, I would like to talk with *You,* to 'get down to business' as *You* put it."

Nothing.

"Or, if *You* are unwilling, send the others—just as *You* sent them to Michael Powers when he sat here."

Nothing.

"Diane, please come."

Nothing.

"Storyteller, will you appear for me?"

Nothing.

Gail coughed nervously, and again looked around. She felt utterly foolish, and on the long drive home, the reasoning part of her brain began the long process of explaining away what she had seen. When she entered her apartment, she felt too tired to eat and decided to go straight to bed. But the persistent pleas for attention from Sigmund gave her comfort. She stroked the cat affectionately, relieved to again touch base with reality. Nevertheless, a turning point had been reached, and no amount of rationalization could erase the recognition that something beyond her ability to understand had occurred, no matter how much of her training went into the effort to prove otherwise.

The cat purred and the apartment held its breath; on the table, a single ash from the burned notebook refused to cool.

Chapter Fifteen

On The Eve Of Moving In

Awake

I woke up this morning from a dream about Storyteller, and its remnants still echo faintly in my mind. I stand in front of the bathroom mirror and, as usual, inspect the creeping effects of age on my face. I hold up my hands, palms down, seeing the blue veins and wrinkled flesh, flecked with dark spots.

Yes, dear Reader, we may think age ultimately prevails, but youth will eventually have its way. Even dead youth. Especially dead youth. Age is the calling back, and death is the homecoming, a reunion with lost youth. Paul Bäumer had it right—being at the Front spares one from all the falsity and artifice that society so slyly nurtures whenever kill-or-be-killed is not dictating fundamentals.

So be it. I know I am being called back. Storyteller calls me. Nature calls me.

Alas, the burden of responsibility keeps me here—where there is something-ness, rather than my destination—where there is stillness.

I mechanically eat breakfast and travel to the cave. Something has me down today. Perhaps it's knowing the iron doors are now irrevocably in place. Only the memory of Buandelgereen's words, "You will pass through the iron doors soon enough" sustains me. Perhaps my funk is because I have given up on Goddess. *She* has failed me, or I have failed *Her*. After all, I am the son, the famous son, the Chosen One *She* so desperately wanted Bai Meiying and John Powers to conceive.

As Child of Buddha and Suling thought, I must be destined for great things if a deity could be so insistent on my birth. Great things! I am an escaped mental patient running trivial errands for a bizarre Mongol woman who is building some massive shrine, or hiding place, or something I do not understand. I have accomplished nothing. The shattered rocks outside the cave try to make me feel better, for they also confide in me that they have only partly completed an inevitable trip to the sea courtesy of gravity, and toward ultimate dissolution as grains of sand. Yet, in their simplicity, they cannot grasp the concept of failure, for it is an alien concept to non-humans. These rocks are perfectly happy to end up as grains of sand, then be recycled into magma, and eventually reborn as new rocks, as all the rest of us are recycled in our myriad of ways.

Somehow, all this recycling does not constitute an existential crisis to them. Yet, for us humans, it seems every jolt, jag, and tumble toward the sea becomes an existential crisis. Well, enough of my own existential crisis, I have word from Buandelgereen that by the end of the month, I can move into my quarters in the cave. And then?

~

Today, I met Temulun for the first time, a female boxer dog. Her human master-slave is one of the construction guys, and she is full of mischief. Temulun has a very hard time keeping her paws on the ground, as she loves to dance and prance and leap skyward for the pure joy of it. I befriended her this morning when she asked for water, and I used a hard hat as a bowl to make it easier for her to drink.

"Thanks! Thanks!" she enthused. "That hit the spot!"

Then she sniffed me for an inordinately long time, wrinkles creasing her boxer face. "Odd," she said. "You are certainly alive, yet you smell of death. Have you recently been dead?"

"Yes," I replied simply.

"Oh, well, that explains it—better to have been dead and now alive than to just be dead!"

"I agree."

So, we talked for as long as she could stand it, then she raced off to find her master-slave, who at that time was working in the cave.

It is now late afternoon, and workers are leaving for the day. Temulun comes bounding up to me.

"Hi! Got a treat for me?"

"Not today, but I'll go to the store and bring some tomorrow."

"Oh, good! Treats are a girl's best friend!" She wiggles in that excited way of hers and starts to bound off but stops suddenly.

"Don't get me wrong," she explains. "My master-slave treats me fine, just a little rough around the edges. Oh! He's calling! Off I go! Off! Off! See ya! Don't be dead again and remember the treats! Dinner time!"

Now, dear Reader, a thought has been picking at my mind. If I can continue to develop my friendship with Temulun, she might be of help to me. After all, she has free rein in and out of the cave. Her slave-owner is a carpenter. He must have access beyond the iron doors to be able to work on the interior construction. He speaks very little English, but Temulun is quite articulate. If I can get past the second iron door, I am sure it is where *she* will reside, and I know it must connect to the tunnel where my friends and Storyteller wait.

~ *A Warning from Goddess* ~

I have not failed you, Michael Powers, and you must not fail Me!

Her words come to me as I am pouring water for a thirsty group of workers outside the cave.

"Where are You?" is all I can manage.

"Standing in front of you," a worker laughs.

Where are You?

Standing inside of you.

You have failed me.

No. When the cave is finished and you are moved in, then you will see. Not before.

Then I will see what?

"Hey!" exclaims a worker. I inadvertently spilled water on him.

"Sorry."

Then I will see what? I repeat.

Then you will see.

You said that about Marie Telles.

We are not done with Miss Telles. Then you will see.

I want to go past the second iron door.

Then you will see.

I snort in disgust.

~

Temulun rushes up all in a dither. "Hi! Wow! Lots of new smells in there! Got a treat?"

"Sure." I dig a treat out of my pocket. "Here you go."

"Thanks! Got another?"

"Nope, that's it."

"Aww."

"Temulun, stop jumping around for a minute."

"Okay, got a treat?"

"No. Is your slave-master still in the cave?"

Temulun looks over her shoulder. "Yeah. He's always working. No time for play. Makes Temulun sad. Got a treat?"

"Sorry, no more."

"Aww."

"Is he deep in the cave . . . I mean far back toward the end?"

"Yeah! It's fun! I must pass tons of workers, and some of them give me treats?" She tilts her head questioningly.

"I'm out of treats."

"Aww."

"Is your slave-master working at the very end of the cave?"

"Yeah."

"Are there doors?"

"Sure, humans love doors. But they're open so I can go in and out whenever I want." She picks up an old glove off the ground. "Want to play?"

"Not right now."

"Aww."

"Do they close them at night?"

Temulun is busy chewing on the glove.

"Temulun!"

"Huh?"

"Do they close the doors at night?"

"Don't know. Want to play?"

"No."

"Got a treat?"

"No. But I'll give you a treat tomorrow if you tell me whether they close the doors at night."

"Okay! I'll try. If I try, but if I don't find out, will you still give me a treat?"

"Sure. We're friends, aren't we?"

"Sure! Here, grab the other end of this glove and let's play tug of war!"

I play with Temulun. After all, I will need her, and besides, she is so damn cute. If she were a human female, she would wear me out. With this thought, Temulun suddenly stops pulling and looks at me with a deep, intelligent expression of sadness and . . . longing, perhaps?

"Oh, Michael," she says. "If you only knew."

~

I have decided. If Temulun tells me they keep the doors open at night, I will make another attempt, but this time go all the way. Buandelgereen might be waiting, but I'll bring Temulun, if her master-slave will allow it. Dogs are immune to deities and all their minions, I think. Besides, it's scary in that cave at night, and she'll be good company. I'll give her master-slave some excuse to have her that night . . . or maybe, just give him money, no questions asked. Cross that bridge when I get there.

Dear Reader, you might ask: why do I want to go past the second door? After all, Buandelgereen said I would go there eventually. But eventually could be years. Doctors Hess and Camara may finally put aside their "demons" and find me, drag me back to the institute. Then what? No—my decision is firm. I'm going to find the connection that will return me to the tunnel where my bones, my comrades, and my young self await. I am abandoning Goddess. Regardless of what *She* said, *She* has failed me.

Good man! booms the voice of God, whom I haven't heard in ages. **You have come to your feeble senses at last. Goddess is a fraud. She and Her faction would have the Mentors violate First Principles!**

I have no response for *Him*. Although *His* last words bother me, I must simply let the world keep turning to the brutal tune of natural selection and leave God to suck the ambrosia of its consequences so *He* may keep *Himself* high and mighty. I am going back. Let people serve *Him* as aphids serve the ant. Just ask the Great Warrior.

"Goddess," I whisper, so the workers cannot hear. "I am abandoning *You*. Time to return to my bones . . . to stillness."

She does not reply, but Buandelgereen suddenly appears next to me, and in a soothing but commanding tone, says, "No, Michael Powers. No need to ask help from a dog when I can show you past the second door now." Her face breaks into a cagey smile. "Besides, I have more treats than you for Temulun, and her priorities are far more straightforward than those of humans." She tilts her head as if questioning her own words. "At least, that's what *she* wants us to think."

I am in no mood for further manipulation and riddle making. "Then take me there now."

"No, tonight. Right now, the chambers are full of workers. You will eat dinner and I will drive you here at eight o'clock."

"No tricks?"

"No tricks."

I throw down my water dispenser for emphasis. "Buandelgereen, if there is some monkey business in all this, if you are not serious, then I will no longer cooperate in the most extreme manner."

"Which is?"

"Turn myself back over to the institution—or suicide. One way or another, I am going back."

"Michael, you are going past the second iron door. What you find on the other side is up to you."

"More riddles?"

"Truth."

"Then, I'll take my chances. Tonight, at eight o'clock. One other condition."

"You don't make conditions."

I feel stronger, so I ignore her and continue. "One other condition—I want to be left alone in the last chamber for as long as I want."

"That's the only condition I'd agree to, since that's what is intended."

"Okay."

She is gone, striding away to join a group that had been patiently waiting for our conversation to end. As for myself, I'm returning to the house. No more water boy.

"You're angry!"

"Oh, hello Temulun. How are you, girl?"

"That human woman scares me."

"Yeah, I can understand that."

"Want to play?"

"Not right now."

"The doors will be closed."

"I know."

"Treat?"

I give her two treats, but in her joy, must tamp down her enthusiasm. "Temu-lun, down! No need to jump. You're welcome."

She suddenly turns serious, her boxer face wrinkling in open puzzlement. "Hey . . . are you really going to the end?"

"Yes, why?"

"I just came back from there. They kicked me out, and my master-slave watched me leave. He looked scared, and I've never seen him scared before. As the door was closing, I saw them moving something around. I caught a whiff of it, and I didn't like the smell! Not at all!"

"What was it?"

"Don't know."

"What did it smell like?"

"Like you."

This really startles me. "Temulun, if it smelled like me, why be afraid of it?"

"Because it wasn't you—and it had that same hint of death you carry. Also, it didn't offer me any treats! No, I didn't like the smell of it at all!"

"Is it a person?"

"It is what it is. Wanna play?"

"Not now."

"Aww."

A bizarre idea crosses my mind. "Temulun, are you Goddess?"

Again, her face becomes intelligent, sardonic. "Goddess moves in mysterious ways. Gimme a treat and maybe I'll tell you!"

I pull out another treat.

"Not that kind," she says, narrowing her eyes.

"What kind do you want?"

"You don't know?"

"No."

"Aww."

From the cave mouth, a draft passed over my hands; Temulun's treat crumbs stuck to my palm like grit from a grave.

~ *Trip to the End of the Cave* ~

Despite Temulun's enigmatic words, I'm looking forward to it tonight. I've eaten dinner and now simply wait for eight o'clock, when I'll meet Buandelgereen out front. I try to think of other things but can't. God and Goddess are mercifully quiet, busy with Dr. Hess and Dr. Camara I suppose. I wonder how it goes for them, as I have not received any visions that would reveal their present predicaments. My own situation is keeping me busy enough. When I reach the end of the cave, I must remember to check my watch (if it happened to Dr. Camara, it could happen to me).

She arrives and says, "We'll walk."

"No car?"

"No."

After we stroll for a short while, I look back and see the house has vanished. Completely gone. My rational brain tells me this might be significant, but I dismiss the thought. *Probably the fog.*

Dew beads my sleeves, and the back of my neck cools, as if the house has stepped away and taken its warmth with it.

~

Buandelgereen and I stand at the entrance. It is dark, and I must admit I feel genuinely nervous. The Mongol woman's white hair fairly glows in the full moon. Fitting. The entrance has been kept wide for easy movement of equipment and materials in and out, but I see the first signs of framing have been installed to close it up. As we step through the opening, Buandelgereen flips a switch and the generator hums to life. Soon the cave fills with light. To this point, my Mongolian Charon says nothing.

She finally breaks the silence. "Shall we?"

I nod, and we begin the long walk. With the cave so brightly lit, I notice many more details. There is a veritable maze of little paths that branch off to side chambers, and presumably to many more beyond. The carpentry and drywall make it look less like a cave and more like a grand hotel, with a multitude of rooms and hallways. I notice the permanent lighting fixtures are being installed.

"It is fantastic," I say in wonder.

"Indeed," replies Buandelgereen.

After moving deep into the bowels of the cave and across the stone bridge, we come to the first iron door. It is closed and locked, but she produces a key and swings it open. Another switch is flipped, and I stare at a large chamber of oak-paneled walls lined with bookcases and massive hanging tapestries. It is as if we've entered the castle of some medieval lord, and I move closer to look at the tapestries, which depict familiar details, but Buandelgereen barks an impatient command with no room for hesitation.

"Come! You want to go past the second door, then come!"

I follow sheepishly.

These chambers remind me of the French fortress and the storage chambers in the tunnel, though their scale is far smaller than this monstrous cavern. We quickly cross the smooth, stone floor to the second door and pause before it.

"Are you sure?" she asks.

The question takes me aback, but I recover quickly and respond more confidently than I feel. "Yes."

She selects a key from her ring and unlocks the door. Before pushing it open, she asks, "Alone? You sure?"

"Alone. I'm sure."

The door swings open, I step through, and she closes it behind me with a metallic slam that bodes no good. I perceive there are no lights, but something on the other side of the chamber glows, its intensity pulsing with regularity. A deep and pervasive mineral stench fills my nostrils, and for a few horrifying moments, I cannot breathe, and fear the chamber has no air supply. Once I regain my bearings, a slight breeze cools my face, and my breathing eases. What is the source of the pulsing light? I reach for a switch that doesn't exist, so I turn on my flashlight, but oddly it has no effect, so I click it off to save batteries.

As my eyes acclimate to the darkness, the glowing object comes fully into view. I am stunned and can only stare to make sure it is real. Now I hear the tapping, a slow, steady beat that transports me back in time.

... Tap. Tap. Tap....

"So, it is you," I say to the Precious Object. "Your journey has been long." These words of calm imperturbability surprise even me.

... Tap. Tap. Tap....

Sound familiar, dear Reader? It should. I can almost see Captain Cairns puzzling over it, Child of Buddha deciphering it, and Clerk Long crying over its loss. Most of my comrades died capturing it, Mr. President died at its feet, and the Venerable Vu Huong understood it, even as Madame Dau, Han Tinh, Feng Shiren, and Captain Tong had glimpses of its true meaning, while Monsieur Davignon and a host of others feared it.

... Tap. Tap. Tap....

When you think about it, that tapping represents a very sparse vocabulary. Child of Buddha could discern the silences between the taps and the variations in tone and tempo, but I cannot.

... Tap. Tap. Tap....

I don't understand the Precious Object. Is this all we will ever say to each other? If so, take me back to the tunnel—there's nothing here for me. Do I sound cynical, dear Reader? Well, wouldn't you be? I am allowed to understand dogs and sidewalks and beds and rocks, but not the Precious Object. Why?

... Tap. Tap. Tap....

Cruelty. Suffering. God. "Enough! I want to go back!" This last thought I evidently verbalized in a primal scream, because I now can hear the echoes.

"Where?" comes *Her* voice.

She is wearing the same outfit *She* wore on that first day in my father's office a half-century ago.

"I knew You would come," I say boldly.

"You are truly a prophet," *She* says, a bit of sarcasm adding an edge to *Her* words. "Now you are here"—*She* pauses and looks at the Precious Object—"what is it you seek?"

"You."

"I am here."

"But why am I here?"

"You came."

"I want to go back."

"To the tunnel in Vietnam? To your bones?"

"Yes, and to Nature and the others."

"They are shades and have joined Mountain Man, Sergeant Dam, your parents, and all the others. You have another Chosen One to meet. You must have a child—the next step."

"I would rather be a shade."

"No. You are the son."

This really irks me. "Look, Goddess—or whoever You are—I'm not some sort of Jesus Christ. I'm a failed husband, a failed father, a mediocre lawyer now out of work, an escaped mental patient, and a desperately ill schizophrenic who is very likely creating this elaborate hallucination in my padded cell."

"You are the son, the Chosen One, the father of the next step."

"Okay, fine, I'm the son. Now, what do *You* want of me?"

"To stay here until it is time."

"Until when?"

"Until *He* comes."

"Who?"

"You know."

"God?"

She nods.

"And then?" I ask quite reasonably.

"Fate starves at Probability's door."

"So in other words—we'll see?"

She nods again.

I shake my head vigorously. "No, no! This won't do! *Your* vague riddles no longer work."

"Then return."

"To the tunnel?" I ask hopefully.

"To the institute."

"No. I don't want to return to the institute. I want to return to the tunnel. To my bones. To my friends."

She suddenly explodes in a fireball of intense light, blinding me as though I stared into the heart of a thermonuclear blast. Throwing my arm in front of my eyes, I hear the Precious Object tapping madly, and when all becomes quiet at last, I peek out and see Goddess in all *Her* glory. *She* wears an angry expression, sparks flying from *Her* gaze, third eye glowing faintly, intricate necklace cradled between two, rounded breasts, left hand resting in *Her* lap, upturned in the shape of a bowl, fingers of the right hand pointed skyward toward the vaulted stone ceiling. *She* sits atop an enormous white lotus, floating above the floor.

Before I have a chance to speak, *She* points to a far wall, where a lone M-16 is leaning.

There is the means to grant your wish, Storyteller.

I look down and see that I'm wearing jungle fatigues. My muscles ache from fever, and my hands are young and strong.

Go, *She* says gently.

I gaze at the M-16. "I could never do this," I say in my old voice. Evidently, I have acquired the trappings of Storyteller, but am not him, yet.

Her head tilts slightly. **Why?**

"I could never commit suicide."

Why?

I have no answer.

She shifts *Her* position almost imperceptibly. **Leave now. You will live here until it is time. Now, go.**

"Wait!" I call.

Buandelgereen's voice bellows from the doorway. "Come!"

The chamber is once again pitch black. I see Buandelgereen's silhouette in the open door, backlit by the chamber she calls from. I start to object but know better than to speak. One last look into the darkness to see the Precious Object or Goddess proves to be fruitless. An urge to stay in this dark chamber chides me. Let Buandelgereen shut the iron door. I will remain and find the connection to the tunnel. Darkness has never been an obstacle to my determination. But. . . .

"Okay, I'm coming."

We leave the cave wordlessly, and I am thrown back into the uncertainties we all must face in life.

Outside, my watch reads 8:07—an hour gone I can't account for.

I had my chance.

Chapter Sixteen

Coming to Terms

Doctor Camara Has A Conversation

A dam stood in front of the information desk at Little Neck Cemetery, staring patiently as a nondescript man put the finishing touches on paperwork for a previous customer. Fastidiously rearranging the documents into a neat stack, the man put them in a file folder and set it aside. He looked up at Adam with a smile.

"What can I help you with?"

"Yesterday I met one of your docents, but it was closing time and we didn't have a chance to finish our discussion."

"Any of our docents are familiar with the cemetery and fully qualified to answer your questions. Mister . . . ?"

"Camara. Adam Camara."

The receptionist motioned someone over. An elderly woman in a docent's uniform appeared wearing a friendly smile.

"This is Mrs. Larkin. Perhaps she can assist?"

Adam nodded toward the woman and returned her smile. "Actually," he said, "I would like to talk with the same docent I met yesterday because we were discussing a particular gravesite."

"Mrs. Larkin is well versed in—"

"No, thank you, but we had been discussing something more personal."

"I see. What is his name?"

"Well, that's just it, I don't know."

"I see." The man's eyes flitted past Adam to a line that had started to form. His tone changed slightly, and his words came more quickly. "Perhaps if you describe him?"

"Older man, big, with gray hair."

The receptionist chuckled. "Mr. Camara, that describes just about all of our docents." Again, his eyes quickly took in the waiting line of people. "Can you be more specific?"

"Well, he was stationed near the grave of Stephen Perrine. Ah, I do not have the plot number with me."

"Sorry, I can't help, Mr. Camara. Our docents are all roving, so they have no particular station. Perhaps if you look around, you might spot him."

"Yes," replied Adam, aware of the line. "I'll do that. Thank you."

He left the main building and began to wander the grounds. At first, he scanned every face, but he gradually became interested in the gravestones themselves. Before he knew it, he had reached the vicinity of Nature's grave.

"Be careful, or you'll end up in his spot again," came a familiar voice.

Seeing his docent walking up, Adam laughed out of nervousness. "Oh—hello. Good to see you again."

The man regarded him good-naturedly. "Another visit?" he asked.

"No. Actually, I came to see you."

"Oh?"

"Yesterday, your words struck me, Mister?"

The man stuck out his hand. "Bud Yancey. You can call me Bud."

Adam took the hand. "My name is Adam Camara, but please call me Adam."

"Okay, Adam."

"Anyway, Bud, what do you mean by Mr. Perrine's spot?"

"Stevie? Oh my goodness, he came every weekend before the war."

"You knew him?"

"Sure. All of us who worked back then knew Stevie."

"What was he doing here?"

Bud looked askance. "You family?"

"No."

Bud waited.

"I know someone who was a friend of his from the war."

"Oh." Bud volunteered no more words, but regarded Adam with a faintly suspicious look.

Adam decided the man was sharper than he'd first assumed, so he decided to be truthful. "Fact is, Bud, I am a psychiatrist. I am treating Stephen's friend, who has often talked about their relationship in Vietnam. I thought by coming here, I might find some clues that would be helpful to my patient."

Bud's gaze shifted to Nature's grave. "So, your patient returned in pain—and Stevie returned beyond pain."

"Yes."

"Poetry."

"Pardon?"

"Poetry," repeated Bud. "Stevie came here to write poetry. That was his spot, so that's where we buried him."

"I see."

A deep smile crinkled Bud's face. "Always wore that silly hat."

Adam pulled out his hat and held it up. "Tam o'shanter?"

"That's it, by God!" cried Bud. "Don't tell me you write poetry also?"

"I do not, much to the relief of the world."

Bud laughed, then turned somber. "Stevie was a great kid. Would've made a great man, but for that damn war."

"Tell me," said Adam, a bit self-consciously. "Do you ever get the feeling some of these folks, I mean the ones buried here, come out?"

"Come out?"

"I mean, as if they were around, their spirits, and you can talk to them."

Bud's eyes narrowed. "You don't sound like a psychiatrist, Adam."

"I know, and I'll take that as a compliment."

Bud visibly relaxed. "Of course I do! Especially Stevie. He comes out and visits all the time."

Adam evidently looked startled, so Bud waved his hands. "No, no, not that way, Doc. I've not gone around the bend yet. What I mean to say is—" he stopped and tried to organize his thoughts.

Adam waited patiently, genuinely interested in how Bud Yancey would explain the unexplainable.

Bud appeared to come to some conclusion. "Come sit on this bench with me, Doc, and I'll try to make some sense of it."

They sat on a bench only a few feet from Nature's grave. Bud looked wistfully at the gravestone and patted the back of the bench. "This is the very bench Stevie sat on to write his poetry. I wasn't a docent then, of course, but a younger man with an administrative job here at the cemetery. Often, I took walks around the place to get out of the office and clear my mind. I still remember the first time I saw this stringy kid, curly hair blowing in the wind out from under his weird hat, hunched over, writing on a notepad.

"So, I walked up to him all friendly-like. 'Hello, kid,' I say. 'Whatcha' doing?' Well, he looks up and smiles to beat the band. 'Writing poetry,' he says, just like that. 'Writing poetry.'

"I say back, 'Poetry? In this place? You're crazy, kid!' I laughed to let him know it wasn't personal. You know what he says back, Doc?"

"No, what?"

"He says, 'Best place in the world to write poetry. Death—and the specter of death—are pure poetry.' I'll never forget those words, coming from the mouth of a young kid like that. Well, long story short, we became friends. Talked a lot sitting on this bench."

"I see," said Adam, waiting for the continuation of the story. When none came, he noticed tears welling in the old man's eyes.

Bud took a deep breath and slapped his knees. "Well, that's it, Doc. Back to work!"

"Wait a minute," objected Adam. "You were going to tell me—"

Bud held up his hand. "I know, I know. Do I still talk to him? That's your question, isn't it? And the answer is yes. I often talk to him, right here, sitting on this bench, just like when he was alive."

"How?"

"Same way I'm talking to you."

Adam shot him a skeptical look. "Well, you have to admit, Bud, not exactly the same."

Bud looked at him oddly. "Close enough to know who your patient is," he said conspiratorially.

Adam felt a jolt of surprise. "Who?" he blurted.

Bud abruptly stood and gazed out at the grounds. "Back to work."

"Come on, Bud, you can't leave me hanging," implored Adam.

"No, Doc. If I tell you, then you'll have too many other questions, and I'm not up to answering them. I stayed on here after I retired to talk to the dead—not the living."

"But—"

"However," Bud interrupted, "I saw you conversing with Stevie yesterday, so he must have picked you out as a person worthwhile talking to, so I'll make you a proposition. I'll write down the name of your patient, who Stevie mentions a lot, and put it in an envelope. After you leave, you can read it, but I will answer no more questions. Agreed?"

"Agreed," replied Adam reluctantly.

They returned to the main office, where Bud went behind the counter, wrote something on a slip of paper, and sealed it in an official envelope.

"Here you are, Doc," he said. "Good luck with your patient, and good luck with Stevie."

With this strange farewell, Bud Yancey walked back out of the building to again wander among the graves.

The envelope seemed to burn in Adam's hand, but a deal was a deal, so he waited until he had returned to the hotel before unsealing it. The note contained a single word.

Storyteller.

~

That night, Adam cursed his promise not to ask further questions of Bud Yancey. Although his flight left the next day, he felt a compulsion to postpone it, return to the cemetery, and convince Bud to give him answers. There were so many questions, so much he might discover, and despite telling himself this rash action would be for the benefit of Mr. Powers, he knew it would really be for his own peace of mind. He even toyed with the idea of sneaking into the cemetery that night and sitting on the bench, but concluded the notion was too preposterous. Besides, he would probably end up in jail. So, the next day, he sat on the airplane returning to San Francisco, contemplating how he would frame his report to Gail.

Was his time at the cemetery a supernatural experience? It seemed to Adam that anything connected with this Powers character contained elements of mystery, if not magic. But ghosts? The more he thought, the more he realized he had been more rattled by Bud Yancey than the ghost of Stephen Perrine. Now, for the first time, he wondered if Bud himself was a ghost, some old Puritan having fun with twenty-first century rubes. On impulse, he pulled out the envelope, felt its weight, and verified its material existence. Retrieving the slip of paper, Adam even double-checked the handwriting to make sure it was not his own—the product of some sort of hypnotic suggestion. It was not his handwriting.

Therefore, Bud Yancey is real, he thought. *I'll still have to verify that when I get home, but it seems likely he exists in the realm of the living.*

Which brought him back to his original conundrum: did he visit with Nature's ghost? All his scientific training told Adam his experience was the product of some unusual but explicable mental anomaly, hidden in the vast thicket of neural pathways that had somehow, some way, been re-routed. The possibility even crossed his mind that someone was playing a trick but dismissed the notion as impractical. A low buzz in the back of his mind kept insisting he find Storyteller (not, as this buzz made abundantly clear, Mr. Powers) as quickly as possible, so that Storyteller would be free to return. Adam knew this persistent exhortation was from Nature, embedded somewhere in his mind. Fight it as he might, Adam renewed his determination to locate Mr. Powers and return him to the institute. Let the chips fall where they may.

~ *Dr. Hess Struggles* ~

After the incident at Michael Powers's house, Gail Hess threw herself into her work, almost doubling the amount of time she spent with patients. She considered writing a final analysis of the troublesome Mr. Powers as a publishable paper and had already begun a rough outline. She thought a post-mortem report combined with an increased workload would put Mr. Powers behind her and let Goddess fade away to a distant memory. Premonitions of personal and professional disaster drove her, and as the hours of unbroken toil piled up, June began to fear for her boss's health and continually scolded her for overworking. Gail blithely dismissed such concerns, telling June to stop acting like an old grandmother. Now, Adam was due back this evening, and she looked forward to being in his arms, notwithstanding her dread at what he might have discovered in Rhode Island, and she was surprised to realize she did not want to know. Gail had already decided some time ago she did not want to see Michael Powers ever again, and only now did she consciously acknowledge that harsh fact. She had not heard from Fred Miller in over two weeks, and fervently hoped his lack of progress might continue. Yet, something deep inside refused to let her move on so easily.

"Gail," came June's voice. "We have a problem with Mr. Lundgren in room 27C."

"Again?"

"It's his demons—he's refusing medication and tried to pummel Mr. Kasper. He's now sedated and in straps, but he wants to see you."

Gail sighed. "Okay, I'm on my way."

When she reached Mr. Lundgren's room, he lay quietly on his bed, the sedative having already taken effect. As she stood next to the bed, his eyes opened, and he looked at her intently, surprising Gail.

"Is it your demons again, Mr. Lundgren?" she asked.

"One of them wants you."

"What?"

"One of them wants you."

"I'm afraid I don't follow you, Mr. Lundgren. Can you be more specific?"

"One of the demons came through my portals and wants you."

"Which demon is that Mr. Lundgren?"

"One I never knew before. Different." Now he seemed to be having a harder time concentrating, and his gaze became rather dull.

Gail felt a constriction in her chest. "Does this demon have a name, Mr. Lundgren?"

"Dunno. Female."

"You know I have said many times, Mr. Lundgren, that there are no demons. It is your mind playing tricks."

"She wants you."

"No, Mr. Lundgren, that is just in your mind. It is not real. Now, you must rest, and we will discuss it when you are feeling better."

Lundgren's eyes widened, panic-stricken. "No! She wants you. I saw her. Snakes, wild, demon woman, wants you. Now."

"What did this demon look like, Mr. Lundgren?"

"Snakes for hair, wild, demon woman, floating, wants you."

"Snakes?"

"Hair."

"What does she want me for?" asked Gail, now deeply shaken.

"Now." Mr. Lundgren muttered the word, then closed his eyes and fell asleep.

Gail left instructions with the attendants and went back to her office deep in thought. On the way, she was astonished to find herself in an internal dialogue with Goddess.

Look, Goddess whoever You are, You want to come after someone, come after me, not my patients.

I hope the snakes were not too much for him.

If You are really a Goddess, You must know he is already on the edge, ready to fall over into permanent psychosis. The human mind is often fragile.

Mr. Powers is the Chosen One. He is not fully human. Your diagnosis is both wrong and dangerous.

Don't give me that. You are obviously a figment of my imagination, or a suggestion of some sort.

Then why are you talking to a Goddess?

Despite herself, Gail let out a dry laugh, causing a few passing staff members to turn and look. *I want You gone.*

Many do.

I should just check myself into this institution right now for talking to an imaginary Goddess.

You checked in when you were born. Humans have turned the planet into an institution.

Look, what do You want with me?

~

"How did it go?"

June's words snapped Gail from her reverie, and she felt annoyed, thinking Goddess would have answered that last question were it not for the interruption.

"Fine."

"You've got a few patients stacked up now."

"Yup."

Gail spent the rest of the day automatically ministering to her waiting patients, but thinking all the while of seeing Adam that night. Periodically, she tried to reestablish conversation with Goddess, but never received a response.

That night, to her great disappointment, Adam called, having just returned home, and begged off meeting her until the next day, citing fatigue and a headache. Gail went to bed early, propped herself up and laid the unfinished outline in her lap, but could not focus and gave herself over to an appreciative Sigmund.

Sleep came quickly, and the absence of troubling dreams helped her feel refreshed the next morning.

When she arrived at work, Adam had still not appeared, so she busied herself with overdue paperwork. Ten o'clock came and went, and he still hadn't shown up for work. Just as she experienced the beginnings of concern, he finally rang at noon.

After the initial greetings, his voice came across as rushed.

"Meet me at lunch, our usual place."

"Now?"

"Yes."

"Okay. Is there a problem?"

He laughed. "Only if you don't believe in ghosts. Any news from our detective friend?"

The ghost comment was most assuredly not what Gail wanted to hear. "No news from Mr. Miller, but apparently you have some."

"Do I ever."

Gail's heart sank. "Your headache any better?"

"Yeah, it's fine. We have a lot to talk about."

"Hopefully more than just shop talk."

"This goes beyond shop talk."

Gail had no response to this.

"See you there," he said and hung up.

On the way to the restaurant, Gail could not help but speculate about the meaning of his words, but her meanderings led nowhere, so she put her foot down and refused to waste more mental energy chasing ghosts. Instead, she fantasized about being in bed with Adam that evening.

Gail saw him waving from a corner booth as soon as she entered, and slid easily into the booth, leaning over and giving him a kiss.

"Hi!" he said cheerfully. "So good to see you."

"Welcome home."

"Before I start," he said. "Tell me how you've been."

"Good, but I missed you."

"Ditto."

Gail decided to cut to the chase. "So, tell me about it."

Coffee came and Adam took a few sips before speaking. At last he said, "Where do I start? I rehearsed what to say, and now I . . . well, there's so much."

"Start with ghosts," Gail sighed.

"Okay. Well, first of all, I don't believe in ghosts."

"Past tense or present tense?"

"Present tense. But having said that, Gail, some very strange things happened." He paused.

Gail knew she should prod him along, but she did not want to hear about ghosts or spirits or Mr. Powers.

Aware he was on his own, Adam poured forth the entire story of his trip to the cemetery.

Gail didn't interrupt or ask any clarifying questions.

When he reached the end of his narrative, she merely said, "Interesting. What now?"

Adam appeared surprised at her lack of engagement, but replied, "Well, I still want to verify Bud Yancey's bona fides."

"Yes."

Adam peered at her. "Gail, are you even interested in this?"

"Of course."

"You don't seem to."

"I admit, when a fellow doctor—an intimate friend—starts talking about ghosts, I'm a bit skeptical. Nonetheless, I am interested to find out where this all comes from." She chuckled. "Childhood trauma in a dark closet?"

"That's great!" he snorted. "Nothing like a sympathetic ear."

"Are you going to work today?" The intent of her non sequitur could not be clearer.

"Tomorrow," he pouted.

"And your plans for tonight?" she asked lightly.

He mulled over his reply. His desire to have sex with Gail trumped his disappointment at her reaction to his news. "Tonight, I plan to be lying next to you in bed—if that works for you?"

"That works very nicely." She was fully aware of his irritation but couldn't bring herself to say anything to smooth his ruffled feathers.

Little did either of them know that their evening together would not turn out as anticipated.

~ *A Fly in the Ointment* ~

When Adam arrived at her apartment, Gail prepared a gin and tonic and handed it to him with a happy smile.

"A drink for the thirsty traveler," she said chirpily. Ever since leaving work, Gail worried that her obvious lack of interest in his trip had been too off-putting, so she was determined to make as many peace offerings as necessary to put their relationship back on track.

In response to his nod of appreciation, she said sympathetically, "Tired from your trip?"

Adam, mid-swallow, grunted his confirmation: "Hmmm." He put down his glass and gazed at her appreciatively. "This tastes good, and, I might add, you are looking very good yourself."

"Thank you."

"It's nice to be back home, although I'm not looking forward to the stack of work that awaits tomorrow."

They conversed in this light-hearted manner for some time, each adeptly navigating around the topic of Mr. Powers and the wreckage he'd left behind. Finally, after finishing off his second gin and tonic, Adam leaned forward in his chair.

"Okay, Gail—what news about your Goddess?"

Gail put down her wine glass. "Oh, nothing much. A few nightmares are all."

"Ah," sighed Adam, clearly disappointed. "That's it?"

Gail understood this cue obligated her to pursue the topic in detail, and she reluctantly acquiesced in the interest of having a more pleasant evening.

"I visited Michael Powers' house," she offered.

Adam blinked and said, "Oh?"

"Yes. On a spur of the moment whim. Mark Powers and his wife had left for the East Coast, so it represented a good opportunity."

"To do what?" Adam stared at her intently, making her a bit uncomfortable.

"I don't know. Maybe catch Mr. Powers living there on the sly. He wasn't." She knew she was lying about her motive, but hoped he would not dig deeper.

"You see anything else?" he asked.

Suddenly, the memory of Ethyl came to her as real and substantial as if she were picturing June, and the dike she had built to control the flood waters was breached. In a torrent of words, she told Adam about her conversation with Ethyl, about the old Black woman's connection to Goddess, and admitted how absurd it all sounded, acknowledging that her description of the meeting bore clear signs of psychosis—hallucination, suggestion, or whatever one wanted to call it. The rush of words would not stop, taking her off guard even as they tumbled out. Adam listened closely but made no comment and asked no questions. When she finished, he sat motionless for a moment, then took a large gulp of his drink.

"Well, and I thought you were uninterested in my story because you had concluded the whole thing is bunk."

"Quite the opposite," Gail sighed.

Adam mixed himself another drink, and refilled Gail's wine glass. "Let's return to first principles," he intoned, his words now somewhat slurred. "First principle: I do not believe in ghosts or spirits. Do you?"

"No."

"Okay, second principle: I don't believe in any god or goddess. Do you?"

"No."

Okay, third principle: find the simplest explanation for this weirdness without resorting to supernatural agents. Agreed?"

"Agreed."

"Then we must accept that this is all in our minds. True?"

"True."

"And that the nature of this mental abnormality is not supernatural, but a form of suggestion, hypnosis, or similar manipulation. Agreed?"

"Agreed."

"Now, the question is, what planted these suggestions? A person? His writings? Circumstances? Coincidence? The water?"

Gail pondered, and said, "If we seek the simplest explanation, the most reasonable hypothesis is that these suggestions were planted by a person."

"Agreed."

"And," Gail continued. "If a person, it could only be one."

"Yes. Mr. Powers, who we already suspected. So, we are back to square one."

"The writer," whispered Gail, horrified.

"What?"

"The writer—the person who puts these thoughts in our heads, these words in our mouths,"

Adam scoffed. "Gail! Not that again. We are real persons, not characters in a book." He gulped the last of his gin and tonic and stood to make another.

"I'm telling you, Adam—if we find Mr. Powers, we'll be reading about this very conversation."

"Nonsense."

"It is not nonsense. I have seen it before. I have seen it, Adam! Read his writings."

"I have. He talks to people and later fills in the details by clever conjecture."

"I know," said Gail in a defeated voice. "But still . . . sometimes I wonder."

"Gail, that idea is even more preposterous than ghosts or goblins or gods or goddesses. First principles, remember?"

"Yes, you're right."

"Damn straight," Adam slurred, a stamp of finality in his tone.

He suddenly whipped out his tam o'shanter and pulled it on his head. "Come on, Nature!" he cried. "Let us in on the joke!"

Gail stared at him in shock, but nonetheless listened.

Only silence greeted them, and Adam laughed humorlessly. "Call out your Goddess and ask *Her* the same thing," he continued.

"I think we should go to bed, Adam."

"No! I want you to call *Her*. Let's really do this spirit calling exercise right."

"Adam—"

"No, I want you to call *Her*."

"Adam—"

"Do it!" he snapped.

Gail had never seen him like this and chalked it up to the booze. She uttered a desultory, "Goddess . . . come out."

Nothing.

"That wouldn't call a hungry dog," grumbled Adam.

"Let's go to bed, Adam, and sleep on it. Perhaps we'll find inspiration tomorrow."

Adam shook his head. "I'm going back home, Gail. I need to think Nature is. . . ."

Gail blurted in surprise, "Nature? What about him?"

Adam stood a bit unsteadily. "Going home. Need to think about it. Nature. Tomorrow." He shook his head as if to clear it. "Tomorrow, I'll see you at the institute. We'll talk then."

"Adam, you can't drive like this."

"Oh yes, I can. Yes, yes. Not drunk on gin. I'm drunk on another kind of spirit."

Gail considered taking away his keys, but he was out the door before she could act.

In the window glass, her face hovered over the red smear of retreating taillights as Sigmund looped once around her ankles and purred.

Chapter Seventeen

Into the Mouth of Goddess

Moving Day

Today, I moved into the cave. My living space is a small room down a side corridor that branches off just before reaching the first iron door. My furniture, such as it is, consists of a bed, desk, chair, chest of drawers, and assorted other smaller pieces. Access to toilet and shower facilities is farther down the corridor, and a veritable maze of piping and plumbing connections is exposed, as no interior walls have yet been constructed for the bathrooms. It feels like living on a submarine, except one is surrounded by rock rather than water. My little room does have interior walls, and is comfortable enough, save for the continuous hum of air mechanically pumped throughout the cave.

I write these words at my desk, having arranged and rearranged the furniture to maximize both space and my own aesthetic proclivities. While satisfied with my living arrangements, I am assailed by wild speculations about what is to come next. I have total freedom of movement except beyond the iron doors. I may come and go as I please and have already chosen a hillside spot near the entrance to the cave where I plan to sit in the evenings and gaze at the brilliant desert night sky, unblemished by the polluting lights of town and city.

Despite my words, this rather idyllic existence is often sullied by the realization that I have nothing to do. I have worked my entire life and earned my own bread as a lawyer, enough to raise a family and send my son to Columbia University. True, since my schizophrenia worsened, I have been unable to work, but I have the uneasy feeling this cave is nothing more than another institution, where I am cared for and fed like any other inmate. I tell myself it is different here, as I am free to leave at my pleasure, whereas I know the institution still searches for me. Only the ongoing existential plights of Dr. Hess and Dr. Camara offer some solace and constitute my only relief from the fear of being found and forced to return to that place. Let me be clear, I wish them no harm.

This feeling of unproductive uselessness drives much of my desire to be Storyteller again and return to Nature and the others in that dark tunnel where my bones wait. My comrades died at the pinnacle of their strength, performing a great task, ill-conceived as it was, and will forever remain vibrant youth rather than old men dissembling about glory days long gone. As I think these idle thoughts, my mind turns to my neighbors in the cave. There are room after room lining the multitudinous corridors and hallways, yet the doors are always closed, and I have seen no one come or go. I seem to be the only tenant in a huge complex filled with empty rooms and deserted spaces.

With this depressing realization, I go to the cafeteria, a vast chamber containing dozens of tables and chairs. Again, it is devoid of people, and when I shout, "Hello!" only echoes rush to greet me. I walk past the tables and enter the kitchen where a huge space is filled with sinks and ovens and pots of all shapes and sizes. I see no one, and again call out, "Hello!"

"Hello," comes a voice, calm and authoritative.

"Buandelgereen," I reply evenly. "Are we alone?"

"No, the cave is full."

I look back toward the cafeteria. "Then where is everyone?"

"Eating."

"I don't see them."

"Of course."

"I don't understand."

"Of course."

"Well, where are they?"

"Eating."

By now, I am irate and confused, and my voice registers anger. "I don't understand!"

"Are you hungry?" she asks pleasantly.

I shake my head. "A little."

She hands me a bowl of rice gruel. "Eat."

I instinctively take the bowl and ask dully, "I don't understand."

Her eyes glimmer. "Remember your famous dinner parties, attended by a dead wife, an absent son, and your younger self?"

"Yes," I stammer.

"Think of this as that type of dinner on a grander scale . . . or, in this case, breakfast."

"You mean the cafeteria is full of ghosts?"

"This from a man who speaks with dogs and beds and rocks?" Buandelgereen snorts, "Go eat."

Duly chastised, I say, "And you? Have you eaten?"

"I've eaten. I must help the cook. Go."

I look around. "What cook?"

She glares at me in a manner clearly indicating her patience has been exhausted. "Go!"

I cannot help but get in a last word. As I walk to a table with my bowl, I say carelessly, "What if I sit on someone?"

To my great surprise, Buandelgereen chuckles and calls out, "They will let you know!"

Indeed, I try a dozen different chairs and always receive the comment, "Not here!" from some invisible patron. Dear Reader, can you imagine my perplexity? For once, I am evidently not the one hallucinating. This gives me an ironic moment of satisfaction.

I wonder if they can they see one another? Am I in the midst of a cacophony of chattering diners, yet can hear only silence and see only empty chairs?

I finally locate an empty chair and slowly eat while mulling over these questions. Perhaps I'm getting a taste of my own schizophrenic medicine. Because I cannot see or hear the people surrounding me, I feel quite normal, even smug. It can give one quite a sense of superiority to claim reality as one's own. Such is life. If I listen carefully, I think I can hear the cave emitting guttural chortles in very ancient mineral amusement.

~

But my brief moment of levity has passed and is replaced by deep loneliness. Where are my voices? My hallucinations? Goddess? I even miss crazy Temulun with her eager wisdom and unvarnished priorities. If she were here, I would gladly give her a hundred treats. But there is only silence and emptiness. Have I been buried alive in some sort of purgatory, away from both the higher world of reality and the lower world of shades where my friends dwell? If that is the case, then I want out. But out to where? I am still a fugitive. I cannot return to my home. My parents are dead. My wife is dead. My second wife was a hallucination. My friends are gone. My twin is dead. My son has betrayed me. And, it must be said, living the life of a homeless person wandering streets and alleys mumbling to himself is precisely what it is cracked up to be: horrific. I look around, hoping all these ghosts will become visible, but I remain alone. I return to the kitchen with my empty bowl, and even Buandelgereen is nowhere to be seen. It is as if some holocaust occurred, and I am the lone survivor. At least in the institution there were others to distract me. But here?

Of course, an inner voice keeps telling me that I can leave any time I want. Venture out into the world. But I reject that voice. I want to again go past the iron doors and find the connection that will lead me back to the tunnel, just as Storyteller found the connection leading him from the tunnel to my house. Lu Zhishen was on to something when he thought of dynamiting the iron doors. If I did blow them up, what then? Whatever is concealed behind the doors would be barren, as *She* would long since have traveled through the connections to other places and times.

Why bring me here? Why shelter me? Feed me? Keep me safe? Of course, I am the SON. And what of it? All of you, dear Readers, are a son or daughter. Why doesn't *She* ask you to stop all the suffering of the world? Will you help to cure God of His addiction? No. Then, why me? Look here, in moments of clarity I recognize the evidence of delusion such questions present, and I am fully cognizant of the fact that the universe is ruled not by gods or goddesses, but by Natural Law. Nevertheless, clarity is brief, and *She* is eternal. Goddess has weaned me with the milk of schizophrenia, and I am sure it must constitute some deeper truth. At least it is more nutritious than the watered-down, canned dreck you normals are raised on.

Nothing personal.

~ *Figures in the Haze* ~

Days have passed, and I spend my time wandering the empty corridors and staring longingly at the first iron door. I have met a few workers who are evidently putting the finishing touches on the interior facilities. Despite my efforts to engage them in conversation, their English is rudimentary, and in any case, they seem ill-disposed to reveal the nature of their work. They are always gone by late afternoon, and after that, I am deprived of even the small pleasure of seeing them. My food is always prepared by the mysterious cook, whom I have yet to see, and is served to me by Buandelgereen (a lowly task for one who rules a vast kingdom of ghostly apparitions).

The highlight of my waking hours comes when I go outside the cave after dinner and sit in my favorite spot, gazing in wonder at the night sky. So attuned am I to the pirouetting Milky Way and all it contains, that I think I can hear the hum of a thousand voices entering and exiting the cave in harmony with its movements, just as Buandelgereen said: a multitude of guests coming and going. From what places and times they come, I cannot know. I can only surmise they are stewarded in and out by forces behind the iron doors, which brings me back to the beginning. I must make getting past those damn barriers my ultimate goal. Indeed, it is tiresome to continually lurch from one abode to another: from the institution to Marie Telles, to the house, and then to this cave. Of course, the irony of all my scheming to escape from one place to another, to hide in one location or another and run to the next, is not lost on me. I am in the service of Goddess, yet *She* has conspired to bring me here. Regardless of my grand plans to find a way behind the iron doors, I still await *Her* pleasure, if only *She* will give it to me in plain English, stripped of riddles and intellectual dead ends. If Buandelgereen would just open the doors for me, all would be well with the world.

I am writing these words while sitting at a table in the cafeteria. Alone, of course. But just a moment ago, I heard laughter. Buandelgereen could not have made such a deep-throated, thoroughly male sound. I scan the tables and spot a barrel-chested man standing in the middle of the room. He smokes a cigar and looks at me with a disturbing grin.

"Well, well, you have been very hard to find, Mr. Powers," he says between puffs.

Something about him makes me uneasy, and I cannot believe he is one of Buandelgereen's ghosts. I'll play along.

"I've been here from the beginning," I say breezily. "Why have you waited so long to appear?"

He gives me a perplexed look, then asks, "You are Michael Powers?"

Something in his tone raises a primal fear, as it has the stench of a normal.

"Yes, and you are?"

He takes a long drag from his cigar and blows out a great cloud of smoke. "Fred Miller."

I decide to be gracious and wave my hand toward an empty chair at my table. "Have a seat, Fred."

He sits and stares, continually puffing away.

I tire of his rude behavior and conspicuously look around the cafeteria. "Are the others going to appear?"

"Others?" he asks, acting innocent. "What others?"

"They're all around. This cafeteria is full."

"Cafeteria?"

His feigned ignorance is irritating. "Yeah," I say curtly.

This gross man makes a sour face. "You're sitting on a rock in a deserted cave, Mr. Powers. So am I. You don't notice how dark it is?" He clicks off his flashlight, then quickly clicks it back on. "See?"

Now I know for sure he is a normal, and my fear redoubles. I am rendered silent by his bluntness. Perhaps he is a spy from God.

He shakes his head. "I'm here to help you, Mr. Powers."

"Can you help me get past the iron doors?" I ask as a challenge to his patently false statement.

"What?"

"The iron doors."

"I'm afraid I don't follow you, Mr. Powers." He throws down his cigar stub and grinds it into the floor. "You are sitting in a deserted cave, and with the help of a woman, a friend of yours, I was able to find you, thank God."

"So, you admit you are working for God?"

"Mr. Powers, we must leave now and get you cleaned up. Then you can rest in a nice bed."

I know he thinks I'm crazy, and my facial expression, I am sure, does not help my cause. He sighs the way only normals can do, in that exasperated way that signals their inability to penetrate our delusions. While thinking these thoughts, he puts his hands on his knees and leans toward me.

"Do you understand me, Mr. Powers?"

I look at him dubiously. "Of course, Mr. Miller. Do you want to eat something? The kitchen is over there." I figure being polite is never a bad idea.

Unfortunately, it turns out to have been a bad idea, for it seems to make him impatient.

He grunts in disgust and says, "Mr. Powers, I am here to take you back."

These words strike me to the core, and I ask a question I already know the answer to. "Take me back to where?"

"I believe you know, Mr. Powers. You can't stay here, and at the institution you will receive the help you need."

I look around, hoping to see Buandelgereen with her rifle to chase this spy away, but she is nowhere in sight. From down the corridor came a single metallic ping, like a key touching a ring; then silence.

Her absence is quite suspicious, and I ask Mr. Miller, "Where is Buandelgereen? What have you done with her?"

"The Mongol woman told me where you are."

This really hits me hard, but I find solace in the knowledge that this man is lying. To drive the point home, I say in a very calm and reasoned voice, "You're lying."

"She is waiting outside the cave."

I have the presence of mind to play the game, so I say, "Send her in so I can talk to her."

The barrel-chested man stands up. "Sorry, Mr. Powers. We must go now. If you refuse, I will call for help from the local authorities."

I stand up and look at him in my most regal pose. "I am a Vietnam veteran, Mr. Miller." I hope this will impress him.

"Yes, I know," is all he says in reply.

"And a lawyer, licensed to practice in this state," I add, hoping this will scare him.

"I know. Now, let's go." He holds out his hand as if I were a child to be led to his room.

I sit back on the chair. "No. I'm comfortable here, and my food has not come. Are you sure you won't join me?"

"No, Mr. Powers, we have to leave."

"Just a bite?"

He gets all puffed up. "Now, Mr. Powers!"

I see that my intransigence is getting to him, and this gives me some pleasure. I notice he keeps looking toward the cafeteria entrance, and I am certain other normals are on their way. My only chance is to make it to the iron doors and hope Buandelgereen has unlocked them so that I might escape. Surely, she and Goddess want me to escape, and I can run into the first connection I come to. Who knows where it will take me, but I know it will be far away in both space and time. Nevertheless, I assess my chances as slim, because though he may be fat, Mr. Miller is younger than me. But I must try.

Wish me luck, dear Reader.

~ *Incarceration* ~

As you can guess, I failed to evade capture, and I am now sitting disconsolately on my bed at the institution.

As I recall, boots hammered stone; a cone of light blinded me; something hissed cold into my arm; the cave tilted and spilled me here.

Although the medication fogs my mind, I am still sharp enough to write these words. Buandelgereen just left, advising me to be patient. Her white hair and ageless Mongol face seem placid, accepting of my incarceration. I have not yet seen Dr. Hess or Dr. Camara, but my anger is at a boil, and I have every intention of working closely with Nature and Goddess to punish them. Please bear in mind, dear Reader, I say "punish" not "destroy." If war has taught me anything, it has taught me the true cost of destruction. Even as a young soldier, I had the sense to realize that those we sought to kill were us, and we were them. The judgment of history might fall on one side as easily as the other, even while our leaders cast us in the role of executioners without the solace of knowing the men we killed had been judged guilty of any crime.

As I've aged, whatever lion I imagined in me has gone quiet. The testosterone script still rattles in the bones, but the lines no longer fit the mouth. Schizophrenia may have loosened a few bolts, but age did the rest. I cry at things I once would have mocked: a headline, a loyal dog, an old song at a stoplight. The younger Michael would have shrugged and called it life. If that is "demasculinizing," then it is the one disorder I refuse to treat. Now, I must prepare for meetings with Dr. Hess and her partner-in-crime, Dr. Camara. It is imperative that I reach the connection and return to where I belong. To achieve this, I must let Storyteller return and take me over. I must seek help from Nature and the others. No more will I try to satisfy the whims of Goddess, who, in *Her* haughty riddles, has laid me low. Suffering continues around the world, and my birth has done nothing to alleviate the scale of such unhappiness. The sacrifices of mother and father have been in vain, and their tragic quest to find *Her* turned to dust. What else is left for me but to go back?

~

There is the Reunion.
Goddess! Thank you for speaking. I have already experienced one Reunion, and that is enough.
At that Reunion, you made a grave mistake.
Yes, I turned my M-16 on You—not on God.
That was not your mistake.
Is this another riddle, or are You going to enlighten me?
What you call riddles are merely the language of the Universe. Let Me be clear: your mistake was not in turning your M-16 on Me and not on God. No, your mistake was in not turning your M-16 on both of Us. Is that clear enough for you?
If I kill You both—what is left?
Everything. As of now, you have nothing but two imaginary deities, which amounts to nothing.
If You are just imaginary—a hallucination, as they would call it here—then what is the point of following Your directions?
If you kill only one of Us, the other will always remain with you. That way leads to madness. That is the path taken by most humans, which you are

most assuredly not. You are the Chosen One, an intermediate, and you must find the other Chosen One and have a child, whose powers will far surpass yours.

What powers? All I have in the way of power is nothing but hallucinations and delusions.

You do not know it, but your unfortunate symptoms and misinterpretations of metaphorical God and Goddess are the side effects of powers you are not yet aware of.

I will ask again: and if I kill you both?

Liberation.

I don't understand how any of this craziness will lead to the salvation of the planet and the death of the human race. How will that end suffering?

It will stop the addiction to suffering.

By stopping the desire for eternal life?

By stopping desire for desire.

Then I will be with my friends and dwell in stillness?

If that is your conception of stillness.

I am tired. I am sick. I am lonely. I just want to go home. I am no powerful Chosen One. I'm just a lowly mental patient.

Another Reunion.

Must I go?

You must.

In the tunnel?

Yes.

How do I get there? You did not protect me, and I am again behind an iron door, but this one is guarded by normals whose blindness makes the door even more formidable.

No response.

~

She would speak no more, despite my entreaties. I call for God to ask *Him* for a rebuttal, but, as usual, *He* does not respond. Perhaps *He* is in a coital haze over the latest atrocity that occurred somewhere in the world. What to do? Naturally, I will go to the Reunion. To get there, I must go through Dr. Hess and Dr. Camara. I can only hope they will be pliable once Nature and Goddess have done what is necessary.

Chapter Eighteen

What To Do with Him?

The Shock

The morning after her aborted evening with Adam Camara, Gail Hess received a phone call from Fred Miller informing her that Mr. Powers had been found and was being transported back to the institution. The call sent shockwaves through her body, and she could not tease out joy from sorrow, happiness from disappointment; it all formed a mash that muddled her mind. Up to this point in her life, Gail felt proud of all she had accomplished, particularly the recognition from the psychiatric community for her research after the long struggle to earn her doctorate. To achieve these goals, she had gladly sacrificed much of her personal life in exchange for the excitement of working on the cutting edge of neuroscience. Many of her more traditional colleagues sang her praises, and secretly wondered when a husband and children would add a satisfying coda to her full life. Aware of these mostly unspoken questions, Gail felt proud and grateful to have found enough fulfillment in her work without succumbing to the distractions of a boisterous family, and she remained unapologetically independent. Now she faced a challenge that stretched her talents to the limit, and presented the likelihood of catastrophic failure encompassing both her professional and personal life. It was at this existential moment that she needed Adam Camara the most, not as a solution, but as a sounding board for her trials.

Gail realized that Adam Camara himself was embroiled in his own existential crisis, and the collision of two parties in the midst of such fundamental disruptions could bode no good for either. Worse, that which threatened his own identity rose from the same source as her own demons, making cooperation an impossibility. Or so she had thought. But, as she mulled over these complications in her office, the revelation that Michael Powers was returning made her reevaluate her fearful conclusions. *Actually,* she thought, *the fact that Adam and I are in the same boat makes our cooperation essential. Divide and conquer must not be allowed!*

With this idea in mind, Gail immediately called June, informed her of the latest, and asked her to summon Dr. Camara. She would not allow her doubts to destroy her relationship with Adam. If anything, this news would strengthen their bond, and together they would fight Michael Powers and whatever spell, magic or otherwise, he held over them. Their unified front would succeed, and ultimately lead to a more permanent and satisfying camaraderie. In the best-case scenario, they would publish their findings about the complicated Mr. Powers, close the case, continue with their rewarding careers, and let their personal relationship lead where it may without sinister gothic melodrama dragging it to ruin.

After overcoming his initial shock, Adam Camara looked at Gail and asked, "When does he arrive?"

"This afternoon."

"I can't believe it . . . I mean—I had almost written him off. Where was he found?"

Gail provided him with the few details she knew from Fred Miller, ending her narrative with the comment, "Interesting that he was found in a cave."

"Yes, I seem to remember something about a cave in his writings."

Gail grimaced. "You need to go back and read everything more carefully. You know, his parents were living in a cave in Mongolia for a time, while searching for *Her*. It can't be a coincidence."

"I admit I focused only on the Vietnam parts. Wow—for a man dealing with his own demons, he takes on the demons that plagued his parents as well? Psychological Armageddon at its most extreme."

Gail looked grim. "Same demons, Adam. Same demons."

"Well, what is your plan when he arrives?"

"Our plan, Adam. Our plan. We are together in this case, are we not?"

Adam blinked. "Yes, of course."

"A dead soldier and a mythical Goddess have given us no choice."

"True."

Gail decided to be brutally honest. "Adam, what do you plan to do about Nature? How do you plan to fight this?"

He shrugged. "Same thing you plan to do about his Goddess."

"Which is?"

"You tell me."

"I've thought about this, and I have an idea that might work."

"Okay, shoot."

"We will switch roles. I will explore Mr. Powers's relationship with Nature while you explore his relationship with Goddess. Call it cross-fertilization."

Adam sat up, appearing more interested. "Yes, I need to know more about Nature . . . and you, of course, about Goddess. I like your idea. It might take him off guard. We must interview him separately, but in a coordinated fashion."

"Agreed. What's more, I think we should be bold and unorthodox in our therapy."

Adam smiled. "That means you are going topless again, are you?"

"If that is what it takes," replied Gail firmly. "I think we should let him stew in his own juices for a while before we interview him. Give him medication and stay away for a few days."

Adam frowned. "What about your idea that we're characters in his writings? According to your theory, doesn't he already know what our strategy is, because we are merely figments of his delusions? Isn't that what you think?" Adam spoke these last words with an accusatory tone.

"No, I do not think that. I was merely offering a variety of speculations. I believe we are real, we are psychiatrists, and it is our responsibility to him that we find a way to help. Nonetheless, what makes this case different is the fact that by helping him we will be helping ourselves. So much the better."

"Okay, but—"

Gail leaned forward in her chair for emphasis and interrupted Adam. "However, know this, Adam, our words will be in his future writings. Look around. Do you see him? No. So, how does he know what we are saying as I speak? That is a mystery on par with your ghost of Nature, and it is the one phenomenon that scares me the most."

Adam sighed. "Before I went to Providence, I would have responded by saying he merely pieced together his knowledge of events and was somehow able to recreate or reconstruct our conversations and our thoughts. After all, he is an experienced lawyer and a damn perceptive schizophrenic. But, having spoken with Nature in that Rhode Island cemetery, regardless of whether my experience involved a real ghost or merely a figment of my imagination, I am not prepared to dismiss your idea entirely. Gail, we must let science lead us where it may, based on evidence, not metaphysical suppositions, and supernatural speculations. Seriously considering your hypothesis leads to madness."

"Yes, I agree. Let me reiterate, Adam"—she rolled her neck and took a deep breath—"I know we are real, but the difficulty is separating out the real from the unreal which evidently propagates from his mind into the minds of others. I suppose his psychosis likely provides the same charismatic basis used by cult leaders and religious mystics."

Adam produced his tam o'shanter and pulled it at a jaunty angle on his head. "After all, if I am to be nothing more than a character in a novel, at least let me be interesting!"

Gail smiled in spite of herself. "Sometimes, Adam, your juvenile humor is really too much."

"Apparently, Nature and I were alike in many ways."

"Are?"

"Okay—he was like me in many ways."

"How so?"

"Humor, kindness, tam o'shanter, curly hair and, of course, quite handsome."

Gail gave him a skeptical look. "And poetry, Adam?"

"Okay, I'm working on that."

"Seriously, Adam—I must be here when Mr. Powers arrives, but I will say very little and have him taken to his room immediately. Attendants can make him comfortable and administer medication while I inform his son. In the meantime, we need to meet and plan how we are to approach the interviews with him."

"Yes, tonight, your place," he replied. "Sorry we were interrupted last night, but this Nature thing. . . . "

"I understand. Now, I think what we should do is each write a synopsis of the strategy we want the other to use. What questions do you want me to ask about Nature, what questions do I want you to ask about Goddess. Does that make sense?"

"Perfect sense."

"If we can catch him off guard, he might slip and reveal some aspect of his psychosis we have not explored."

"Give me a break—he's an ocean of psychoses! Do we really need to find more? We already have an abundance of . . . symptoms."

"True."

Adam frowned. "Yet, if we dive too deep, we ourselves might drown in his troubled sea."

Gail reached out and took his hand. "Adam, together we can crack this case. After that. . . . "

"After that?"

"Maybe we can have a normal relationship without all this drama."

"Gail," said Adam gravely. "Drama and all its manifestations are the symptoms—the observable lesions if you will—of the mentally ill, and we must seek them out to find the underlying causes. You may very well play the role of Goddess and I of Nature in order to get under his skin and probe around to find the malignancy, but it will be pure drama, and any unorthodox treatment may be very dangerous."

"As long as we know they are only roles, Adam."

~ *The First Interview* ~

Gail decided to interview Mr. Powers in a small conference room separate from her office. Her plan was to keep it short and to the point. She would avoid how he ended up in the cave and instead plant the first seeds of doubt in his mind about where her line of questioning would lead.

"Hello, Mr. Powers, so good to see you again."

"Thanks, I guess, except I don't want to be here, nor does Goddess want you to keep me here."

Gail kept her face poker-still. "Mr. Powers, tell me about Nature."

Michael Powers, to her satisfaction, appeared a bit startled. "Aren't you going to ask me about the cave?"

"No, I am more interested in Nature."

Mr. Powers chuckled knowingly. "You'll have to ask Dr. Camara about Nature."

"No, I am asking you. After all, he was your best friend in Vietnam, wasn't he?"

"Yes."

"How did you feel about his death in the ambush?"

"We have already discussed this."

"Yes, but I do have a few more questions about it. Did his death affect you more than the others?"

"Will the death of Dr. Adam Camara affect you more than the others?"

"You know," she continued casually, ignoring his attempt at deflection, "some would call Nature a coward."

Michael Powers flinched, his face turned red, and he appeared about to jump out of his chair. Gail watched in fascination as he seemed to listen to some inner voice, and almost immediately calmed, even smiling as he gave his answer. "Very clever, Dr. Hess. It is my turn to play this game and ask you why you say that? So, let's play. Why do you say that, Dr. Hess?" An exaggerated expression of curiosity lit up his face, and he tilted his head quizzically to add to the farce.

"You may find it amusing, Mr. Powers, but I have learned that the Army inquiry into that ambush raised the issue of cowardice on the part of your comrades who left you alone in that tunnel."

"I wasn't alone."

"Sorry, alone with an unconscious Idaho."

"Nature was no coward, unlike you, Dr. Hess. And that is a fact."

"But we are not speaking about me, Mr. Powers. Did his cowardice cause you much grief?"

"Ah! Objection! Introducing facts not in evidence. The Army never found any evidence of cowardice on the part of my comrades."

"How do you know?"

"Because they never asked me whether I thought they were cowards, and I would be the only one to know."

"Come, Mr. Powers, you know that is not correct."

Mr. Powers put his elbows on the table and made a tent of his fingers. "Dr. Hess, this line of questioning is a red herring. You have no interest in Nature, except insofar as he affects your precious lover. What does any of this nonsense have to do with my schizophrenia?"

"Perhaps, Mr. Powers, you developed your psychosis when you realized you had been abandoned by those you loved in Vietnam, just as you had been abandoned by your father and mother."

"I will not rise to this bait, Dr. Hess. My father and mother did not abandon me, as you well know. However, your theory is interesting, as there is some truth in it, although not of the type you are implying."

"What truth?"

Michael laughed. "Dr. Hess, for that I must speak with Goddess."

"Why? To see my breasts again?"

Michael leapt up and banged his fist on the table shouting, "No! For you to see the truth, Goddess, the truth! The crazy man with his portals was right, *She* wants to see you!"

Gail instinctively fell backward in her chair and grabbed the edge of the table to keep herself from tipping over.

Michael continued to rant. "*She* wants you, Dr. Hess! Take my word for it, *She* will get what *She* wants, even if God objects! You have clumsily and inadvertently touched upon some truth regarding me. Pursue it! Go with *Her*!"

As he screamed these nonsensical words, she calmly watched attendants rush into the room and forcibly remove Mr. Powers. In the midst of projecting a calm demeanor, she found herself exclaiming, "Careful! Be careful with him! He is not violent!"

Bombarded with concerned inquiries about her well-being, she relaxed her grip and repeatedly muttered, "I'm fine. How did this happen? I'm fine. How did this happen?"

Once the uproar died down, Gail smoothed her lab coat and continued to assure the attendants she was fine. After receiving sufficient confirmation, they left and she returned to her office, instructing a nurse to administer a sedative to Mr. Powers.

~

Later that afternoon, she sat in her office with Adam discussing the interview. In her recitation of events, she could not help regaling him with self-impugning comments about her performance.

"How could I have been so foolish?!" she exclaimed. "I seem to have played right into his hands—or those of Goddess. At the end, we were on *Her* instead of Nature."

Adam, inwardly feeling he would do better when his turn to interview Mr. Powers came, did his best to console her.

"Gail, you did all you could. After all, you cannot expect to control the words that come out of his psychotic mind. This may have been a real breakthrough."

She refused to be mollified. "Adam, I am a psychiatrist, and it is up to me to guide the discussion into areas useful to me—not to my patient."

Adam smiled in the manner so infuriating to her. "I hope you heard what you just said. If we follow what's useful to him, we may find what's useful to us."

Gail cringed inwardly, but knew he was right and changed the subject.

"When do you interview him?"

"Two days."

She managed a self-serving comment that made her feel a bit better.

"Well, discussing Goddess will certainly be easier than delving into Nature."

Again, his smile. "Yes."

Gail considered making a snide remark about his superior attitude, but decided against it. Adam Camara was the only person aware of the immensity of her (and his) problem, and she wanted his support, painful as it was to admit.

"Will I see you tonight?" she asked.

Adam's rather patronizing smile melted away to reveal a genuine grin, his face beaming with both joy and relief. "Yes, absolutely! We have unfinished business, both professional and personal."

This tendency of his to morph from condescending man to mischievous boy made him both ingratiating and insufferable to Gail, causing her to always be on edge yet fully alive when in his company. His response made her heart flutter and she found to her surprise how much he had ignited her long-repressed libido.

"Good. I'll make dinner," she smiled.

At that moment, it seemed the return of Mr. Powers actually brought them closer together and pushed the specters of Nature and Goddess aside.

~ *The Second Interview* ~

Gail and Adam enjoyed two days of uninterrupted work and pleasure. They were not bothered by voices or ghosts or any reminder of Michael Powers. By the day of Adam Camara's scheduled interview with Mr. Powers, they had both cautiously agreed a corner had been turned.

~

(Dear Reader, you and I both know that could not be allowed to happen. Nonetheless, the beginning of the interview did not go as I planned. Dr. Camara is clever.)

~

When Adam sat down with Mr. Powers, he had mapped out a strategy that he thought might prove fruitful. He would focus on Goddess by confronting the patient with his delusion about Dr. Hess being somehow possessed by *Her*. Michael Powers was escorted into the same meeting room where he and Dr. Hess had met.

"Hello, Mr. Powers," said Adam rising to shake his hand. "So good to see you again."

"Sure, Doc."

"I would like to discuss a few things with you regarding the Goddess, if that is okay with you?"

"As I have pointed out to Dr. Hess many times, *She* is not *the* Goddess, *She* is simply Goddess. Do you call God *the* God? No, just God. Anyway, moving on, how is Nature?"

Expecting this, Adam coolly replied, "It is not Nature I want to discuss today, Michael. It is Goddess and Dr. Hess."

"I see. Both have beautiful breasts."

"Well, that is one of the subjects I want to discuss. First of all, do you believe Dr. Hess is somehow connected to Goddess?"

"At the hip."

"How so?"

"Both have beautiful breasts."

"Come, Mr. Powers. We both know you are not playing straight with me. I believe you know the meaning of my question."

"Which is?"

"Do you believe Dr. Hess is somehow connected to Goddess?"

"Do you believe you are somehow connected to Nature?"

"That is not my question."

"It is mine. Answer me first, then I'll answer you."

Adam laughed as if in on a little joke. "You know we psychiatrists prefer to ask questions rather than to answer them. I am here to help you, Mr. Powers. You do have schizophrenia, which you acknowledge is accurate, correct?"

"Indubitably."

"So?"

"Answer me first—I am very interested, as a schizophrenic, whether you believe you are somehow connected to Nature?"

"If I answer, will you answer my question?"

"Indubitably."

Adam cleared his throat. "No, I do not believe I am somehow connected to Nature, except insofar as he is a major character in your history and has played some role in your psychosis."

"Why did you travel to a cemetery in Rhode Island, if not to make a connection with Nature?"

"I have answered your question, Mr. Powers, now you must answer mine."

"Dr. Camara, war has ruined me."

"How do you mean?"

"The war—Vietnam—the killing—the horror—all that shit has ruined me."

Adam Camara was waiting for deflection by Mr. Powers, and he had prepared responses to many different topics that deflection might take, including the war in Vietnam.

"No, Mr. Powers, war provided the excuse for you to ruin yourself. War removed all impediments to expressing the worst in you, rather than nurturing the honest struggle to express the best."

Michael settled back in his seat, taken off guard by this response. "Very good," he muttered. "So, Dr. Camara, do you think the war ruined Nature, or merely removed the excuse for him to continue living?"

"I don't follow."

"You said I ruined myself, not the war. Now, Nature is trying to reach me through you, so that I may return. Given your theory, wouldn't it be better for me to return before I ruined myself?"

While Dr. Camara struggled to find an answer, Michael continued. "Nature is possessing you so that I might return. Once he has succeeded, you—meaning Nature—will take me to the connection."

"Mr. Powers, that is very foolish of you, and I think you know better than to believe such a thing."

"Look at your hands, Nature."

Adam involuntarily looked at his hands which were resting on the table. They were shaking.

"This interview is over, Dr. Camara. I want to talk to Nature."

Adam tried to speak, but his trembling hands continued to mesmerize him.

"I want to talk to Nature. How did it feel, out there in the jungle, ambushed, dying? How did it feel, Nature?"

Adam stood and forced himself to speak calmly, holding his hands together tightly. "Mr. Powers, we need to stick to the topic. I want to know about your view of the relationship between Dr. Hess and your Goddess."

Michael simply stared at Dr. Camara's hands. "He's going to succeed, Doc. The process has already begun. His spirit is not limited to that grave in Providence, it is inside you, and it wants to express itself. It wants you because it wants me."

Adam forced himself back to his preplanned topic. "Dr. Hess and Goddess, what about them?"

"Same as you and Nature."

"Why does Goddess want to possess Dr. Hess?"

"Possess is not the right word. It is for you and Nature, but it's not for Dr. Hess and Goddess."

"How so?"

"Goddesses do not possess."

"What do they do?"

"Dominate."

"Does *She* dominate you?"

"In a manner of speaking, *She* created me."

"How?"

"You can read."

"Yes, I've read your stories. But, Michael, they are part truth and part figments of your illness."

"Can you tell which is true and which is 'a figment of my illness'?"

"That is the entire nature of your illness, Mr. Powers. It is the inability to tell the difference."

"That does not answer my question, Doc. Can you tell which is which?"

"I think so. Goddesses, Gods, spirits, ghosts, magic statues—none of them are true. Our job here is to tease out the truth from the . . . delusions. Perhaps a better way to put it is that we are here to help you recognize fiction from non-fiction."

"Clever, but wrong. Your job here is to keep yourself and Dr. Hess from traveling the same road I already have. Nature made it clear to you at the cemetery, but you have not yet accepted it."

"Accept what?"

"Either both of you are delusional, or there is something else going on—something neither of you can explain. If you insist on this absurd notion that I'm planting 'suggestions' in your minds, you will never get to the truth. Using your own words, you will never distinguish fact from fiction."

Adam sat back in his chair, stunned. As far as he knew, neither he nor Gail had mentioned the concept of 'suggestions' to Mr. Powers. He continued to hold his hands tightly together, as if in prayer, and strove to maintain an even tone in his voice.

"We are off the subject, Mr. Powers. Let's get back to Dr. Hess and Goddess. Please explain this relationship as you see it."

"Let's get back to Dr. Camara and Nature. Please explain this relationship as you see it."

"Mr. Powers, I'm afraid we're not making much progress."

Michael gestured toward Camara's tightly clasped hands. "I'm afraid you're not making much progress, Doc."

Adam put his hands under the table. "Why don't we try this another day, Mr. Powers? It is clear you are not taking our conversation seriously."

"You seem quite put out, Doc. We can keep going if you want. I'm having fun."

Adam forced a smile. "I'm glad, but I do have other patients—clients, if you prefer."

"Can they tell fact from fiction?"

"Most of them are very cooperative. They understand that we are trying to help them overcome their illnesses. The other patients are grateful for our care and attention."

"The other patients needing the most attention are Dr. Hess and you, Doc."

"I think not, Mr. Powers."

"I think so, Dr. Camara. Soon, in these interviews, I will be talking with Nature."

~ *Debriefing* ~

That evening, over dinner at Gail's apartment, Adam recounted the interview. Unlike Gail, his personality wouldn't admit to egregious error, so he framed his summary in neutral terms to preserve what little confidence he had left in handling Michael Powers professionally.

After giving her a brief summary, he admitted, "Gail, I don't think I achieved much in the interview. He is clearly well-versed in the art of testimony, both on direct and on cross-examination."

"Yes, he can be very elusive. But, as you said, our job is to find the cracks and crevices where deeper issues lie hidden."

The reminder of his own superior words smarted, but he kept an even keel, and said, "I do think I found some of those cracks and crevices, Gail."

She took a sip of wine. "And?"

"Well, for example . . . I don't know . . . his take on Goddess and Nature as they pertain to you and me."

"Yes?"

He shook his head and took a sip of his gin and tonic. "For example, how could he know about 'suggestions' being planted in our minds? Are you sure you didn't mention that to him in the past?"

"Quite sure. That is a topic I would never have raised with him. How about you? Might you have forgotten mentioning it? A slip of the tongue?"

"Absolutely not!"

Gail refilled her wine glass and sat silently for a moment. She crossed her legs and leaned forward in her chair. "Adam, tell me how his words affected you."

"What do you mean?"

"I mean, did he get to you? Did you get angry or irritated?"

Adam avoided mentioning his shaking hands. "Not that I recall. True, his constant deflections are irritating, but I think I kept my cool."

"Are you sure?" she pressed.

"Of course, why?"

"Because your hands are shaking, Adam. You didn't notice?"

He stared at his hands, trembling enough that he was afraid he might not be able to pick up his drink.

"We must stay away from him, Adam. At least for the short term. Being near him magnifies our risk."

"Yes, yes." Adam shook his hands in frustration. "This is crazy!"

"I agree," said Gail. "This situation is crazy, but are we crazy?"

Adam managed a weak laugh. "We may be crazy, but at least we're crazy together. Let's go to bed and break the springs together."

Gail smiled and lifted her wine glass. "Like crazy people!"

Chapter Nineteen

Mind Games, Chess Matches

Who Rules Here?

You may wonder, dear Reader, who rules here? I mean, who or what is the real force behind the Moving Finger that writes these words? Goddess? *Her*? God? The Precious Object? Buandelgereen? Nature? Or, perhaps, me. Ha ha, that is the question I'd like answered. I have asked the tiles in this room, and they are utterly clueless. My bed only groans, and the chairs huddle close together, evidently involved in a conspiracy of silence; they do not speak to me and only wince when I come near. In fact, their apparent fear makes me sit almost exclusively on the bed. Joe is no longer working here, fired on suspicion of helping me escape. I feel bad about that. I would advise him to sue, but he is already gone, and he was only an at-will employee anyway. There might be a racial angle to pursue in court, but it doesn't matter, he is gone. My new attendants are monosyllabic, obviously having been warned off about conversing with me. I got word that my son and his wife will visit as soon as possible. Perhaps I can convince Mark to get me out of here, assuming he isn't possessed by Sergeant Dam anymore. However, his wife is certainly a bridge to the figures who touched my past—Tuyet Mai, Han Tinh, Captain Tong. Ah! What to do? What to do?

The other day, I shouted at the ceiling, "Who rules here?!" You can guess there was no response (except the displeased grunt of the ceiling itself, unhappy I threw unaccustomed sound waves in its direction). Buandelgereen said she would return, but I have not seen her. Speaking of fact or fiction, is that great Mongol woman real, dear Reader? Although I know I have the upper hand over Drs. Hess and Camara, they have succeeded in planting doubts in my mind. It's natural selection. Between them and me, it is a race to see who adapts first—whose genes will mutate first to give that one crucial survival edge? Nature (aptly named) must succeed in possessing Dr. Camara. Goddess must succeed in dominating Dr. Hess. Their success will be my success. The doctors have an alliance with each other to fight against their fate, and I have deities and ghosts on my side. Who will win? Ah, fate starves at probability's door.

~

A few days have passed since I wrote the words above, and I have cooled down somewhat. I can think more rationally now, and my planning skills center on finding a way to the connection. Neither Hess nor Camara has bothered to contact me since their last interviews, and I am getting restless. I am toying with the idea of breaking the logjam by requesting an interview with Dr. Hess, and sweetening the proposal with something new, something that would intrigue her. Ditto for Dr. Camara. But first, I need to ask about Buandelgereen. Unfortunately, I need to know for sure whether she is real. I know Marie Telles is real, but Buandelgereen? We'll see.

~

Over the last few days, I've sought out Mr. Lundgren of seven-portals fame. Apparently, he has been isolated and not allowed to eat in the cafeteria. But today is different. Evidently, someone decided he could be let out. He sits in the corner, as usual, talking to himself. Crazy schizophrenic! It's imperative that he and I talk, as Goddess seems to have chosen him as a medium of communication. I need to know why. I sidle up to him, very slowly, and sit with my Styrofoam coffee cup.

"Hello, Mr. Lundgren," I say as warmly as possible.

He ignores me.

"Mr. Lundgren?"

Nothing. Flat affect.

"Hello, Damien," I try again.

"Hum," he grunts, a glimmer of recognition in his eyes. "You are the one who tried to tell me your voices were more powerful than mine."

This last statement is a revelation. Okay, I'll play. "They are."

"If they were once, they aren't no more."

"What's changed?"

"A powerful lady. A powerful voice. She's the Queen of the Night."

Best not to tell him about *The Magic Flute*. "How do you know?"

"That's when she comes to me."

"At night?"

"Yeah, that's why I call her the Queen of the Night."

"What makes her powerful?"

"Her voice, her presence in my head, and she can tell the future."

"How do you know?"

"Because she said you would come and talk to me in the cafeteria, and I should talk to you. So, I asked her why. She said, 'I will rid you of the other voices.'" He waves his arms and laughs. "And here you are, as I knew you would be. I'm talking to you, aren't I?"

"Are the other voices gone?"

Damien turns glum. "She had better keep her bargain."

"Are the other voices gone?" I ask again.

"They will be, after we talk. Damn Akkadian Udugs! That was the bargain."

"Who?"

"Akkadian Udugs! Udugs!"

I shake my head, figuring I'll Google them later. "What if they're not gone?"

He gives me a look that sends chills down my spine. "Look, Michael, when she speaks, they cower into silence . . . not even a grumble. And she wants you, and she wants Dr. Hess, and she wants Dr. Camara, and she wants me . . . Lord, she wants all of us! Did she enter any of your portals yet?"

His eyes develop that crazy look, but I press him.

"What does she want all of us for?"

Damien's eyes narrow and bore into mine. "Are you one of the Old Ones?"

"I'm old, but not that old."

"Are you one of the Old Ones?!" he shouts.

I grab my coffee to keep it from spilling, as he is slowly banging on the table. "No, Damien, I'm not one of the Old Ones."

"Oh? Are you sure?"

"I'm sure. Damien, what does your voice want us all for?"

"I can't say."

"It's for your own good, Damien."

"That is a cosmic secret. She swore me to secrecy."

"Damien—" I start to say, but he is adamant.

"A secret. If I tell, she won't get rid of the voices!"

This time an attendant walks over and I tell him we are just having a lively conversation about football. Damien remains silent until the man leaves.

"Come closer," he whispers.

I lean forward, knocking over that damn cup of coffee. Fortunately, only the dregs.

"She has an enemy," he says dramatically.

"Who has an enemy?"

"The Queen of the Night."

"Oh, who is the enemy?" I ask innocently, knowing full well he means God.

"You."

~ Shock ~

Dear Reader, you must surely understand my shock. Could it be, after all these years, that Goddess is my nemesis, not God? Could *She* be the cause of my father's illness? The death of my mother? My own schizophrenia? Were all of these horrors accomplished to advance the false narrative of ending God's addiction to suffering?

I must pause and consider soberly and carefully before jumping to any conclusions. Damien Lundgren is a schizophrenic, prone to bizarre conspiracy theories and crazy delusions. He most certainly is wrong about my being an enemy of Goddess. All these years of travail in service to *Her* cannot conceivably have been wasted on behalf of a traitor. I am not so gullible, am I? Surely not! I have read about those people who suffer from over-allegiance to a cause, and that when proven to be false or in error, swing wildly to its opposite with the same unquestioning zeal. I am here to tell you, dear Reader, I am not so fickle.

These thoughts pass through my mind as I continue to sit at the table with Damien. I clean up the spilled coffee and get a fresh cup, but haven't taken a sip, and it's getting cold. My foam cup squeaks foam protests that I will not drink and mercifully relieve it of its uncomfortable, bloated feeling. I decide to question Damien a bit more, though he no longer has much credibility. As I am about to speak, I notice he is staring vacantly off into the distance. It is an unmistakable sign that the voices are speaking. Or one voice. Take my word for it.

"Damien," I say softly.

He does not respond.

"Damien!" I am more insistent.

"What?"

"Focus."

"What?"

"Who am I?"

He laughs. "You are *Her* enemy, and I am talking to you."

"Is *She* talking to you now?"

"Of course. Leave me alone!"

"What is *She* saying?"

He waves his arm dismissively. "Leave me alone!"

"Damien, what is *She* saying?"

But it is no good. He is beyond reach now. He just sits and mumbles to himself, vacant look once again on his face. I know when to quit.

Therefore, I have returned to my room (accompanied by an aloof attendant who promptly locked me in) and now sit in contemplation. I feel deathly tired . . . and old. I want to turn myself over to Storyteller in the tunnel. No more Goddess, God, talking dogs, or anyone. Just rest in the dark. But how? I will not commit suicide, as I believe that will cut me off from everything we struggled for in Vietnam. What was that? Life, dear Reader, life!

If that is true, you may ask, you're not even that old. Why do you want to return to stillness? Because stillness is not stillness. My bones, Nature, my comrades, all inhabit stillness, which is not really stillness. Just as physicists tell us virtual particles pop in and out of existence throughout the universe, so too do my ghosts and demons. So, don't you see, I am like a virtual particle. *She* allowed me to pop into existence from the nothingness of the tunnel at the beginning of this bloody story, and I have dwelt among you, the living, all this time. Look what it has gotten me! From the perspective of Dr. Hess, I was curled in a fetal position, locked in a coma or trance. From my perspective, I was tucked away nice and cozy in a dark tunnel, having re-inhabited my bones, glorying in the company of my dead friends. Well, my sojourn among you normals has not been so pleasant, and *She's* jerked me around once too often. I shall return, as General MacArthur famously said, and I won't have to make a show of wading through water to get there. Question is, how? How? How?

~

You will stay among these people until I give you further direction.

"Goddess! I am not playing that game anymore. *You* are merely a hallucination. A schizophrenic voice. And, worse, apparently my enemy all these years! Besides, I thought *You* wanted me to turn my M-16 on both *You* and God."

You will stay.

"Damien Lundgren told me—"

I gave him a story merely to get to you.

"Yes, really? I mean, Queen of the Night? Been listening to Mozart? *You* can do better than that. Besides, *You* can talk to me any time you want, even if I don't want *You* to."

You will stay.

"Why?"

The Reunion.

"That again? I am not listening. I thought finding a mate was more important than *Your* stupid reunions."

I am sending You a visitor. You will receive him and listen.

"Who?"

He will visit soon, and you will receive him and listen.

"No. *You* are my enemy!"

No. Listen to the visitor.

"No! Why should I when *You* are my enemy? I will go to God and pledge allegiance to Him."

You have been halfway there since you were born, Chosen One.

"What do You mean?"

No response, of course.

"Goddess!"

I know Dr. Hess is watching and listening to me via the security camera, but I can't help shouting again, "Goddess!"

No response.

She is infuriating. But is *She* my enemy? Perhaps God is the benevolent One, and *She*. . . . ?

~ A Visitor ~

It has been many days since I have written anything. I am so down that I have put in multiple requests to see Drs. Hess and Camara but have received no reply. I know this is their strategy, nonetheless, I am depressed. How long will it take Nature to finish his possession of Dr. Camara? And as for Goddess, what is delaying *Her* with Dr. Hess? This waiting is positively discouraging. At least, that was my mood five minutes ago. Now, it is completely changed. I have been informed I will have a visitor tomorrow, and it is not my son. Is this the visitor

Goddess promised? One can only hope. Movement, any movement, is preferable to rotting in the doldrums of this sterile trap any longer.

~

It is the day of the visit. I am waiting patiently in my little white and green room. Who could it be? If Marie Telles, I will be disappointed, not because I don't like her, but because she would be too prosaic a visitor for such anticipation. Buandelgereen? No, they would have told me. Finally, I hear a knock on my door.

"Yes?"

Keys unlocking.

"Mr. Powers?" It is an attendant.

"Yes?"

"You have visitors."

"Yes, come in, come in." *Visitors? Plural?*

To my great disappointment, my son and his wife enter. Now, don't get me wrong. I love Mark and have mostly given up that old delusion he is possessed by Sergeant Dam, and I find his wife My-duyen very sweet, but I had envisioned a visitor more . . . interesting. After all, were it not for Mark's acquiescence, I would not be here, but that is for a different time.

"Hi, Dad!" Mark exclaims chirpily as he enters and gives me a hug. His wife stands quietly behind.

"Hello, Mark," I say, trying not to communicate any disappointment in my voice. I turn to his wife and nod.

"Hello, My-duyen." I bow.

"Hello, Mr. Powers," she says demurely, bowing back.

Charming woman.

"Have a seat wherever you can find it," I say.

My-duyen sits on my one chair, which moans in pleasure under her light frame, while Mark continues to stand, claiming he prefers it. I sit on the bed, my throne, suitably unregal for this sorry paterfamilias. At least I had the foresight to put on my shirt and trousers in honor of my visitors. Wouldn't do for me to be wearing a dreary hospital gown. After a smattering of pleasantries, I grow impatient.

"So, Mark, what brings you here?"

"Well, it is always good to see you, Dad."

"Yes, and?"

To his credit, he chuckles. "You always taught me to get to the point, Dad. Must be the lawyer in you."

"Get to the point, Mark."

He chuckles again, this time self-consciously. "Dad, there is someone who wants to see you, but we"—he glances at My-duyen—"were not sure you would want to see her."

"Her?"

"Yes, My-duyen's mother."

With these simple words, it seems my heart stops beating; the universe joltingly grinds to a halt.

"You mean, Nguyen Tuyet Mai?"

"Yes, Dad." Mark looks at My-duyen. "I'm told she wants to meet you."

I look at My-duyen for confirmation. She nods.

"Yes, Mr. Powers, it is true. She is quite old and feels the ancestors calling. Her husband"—she looks down—"my father recently died."

"Han Tinh?"

"Both of my fathers have joined our ancestors, and she wants to meet the sole survivor of that old battle at the fortress."

"Why?" I ask weakly, still stunned.

"Restless spirits," she replies, then looks at Mark. "I know Americans do not believe in such things, but she is certain a particular spirit is asking her to come to America and meet with you."

"What spirit?"

My-duyen shrugs. "She will not tell me. There may be one, there may be many. My village is home to many, many restless spirits."

I can barely keep my balance on the bed. "But, my God, Tuyet Mai!"

My-duyen jumps a bit at my outburst.

"No, no, don't worry, My-duyen," I hasten to assure.

"This is my mother's first time in America. She is, well, I mean to say, she is . . . a little. . . . "

"Shy," says Mark, jumping in to help his wife.

"Funny," I say. "I don't think of Tuyet Mai as shy about anything. In fact, my dear"—I look at My-duyen to show my sincerity—"she is one of my heroes."

My-duyen replies quite solemnly, "Mother is a hero."

"Yes."

I turn to Mark. "So, tell me, Mark, when do I get to see . . . ah . . . sorry, I am at a loss for what to call her."

"Please, you may call her just Tuyet Mai," says My-duyen. "Mother is very independent and does not prefer Mrs. Nguyen, and certainly not Madame Nguyen."

Again, I turn to Mark. "So, when do I get to see Tuyet Mai?"

"If it is okay, Dad, tomorrow during visiting hours."

"Of course! Of course!" I suddenly feel a premonition, not of something dreadful, but something I cannot put my finger on.

Mark says, "She is staying with us at your house, Dad. She arrived just yesterday in San Francisco and is resting. We flew here specifically to meet her and see you."

"Ah." I turn to My-duyen. "I'm still a little confused as to why she wants to see me. Is there anything you can tell me?"

My-duyen mistakes my comment. "Oh, Mr. Powers, if you'd prefer not to see her—"

"No, no! It's not that at all. I want to see her. I look forward to seeing her."

My-duyen assumes a puzzled look. "I do not know why, Mr. Powers, but she is quite. . . . " she struggles for the right word.

"Adamant," says Mark.

"Yes, adamant," repeats My-duyen.

"Okay. Well, then . . . good." I admit, dear Reader, I'm nervous. Of course, I have written about Tuyet Mai, and I have seen her at her worst when she was a prisoner of ours in the old fortress, but to see her again is almost too much. The memories, you know.

"Dad?"

"Yes, Mark?"

"You were gone for a minute there. My-duyen and I have to go now, as we don't want to leave Tuyet Mai alone for too long."

"Yes, yes, I understand. I'll see you both tomorrow?"

Mark glances at My-duyen. "Yes, sure thing, Dad. Before we go, I think you should know that Tuyet Mai wants to see you alone . . . well, My-duyen will be there also."

"Why? I know Tuyet Mai speaks English, but does she prefer not to?"

"Oh, My-duyen will interpret for you. I'm afraid I was banished from the meeting. Something about old veterans needing to be alone with their stories."

My-duyen interposes. "Mr. Powers, it is nothing against your son, it has something to do with you in the war, the battle that happened there, that old fortress, and. . . . " she looked down.

"And?"

"The tunnel, Dad," said Mark.

Ghosts! They call!

"The tunnel?" I ask innocently.

"Yeah."

"You were in that tunnel not too long ago, Mark. Did you notice anything odd?"

"Dad, you already know about this—I told you."

"I forget. I have schizophrenia, remember?"

"It's schizophrenia, Dad, not amnesia."

"All right, all right. Let's not get into that. Besides, you have to go."

"Yes, we're already a bit late."

"But, when you were in the tunnel, Mark. Tell me."

"Dad, it's late."

I glance over at My-duyen, whose face betrays impatience to leave.

In deference to My-duyen, I stand and hold out my arms to hug Mark.

"Okay, you'd best go."

As I hug him, I am comforted by how solid he is.

No hallucination. No delusion. No Theresa. No ghost.

My son is real.

He gives me one last slap on the back and steps away.

My-duyen bows to me, and I return the bow.

After they leave, I wonder how long it will be before Dr. Hess contacts me about the visit.

~ Not Just Another Visitor ~

It is the day I'm to be visited by Tuyet Mai and, to my surprise, I have not heard from Dr. Hess. No matter, I'm nervous enough as it is. If Tuyet Mai triggers the memories before I am ready, I don't know how I'll respond. What makes her dangerous is that I know she is real. For certain, she is real. And everything real either turns up dead or is intent on locking me up. Dear Reader, I do have my moments of clarity, and I may not know whether certain things are real or not, and, in the back of my mind—my sane mind—I can catch glimmers of the difference. As I have said, Marie Telles, Dr. Hess, and Dr. Camara—these people are real. Buandelgereen is in the gray area. Mark and My-duyen are real. On the other hand, my twin is not real. My friend Paul and his family are not real. Theresa, my second wife, is not real. But, Tuyet Mai? Yes, she is real. You see, even in these moments of clarity, moments of confusion are also present. Did I hallucinate the visit of Mark and My-duyen as a preliminary to seeing a non-existent Tuyet Mai?

Knocking.

"Yes?"

"Visitors, Mr. Powers."

"Thank you."

The door opens.

My-duyen enters first and bows. Behind her comes Tuyet Mai, swinging her torso through the door with a gymnast's ease. (For those of you who do not know, Tuyet Mai lost her legs in the war.) Her hair is gray, her face lined, and she has a new set of teeth, but the depth of her great beauty shines through. Even now, she takes my breath away, and instantly, the memories come in an unstoppable flood. I bow to both and take a seat on my bed to leave the chair available. The intelligent eyes of Tuyet Mai examine my room, then she says something to her daughter in Vietnamese, whereupon My-duyen sits on the chair. Tuyet Mai moves next to her and scrutinizes my face for a long time, even as I steadily return her gaze.

"Welcome, Nguyen Tuyet Mai," I say respectfully.

"Thank you," she replies in English.

I glance at My-duyen, then turn my attention back to Tuyet Mai. "I know your English is quite good, Tuyet Mai. Perhaps we may converse in that language?"

Her face is stern, yet sorrowful. "You'll forgive me, Mr. Powers, but my daughter is better at the language, and she can pick up the subtleties of your words."

Still the clever intelligence officer, I think. "I was very sorry to hear of the loss of your husband."

Tuyet Mai blinks and responds in Vietnamese while My-duyen translates. "Ah, yes, Han Tinh was one of a kind. He is certainly making the ancestors laugh."

"What do you think of America?" I ask with genuine interest.

"Big. Noisy."

"Have you come only to visit your daughter, or do you plan to travel elsewhere in the country?"

"I didn't come to visit my daughter, though it's good to see her. I came here to visit you."

"Oh?" Now I am alarmed. What possible reason could she have to visit an old enemy? To see an American veteran in a mental hospital who she saw only briefly under horrific circumstances?

"Now that My-duyen is married to your son, we are connected by family as well as by our experience of war."

"Yes.

"Furthermore, I am finding other things connect us, Mr. Powers. My husband often told me to believe in his ghosts, but I have always resisted superstition. I am no wooden-headed peasant."

"What is it you are finding that connects us?" I ask, breathless.

Tuyet Mai's eyes bore into me. "A fortress, a tunnel, and one of your comrades."

"Nature," I whisper.

"Earth," My-duyen translates her mother's word.

"Same person," I say, feeling tears roll down my cheeks.

"He's been keeping me awake," Tuyet Mai continues. "Spirits from the tunnel hover over my village. At last, I could bear it no longer. I went back to the old fortress to ask Earth what he wanted. Of all you American soldiers, he seemed the kindest—not crazy like your Man From The Mountains or your disgusting captain!"

Tuyet Mai shakes her head and continues. "Perhaps I am a wooden-headed peasant, but I went back to that fortress and down that cursed tunnel, where your captain tried to rape me."

"And?"

For once, Tuyet Mai seems to lose her iron composure. "After going into the tunnel, I heard many terrifying things and saw many astonishing sights. As a result, I came here to rid my village of the restless spirits that haunt it and make it unbearable to sleep!"

"What can I do?" I ask, shaken by Tuyet Mai's passion.

"Your son's visit stirred them up, and they have gradually become much worse. That is the only reason I returned to that fortress, into that tunnel, and walked among those spirits."

"Spirits? I thought you only spoke with Nature?"

"I have not told you what I saw in that tunnel. I have not told you who I spoke with."

"No."

She remains silent for a long time. I am too shaken to say a word. Her presence rivets me in place, and I can only wait.

"I am told you are ill. A mental illness. Is that correct?"

I look around my room. "I must be ill; I'm locked in here."

Her eyes bore into me. "I did not ask you about *their* opinion of your mental health, I am asking *your* opinion of your mental health."

"Nguyen Tuyet Mai, I am aware of your background."

This seems to surprise her. "Which is?"

"Intelligence officer for Hanoi. I assume that is where you get your excellent interrogation technique."

I notice My-duyen blanch as she translates my words, though I know Tuyet Mai completely understands them.

"Mr. Powers, our backgrounds are not relevant to why I am here. I am here to speak with you about certain things I learned in that tunnel."

"From Nature?" I ask breathlessly.

"From Earth and from others," she says with an unspoken air of mystery.

I look at My-duyen sharply. "My-duyen, my dear, please use the name Nature instead of Earth, as they are two different words and mean two different things."

"So sorry, Mr. Powers." She speaks for a long while to her mother in Vietnamese, after which Tuyet Mai looks at me, and for the first time with a smile on her face, says, "Nature" in English. "My daughter has explained the difference in these words, and your friend is well-named. *Thiên nhiên*. Good. I will call him Nature from now on."

She enunciates these sentences in perfect English. Formidable woman.

"Tuyet Mai, what did he say to you?" I ask anxiously. "What did they say to you?"

She looks up at the security camara and shakes her head. "Mr. Powers, if I tell you, they may lock me up in here with you. I'm no *tâm thần phân liệt*."

"Schizophrenic," interjects My-duyen.

I laugh heartily. "My-duyen, you have that word down perfectly in English! Tuyet Mai, don't worry about the camera; they won't care what you say. Anyway, you're a foreign national. They won't lock you up." I look directly at the camera. "Will you, Dr. Hess?"

Tuyet Mai suddenly barks an order at her daughter in Vietnamese. My-duyen stands and bows. "We must leave now, Mr. Powers."

I am stunned. "No, you can't. I . . . I mean your mother . . . she hasn't told me what was said in the tunnel!"

"We must leave," said Tuyet Mai in English.

I jump up. "Tuyet Mai! You can't! You've only been here a few minutes!"

Her face softens. "Tell your doctors I will not speak with you until there are no camaras or microphones."

"But . . . but. . . ." I stammer. "You must tell them. They will not listen to me. I'm just a patient. Call Mark—he must tell them!"

Tuyet Mai signals me to lean close to her. Once I'm inches from her face, she whispers, "Trust me, Storyteller. I will return and speak with you."

Chapter Twenty

What World Are We In?

Another Legend

The minute Gail heard that Nguyen Tuyet Mai wanted to visit Mr. Powers, she felt intense excitement and almost unbearable curiosity. First, it was Buandelgereen, and now Nguyen Tuyet Mai. Two people from Michael's past who, in the most unlikely of circumstances, came from distant countries to visit him. Gail felt conflicted, as if she were an emotional yo-yo, first wanting to be rid of the entire Michael Powers case, and then drawn into its strangely hypnotic complexities. Her fascination was shared by Adam, and they both agreed to stick to their plan of leaving Mr. Powers alone but to continue monitoring his conversations.

On the day Tuyet Mai was scheduled to arrive at the institute, Gail made sure she was near the reception desk, surreptitiously observing this amazing woman, made famous to her in Michael's writings. Her ability to move without legs, yet display the grace and flair of an athlete impressed Gail to the core. She could easily see past the aged face and body that this woman had once been beautiful, and imagined how easily she could entrap the victims of her espionage assignments.

After watching Tuyet Mai, Mark, and My-duyen enter the elevator that would take them to Michael Powers' room, Gail rushed to her office where a monitor provided audiovisual feed of the visit. Adam promptly joined her, and they both sat in rapt attention until Tuyet Mai and My-duyen departed. Neither could hear what Tuyet Mai whispered into Michael's ear at the end, despite numerous attempts to rewind and pick up her words.

"So, Nature again," sighed Adam. "He is everywhere."

Gail noticed for the first time his pale face and fatigued look. "Are you feeling well?" she asked.

He looked at her forlornly. "Lack of sleep. What do you think?"

"Of the visit?"

"Yeah."

Gail pondered. "Well, the center of Mr. Powers' mania is the tunnel. His writings are full of incidents in the tunnel. Spirits inhabit it. Then there is Goddess, who evidently dwells in tunnels, caves, mental institutions, behind iron doors, in dark spaces—all those symbols are centered in the belly of the beast."

"Don't forget, Gail, Michael was abandoned by his comrades in a tunnel. There lies the belly of your beast."

"Absolutely. Does he subconsciously blame them for leaving him, or does he blame himself for being the sole survivor and leaving them?"

Adam shrugged. "How different is Storyteller from Michael Powers? Are they separate personalities, a sort of modified dissociative identity disorder on top of his schizophrenia?"

"Yes, I believe so. That is partly why his case is so complex and difficult to sort out."

Adam threw up his hands. "I don't understand! That doesn't explain why Buandelgereen and Nguyen Tuyet Mai would go to so much trouble to visit him! They are real people, not hallucinations!"

"Perhaps as much as we are real people," murmured Gail.

"Gail, I won't listen to that nonsense anymore. We have agreed to dismiss that thought as . . . ridiculous! I repeat, why would Buandelgereen and Tuyet Mai visit Michael Powers from such great distances?"

"Orders," said Gail.

"Orders?"

"From Goddess."

"Oh, come on, Gail! Let's try and stay away from supernatural explanations. We have gone over this before. Anyway, you don't believe there's a Goddess any more than you believe we are simply characters in his book."

"No, you are right, I don't literally believe it." She looked at him sharply and continued. "Any more than you literally believe you spoke with Nature's ghost. But, both Tuyet Mai and Buandelgereen are superstitious, despite Tuyet Mai's protestations to the contrary. Perhaps Michael is a sort of cult leader, communicating with them, giving them orders that he claims are passed through him by Goddess. In that case, they would follow him, seek him out, do what he directed them to do. How did he convince Joe to help him escape? Charisma. A cult-like charisma."

"Perhaps," said Adam doubtfully. "But, judging from that tape, Mr. Powers was taken by surprise at Tuyet Mai's visit. What's more, she seemed in control, not him."

"What did she whisper at the end?" wondered Gail.

"Whatever it was, Gail, she summoned him to come close enough to ensure privacy. He did not summon her."

"True."

"Maybe we should meet with Tuyet Mai," said Adam. "You know, let the mountain go to Muhammad."

Gail appeared startled at this suggestion and shook her head. "Maybe, but under what pretext?"

Adam smiled. "The truth. We need her help to treat Mr. Powers."

"We don't know how long she will be here, in the States, I mean."

"Easy enough to find out."

She sighed. "I did not have much luck with Buandelgereen, and Tuyet Mai looks to be a very tough nut to crack, even assuming she would agree to meet."

"One way to find out."

"I don't know," wavered Gail.

"Are you intimidated?" asked Adam with his patronizing smile.

"Yes!" exclaimed Gail. "This is no ordinary woman!"

"Nor is Buandelgereen."

"Exactly, and I got nowhere with her either."

"Then let me have a crack," said Adam. "I am quite interested in Tuyet Mai's contacts with Nature."

"You say that as if he really exists."

"He does. And so does your Goddess." He pointed to his head. "Up here, where everything exists, corporeal or spiritual."

Gail had no response to this rather metaphysical reply, and inwardly welcomed his willingness to contact Tuyet Mai. It is true she felt drawn to this woman, whose exploits in Vietnam, even considering Mr. Powers's penchant for exaggerating, were no less than harrowing and heroic. Yet, at the same time, Tuyet Mai made Gail feel inadequate and small, and the legless Vietnamese woman's steely character and powerful presence intimidated all around her. Lack of success with another larger-than-life woman, Buandelgereen, also contributed to her wariness and feeling of inadequacy.

"Go ahead, contact her. Let us see what you can get out of it."

Adam put his hand atop Gail's and said softly, "What would you like me to ask her?"

She blinked back tears. "Ask her if she has seen Goddess."

"Yes."

"I mean, if she has seen Goddess, what did they discuss?"

"Of course."

Gail sat up straight. "This Goddess figure seems to be at the center, therefore the more we learn about her the better."

Again, his smile. "Yes, of course. Anything else?"

She had a sudden impulse to withdraw from her position as Michael Powers' therapist. She wanted to tell Adam to take over the case and leave her out of the loop. He could have all the glory, all the publicity, all the kudos. Instinctively, she knew something threatened her, an unspecified existential crisis with the potential to destroy her identity, her confidence, her life. All Gail knew is that her anxiety could be traced to Goddess, and that this imaginary deity occupied the core of her fears.

"No, nothing else," she said bluntly. "I am going home early, Adam, and think a few things through. I want to meet with you tomorrow at ten o'clock if that works."

"That's fine. Are you all right?"

"No."

"Is there anything I can do?"

"Yes, I'm thinking of turning this case entirely over to you, but I need some time to make that final decision."

Adam's face registered shock. "No, no, Gail, you can't do that! I don't want you to do that!"

"I don't think I'm up to it anymore."

"Gail, please do not make that decision. You're tired, and this case presents unique complications that I can't deal with alone."

She looked at him with as steady a gaze as she could muster. "Contact Nguyen Tuyet Mai and find out everything you can."

"In the meantime?" asked Adam.

"In the meantime, neither of us meets with Mr. Powers."

"Agreed."

"Let him continue to stew," added Gail.

~ *Adam Camara and Nguyen Tuyet Mai* ~

Adam Camara could not sleep that night. He worried about Gail, he worried about calling Tuyet Mai, he worried about Nature, and he worried about his own ability to deal with his worries. A headache and the disquieting presence of Nature lurking in the background forced him to pace the kitchen for hours. The next morning, as he arrived at work, Gail called and postponed their meeting until the afternoon. After dealing with a few urgent matters concerning his patients, he resolved to sit down and call Mark Powers before seeing Gail. Closing his office door, he sat for a few moments, then telephoned Mark. With a few preliminary courtesies, he came straight to the point.

"Mr. Powers, would it be possible to meet with Nguyen Tuyet Mai?

"Why?"

"I think your mother-in-law has some insights that would help us in treating your father."

"Like what?"

"The fortress, that tunnel."

"Look, we've gone over this time and again. These things are traumatic for all of us, including Tuyet Mai, I'm sure."

"You told Dr. Hess you've been down there, Mark. You know there is something going on in that place, and it is affecting your father's brain."

"I've already told her what I know, what I experienced. Enough."

"However, Mark, the issue is that Nguyen Tuyet Mai has not told us what she knows, and that is what I think might be valuable to find out."

Mark lets out a long sigh. "When do you want to see her? She does not plan to be here much longer."

"How long?"

"A week."

"As soon as possible. I will work my schedule around her."

"What about Dr. Hess? She is the treating physician, isn't she?"

"Yes, but we work together."

"Is there something wrong?" asked Mark.

"Why do you ask?"

"Doc, I wasn't born yesterday. I know my father has been a difficult case, to say the least. And all of us, I mean all of us, have experienced weird things with his delusions and hallucinations. Sometimes, I can't help feeling liberated when a continent separates me from him. What I saw in Song Nhan village, what I heard in Song Nhan village, will never leave my head. When there is distance between me and Dad, I feel better. I know that sounds bad, but it is what it is."

"You have been very fortunate, Mark. Your grandfather suffered from schizophrenia, and so does your father. You have been spared that terrible legacy. But, with that good fortune comes responsibility. Please help us. I know you already have, but we need more help."

"I'll do what I can do, but I don't know if Tuyet Mai will agree. She does not trust . . . certain people."

"Americans?"

"Yeah. And the American government. And many other things. Her intelligence training has never really left her."

"I understand."

"I really do not think you do. Have you any experience with Vietnamese who survived the war?"

"Yes, we have some refugees who fled by boat here whose traumas have led to severe depression."

Mark spoke with irritation, producing an edge to his voice. "No, I don't mean boat people. I mean . . . oh, never mind. Anyway, let me talk with Tuyet Mai and I'll get back to you."

"Great, that is all I can ask. Just call me at the institute, and if I'm unavailable, leave a message. By the way," added Adam, "Someday I would like to explore what you just said about being liberated when you are some distance from your father."

After the call, Adam pondered the "liberation" comment, and thoughts of Gail's desire to leave the case came to mind. Perhaps distance from Mr. Powers would make troubling hallucinatory episodes like the ghost of Nature disappear, but he knew he was in the grip of something too strong to walk away from, even if Gail decided to withdraw.

The next day, Adam received a message saying Nguyen Tuyet Mai would be at the institute that afternoon, at four o'clock.

~

Tuyet Mai, My-duyen, and Adam met in a private conference room. Once everyone settled in, with My-duyen taking a chair next to her mother, who opted to stand, Adam coughed nervously, and opened the proceedings.

"Is Mark going to join us?"

"No," said Tuyet Mai in English.

"Okay, well let me start by assuring you that there are no cameras or audio-recording devices documenting this meeting unless you agree. There-fore, I must ask your permission to record what we discuss. Will that be all right with you, Tuyet Mai?"

Without waiting for her daughter to interpret, Tuyet Mai said in English, "No, it is not all right. You may ask me questions and take notes, if you must, but no recordings."

Adam nodded tentatively. "Yes, okay, that will be fine. No recordings."

"Good," said Tuyet Mai without smiling.

"I have read the writings of Mr. Powers," said Adam. "He wrote extensively about Vietnam, about the tunnel, about Song Nhan village, about the battle, well, about all of it. In fact, I have reread his words many times, but there are so many questions that need to be answered before we can make progress in his treatment."

Once My-duyen translated, Tuyet Mai looked at Adam, smiling for the first time. "I have not read these writings you speak of. My daughter and son-in-law have seen them but have not studied them in detail. From what I hear, they are mostly true."

"What parts are not true?"

"You misunderstand me, Dr. Camara, there are many details he could not include. His knowledge of my background, my experiences, the war, the village, the fortress, and my own comrades, could not have been based on his own personal knowledge."

"Yet, they are true?"

"As I said, they are mostly true, minus some details."

"And the voices he heard, Goddess and God?"

"I cannot speak for those."

"Tuyet Mai, did you ever see or hear Goddess?"

Tuyet Mai looked at Adam with a faint smile. *"Xa mặt, cách lòng."*

My-duyen stumbled over the translation when she was interrupted by Tuyet Mai, who said in perfect English, "Out of sight, out of mind."

"What do you mean?" asked Adam.

"I do not see Goddess, so She is not in my mind."

"And God?"

"Xa mặt, cách lòng," she repeated.

"Do you believe Mr. Powers sees Goddess and God?"

"They are in his mind, and rarely out of his sight."

Adam appeared agitated. "But you, Tuyet Mai, have you seen the ghost of Nature?"

"Xa mặt, cách lòng," she said once again, adding, "However, Dr. Camara, I know he is in your mind, and rarely out of your sight."

"Tuyet Mai," said Adam, picking his words carefully, "I am a psychiatrist, a scientist. I don't accept ghosts, only mechanisms of the mind that make us think we see ghosts or spirits. Nature is of interest to me because he is of importance to Mr. Powers." He leaned forward. "What was he like?"

"Nature?" asked Tuyet Mai in English.

"Yes. You did know him for a while in the fortress."

"He was kind."

"Yes, and what else?"

Tuyet Mai gave Adam a hard look that took him aback.

"I stabbed him. I killed him." She immediately swung her body around toward the door and gestured to My-duyen. "Now, we leave." She stared hard at Adam and spoke in English. "Tomorrow, at ten o'clock, I return to talk with Mr. Powers, in this room, no cameras, no tape, no doctors. I killed Nature, I must provide *sự bồi thường.*"

Adam looked at My-duyen in confusion. "My mother believes she killed Nature, and she must provide *sự bồi thường.* Restitution."

"Tuyet Mai!" exclaimed a startled Adam. "There was an explosion! Perhaps you did not—"

Tuyet Mai was already out the door, and My-duyen awkwardly twisted around to bow to Dr. Camara while she followed her mother. "Sorry, Doctor, but these questions . . . they are too much . . . she cannot."

Before he had any more time to think, the two had disappeared, leaving him alone in the room to reflect on the truncated interview.

His first inclination was to blame himself for learning so little from someone with so much to reveal. He had asked such clumsy questions! After these initial self-recriminations, he went back over what was said, and found to his amazement that he had not written a single note. Again, he lambasted himself for being so sloppy.

Yet, when he allowed himself some time to ponder more carefully, he realized Tuyet Mai never actually denied seeing God or Goddess. In fact, she took great pains to hint that she had, but deflected this admission with a Vietnamese proverb.

She saw them, I know she did! he thought excitedly. *They were just not in her sight when we talked, and thus not in her mind. But she has seen them! All of them, God, Goddess, Nature, and the others. I must know more about her time with Nature. How was he kind? How did he express his kindness? How did he face his death? What did Nature's ghost tell her? What did he think when her knife slid into his side? Is Michael Powers's narrative accurate?*

As he thought further, his mind focused on the tunnel. *The spirits are restless, so she goes to the tunnel. Why? What did she see? What did she hear? What did Nature tell her?*

These questions drilled holes deep in his psyche, and he felt an overwhelming desire to have them answered.

~ *Gail Hess Tries to Withdraw* ~

That afternoon, Adam invited Gail to dinner at their favorite restaurant after work to discuss the interview and her feelings about continuing with the case. When they arrived, neither felt anything other than a gloomy pessimism at the prospects of resolving the manifold mysteries surrounding Mr. Powers. Adam's usual self-confident demeanor was absent, his tam o'shanter remained buried in his pocket as he described his meeting with Tuyet Mai. He blamed himself for its failure to elicit any useful information. Gail responded sympathetically, but refrained from asking questions and kept her comments short and noncommittal. Adam finished his discourse and shifted uncomfortably, absorbing the silence and looking forlornly at Gail.

"Well, what have you decided?" he asked.

"I am leaving the case."

Adam gave a deep sigh. "Gail, you know you must proceed with great caution. You're leaving yourself open to being sued for abandonment by his family. If that happens, and you lose the case, damages awarded, both direct and indirect, could be a fortune, not to mention your career."

"Yes, I know. I've investigated the consequences of violating a fiduciary duty, but, as I understand it, damages would be awarded only in cases where the patient needs continuing therapy, and there is no suitable substitute. You, my dear Adam, are the suitable substitute."

"What if I were to tell you I would not accept it? You know, we've never really formalized our cooperative relationship, and I would be viewed merely as a colleague you occasionally bounce ideas off, on a casual basis."

Gail blinked, took a sip of wine, and said, "But, Adam, you would not do that."

"Oh?"

"I cannot believe you would."

"Try me."

Her face reddened. "Trying to blackmail me into staying, Adam, is a very bad idea. However, I will ignore your threat and ask you to step into my place. Please be the sole therapist on record in this case. I am not helping Mr. Powers or myself at this point."

"Do you think I can help him better than you? Alone, with my own demons, pun intended?"

"Yes, I do."

"Why? I think I'm having a harder time with my ghost Nature than you are with your deity Goddess."

Gail started to respond, but a fiery upwelling in her mind made her gasp for breath, as if some deep ocean ridge had split open and molten lava flowed into the cold sea of her thoughts. She threw her head forward, then backward, wheezing for air, dimly conscious that Adam had rushed to her side.

"Are you choking on something?" he asked frantically.

But she could not utter any sound other than gasps. He started to assume the Heimlich position, but suddenly she stopped fighting for air, and pushed him away, rasping, "It's okay, it's okay. I'm fine now."

After assuring the dubious waiter everything was fine, Adam returned to his chair and looked at her questioningly. Before he could speak, a concerned manager inquired about her condition and Adam politely waved him off.

"What happened?"

"I . . . I . . . this is why I want off this case, Adam."

"What do you mean?"

"It was Goddess."

"Goddess?"

"Yes! Goddess! Adam, I had this irresistible urge to tear off my blouse and expose my breasts, jump up on the table and sit cross-legged, then . . . and . . . and. . . ."

"And what?"

"I don't know . . . levitate . . . and . . . but it is all so stupid!"

"Try to remember, Gail, while it is still fresh."

"No! Let's go. I need to go home. Adam, you must take over this case. I cannot do it any longer. I cannot!"

"I didn't know it was this bad, Gail. Why didn't you tell me?"

"Listen, dear Adam, you've got your own problems. Nature, remember?" She chuckled weakly. "We are a pair. You talk to a ghost; I am possessed by a Goddess. What else is new? Just your average run-of-the-mill psychiatric problems."

They paid and stood in the dark parking lot by Gail's car.

Adam pulled out his tam o'shanter and put it on at a cocky angle. "Well, since we're both certifiably crazy, let's go even crazier together, okay?"

Gail did not respond.

Adam's face darkened. "Gail, I mean it. I cannot do this alone. If you leave, I don't know what will happen."

"Then come see me, and I'll treat you."

"To what? I've never made love to a Goddess."

"Very funny."

"Seriously, Gail, during the telephone call I had with Mark Powers, he mentioned being liberated by putting distance between himself and his father. A continent, no less. Perhaps . . . well, perhaps we should both quit the case."

"And Nature?" asked Gail.

"And Goddess?" replied Adam.

"Adam, you don't understand. Total abandonment of Mr. Powers is out of the question, but I'm afraid. I'm terribly afraid."

"Of what? An imaginary Goddess?"

"Yes. And what She will make me do. It took all my willpower tonight to stop myself from taking on Her persona. Had I done what She wanted me to do, I would have been arrested. It would have ruined my career!"

"Okay, I understand," said Adam. "But hysteria will not help."

Gail hated it when Adam slipped into his patronizing male smugness. She spoke in the steady, even tone of one who has lost her patience. "Adam, I'm not hysterical, I'm afraid. Do you understand that? I don't know what world we are in. It's as if I have awakened to find myself in some alternate universe. I am afraid."

Adam doffed his tam o'shanter and waved it before burying it in his pocket. "So am I, Gail. So am I."

Chapter Twenty-One

Being Sane Is Not Sanity

Time for Reflection

Dear, dear Reader, you can see for yourself that Dr. Hess and Dr. Camara are having difficulties. At least I'm not the only one suffering from mental illness. Perhaps Mark is right. Perhaps I'm contagious. Not with pathogens, with stories. The mind catches what it longs to prove. Anyway, as I have said, the entire human race is schizophrenic, and its creator has established brutal rules to stay in the game. Whoever or whatever controls this competition (and I have my suspicions) is spending a great deal of energy moving chess pieces in apparently random, improbable ways. Fate starves at probability's door. It does indeed. How does one anticipate the next move? Prediction is useless. Welcome to mental illness, dear Reader. Or perhaps, if one believes Goddess, welcome to the beginning of the end of the human race.

Needless to say, being locked up again in this institution, forced to imbibe awful medication, has lessened my psychotic episodes but increased the intensity of my psychotic appetites. I want out. Am I to be denied sustenance while Dr. Hess and Dr. Camara enjoy ever more lavish psychoses and gorge themselves on delusions and hallucinations? No. That must not be. Fine, leave them the field of victory, but let me return to stillness with Nature and the others. Let me be Storyteller again!

Knocking.

"Yes?"

The door opens and an attendant enters. I don't recognize him. He must be from another ward.

"You have visitors. Put on your slippers and follow me."

I follow him to a private conference room. When I enter, I see Tuyet Mai and My-duyen waiting.

My-duyen bows, and Tuyet Mai appraises me with her discerning eyes. I return the bow and sit. As usual, Tuyet Mai balances on her stumps beside My-duyen.

"I'm glad to see both of you again," I say.

"I want to talk with Storyteller," says Tuyet Mai without wasting words on formalities.

"Tuyet Mai, I have schizophrenia, not multiple personality disorder. I can't just call up Storyteller."

"You are Storyteller. Storyteller is you. I wish to speak with him. These are the wishes of the one you call Nature."

"I can't. I've tried."

Tuyet Mai tells her daughter to turn off the lights, and the room is plunged into windowless dark. The switch clicks; the HVAC hum swells; somewhere a diode winks and dies. The dark has weight, as if the room itself leans closer to listen. I hear her voice.

~

"It's dark. There's lightning and thunder. The jungle steams and hisses like a giant snake. Inside the fortress, your comrades prepare to leave. You are to be left in the tunnel. Malaria. High fever. They cannot take you with them. I am tired but forced to go. Your friend Nature helped you into the ruined church, where the tunnel entrance waited. You both sat on a large, flat stone. You squeezed Nature's hand while waiting to descend into the tunnel. I listened.

"Nature asked if you would be okay until he returned. You moaned and complained about how dark it would be in the tunnel, worried you wouldn't be able to breathe.

"Your wounded friend was taken down first, and you told Nature how terrible it is to be alone with a dying man in a dark tunnel. I saw the look in Nature's face when he replied. He said, 'I'll make it. I won't leave you here for long. I'll make it. That is a promise, brother. All of us will make it and come back for you.'

"You said, 'Yeah,' and tried to wipe away your sweat.

"Then, I remember very clearly, Nature told you that your ghosts would not let anything happen to you. He told you that if anyone made it through this ordeal, it would be you, not the rest of them.

"While waiting, you talked some more, and Nature rubbed your shoulder. After your friend was carried down, it was your turn. Your lieutenant said to make it quick. I watched you disappear down into the tunnel and saw Nature rush after you to say goodbye. At that moment, I turned away to await my own fate.

"It is from this point that Nature's ghost told me the rest. His ghost told me many years later when I returned to the darkness of that tunnel. Nature told me you asked where birds go to die. There was soldierly banter, joking, but you kept asking through your fever where birds go to die. He pressed a flashlight into your hand and sang you a song. Years later he sang it to me, and I cried. Then, after placing in your hands the so-called flock bag (the mysterious pouch carried by your Man From The Mountains), he left you with a promise: he would return to free you and, when the war was over, go back to America to tend his graves and write his poetry. He left with the others and died in the ambush. He died at my hand while trying to help me. A knife. Now, he wants you to return to be with him and your other comrades, Storyteller. I understand. I too, lost many friends."

For the first time, I see tears gather in her eyes.

"Kim Lan," she whispers. Her comrade from the village—the one who didn't come back.

~

Something rumbles in my mind. I feel dizzy. A pressure change, like stepping into a tunnel: sound thins, edges blur, and heat lifts from my skin. I know it is Storyteller. He is here, pushing me aside. I don't fight it. I acquiesce, happy to be buried, happy to turn over control.

~ *Storyteller* ~

Michael fainted and he has been brought back to his room. I have taken over, but too late to inform Tuyet Mai. She will be back, and I will talk to her then. This aging body of Michael is inconvenient, but I'll manage. There is much to do. I am confident Dr. Camara will want to meet soon, despite the agreement with Dr. Hess, who is anxious to put distance between Michael and herself. How do I know these things? Ghosts, you know, are everywhere and nowhere. They slip into the crevices of your mind like water seeking the slightest crack, then set about to widen the fissures at their leisure. I am not a ghost, in the literal sense of the word, unless we consider our past to be ghostly. I am from a past that bears many secrets, unknown consciously even to the one who is the vessel of the present. Michael's writings are like prehistoric paintings on a cave wall, full of distorted beasts and fading spirits. But those beasts were once alive, pumping blood through their bodies, desperate to eat and not be eaten. To be alive! Nature is a shade. Mountain Man is a shade. All the rest of my dead comrades are shades. Memory is not a shade. It is, instead, a map whose boundaries shift, and whose directions change, confounding us with its unreliability. Soon the entire human race will be a shade.

Can you pour a living body from the present into an insubstantial memory from the past, like pouring blood and guts into an empty container? In this case, my comrades and I are the memories, and the empty container is the tunnel. I want him back and intend to get him back.

Knocking.

I know one of the doctors will want to see me. Is this the summons? They don't know they are now dealing with Storyteller, and they must not find out. Not yet anyway.

"Yes?"

"Medication time, Mr. Powers."

"Okay, come in."

I palm the cup and pretend to take the medication. When the attendant turns, I cheek the pills and wash down nothing. The chalk ghosts my tongue; bitterness sears metallic at the back of my throat. I can't be weak at a time like this. When will they call me?

~

Two days have passed, and I'm finally told I'll meet with Dr. Camara tomorrow. Michael is submissive. He's broken, I think. My thoughts turn to Tuyet Mai.

"Goddess?"

Yes?

"Soon, I meet with the woman who killed my best friend. A woman who is older and more experienced in the ways of the world than I. What will she say to me?"

You, as much as anyone, have experienced suffering. Some have suffered far more than you, others less. You are a memory, a ripple, a passing wave. How can you understand?

"Michael always complains that You speak in riddles. I think I can understand You because memory itself is a riddle. What part of memory is true, what part false? You have said You want to end God's addiction. That's all I know. The rest is vague and unsatisfying. I'm the saddest of all things—a memory that wants to be alive again. I know how much I lived, how vital living was to me, every moment I breathed in Vietnam. Since the war, since I became a memory, Michael has not truly lived, and he knows it. The older he gets, the more desperate his yearnings to recapture the exuberance of life on the edge. You see, we are all dead, even I, nothing more than a memory, given form only by a set of bones in a tunnel. I know what You want of me, but what do You want of Michael?"

He is the son. Your parents sacrificed all to give birth to you and him. It is the son that must take the next step. He must mate with another to produce the next Chosen One.

"But I must bring him back to us."

Yes, the Reunion, but only after he has bred with one We have chosen.

~

"Good morning," Dr. Camara says to me.

We're meeting in the same conference room we met last time.

"Good morning."

He looks at me funny, and for a minute I cannot anticipate what he will say.

"Are Tuyet Mai and My-duyen going to join us?" I ask.

"No. I just wanted a chance to see you first," says Dr. Camara.

I put on my best confident attitude and speak like an old person. "What can I do for you, Dr. Camara?"

"I want to know more about Nature."

Just as I suspected.

"Oh?" I say innocently.

"You knew him as well as anyone."

"Is this part of my therapy?"

He hesitates. "No. Mr. Powers, this is purely to satisfy my own curiosity about this person called Nature. I'm aware that asking you here blurs roles; this isn't treatment—it's me, not the doctor, trying to understand the man who . . . seems very important to you."

"Why are you so curious?"

"He interests me."

"As a psychiatrist?"

"No, as a person."

I shrug. "What do you want to know?"

"You say in your writings that Nature came to believe in your ghosts. Correct?"

"I don't know about any writings."

"But, Mr. Powers, we have reams of them. It's the history of your parents and your war experiences."

"Oh, that is Michael Powers." I know this will give me away, but I'm having too much fun. His look of confusion makes me chuckle.

"And who are you?"

"Come on, doctor, just joking. I'm Michael Powers. Can't a schizophrenic have a little fun?"

He does not laugh. "You know, Dr. Hess and I have discussed the possibility you sometimes exhibit dissociative identity disorder when you suffer a psychotic event? I would not joke, Mr. Powers, or I might take it seriously."

I'm young and my back is up. "Give me a fuckin' break, Doc. What can you do to me that is worse than being locked up in here?"

He appears surprised at my words. "Keep you under sedation. Restraints."

"For making a fuckin' joke?"

"This cursing is not like you, Mr. Powers. It fuels my suspicion you might be having a psychotic dissociation as we speak."

I feel compelled to back off, for now. "Sorry, you're right. I won't joke anymore."

He looks at me a long time, sort of undecided, then says, "Thank you. Now, about Nature?"

I want to mention his meeting Nature's ghost in the Providence cemetery, but that would freak him out way too much. Besides, it might get me sedated and in restraints. So. . . .

I say, "He was kind. Had curly hair. Wore a tam o'shanter when we were not in the bush. Wrote poetry, smiled a lot, and is now none of those things."

"How so?"

"He's dead. Stillness, Doc."

Dr. Camara looks at me with this piercing gaze. "Do you blame yourself?"

I laugh. "So, this is therapy, eh, Doc?"

"Sorry. I slipped into my professional mode. Hard to shake. By the way, Mr. Powers, why this sudden urge to curse?"

"Sorry. I slipped into my young soldier mode. Hard to shake. By the way, Dr. Camara, why this sudden urge to analyze me when you said I'm not here to be analyzed?"

"Touché."

We remain silent for a few moments, then he says, "Did Nature ever do anything that you would consider mean or cruel?"

"Yeah."

"What?" he asks in some surprise.

"Killed Vietnamese."

This takes him aback.

"Wellll," he draws out the word. "Didn't he kill in self-defense?"

I want to rant and rave and bang my fist on the table. I want to punch him in the face. That's all these pricks who've never seen war can say. "Oh, you did it in self-defense. Kill or be killed." Bullshit. No one in war kills in self-defense. We just kill, like we are told to do. However, I control myself.

"If you say so," I reply.

"I mean, other than the war, did he do anything mean or cruel?"

I must admit, I'm a bit confused at his motivation for asking such a question. In return, I make a reasonable inquiry.

"Why do you ask?" I look at him with raised eyebrows.

He tilts his head and smiles. "It might surprise you to know, Mr. Powers, that your description of him—I mean, in your writings—is intriguing. I want to know more about him."

"You are writing a book?"

He laughs uncomfortably. "No, just curious."

"Truth is, Doc, Nature is preying on your mind. Am I correct?"

"Well, in a manner of speaking, yes."

"Doc, in a manner of speaking you're obsessed with him."

This has an effect.

"Now you are analyzing me, Mr. Powers."

"Someone has to."

He grunts and I can't tell if it's a laugh or something else. "Can we get back to Nature?" he asks.

"What do you want to know?"

Now he groans. "Other than the war, did he do anything mean or cruel?"

Getting to him like this is too easy, but I feel sympathy. Poor guy has no idea what is going on in his mind.

"Doc," I say very patiently. "You have read Michael Powers. What he wrote is true."

"He?"

Oops, I slipped. Oh well, too late now. I do what I can to recover.

"I sometimes refer to myself in the third person. It's an affectation of mine. Bad habit."

Again, his eyes bore into me. "Am I talking to Michael Powers, or someone else?"

"Michael Powers, of course."

"Are you sure I'm not talking to Storyteller?"

"Same person, Doc."

"Is he?"

"You know he is."

He appears excited now. "No, I don't think he is. You are Storyteller, aren't you?"

"Yes, I was called Storyteller in Vietnam."

"Not your twin?"

"That particular delusion is long gone, Doc. Old news. Dead horse."

"May I call you Storyteller?"

"If you want, as long as you don't insist that I am some multiple-personality shit."

"I promise."

"Is calling me Storyteller part of my therapy, Doc?"

"Could be. Depends."

"On what?"

"On what you say next, Storyteller."

We fall silent while his brain races to figure out where to go from here.

"Well," he finally says. "As long as I am calling you Storyteller, tell me about Nature from your perspective."

I laugh. "You mean from Storyteller's perspective and not Michael Powers?"

"Yes."

"I see. You're not interested in Storyteller, only Nature."

"I can talk to Storyteller anytime, but I can't talk to Nature, ever."

"Not true."

"What?"

"You did talk to Nature."

This makes him blink. "What do you mean?"

"A certain Providence, Rhode Island cemetery."

He starts to sweat and dabs at his forehead with a handkerchief. "How did you know about that?"

I shrug.

"Did Dr. Hess tell you?"

"No, Doc. Nature told me."

Now I've done it. Fuckin' adolescent mind craves melodrama. I know I'd better get out of the mess I just got myself into. Dredging up faint memories of a few bad movies, I pretend to nod off, then awaken as if I do not know where I am.

"Oh, hello Dr. Camara," I say. "How long have I been here?"

I think my acting is decent, but he seems doubtful.

"Mr. Powers?" he asks.

"Yes."

"Do you know I just spoke with Storyteller?"

Now, how would a person suffering from multiple personality disorder respond to this question? Whatever it is, I must do the opposite.

"Of course, doctor. But, as we agreed, I did that for your benefit. I assure you; I don't suffer from dissociative identity disorder. I can't help myself from pulling these ridiculous little jokes. Must be the medication getting to me."

"Whoever you are now, Mr. Powers, you still haven't answered my question about Nature. Do you remember it?"

I know this is a test. "Okay, of course I remember it. The answer is that Nature never did anything mean or cruel the entire time I knew him. Period. Now, I want to go back to my room. I'm tired and these questions are too disturbing."

Next thing I know, I'm back in my room. I don't think he wanted to take any chances. After all, I might have a real psychotic break, like Michael did with that whole tunnel business. I now anxiously await word that Tuyet Mai is ready to meet.

~ *Tuyet Mai Meets Storyteller* ~

It is the day after my meeting with Dr. Camara, and I have learned Tuyet Mai is to visit this afternoon. She has kept her promise to return! The old heart in Michael's body is beating fast, and, I fear, irregularly.

It turns out the visit with Tuyet Mai is in the same room as before. I assume it's wired for recording, and I tell her so, but she waves off my warning. Mark, as usual, is not present, and My-duyen sits demurely.

"No problem," says Tuyet Mai breezily. "This will not take long."

I do not respond and sit quietly, waiting for some transcendent revelation, but none comes.

"Are you treated well here?" she asks.

"Reasonably so."

Tuyet Mai rocks on her stumps for a while, seemingly lost in her own world. My-duyen shifts uncomfortably.

"Ma?" My-duyen directs this to her mother as if to draw her out of a trance.

"My daughter is with child," blurts Tuyet Mai. "I came here from Vietnam to be with her and to see Mark's father."

For a moment the fluorescent hum drops a note; an unseen heart stakes its claim, the line quickening: hope and dread arrive as twins.

"Does Mark know?" I ask in a voice made shrill by shock and a welter of complicated feelings jockeying for position.

"Yes and no, Storyteller."

I have no idea how to respond.

"When we first met," continues Tuyet Mai through My-duyen, "I found I was really speaking to Storyteller rather than Michael Powers. I know you are Storyteller."

I remain speechless, quietly stunned.

Tuyet Mai says, "In Vietnamese culture, grandfathers are revered. However, I was weaned on revolution and communism, and find the old notions absurd."

I listen and can think of nothing to say.

"So," continues Tuyet Mai, "I want to see for myself this grandfather, who I know only as an enemy many, many years ago."

"Here I am," I say tritely.

"No, here is Storyteller."

"Same person." I feel a sense of *déjà vu*.

"If that is true, then Michael Powers must be kind. Is this so?"

"Yes."

"Does his illness make him a danger?"

"A danger?"

"To others," says Tuyet Mai. "To children."

"God, no!"

"That is good, but I do not know about this disease, what you call, *tâm thần phân liệt*."

"Schizophrenia," I say reluctantly. "It is hearing voices that are not really there, so they say. If Michael Powers harms anyone, it would be himself."

"And you with him," replies Tuyet Mai.

"I'm only a memory. You can't kill me. I exist in the cloud of memory, passed on from one to another until only a wisp remains."

With this poetic statement, one that would make Nature proud, I expect Tuyet Mai to be suitably impressed. But, to my surprise, she laughs.

"Look at my legs, Storyteller," she finally says.

I am speechless.

"Look at my legs!"

"I can't, Tuyet Mai. You have no legs."

"They are memories, and yet more real than the empty air that has replaced them."

"I understand."

"You are real, Storyteller, that's why you have taken over from Michael Powers. But hear me well: he is to be the grandfather, not you."

Chapter Twenty-Two

The Spirit of God is in the Flesh; The Flesh of Goddess is in the Spirit

Dear Reader

Dear Reader, by now you must understand my state of mind. I am trapped between two powers: Goddess and *Her* faction, bent on curing God of *His* addiction to First Principles, and God, who wants to erase any remaining vestiges of Goddess and *Her* meddling so that the human race can proceed on its natural course, thereby destroying the planet. This situation threatens Armageddon, or at least threatens the remaining fragments of my sanity. Drs. Hess and Camara believe they are victims of the "suggestions" I planted. Dr. Tavaris, on the other hand, is closer to the mark, though he does not realize it is happening to him as well. No, that is not quite accurate. He welcomes possession; in that, he is more foolish than the other two combined.

Dear Reader, do you really think I wish any of them harm? I am nothing more than a leaf in a storm, and where I land is irrelevant, at least on the surface. You see, I am background-independent, as a physicist might say (look it up, curious ones). Unfortunately, when I do land, corruption begins, just as it did when Father lowered his hand for the ant to escape. Must one always die inside to set another free? Yes, a little . . . or a lot. You see, these shrinks believe their troubles emanate from my schizophrenic brain, but they are entirely wrong. Their troubles come from beyond the feeble walls of this institute . . . as do mine, which is why I again feel compelled to escape to the dark womb of the tunnel. Let Her reunion take place here, in this sterile morgue, but I plan to be long gone. No more allegiance to Goddess. No more conspiracy against God. Born alone, die alone. Okay, so be it.

Dear Reader, who am I? Storyteller? Michael Powers? A father? A walking facsimile of corrupted DNA? A heroic veteran? A murderer? A lawyer? A madman? All of these; together they make my life untenable. Hero, madman, murderer: do you see? I am torn limb from limb. What remains?

I will tell you. What remains is a walking dead man whose business is with the dead. While amusing to watch the living, I have become bored with their trivial concerns. Alas, there is a fatal catch to my conclusions: at heart, I am a coward. Sure, I have medals from Vietnam, but Madame Dau (to name only one) was a far braver person. Suicide is out of the question. Where am I to find amusement? Hess and Camara? Hardly. They are already marinating, soon to be cooked. Tavaris? Maybe. He is an unusual prize worth the effort. Before I set his trophy among my collection, I will be long gone, back to the tunnel.

~

I am sitting across from Damien in the cafeteria, waiting to hear his latest intelligence from Goddess, who speaks to me less and less. The coffee tastes of tin; the lights buzz like insects. As usual, Damien sits in silence, tilting his head side to side as if listening to an internal cuckoo, which is an image apt on many levels. As if a switch is pulled, he stops rocking and looks at me.

"She is angry with you."

"I can imagine."

"She is sending a messenger."

"What, another one? I have had many. Buandelgereen, Tuyet Mai, the Great Warrior, all my nightmares."

"She is sending a messenger."

"You said that."

"She likes me best."

"Yes."

"Your power is gone."

"How so?"

Damien holds up a half-eaten hamburger. "Do you hear the cow screaming?"

"No."

"I do. You have lost your power. I have it now."

"Welcome to it, friend."

I appear calm, but terror takes me by the throat—what now?

"When did She tell you this?" I ask weakly.

Damien merely returns to his nodding insensibility.

I admit, dear Reader, his drifting in and out makes me jealous that Goddess should choose such a sorry mental patient over me.

"Hey, stupid!" I shout a bit too loud. "Answer me!"

Damien draws back and throws up his hands as if I were about to hit him.

Pedro, one of the attendants, comes over and chastises me. I plead *mea culpa*, and feel grateful Dr. Tavaris is not here to see my little exhibition. Moments of weakness are not to be witnessed by those we consider enemies, or, if not exactly enemies, then antagonists, rivals, or whatever.

Dr. Tavaris is definitely a whatever. He is not my enemy, or rival, but he is someone I view as an opponent in a game of chess. More so than Dr. Hess or Dr. Camara. Why? His reputation for unusual approaches to treatment intrigues me, piques my interest, and challenges me. In moments of weakness, I would wish to see him completely possessed by Bowls, rendering him harmless to future patients. I can see him now: sitting behind his desk with an empty pipe protruding upside-down from his mouth, occasionally removing it to chatter to himself and bite his fingernails to the quick, like Stretch.

After Pedro leaves, I turn my attention back to Damien.

"Look, Damien," I say gently. "When Goddess talks to you, does She mention God?"

"God?"

"Yeah, God."

Mustard is dripping down his chin. "God is the Father."

"Yes, but does She mention Him?"

"God is the Father."

I am getting nowhere, but I keep trying. "I mean, does She talk about God being addicted?"

"Addicted?"

"To suffering."

"God's only son suffered."

Ever the optimist, despite an intense desire to wipe his chin, I press on. "Is God addicted to suffering?"

"Demons are everywhere. They enter the portals."

"Are you possessed, Damien?"

He begins to shiver uncontrollably. Pedro notices, walks over, and looms above me. "Are you egging him on, Mr. Powers?"

"Me?" I ask innocently.

"Yeah, you." He peers at the still shivering Damien and says accusingly, "Maybe you should just leave him alone. You're egging him on, aren't you?"

"Not me. I'm trying to help. He thinks a Goddess possesses him. Talk about crazy."

Pedro gives me the evil eye. "Comments like that are not helpful, Mr. Powers."

Damien suddenly sits bolt upright and exclaims, "She likes me best!"

While Pedro stares at him in confusion, I slip away and return to my room. The corridor smells of bleach; the walls close in. For some reason, the exchange with Damien has brought on a deep depression. Is it because I am left bereft? Abandonment by Goddess is less desirable than I thought. I mean, isn't that what I want? Or, maybe I just got a ringside seat to see for myself how crazy and pathetic I must seem to others.

"Goddess!" I shout at the walls. "Explain Yourself!"

You will have a visitor.

Not having expected Her to respond, I can only reply, "Who?"

Silence. Of course, She does not answer. By now, I really should expect this, but I was born to be surprised. As usual, I am left to speculate.

~ *A Visitor. The Visitor.* ~

This morning, I am told I have a visitor. Arrangements have been made to meet in a private therapy room. When I enter, I freeze. It is *Her*! *Her*! The famous *She* whom my parents sought through war and famine. The famous *She* who drove my father to despair and my mother to distraction. *She* sits with legs crossed, just as *She* did when my father first met *Her* in his office almost a century ago. I find myself in a chair across from *Her*, waiting for the famous question.

However, instead of that question, another comes, and it takes me by surprise.

"Are you not the Chosen One?"

Before I can answer, Dr. Tavaris bursts into the room holding his damn pipe. "Sorry, Storyteller!" he bellows. "I am late!"

Taken aback, I look to *Her*, but *She*, of course, is gone.

"You are the visitor?" I ask Tavaris.

"What?"

"The visitor! The visitor! They told me I had a visitor. It's you?"

Tavaris looks around conspicuously. "Apparently."

I am furious. "*She* is gone, thanks to you."

"Who?"

"Never mind."

Tavaris is on full alert now. "Storyteller, who is she?"

"Never mind, and I'm not Storyteller. Furthermore, I don't want to talk with you. Please leave so *She* will come back."

"Wouldn't it make you feel better to tell me who this person is?"

"No. Just leave."

"I'm afraid I can't do that, Mr. Powers."

"Then I will." I really am in no mood to deal with Tavaris. Thoughts of *Her* are swirling so rapidly through my mind I feel dizzy. Tavaris is saying something, but I don't hear. I find myself on my feet, leaning across the table toward him. He barks out a name, and before I know it, I'm back in my room. To my great relief, *She* is waiting.

Once the door closes behind me, I say to *Her*, "So glad to see you. I was afraid."

She sits in the same position, legs crossed. *She* does not blink and asks the same question again. "Are you not the Chosen One?"

The words fall like a key into a lock I've heard turning all my life. Still, I am not prepared to answer that. Instead, I ask, "If I am the Chosen One, why has Goddess abandoned me?"

"You have abandoned *Her*. Are you not the Chosen One?"

"If so, Goddess has chosen a fool to replace me."

"Your mother suffered."

"Which mother?"

"Bai Meiying."

"I am her chosen son."

"No, you are *Her* Chosen One."

Before I can reply, Tavaris again barges into the room unannounced. He looks around. "Is she here?"

"Who?" I ask innocently.

"We have been observing you talking to someone."

"Damn cameras! I have constitutional privacy rights—Fourteenth Amendment, to be precise."

"Be that as it may, Mr. Powers, is she here?"

"You merely observed me practicing a speech I'm trying to memorize. Just because my lips are moving doesn't mean I am hallucinating."

"What speech?"

"Lincoln's Second Inaugural Address." I try to sound serious in order to maximize the impression of insanity. Tavaris is not buying it.

"Mr. Powers, who is she?"

"With malice toward none, with charity for all—"

"Mr. Powers!"

I decide to have a little fun. "I'm fuckin' Storyteller! Why are you calling me Mr. Powers?"

I enjoy watching his expression as he instinctively looks down at the pipe still clutched in his hand. He makes a weak move to put it in his mouth, and then apparently thinks better of it.

I laugh. "Don't bother, Bowls, I know who you are."

He makes a feeble recovery and asks again, "Who is she, Mr. Powers?"

"Christ!" I exclaim in disgust, and then make a firm decision to clam up.

Tavaris chatters aimlessly for a while before finally withdrawing from the field. I wait for *Her* to return, but I have a sinking feeling *She* will not appear.

~

I was right. Dear Reader, *She* has not appeared. However, *Her* brief words have given me renewed hope I am not forgotten. Yes, yes—I know. You have read my words about being done with Goddess, about turning my back on *Her* quest, but such is the fickle nature of a schizophrenic. I reserve the right to change my disordered mind, as I am nothing more than a perplexing blur of masks flashing on and off in the hands of a skilled Chinese face changer. Besides, we all need a little love. Yes? Besides, after all, I might really be the Chosen One.

~

It has been days without a word from anyone. Again, I sink into depression. The bed no longer speaks to me, nor does the chair or the walls. Why hasn't *She* returned? And where are Buandelgereen and Tuyet Mai? Even my son has deserted me. You would think My-duyen could use her Asian sense of familial responsibility to convince Mark to come. Even Damien has clammed up, and eating at the cafeteria is an exercise in isolation. I have even lost my connection with our illustrious doctors—all three of them. I know the game they are playing. Let him cool his heels. I'm not sure I can outlast them in my weakened state. I don't know how far Goddess has progressed in Her possession of Dr. Hess, or Nature in his hold over Dr. Camara. I have won a few rounds with Dr. Tavaris, but he is winning this one. Dear Reader, I am close to breaking.

~

She is back! Like the cavalry, *She* has arrived just in time. In fact, *She* is kind enough to let me write these words even as we speak. Hours ago, already past midnight, my usual nightmares would not permit sleep, so I got out of bed and turned on my weak desk lamp. Lo and behold, the dim light revealed *Her* sitting in the corner, legs crossed. *Her* smile beckons me to be bold. Before *She* says a single word, I ask *Her* an impertinent question.

"Can you take me to see my mother?"

"Which one?"

"Bai Meiying."

She registers no surprise, and replies, "Your mother is dead."

"Exactly."

"Are you the Chosen One?"

I now have no doubts. "Yes!"

"Then you may see your mother."

"Bai Meiying?"

"Bai Meiying."

"How?"

"She is with your dead comrades. Why? She roams among them seeking knowledge about your life. As a shade, she seeks those fellow shades closest to you when they lived, that she may share parts of you she never had the opportunity to see."

My heart leaps in my throat. "She is with Nature?"

"Of course."

"Mountain Man?"

"Yes."

"Father?"

She does not respond.

I am worried, so I repeat, "Father?"

"Do you wish to see for yourself?"

Some stern warning comes to me, a flashing red light signaling 'go no further!' *She* waits patiently, watching my hesitation.

"I am unsure," I falter and release a slight tremor. "I have been there before."

She nods. "I know."

"What if I cannot return? I am ill, after all. Schizophrenia plays tricks."

"Do you believe I am not real?" *She* asks.

"*You* are real. More than real. *You* are the reality behind the real. That is what makes me hesitate . . . that is what scares me."

"Then I shall leave you to your room."

"No! Please! I want to go!"

She flies toward me with arms outstretched. I close my eyes.
Then—darkness.
I open my eyes.

~ *Shades* ~

The Underworld extends before me to a vague horizon. Emaciated shades in dark, wobbly hordes file back and forth like ants in a disturbed colony. Ribbed, bony walls pen the wanderers to a vast, alabaster tomb, wherein the marrow of souls ebbs and flows. It all comes back to me in a rush of memory. I look past the infinite and can only blink in wonder. Has *She* set me down close enough among this multitude of spectral sighs to find Mother? Or, perhaps, Mother will find me?

I strain to locate a familiar outline. Is this passing shade Mountain Man's slouching figure? Is that fleeting smudge Nature's tam o'shanter? It is hard to distinguish such insubstantial, mummified forms. They brush past as airily as the lightest of breezes. A wave of panic rolls over me, and like a lost child, I rake the milling throng to find Mother. How will I recognize her? There are pictures, of course, but these shades have blurred faces, and lack even distinguishing smells. They are as ethereal and strangely brittle as Autumn's desiccated leaves.

She appears at my side.

"Where is Mother?" I ask.

She points toward a tremulous shade hovering nearby. "Go to her."

My body is rooted, and I cannot move. Instead, the shade glides up to me, shy and hesitant.

"Is this my son?" These words are not a question. Is this truly her? How does one identify the shadow of a mother one has no memory of? I force myself to calm and let her presence wash over me.

Yes! Yes—it is her!

"Yes, Mother."

The shade seems to exhale a profound sigh.

"My son."

Chapter Twenty-Three

Psychiatrists in Distress

Hess and Camara Falter

Dr. Tavaris had been gone for ten days at a conference in New York, and when he returned, called for a meeting with Drs. Hess and Camara to review Mr. Powers's progress. When he observed his two colleagues, his concern for Mr. Powers melted away as his shock at their demeanor took over.

"You both look tired," he commented, biting back his first read: hollowed eyes, paper skin, hands that can't quite be still. *They look incredibly worn and haggard,* he thought. *Has Mr. Powers been up to his usual tricks?*

Neither answered directly but instead offered banal questions about the conference. Both seemed distracted by inner conflicts.

Unwilling to dance around delicate subjects, Tavaris pressed them. "Actually, you both look terrible. Has something happened during my absence?"

His colleagues looked at each other warily, neither inclined to speak first.

"Well?" asked Tavaris.

"Yes, well, we are a bit tired," answered Gail.

"Goddesses don't get tired!" snapped Adam. "Especially while dealing with us mere mortals." Suddenly aware of his jarring outburst, he laughed weakly and added, "Just joking."

However, to Tavaris's keen ears, Pandora's box had been opened. "Dr. Camara, you and I both know that 'joke' came from some other place. I am going to assume you are professional enough to realize this and explain yourself."

Camara stared at Tavaris angrily. "Dr. Tavaris, I am not obliged to explain myself to you, or anyone, for that matter. We are equivocating ourselves into oblivion."

"What does that mean?" asked a perplexed Dr. Tavaris.

Gail spoke quite calmly. "It means, Dr. Tavaris, that Nature keeps calling him back to Providence—graveyard and all."

"What do you mean?" asked Tavaris.

"It means, Dr. Tavaris, that Adam wants to return to the graveyard in Providence."

"Is this true?" asked Tavaris, turning to Adam in surprise.

"Yes. I want an opportunity to interview the docent I told you about."

"Maybe write some poetry while you're at it?" asked Gail sarcastically.

"What the hell has been going on here?" demanded Tavaris. "When I left, you two were thick as thieves . . . and now—"

"And now, Dr. Tavaris, I am leaving, unless you have something relevant to ask about our mutual patient," said Adam curtly.

Without waiting for an answer, he walked out of the room.

Tavaris looked questioningly at Gail, raising his bushy eyebrows. She stared back at him with a look of defiance.

"It's Nature," she said.

"Nature?"

"The . . . suggestion, or whatever you wish to call it, is growing stronger—very much stronger. I have tried to help, but Dr. Camara is a stubborn man. I advised him not to go, but he insists. Stubborn man!"

"Stubborn enough to defy a Goddess?" asked Tavaris with a humorless gleam in his eye.

Gail sat upright and peered at him without any apparent emotion. "It is true; the pull of Goddess has been stronger in me as well." She faltered. "Do you have any recommendations?"

Dr. Tavaris heard this distant plea for help and felt an odd twinge, some unfamiliar urge. He pulled out the empty pipe he kept in his pocket.

"Actually, I do," he said, then clamped the pipe between his teeth. It tasted like chalk.

Gail waited, staring at his pipe quizzically.

As if aware of the object of her attention for the first time, he quickly put it back in his pocket. "You can tell me what you're experiencing," he said in his best professional voice.

Gail frowned. "Ahab beware Ahab," she said. "Perhaps you can tell me about your own demon?"

Tavaris reddened, but slowly a grin spread across his face.

"You're right!" he exclaimed. "We both need to talk."

"You first," said Gail.

"At the conference, I kept looking for Mountain Man, just like Bowls would do."

"You don't know what he looks like."

"True, true. Mr. Powers has described him very well. Every time I caught myself searching the room, I had an uncomfortable urge to put this stupid pipe in my mouth. And you?"

Gail shook her head, hesitating. "I assume the rules of confidentiality apply between us," she said.

"Of course."

"I keep wanting to expose my breasts, and I am quite sure it is not some Freudian drive."

It did not escape Gail's notice that Tavaris moved almost imperceptibly in his seat.

"And God?" he asked.

"I feel a compulsion to oppose Him, although I am not religious."

"You don't believe in God?"

A stern look came over Gail's face. "Do you?" she demanded.

"No."

"Then you are a fool."

Tavaris appeared more perplexed than he actually was. "But you just said you are not religious."

"So I did."

"Have you seen any of Mr. Powers's writings lately?"

Gail flashed an ironic smile. "Yes."

"Well?"

"Mr. Powers is currently in the Underworld."

"What?"

"He is with the shades."

"You found that in his writing?"

"We have a little game, you see. He hides his latest work under his mattress, and when he is not in his room, we take the pages."

"He doesn't notice?"

"Of course he does, but he doesn't complain. It's like the Tooth Fairy. We take the writing and leave him blank paper."

Tavaris looked past Gail. "Why does he do it?"

"Do what exactly?"

"Write."

Gail shrugged. "Therapeutic, I guess."

"No, no, no. That can't be." Tavaris seemed inspired by a thought.

"What do you mean?" asked Gail.

"Someone else is writing through him—using him."

"Oh, that again!" laughed Gail. "Dr. Camara and I have already thought of that. In fact, we have discussed it many times. If you asked Mr. Powers who controls his writing, he would say it is me . . . or, rather, Goddess."

"Is it?" asked Tavaris.

Gail ignored the question.

Tavaris continued. "Didn't you say he is in the Underworld?"

"Well, that's the last he wrote. Who knows what's happening as we speak?"

"Come here!" exclaimed an excited Tavaris. As he spoke, he grabbed Gail's hand and pulled her with him.

"Where are we going?" she asked.

"I want to check on the surveillance feed."

They raced down the hallways past startled patients and staff, entered the private surveillance room, ran the tape, and scrubbed forward to the live feed of Mr. Powers's room. To Gail's surprise, he sat on his bed, writing, but Tavaris nodded in confirmation.

"As I thought!" he cried. "Follow me!"

Again, the two psychiatrists hurried down the hallways and reached Mr. Powers's room out of breath. Before Gail unlocked the door, they looked through the window and saw an empty bed. When they entered, Mr. Powers sat curled on the floor in a corner, by all appearances comatose. Tavaris paused, blinking in wonder, then lifted the mattress and recovered a sheaf of papers. Gail stood with her arms crossed, unperturbed by Tavaris's sense of urgency.

~

Tavaris flipped to the last page, read it aloud, and mumbled, "My God!"

Gail listened impassively and replied calmly. "Yes, Dr. Tavaris, I have experienced this many times. Michael Powers would've responded to that incredulous exclamation by saying something like, 'When you say 'my God', I know that He is your deity, your God. But you must understand—He's an addicted deity who needs more help than the inmates of this institution.' What's worse, I'm beginning to believe him."

Tavaris listened to Gail with an expression of dawning awareness. "Who are you now?" he asked.

"Do not worry, doctor, I am still Gail Hess, but his Goddess figure is close. Very close."

"How can I help?"

Gail looked down at the unmoving Mr. Powers. "You can't."

Tavaris followed her eyes. "And him?"

"I told you, he is in the Underworld. We call it a psychological, self-induced coma, but he is there among the shades. Do you want to follow him?"

Tavaris's eyebrows jumped up. "Actually, I do. Not only that, I want to go to a certain Providence cemetery with Dr. Camara. It is our professional duty to learn by immersing ourselves in their delusions."

"You're a bigger fool than I thought," said Gail.

Tavaris ignored her words, leaned over Mr. Powers, and moved his examination light across the sightless eyes.

"No response," he said flatly. Testing again, then lifting the lids to the same fixed stare.

Gail released a scornful laugh. "Of course not. I told you, he is in the Underworld."

Tavaris listened patiently, and with deliberative and exaggerated skepticism, narrowed his eyes. "How do you know that? You haven't even read his latest writing."

Gail shrugged. "You'll get used to it."

"Have you?"

"Have I what?"

"Gotten used to it."

"No, not really."

"And your lover, Adam—has he?"

Gail ignored the prod. "Nature has made great progress with poor Adam."

"What does he think he will achieve in Providence?"

"He isn't thinking anymore."

"Due to Nature?"

Gail nodded.

"And how about you? Has Goddess made similar progress?"

"Goddess grows stronger while Gail Hess grows weaker. And you, Dr. Tavaris? What about Bowls?"

Tavaris took out his pipe. "At least I still control this."

"Are you sure? Adam said the same thing about his tam o'shanter, and now. . . ."

A shadow fell across Tavaris's face, and his tone became rough. "Let me see your breasts, Great Goddess!"

"You are not the son," replied Gail haughtily. "You'll have to meet Her at some point, and. . . ."

Gail started to unbutton her blouse.

Startled, Tavaris threw up his hands. "No! Stop! Don't!" He rushed to physically stop her, but Gail smiled at him and rebuttoned her blouse.

"Just checking," she said with a dismissive wave of her hand. "Did you really think. . . ."

Tavaris breathed a sigh of relief and wagged a finger at her like an annoyed father scolding a child. "Gail, I'm not a dirty old man."

Gail replied scornfully, "No, I don't think you are a dirty old man. I think you are a frightened young soldier sucking on an empty pipe, chewing his fingernails, and following his pig farmer savior, Mountain Man, wherever he goes."

Tavaris laughed nervously and held up his hand, spreading his fingers before his eyes, turning them in the light to see the mangled nails and torn skin. "Strange, I've never chewed my fingernails before."

"So, you have read everything he has written. Does this surprise you even now?"

"I have read every word. Stretch had Tourette's, correct?"

"Good. Sounds like you're blending a little Stretch with Bowls. When will you give in to them, Dr. Tavaris?"

Tavaris tilted his head and gave a patronizing smirk. "You don't understand, my dear Gail—I'm ready to give in anytime."

"For purposes of your research?"

"Of course."

"Your foolishness truly knows no bounds. Are you so sure you'll make it back from wherever this takes you?"

"Always have."

"I bet you've never been in quite this same situation, have you?"

Tavaris sat on the bed and spoke calmly, reflectively. "No, I have not, which is why it holds such utter fascination and is so important to pursue."

Gail lashed out. "You're out of your depth! We're all out of our depth!"

Tavaris looked at her wryly. "So, shall we all just give in?"

This response took her aback. "No, but. . . . "

"No but!" mimicked Tavaris. "Now that's an answer!"

Both fell silent and looked glumly at Mr. Powers.

~ *The Providence Cemetery Beckons* ~

Dr. Camara departed alone for Providence after vehemently opposing Tavaris's request to accompany him. This time, Adam didn't have to make a dry run to find Little Neck Cemetery. Driving a rental car straight from the airport, he stood at the front entrance, scanning the gravestones for a glimpse of Mr. Yancey. Something drew him to Nature's grave despite his resolve to meet with Bud Yancey first. He whipped out his tam o'shanter and pulled it on, appreciating the warm protection it offered against the cold Rhode Island breeze. Little Neck seemed to exhale a sigh of overdue welcome, as if relieved that he had returned at last. Adam felt curiously at home among the pockmarked gravestones and fallen leaves scurrying in acrobatic swirls. He felt as if he could sit there indefinitely—one more marker among markers—joining the other stones that perch above their own precious clutches of bones.

Adam had no sense of how much time passed when a shadow fell across the bench. Without looking up, he said, "Hello, Nature."

"Not Nature, son," came a familiar voice.

"Oh, hello Mr. Yancey."

"Bud, to you. I take it you've returned to see your ghost?"

Adam smiled. "And yours as well."

Yancey returned the smile but said nothing.

"Have you seen Nature lately?" asked Adam casually.

Bud squinted against a gust of wind. "Must I remind you, Doc, that the person you call Nature is dead?"

"But you and I know better, don't we Bud?"

"Do we?"

Adam shook his head in disappointment. "No reason to be coy, Bud. You told me yourself that you often see him."

"Then perhaps I should ask if you have seen Stevie—I mean Nature—lately?"

Adam fell silent.

"Well?" prodded Bud.

"Yes," whispered Adam.

Bud tapped his temple. "In here?"

"You might say that."

"Oh, he's really got you, hasn't he?"

Adam flashed anger. "Yes! . . . No! Look, Bud, I'm not even sure you're real, let alone whether Nature is here."

Bud laughed heartily, momentarily resting his hand on Adam's shoulder. "I'll leave you alone. Maybe he'll deign to appear. I mean, returning from the Underworld is not easy, you know?"

"No, I don't." grumbled Adam, feeling an odd numbness spread through his body at Yancey's touch. A weight settled under his left collarbone; the wind anesthetized his bones.

Bud laughed again. "You will!"

"Look, who are you really?" demanded Adam, but even as the question left his lips, Bud Yancey had disappeared.

Adam did not bother looking for him, instead sinking into a state of granite immobility. Only the fabric of his tam o'shanter displayed any movement from the blustering wind.

~

At closing time, staff found his body sitting in the same position, eyes open in wonder. There were no witnesses to explain what happened. The coroner's report concluded that Dr. Adam Camara had suffered a massive coronary event, and after a flurry of phone calls to the West Coast, his body was shipped back to California, accompanied only by Dr. Gail Hess—a colleague who had flown to Rhode Island to make sure the final arrangements were carried out without a hitch. Her repeated requests to meet with Mr. Bud Yancey were met with confusion, as he had not worked at Little Neck Cemetery for years.

~ *Ashes of Goddess* ~

The next few weeks were spent by Gail Hess in a confusing miasma of funeral arrangements, complicated by visiting relations of Dr. Camara—some close, some distant, some friendly, some frigid. His parents were dead, and his only sibling—an older brother—viewed Gail with wary gratitude. A variety of aunts, uncles, cousins, nephews, and nieces, came and went in sorrowful anticipation and dutiful solemnity. Twice she reached for her phone to text him—out of habit, out of hope—then remembered. For a while, Goddess seemed content to withdraw from Gail's mind. Mr. Powers remained in a psychological coma, receiving liquid nourishment intravenously. One night, in the depths of her despair, Gail stole into his room and leaned close to his ear.

"Dr. Camara is dead," she whispered.

His eyes fluttered beneath the tears dropping on his face, and his lips moved in silent mimicry of speech.

Gail leaned closer.

"He is with Nature and me," he rasped, the words barely audible above her beating heart.

"Where are you?" she asked.

No response.

Suddenly, his eyes burst open, radiant, probing, demanding. "Goddess?" he asked in a tone of pleading obeisance.

Gail felt herself gain height and lose clothes, the constraining fabric falling away from her as lightly as freedom. Low humming vents sighed restless air across her naked skin, producing little erotic waves as she gazed at Mr. Powers staring back at her. Normally, Gail Hess the psychiatrist, viewed men's fascination with women's bodies as amusing in its absurdity, for she understood the physiology of bodily functions, the scarlet liquid, the slick layers of tissue, and the glutinous organs that gurgled and burped beneath the smooth sheen of femininity. Nonetheless, when possessed by Goddess, she acknowledged the power and glory of deistic luminosity shining forth from the revelation of naked skin and fertile breasts.

She watched his eyes take in her body, and she briefly wondered if Dr. Tavaris even now leered at her in the surveillance room. With this thought, she felt oddly detached—why bother with the petty obsessions of mere mortals? As she stood above Mr. Powers, a roundness came over her, smoothing all sharp edges, granting her a spherical view of the world, as if every patch of skin, front and back, up and down, prickled with the sensory input of innumerable eyes.

Something startled her from behind—perhaps a shadow passed by the window—and she hurriedly put her bra and blouse back on.

"My God, what am I doing!" she exclaimed aloud.

Mr. Powers had sunk back into his comatose state, eyes open but glazed, unseeing.

Thank heavens he was unseeing, she thought, palming the heat out of her cheeks as she smoothed her skirt. *Truthfully, I have been unseeing myself. What do I want? Success? Fame? Happiness? Contentment?*

These questions she had asked since she was a girl, but back then, they were hollow intangibles about an uncertain future. Now, they bore the gravitas of real choices with real consequences, and her rash actions had just jeopardized the harmlessness of those once-harmless conjectures.

Mr. Powers was to have been her ticket to fame and fortune, and now he represented an irresistible threat.

With the death of Adam, she knew her patient had the power to destroy her. The thought jolted Gail into action. Casting a last glance at Mr. Powers, she rushed straight to the surveillance room, and experienced immense relief at finding it empty. Relief is a fool's contract; the footage persists whether or not anyone is watching.

She wanted to smash the screens and dismantle the cameras, erase from the world all hint of her latest indiscretion. Yet, as she looked at the machinery, she felt utterly impotent and knew she could not simply expunge her latest indiscretion. Like life itself, nothing recorded on the entropic cloud can be erased; only garbled.

Nonetheless, that snippet of film settled coldly into the hot core of her being, and instead of melting, it spread its coldness outward and upward.

Is this how Goddess feels? she wondered. *Detached. Impervious. Cold. Hot. Caring. Indifferent?*

You are close to it, my dear!

Goddess's voice came to Gail like a trumpet of doom.

She fled the room and ran to her office and the comfort of inconsequential conversation with June.

June closed the door and didn't offer small talk. "Heads up—HR pinged me. Risk flagged last night's tapes. They're talking administrative leave and a fit-for-duty screen."

Gail scanned the bullets; Fit-for-Duty bloomed like a bruise.

~ *Operational Fallout (Internal)* ~

From: Risk Management

To: Medical Director; Compliance; Legal

Subject: Sentinel Event — Deceased Visitor Hallucination (Dr. Adam Camara)

Effective immediately, all one-to-one off-unit visits are suspended.

Surveillance retention extended to 180 days for Units C–E.

External review initiated; counsel advises no staff statements without representation.

Dr. Tavaris to submit written account; Dr. Hess remains on leave pending Fit-for-Duty.

Policy addendum: dual-role conflicts (treating physician vs. research observer) require prior approval.

—End memo—

~ *Home* ~

Gail successfully avoided Dr. Tavaris the rest of the day and returned home to the ever-patient Sigmund. Adam's death always hit her hardest at this time of evening, and in a gesture of self-pity, she went to bed with *Lady Chatterley's Lover*—to twist the knife deeper. But she could not concentrate on the words, and after the final shudder of joy granted by her own dexterous fingers, she felt more bereft than ever, and wondered at Adam's rapid demise at the hand of . . . of who? Or what?

Has Nature pulled Adam's soul into the confined space of a coffin, or is Adam cavorting somewhere among the shades? Can I visit him now if Goddess agrees to be my guide, and, like Virgil, shields me from the outrages of hell?

Yes, everything is possible. Almost.

Gail trembled at the thought of her sanity falling away like the fabric in her moment of weakness, leaving her naked and vulnerable to the predatory world. She pulled the covers over her head, fully aware she had regressed to the behavior of a frightened child, and yet, in the entombing darkness, thought recklessly. *Yes! I want to go!*

You will, child, you will. In good time. But you are not yet properly prepared. Adam is ashamed to see you just now.

Thinking of Adam's naked body made her shudder, and she felt for *Lady Chatterley's Lover*. "I don't need you anymore," she whispered to the book. "I'll donate you to the institution and let you work your magic on all the lonely, helpless patients."

Chapter Twenty-Four

Dog Days

A Defense

Dear, dear Reader, you must believe me when I tell you I had nothing to do with the death of Dr. Camara. I liked him. Truly. Do you finally accept my conviction that there are powers far beyond these meager words of mine? It is true, I am schizophrenic, but you, dear Reader, all of you Readers, are fellow schizophrenics! You all hear voices. The problem is that you 'normals' filter out the truest warnings, bleakest lamentations, and most accurate prophecies. Instead, you focus on relationships: family, friends, money, power, escaping loneliness, and so on and so forth, with the obsession of dedicated navel-gazers, while all around you, the universe shouts to be heard. Yet, you remain deaf! Sorry—I had to get that off my chest. After all, according to Goddess, I'm not schizophrenic at all, but I am the Chosen One.

Oh, enough moralizing for today! Well—speaking of today, or more specifically, where I am today, I have discovered there is no 'today.' The Underworld seethes with restless shades drifting rudderless in perpetual twilight. I stand, swaying to my mother's shade, her dark form gently rippling like the surface of a placid lake at night. I sense those ripples long to spread and take me in, but the rigid barrier of flesh deflects them.

When I first went to her, I felt at a loss and could only say, "I love you, Mother."

She communicated with me inside my head, as the shade itself emitted no sound.

"I love you beyond words, my son. I am sorry I cannot be with you in your distress."

Mother! Your words pierce me to the core! I put together a string of sentences and reply, "I miss you, Mother. I write about you. I will continue to write about you, and I dream you look over my shoulder with the creation of every word."

Her ripples quicken. "I am astonished you bother to write about me, my son. I am such an uninteresting Chinese girl. One among the many; now merely a shade among shades."

"Never has this world experienced such fascination as your life, Mother. You are the great Bai Meiying—pianist, and seeker after truth. Mother of a sad, ill boy, but friend of the Powerful Ones." My statement seems to make the ripples move even faster. It is during this conversation that Dr. Hess, aka Goddess, whispers in my ear, "Dr. Camara is dead." With these words, I am jerked back to the institution. It seems only a momentary absence from the Underworld, but when I return, Mother is nowhere to be found. Who knows how much time—or no time—or all time—elapsed during my absence? At any rate, I'm once again walking among the shades, scanning their somber outlines, looking for her. Instead, *she* appears at my side.

"You know, your father is also here, Michael Powers."

"My father!" I cry. My poor diseased father who bequeathed to me the schizophrenia that has defined my life. I am shocked that I have not thought of searching for him. I can only stammer, "What about Dr. Camara?"

"Ah, yes, he is here."

"Is he close?"

"Yes."

"Is Diane here?"

"Your wife is elsewhere. We must not have her wake you."

I look long and hard at the multitude of shades passing here and there. I turn to *her*. "Superman would want to know. Is Jesus among these shades?"

"Of course, both Superman and Jesus."

"And Buddha and Mohammed and Abraham and all the rest?"

"Yes, but all of these shades are very far away."

I nod. "That doesn't surprise me," I say smugly. "No doubt keeping their distance from Darwin."

She stares at me. "Nature has requested to see you."

"But, where is my Mother? I was speaking to her when—"

"She will wait. Bai Meiying is marvelously patient."

I look at *her* in wonder. "Are *you* in charge?"

"Fate starves at Probability's door."

"And are *you* starving?"

"Yes."

"Then *you* are fate!"

"I am assigned to you."

"By Goddess?"

"Enough! Here is Nature."

I turn to see a shade staring at me with what can only be described as a grin. My old comrade! As with Mother, he speaks to me in my mind.

"Storyteller!" he cries, with that distinctive Rhode Island accent. "I have followed your adventures since the war!"

I grin back. "You seem to have had your own adventures. You have been busy!"

"Oh—him." He nods toward another shade standing off to the side. Somehow, I know it is Dr. Camara.

"Hello, Doc," I say awkwardly.

"It seems I made a terrible mistake," says Dr. Camara.

"How so?"

"Allowing Nature here into my mind."

Nature looks at me and says something that shocks me. "Michael Powers, otherwise known to some of us as Storyteller—my fellow grunt—is the culprit."

"Me?" I say stupidly.

"You're sick," says Nature. "But I love you for it. I have always loved you for it. Your illness connects you to all of us. Dr. Camara did not love you for it. He wanted to fix you so you would have no more voices, kind of like fixing a dog so it would have no more offspring. You lashed out unconsciously. I merely accommodated."

"Then I am responsible for his death."

Both shades remain silent, but I see agitated ripples in Dr. Camara.

"No, not really," says Camara. "The universe is not deterministic. The probability that I would turn out to be so suggestible did me in. Three nights without sleep on the wards, Storyteller. I opened a window; something flew in. Probability did the rest."

"Do you truly miss being alive?" I ask.

"Yes!"

"Do you miss Gail Hess?"

"I would if she was totally Gail Hess. But, alas, now she is only partly Gail Hess."

"And the other part?"

"You know."

I suddenly feel a horror rising in my gut, and I say, "What will happen to her?"

She breaks in. **Fate starves at Probability's door.**

"Then Dr. Hess has a chance?" I reply in a pleading tone.

"There is always hope." These gentle words come from a different shade—Mother. Her words are a comforting balm to my guilty mind. I rush to her—I want to ask her about Meili, about Lihua, but all becomes black.

"Mother!" I cry into the darkness, but there is no reply.

I know it's no use. I'm back at the institution. Back in my room! It's the one place I do not want to be. I want to be back among the shades, with Mother and Nature and all the others I love the most. I want to be back in the tunnel. Anywhere but here. I deserve what I get. Don't tell me otherwise, dear Reader—I have blood on my hands—more and more blood on my hands!

~

It has been some time since I have written. A guilty conscience, I suppose. It suddenly comes to me that I need a woman. I saw a copy of *Lady Chatterley's Lover* in the recreation room a few days back, so I spirited it away to read at night before lights out. It has awakened old longings. Damn antipsychotic medication kills sexual desire, but I've killed the medication, and now—I need a woman. Why this sudden urge? Dunno. Sex? Yes and no. Companionship? Get a dog.

Intimacy? Of course. You see, dear Reader, I have only you to talk with, and you cannot sit with me without my having to perform the dreary task of feeding words into your mind. The death of Dr. Camara has rendered me unsure of anything. My time in the Underworld taught me the true meaning of transient life. I feel like Ahab. Why this restless searching for some unknown, nameless thing, Starbuck? Is it because of *Her* and *Her* ceaseless quest to end suffering? Yes . . . perhaps. If I boil it down to its shameful core, it is this: *Her* breasts. Dr. Hess has lovely breasts, but, well . . . still mortal and subject to decay (yet young enough to give me an erection). When my cock is erect, I am alive! A simple, unadorned truth . . . primitive perhaps, but there it is. Soon, Gail Hess's breasts will be impervious to age when she morphs into Goddess, and the world of cocks will fall to their knees in supplication.

Once again, I stray from my point. Dr. Camara is dead, and I am to blame. I might cast aspersions on Goddess and claim it is *Her* fault, but the fault is mine. The bell is now tolling for Dr. Hess as well . . . and Dr. Tavaris. They're unaware, though both are suspicious (and afraid) in their own ways. Do I continue to obey Goddess in Her noble quest, or do I warn Hess and Tavaris with dire predictions? Ah! They would laugh it off. No, perhaps not. They can feel it for themselves. At least Gail Hess knows it is coming. Tavaris remains a fool in his juvenile convictions. And I? Schizophrenics cannot be fools any more than cancer patients can be jesters.

~

Back to the woman idea. Diane has not communicated with me in ages, and without her, my nightmares continue unabated. Is there anyone in this nuthouse that can give me comfort and satisfaction? Decidedly not. The depression patients are out of the question, and the assortment of schizos, psychos, and bipolar banshees is enough to induce suicide. That leaves the nurses, all of whom have heard of my reputation, and all give me a wide berth. Once again, my only hope is escape.

~

Dog days. Dr. Hess has taken a leave of absence, and Dr. Tavaris is playing hard to get again. He won't respond to my requests for a meeting. Rumor has it he plans to return to NIMH, but I don't believe it.

No one's removing my finished writing, and the papers accumulate under the mattress. I even had to ask for more paper.

I cannot write any more than this today.

I am depressed beyond words. I want to go back to the Underworld. Permanently.

I keep having nightmares about Dr. Camara. Where are you, Diane? Wake me from this bad dream.

And where are you, Mark? You can get me out of here, but if you did, you would have my carcass to burden you with.

~

Just when I am at my lowest point, a miracle! Standing before me is a gorgeous, entirely naked woman. She smiles at me, and evidently has no relationship with modesty.

If you have read my scribblings, you should already know her identity.

"Theresa!" I cry, for she is my long-lost hallucination—my imaginary wife—a spy sent by Goddess years ago.

"Hello, Michael," she says with a voice husky and sensual, created specifically to drive me madder than I already am.

"It's been a long time," I say, greedily drinking in every inch of her glowing body.

"Sent by Goddess?" I ask.

She nods, and quite casually runs her index finger in circles around her nipple.

"Theresa," I manage to say with some difficulty. "No need for that yet. Can we just talk for a while instead?" I can't believe I am saying this, but the urge for emotional rather than sexual intimacy overcomes my physical need . . . for the moment.

Her arms fall gracefully to her sides, and she replies, "Of course."

We sit on the bed and converse for hours. Our imaginary marriage had ended when I returned to the tunnel, so we have a lot of catching up to do.

"Does *She* know I am done with *Her*? That I have blood on my hands?"

"*She* does."

"Does *She* accept that our on-again, off-again relationship is off for good?"

"I am here."

"What does that mean?"

"It means, Michael, that you do not have the power to sever the relationship."

This angers me. "And what if I find God? If I go to *Him* for help?"

Theresa shakes her head. "God will find you. *He* will entice you with *His* stories of candies and cakes, but you must resist."

"Why should I?"

Theresa stands up and spreads her arms, revealing the full magnificence of her body. "When you ask for a woman, *She* gives you one."

"Yes, but you are not real."

Theresa laughs. "There is very little about what you see that is what you call 'real,' and yet I am a part of you that is more real than most of your delusions."

She reaches out, and I quiver under the touch, for it is as real as if I were touched by Dr. Hess or Dr. Tavaris.

I pull her toward me, but she resists. I let go of her wrists and lean back on the bed, drinking in the flawless translucence of her nakedness.

"What about my life is real?" I ask, recognizing the childish pleading in my voice.

"The bones of your life are real; your parents, your childhood, being a soldier in war, being a lawyer, Diane, your son Mark, and, of course, being a misdiagnosed schizophrenic who is, instead, the Chosen One. The tunnel is your anchor, not your prison."

"That tells me nothing!" I cry.

"It tells you everything."

I have a sudden, pleasant thought. "Isn't it true that this room, this institution, are dreams, and I'm in bed with Diane, dreaming?"

"No, that is not true."

I knew the answer before the question, but it stings nonetheless. "You're cruel to be so blunt," I say.

Theresa shrugs and shows me her bruise. "The world is cruel."

"Is Buandelgereen real?"

"Yes."

"Is my son's wife, My-duyen, real?"

"Yes."

"Thank God!"

Her face darkens. "You need not thank *Him*, for their days of suffering will come under *His* rule."

I hold up my hand. "Don't tell me that."

She nods.

"When you say things like that, I think of Tuyet Mai, Madame Dau, Lihua, Meili, Feng Shiren, Mountain Man, Sergeant Dam, and all the rest. I do not want to think of them and their suffering. Please—tell me they were not real, that their suffering was dreamed up by my diseased mind."

She looks pained. "No, they were, and Tuyet Mai still is, real. I say this with the caveat that their experiences were real, and not real, as you've mixed together much that complicates the laws of physics."

"You violate the laws of physics!" I say resentfully.

"The schizophrenia in your human genes is a serial rapist of virgin reality."

"You must tell me!" I plead.

"Tell you what?"

"Is there one core reality, one anchor, on which I can rely as real, even as the delusions and hallucinations storm all around?"

"Yes."

I wait.

"The tunnel."

"Ah." The word hits me hard, and it rolls around in my mind until I grip it tightly. "Then, that is my home. That is where I belong. It is the only reality, as I have known all along."

Theresa chuckles softly. "No, that is not the only reality." She waves her arms. "This room is real, Dr. Hess is real, although possibly soon to be among the shades with Dr. Camara. The tunnel is your reality, but Goddess has other plans for you."

"Is *She* real?" I demand.

"As real as I am standing before you."

"But you are not real!"

"You can't actually fuck physics, but you can fuck me. How much more reality do you need?"

As she says these words, she moves forward and strokes my erect cock.

I'm helpless. It's been so long. . . .

~ *Reality?* ~

Yes, yes, I know, dear Reader, by your "normal" lights, since Theresa is not real, I merely masturbated. However, to those of us conscripted into the supernatural, it was so much more real with her. I have often heard it said we must live in the moment, but, in fact, there is no such thing. If healthy, one lives in the future. If ill, one lives in the past. Only subatomic processes ever brush the now. Although humans are constructed from such particles, the whole somehow becomes less than the sum of its parts. Where do we schizophrenics live? We live amid un-collapsed quantum states; our hallucinations exist here, there, and everywhere at once—mere tendencies to be. Psychiatry calls in the measurement, collapses the swarm to one narrow fact, and names it health. Fate starves at Probability's door. Even you, dear Readers, are as insubstantial as these erasable words. The goal of our esteemed psychiatrists is to collapse the entangled swirl of our delusions and hallucinations to a certainty and shrink reality to the realm of normals. Very well, let us grant them their wish. Let's assume psychiatrists succeed, and all probabilities fly away, leaving us with the certainty of what is real—a most lamentable state. You would have us schizophrenics be as narrow and constricted as you.

I do not mean you, dear Reader. I do not cast aspersions on you. After all, if you are still reading, you have endured the unendurable. I speak of the others—you know the type: smug little people who revel in their own stupidity. However, again I digress. Theresa has convinced me to stick with Goddess. Why? Isn't it obvious? Deities, the gods and goddesses to whom you pray, are the voices that we all share. They speak the universal language of mental illness, which is why people kill and slaughter for them—desperate acts by the desperately ill. We cling to the voices of the unreal because the voices of the real rarely satisfy.

There I go again, dear Reader. Ignore these detours and focus on this: I plan to escape again—it's true! If I am to help Goddess, I can do no good in here. She has renewed confidence in me. I have something to live for again. Isn't that what we all want? She gives me a reason to wake up every morning. That's enough—for me, at least. If I cannot return to the tunnel, I will return to the world. Again. Oh, Goddess! You, being immortal, do not get weary. But I? . . . Never mind, I ramble. And now, I'm ready to escape.

So, once again, like a general in a war, I search for weaknesses in their defenses. Now there is no Joe to exploit, so the task is rendered more difficult. Sure, there are foolish employees who perform the unpleasant daily tasks of care, but most are clearly more impervious to manipulation than Joe was, for a minimal amount of sentience is required to even be manipulated, and I fear many do not rise to that level. There is one with potential—the heavyset nurse with the jangling key ring and the weary eyes. Maybe I can start working on her. At 06:55 she always counts meds before the south-wing handoff; when the laundry cart hits the stair threshold, the camera blanks for eight seconds. Weaknesses, plural. Better yet, patience. I'll wait a little longer. If Goddess succeeds with Dr. Hess, then the path is clear. That, of course, assumes Dr. Hess avoids being fired for her indiscretions.

Where is Theresa? Ah. . . .

~ *Dr. Hess?* ~

Dr. Hess has not returned, and no one will tell me when she will resume work. In the meantime, Dr. Tavaris has also been scarce. Since Dr. Camara's funeral, he has seen me only once, exchanging no more than a dozen words. Either he is playing games with me, or Bowls is on the verge. I go to the cafeteria, accompanied by my morning keeper—Mr. Greene—a rather dull nurse's aide, impervious to any form of conversation or banter. The coffee tastes burned; the linoleum hums beneath the fluorescent lights. With my mind swimming in impractical escape plans, I see my old friend, Damien Lundgren, sitting in his usual spot, nodding with the regularity of a pendulum. Mr. Greene moves over against the wall to talk with one of his buddies.

I set my tray at Damien's table.

"How is Goddess these days?" I ask in my best jocular, hale and hearty manner.

He stops nodding and looks at me with a hound dog expression. "*She* has returned to you," he says, drawing out the words in a lugubrious tone.

This takes me aback. "Why? I mean, what makes you say that?"

"I asked *Her* that very question, and *She* said you are the son."

"Oh." I do not know what to say.

"Now I know," he adds, even more morosely.

"Know what?"

"You are Jesus Christ, and I am not."

~

Now, dear Reader, this would make anyone stop and think. It isn't that the thought had never occurred to me, but I had always dismissed it as too stereotypically schizophrenic—I have my pride. I have never believed I was Napoleon Bonaparte or Abraham Lincoln, or, for that matter, Jesus Christ. I have never—ever—

Well, look at it this way: I am not *His* lamb, but *Her* instrument—a soldier repurposed.

"You are the son," keeps echoing in my mind. And why not? End suffering; bring love and peace to the world? Of course, I'm *Her* son, not *His*, and that makes all the difference.

What drives these thoughts, or, as you might call them, these fantasies? The answer is obvious: the war. Jesus Christ never carried a weapon or wore a uniform, much less killed others in battle. That alone disqualifies me from being legitimately some sort of reincarnation of Jesus. You see, Goddess works differently than God, and *Her* methodology may be counterintuitive. God concerns *Himself* with redeeming suffering Man, while Goddess concerns *Herself* with redeeming addicted God. While, intuitively, it might seem that a warlike, angry God should have a son who would fulfill the Hebrew prophecies of a vengeful King leading them to victory over their enemies, it turns out to be the opposite. Alternatively, while it would seem that a feminine, domestic Goddess should have a son that promulgates peace and nonviolence, the opposite appears to be the case. That is where I come in. Perhaps Damien is correct. Perhaps the son of Goddess—me—can be a reformed soldier who will lead humanity down the path of enlightenment. Oh—it hurts my head to think about.

I look at Damien, who has reverted to nodding his head idiotically. I am curious.

"Damien, do you think I am Jesus Christ?"

"You are the son," he murmurs without looking at me.

"But am I Jesus Christ?"

Mr. Greene moves closer to our table and guffaws rudely. His mocking voice booms, "Of course you're Jesus Christ, Mr. Powers! You are definitely Jesus Christ, plus the Pope and God, all rolled into one!"

"Fuck you!" I shout, but my retort only makes him laugh harder.

Still, his hurtful words snap me back to the grim reality of this damn institution. I really wish I had my M-16 to empty into Mr. Greene, but that's certainly not how Jesus would react, is it, dear Reader? No, of course not. And it is certainly not how the Chosen One should act.

So I gather up what remains of my dignity, and return to my room, his laughter trailing behind, sharp as gravel in a shoe.

Chapter Twenty-Five

Doctor Hess Suffers

Downward Spiral

~ Fever Dreams[1] ~

Gail Hess had confined herself to bed for days, struggling with a high fever and grotesque hallucinations. In moments of clarity, when the burning lessened, she felt certain she had survived a deathbed night, but the fever kept returning, warping her mind with the most terrifying visions. Every inanimate object in her room, at one time or another, transformed into animate monstrosities with evil intentions, ready to tear her limb from limb. Even poor Sigmund, innocently cuddling next to her heated body, morphed into a voracious beast with a human face and claws that raked her fevered flesh. She violently kicked him off the bed and he wisely kept his distance, curling up in another room, resentful and watchful. Now, she lay exhausted, between life and death, her thoughts wandering down strange and alien paths.

Gail's mental landscape unfolded in ways unfamiliar to her accustomed view of the world, and the view took her breath away. She no longer regarded herself as a psychiatrist, or, for that matter, a woman, but rather as some omniscient being. The room could not keep its shape, and Gail watched in amazement as the walls and ceiling ballooned outward, encompassing the neighboring houses, then the city, the countryside, the Earth, then, it seemed, infinity. *You cannot encompass infinity,* she marveled, whereupon the rational Dr. Hess blinked out, and she lost sight of the tiny kernel that remained of her soul. All of life, all that exists, filled this infinite space, and she surveyed it through the eyes of Goddess.

And what a view! Gail had never felt such power. Awareness transcended the abilities of her feeble human mind to comprehend, suffusing every molecule of the universe with all-encompassing knowledge. Just as she began to adjust to the dizzying sense of oneness with all that exists, she saw a faint, pulsing light among the galaxies. Somehow, she knew it was the beating enigma of Mr. Powers. As if her body drew into a filament of light, she sped toward the center of its reddish pulse, and knew Mr. Powers's holy of holies would soon be revealed. As she plunged into the pulsing core, she felt herself instantly bounce backward, like light striking an impenetrable mirror, and she stared at herself, drenched in sweat and standing limply in her own bathroom. Her heart clattered and fluttered for an indeterminate span until finally slowing to a survivable pace. Somehow, she knew she had escaped something either wonderful or terrible, and she speculated whether this was how Adam died. The recoil from the core that stopped his heart—was that his last sensation? *It must be*, she thought. *It must!*

~

Gail staggered to her bed, fell clumsily on her back and stared in a blind stupor at the ceiling. Gradually, for the first time, the idea of freeing herself from Mr. Powers's physical presence took root. *Either I leave or he leaves*, she thought. *One way or another, I must rid myself of him!*

This realization—sudden, definite, and irrevocable—rejuvenated her. *I cannot release him from the institution, so I must quit. Get a job as far away as possible. Go to the East Coast. Go to Africa. Just go. Go!*

The next morning, still officially on leave, Gail went in to the hospital with single-minded determination, her spirits high, borne by the rare exhilaration of resolution. She said "Good morning" to June, and after dropping off her purse, walked directly to see Mr. Thomas Jones, the CEO of Smythe-Haines Psychiatric Hospital. After waiting a few minutes, the secretary sent her into his office.

Mr. Jones rose in greeting. "So good to see you, Gail."

"Thank you."

"Please have a seat. What can I do for you?"

Gail had been rehearsing her words all night. "Tom, I am going to resign my position here, effective as soon as possible."

"But—"

Gail held up her hand. "Let me explain, Tom. It has nothing to do with this institution or with the death of Adam Camara. I have been quite happy here, and you have been most helpful and understanding. My decision is for private reasons, personal reasons."

Mr. Jones remained quiet, processing what he had just heard. His initial inclination had been to make a sincere effort to convince her to stay, but on further consideration, he saw an opportunity. After all, Gail Hess had been controversial, and her role-playing stunt had caused intense embarrassment and widespread consternation among the staff. Furthermore, with her youthful brilliance, unorthodox methods, and occasional disregard of protocol, she represented a threat to many other psychiatrists.

Yes, he thought, *this might be the perfect opportunity to have her gone without the disruption of hearings, paperwork, and possibly lawsuits.*

"Well, Gail, I am so sad to hear this. I can see any attempt to talk you out of this would be in vain. I will not ask what personal reasons have led you to this decision. You have been a valued and integral part of this hospital since I got here. Your presence will be sorely missed."

Gail felt her heart constrict. She knew he was secretly pleased, and her pride suffered a blow. Surely, he could have at least tried harder to convince her to stay. *Stupid woman*, she thought. *It is exactly what you want.*

"I am sure I can count on a positive recommendation from you and this institution in the event I seek a position elsewhere?" she asked.

"Of course, of course, that goes without saying, Gail. Do you have another position in mind?"

"To be honest, I do not. It is sudden. I made this decision very recently, and have not had time to consider the next step professionally."

"Before we get into coverage," Jones said, steepling his fingers, "HR still has your Fit-for-Duty review open following the incident. Technically you're on administrative leave."

"Understood," Gail said. "My decision stands."

"I see." Mr. Jones's face darkened. "Your other patients are easily transferred, but one particular patient, Mr. Powers. . . . " He coughed, searching for the words.

"Yes?"

"Could your decision have anything to do with him?"

"What makes you say that?"

"Well, I have heard rumors."

"What rumors?"

"Oh, just how unique his condition seems to be." He leaned forward. "And I know the death of Dr. Camara may have had something to do with the case."

"I don't know about that. Anyway, you have Dr. Tavaris to take over the treatment of Mr. Powers."

"Well, as you know, Dr. Tavaris is here temporarily. I am not sure he is willing to take over the case completely."

"He seems pretty interested."

"No, I don't think so. He has too much going on at NIMH."

Gail smiled. "There are many qualified psychiatrists out there who can fill my shoes more than adequately."

"Perhaps, perhaps," he mumbled.

"Of course they can."

As if remembering himself, Jones straightened and said brightly, "But I am sure not as well as you."

"You're very kind."

"Well," he said. "If you're sure, I will have the paperwork drawn up. Will you stay another few months until we can find a replacement?"

Gail knew this question would be coming, and she negotiated him down to thirty days. *How will I stay away from Mr. Powers for thirty days?* she wondered as she left Mr. Jones's office.

The remainder of the day unfolded routinely, and she put off telling June until her emotions were in better check. Somehow, as she walked the halls and chatted with a few patients, she felt an unexpected sadness.

"Once I cross the Rubicon," she said aloud, "will he follow?"

~

The next day, after she completed the unpleasant task of informing June about her decision, Gail felt a heavy weight lifted from her shoulders.

It seemed telling June truly meant there was no going back.

~ *No Second Thoughts* ~

Two weeks after her meeting with Mr. Jones, time had passed rather quickly and uneventfully. Gail felt a sense of relief, and believed she had "turned the corner" to lead a normal life once again. HR had reinstated her to restricted, transition duties for her thirty-day notice, and one morning, June announced that Mr. Powers insisted on a meeting.

"That's not going to be possible," said Gail flatly. "Mr. Powers will have to accommodate himself to a new psychiatrist."

June rolled her eyes. "He said if you refuse to see him, he will go on a hunger strike."

Feeling untouchable by the closeness of her impending departure, Gail shrugged. "The institute has ways of dealing with that. Enteral feeding is policy if necessary. I understand replacement psychiatrists are already being interviewed. Soon, it will be their problem. Meanwhile, Dr. Tavaris can handle it."

"That doesn't sound like you," grumbled June, still resentful over her boss's departure.

"Aren't you the one who always worries when I am in the same room with Mr. Powers?"

June did not reply, merely grunting her displeasure and walking out of the office. Gail felt a surge of imperial pique at June's attitude and stood tall and proud while looking disdainfully at the closed door. In the back of her mind, she searched for her usual good-humored imperturbability when dealing with June but could not find it. With reluctance, she soon began her rounds, and as she passed by a large window in the hallway, she glanced at her reflection and its haughty demeanor, recognizing someone or something not part of herself. Again, the old fear returned, and she rushed past the reflection, mumbling whatever Ave Marias and clinical mantras came to mind. The image of poor Adam Camara slumped on a cemetery bench, tam o'shanter askew, haunted her thoughts. Yet, often, the thought of Adam Camara brought forth no human emotion, only the chilling frigidity of omniscience. When he was alive, Gail often fantasized about marrying him and raising a family together. *Two children*, she told herself in those days. *That is all I want, two children: a boy and a girl.* Suddenly, quite out of the blue, her womb ached with two conflicting sensations—a mother's teeming biological fertility and Goddess's arid, deistic desolation.

Gail's body reacted to these polar states-of-being as if attacked by a virulent disease, and she rushed to the nearest bathroom to retch and pant away her anxieties. After what seemed hours, she gradually regained control of her senses.

In her weakened state, she canceled all appointments and returned home to seek comfort in the solitude of feline companionship.

~

Once home, wrapped in comfy pajamas, Gail stroked the soft fur of Sigmund and contemplated her condition. She knew she was again losing her sanity, but this time, her mental processes slipped away more quickly, and the realization caused her to fall into deep despair. It now seemed evident that distance from the institute and Michael Powers would not matter. After all, Adam died a continent away. Why not end it now, on her own terms, while she still retained a modicum of her own self? She knew she was a long way from surrendering to the lure of suicide, but, like Alzheimer's, it would just be a matter of time. Even as these thoughts roiled her mind, she felt an inexplicable urge to remove her clothes and walk back to the institute. Why? She knew. She would not walk, but rather float through the walls and hover over Michael Powers. To what purpose? In a blinding flash, she understood . . . purpose engulfed her, smothered her. Knowing the consequences, she released her last grip on the woman known as Gail Hess.

Doors are for mortals, she thought; *to deities, walls are only weather.*

Without a backward glance at Sigmund, she removed her pajamas and drove to the institute

~ *Dr. Tavaris Confronts the Unthinkable* ~

Mr. Jones and Dr. Tavaris stared down at Gail's body. Psychologists and staff hovered on the other side of the cordoned area.

"The forensics people are on the way," said Mr. Jones, unable to tear his eyes away from the naked body.

"Yes, yes," mumbled Dr. Tavaris.

Her body lay slumped against the door of Michael Powers's room.

"Still locked," continued Mr. Jones. "Couldn't have been Mr. Powers. See how her body rests against his door from the outside?"

"Yes, yes," again mumbled Tavaris. "How did she die?"

"Dunno yet. We checked the security tapes, and she entered the hallway and walked straight into the door, then just collapsed. Mr. Powers remained in his bed the entire time. Maybe a heart attack?"

"I see, I see. Is Mr. Powers awake now?"

"No, still asleep."

"Or something," whispered Tavaris.

"What?"

"Nothing. Look, can't we move the body so I can check on Mr. Powers?"

"Police told us to leave it as is. I guess they suspect foul play."

"But there are no marks!" protested Tavaris.

"I know. Odd. So young to have a heart attack. And why is she naked?"

"Raped and dumped here?" asked Tavaris with a catch in his voice.

"No one else on the tape."

"Oh, yes. Of course."

At that moment, Jones and Tavaris simultaneously turned their heads and saw the eyes of Mr. Powers staring at them through the little window. Both gasped and instinctively flinched backward. The eyes were open wide, probing, yet otherwise indecipherable. The eyes rolled downward but could not see the body slumped beneath their view. The eyes shot back up to stare at the two men, then disappeared as quickly as they appeared.

"We must move the body so I can go in!" said Tavaris urgently.

Just as Jones was about to respond, the forensics team arrived in hooded Tyvek **suits** and asked both men to leave the cordoned area while they did their work.

"Please hurry," said Tavaris. "We need to get to the patient in that room."

The aliens nodded and went about their business.

As he moved away, Tavaris felt real fear for the first time. Borderline terror. His usual professional imperturbability had vanished in the face of this latest shock. He had the urge to run as fast as his legs could carry him away from this cursed institution, away from this cursed patient. He reached in his pocket and fingered the pipe, now seeming an inert malevolence that mocked his powerlessness. *Bowls was terrified, but he had Mountain Man,* he thought. *And me?* The dark vortex that destroyed Adam Camara and Gail Hess swirled nearby, tugging at the loose thread holding his grip on objective reason together. *It happened to them so quickly!* he marveled, even as he felt his own sense of self unraveling.

Excusing himself from the presence of Mr. Jones, Tavaris hurried to the security room. He wanted to see the tapes, but two plainclothes police detectives were already perusing them.

"May I join you, gentlemen?" he asked in his most authoritarian voice.

"And you are?" asked a detective.

"Dr. Alfred Tavaris, on a special assignment here from NIMH."

"What's that?"

"National Institute of Mental Health."

"Oh. Well, these tapes are evidence, but I guess you can take a look. Perhaps you can help explain what happened."

One of the men took out a notebook and pen while the other rewound the tape. All three leaned forward and watched. Gail Hess appeared like a ghost in the grainy footage, entering the frame from the right, naked and walking with the calm assurance of routine rounds, only this time on a beeline for one room. As she veered toward Mr. Powers's door, Tavaris's hand rose on its own; the dead stem of his empty pipe **tapped his teeth—a soft click—and he flinched, pocketing it as if burned. Gail's face was indistinct, and when she turned toward Mr. Powers's door, she simply walked straight into it as if it did not exist. Her body crumpled at the foot of the door and did not move. No startle, no bracing, her arms never lifted; the body simply switched off and folded. That was all. They replayed the tape many times, with Dr. Tavaris's attention riveted to the little window. He thought he saw eyes but could not be sure. When he mentioned the possibility, all three men strained their attention to make out what was on the other side of the window, but none could swear to eyes, a face—anything.

"We'll take this to our tech people," said a detective. "They can resolve the image to make it clearer. Then perhaps. . . . " He shrugged. "We'll see. Now, Dr. Tavaris, why do you think she was here, naked, walking into doors?"

"I cannot imagine," he lied.

Clearly the detective was skeptical. "Confidential?"

"No. I just do not know."

"Doctor, if there is foul play here, we can get documents, witnesses—this type of thing never stays confidential."

"Foul play?"

"We've seen everything, doctor. We've seen people forcing other people to do weird things using drugs, threats, hypnosis, you name it."

"I still do not see why you suspect foul play."

"You don't? A respected psychiatrist found dead, naked, in the hallway of a psychiatric hospital, having apparently walked into a door as if it did not exist. Is this the type of behavior you would expect of Dr. Hess?"

"Of course not."

"Well then, let us do our job. If you know something, or suspect something, please let us know. We'll find out anyway. Maybe one of her crazy patients did something?"

"Sorry, I do not know, but I will check her notes and other records and let you know if I find anything."

"Doctor, we will be checking those notes and records ourselves, but your insights would be helpful."

"I will do everything I can."

"Thank you."

Once alone, Tavaris immediately went to Gail's office. June was being questioned, so he waited patiently. Mr. Jones entered and nodded at Tavaris, then, after the detectives left, went to June and gave her a consoling hug. "June, go home. There's nothing more you can do here."

Through her tears, June said, "It was him."

"Who?" asked Jones.

June looked at Tavaris. "Dr. Tavaris knows who I am talking about. It was him."

Mr. Jones sighed. "Michael Powers?"

"Yes."

"June, we looked at the tapes. He was nowhere to be seen."

"Where did she die?" June challenged.

"I know, I know, but he was locked inside, asleep. Security tapes have it all. Now, go home. That's an order. We and the police will find out all there is to know about this terrible tragedy. Go home."

June left, shaking her head, and between sobs kept repeating, "It was him, I know it. It was him!"

Tavaris talked for a while with Mr. Jones, then pretended he had an appointment. When he observed Jones disappear around a corner, he slipped back into Gail's office, boxed all of Michael Powers's binders, and walked to his car as casually as he could manage. He put the binders in the trunk, clenched the pipe in his teeth, and walked back into the institution to confront Michael Powers.

Chapter Twenty-Six

To Freedom?

First, The Cave

I am just as puzzled as you, dear Reader. Dr. Tavaris and I are in his car, driving to the cave. Maybe you think I'm hallucinating again? Dreaming this all up? Perhaps. But now, even I am afraid. If I'm not in the throes of some delusion, then Adam Camara and Gail Hess are truly dead, and something terrible has been loosed upon the world. A cradle rocked by the hand of Goddess, or blood-dimmed tide churned by the hand of God. Anyway, that's neither here nor there. First the cave; next the tunnel; then—nothingness.

"What?" asks Dr. Tavaris.

"Nothing, I'm schizophrenic, remember, Doc?"

He emits a strange little laugh. "Yeah."

He has that pipe constantly in his mouth, just like Bowls. As I said, I am very afraid. But if this is a hallucination, the desert outside the car looks very real. Like fugitives, we've stayed off the main roads knowing the police are searching. We sleep in the car when we can and travel mostly at night. At 3 a.m., Bowls—Dr. Tavaris—borrowed a laundry cart and a smile; my bracelet became a relic under a folded towel, and the back gate forgot to care. I must be dreaming; all this has happened too quickly, even for a schizophrenic. I try to impose order on my mind and repeatedly fail. Nevertheless. . . .

"Dr. Tavaris?" I ask.

He looks at me funny and takes the pipe out of his mouth. "Shit, Storyteller, you can call me Bowls. Dr. Tavaris is no longer available."

"Christ, Doc, you're crazier than I am now." I look at his fingers, the skin pulled back from constant fidgeting, and fingernails all chewed to the nub. His head bobs and shoulders twitch, just like Stretch. Christ, who is he? Bowls or Stretch? Are they all morphing together, or has Tavaris just got it all wrong in his head?

"Got to see Mountain Man again, Storyteller. Fuckin' got to."

"Dr. Tavaris, Mountain Man is a shade."

"I'm, not Dr. Tavaris."

"Okay, but Mountain Man is still a shade."

"I know."

"In fact, if you're Bowls, you're also a shade."

"Not no longer."

The cradle rocks, the tide advances.

I revert to Vietnam lingo, hoping to make a connection. "You're fuckin' too old to be a grunt, Bowls. Look at you!"

Tavaris laughs. "Look at you, motherfucker! Look who's talkin'!"

I peer at him closer. It is utterly bizarre. A few days ago, Tavaris was a respected psychiatrist from NIMH in full control of his own delusions, and now he's a shit-faced grunt in a scorched Vietnam as if Vietnam had been repoured as sand and dust. The question is, will he die like the other two? And if he does, what is the point of it all? Goddess? God? Neither of You have answers, do You? Memories are never still. They are shape changers, and the shapes they assume are more joyful and more horrifying than anything in the real world. Perhaps Dr. Tavaris, the car, the desert, and the cave, are all delusions . . . or, hallucinations, and I am lying in my bed back at the institute. Or, perhaps, that is just what memories are. We see them as flowing rivers and streams and tributaries, forever changing their course and sculpting new landscapes. But once I succeed in stilling the stillness, they will solidify into reality—perpetual, permanent reality. The trick is to still the stillness at just the right moment; catch the morphing shape of memory when it is joyous rather than horrifying, and then freeze it in place.

"Hey, Storyteller!" cries Tavaris as he pulls off the road and slams on the brakes. "Look at that naked woman up ahead runnin' that lipstick thingy around and around her nipples! Your tab, man! Your tab!"

His jaw goes slack; a thin string of saliva silvers the stem. One soft wheeze—then nothing.

By the time the car rolls to a stop on the dirt shoulder, he is dead, slumped over the steering wheel.

~

Hours have passed. I have dragged his body from the car and laid it on the desert floor, and now I just stare at the corpse. The deaths of Doctors Camara, Hess, and Tavaris have happened too quickly for me to deal with. I am left with memories made jagged by the unending permutations of horror, and I must continue to live until I see their gruesome shapes shift back into the beauteous fabric of joy; then, I must stop them dead in their tracks—freeze them in place—before they become gruesome again. I decide to leave Tavaris's body in a conspicuous place, so he may be found and buried by whatever relatives or loved ones he has in the world. I've left his body close to the main road, and now I drive on. To the cave. To Buandelgereen. My first step to stilling the stillness.

I clutch the steering wheel and drive slowly over the narrow dirt road that parallels the main highway, more than a mile away. My good fortune only now washes over me in pleasant sensations, like cool baptismal water on a hot day. Those jagged, guilt-ridden memories of Gail Hess and the others melt to a waxy slag; still there, but formless and partly transparent, through which I can perceive the distorted image of my ultimate goal. This endless stretch of desert sand, surrounded by a necklace of purple hills in the distance, is my antivenom, my anti-Vietnam, my antidote for the poison that has collected in the craters of my soul. Yes, father, I remember your words. Memories, here in this desolate place, have room to swell and bloom spectacularly, like hardy desert flowers flinging open their brilliance in colorful bursts of inspiration and insight. By mid-morning the heat turns the asphalt to a mirage, and the sky hums with thermals.

Up ahead, I see a dust devil swirling madly, locking its tortured grains of sand in violent bondage, twisting to form a column writhing and spiraling upward, like one of Michelangelo's agonized slaves struggling to break free from the marble.

"Triggers," I hear a voice say from the back seat.

I snap my head around but see nothing. When I look forward again, the voice returns.

"These images, my death, this desert, Dr. Tavaris lying in the sand behind us, are all from the real world, and are triggers that set your psychotic episodes in motion."

I look in the rearview mirror and see Dr. Hess's eyes locked on mine. Her ghostly presence is somehow soothing, and I slip easily into my Michael Powers persona. "No, Doc, only your breasts are my triggers. If you show them to me, I'll share with you deep insights into my childhood."

The words ring hollow, even to my sarcastic ears.

She does not respond; she only points a finger straight ahead. I follow it, and now see two dust devils, side by side, churning the desert floor. Two human figures emerge from the amorphous twisters. I have seen this film before, and in resignation of the inevitable, I stop the car and wait. As usual, the shapes change in dizzying progression, as if carved by a mad sculptor. They change from humans to birds—then to fishes—to trees—clouds—mountains—reptiles—all the while talking in the low rumble of an approaching tornado. Finally, their shape-changing stops and two human-sized ants stand upright. Antennae waving, legs gesturing, their words become distinguishable.

He has turned from You, Goddess, and I am pleased.

No, God, he long ago turned from You. He embraces the future.

Ha! He embraces Your breasts. He still thinks you are nothing but a voice in the mind of a schizophrenic.

On the contrary, Dearest God, he drives to liberation. He is beginning to understand his power. He is beginning to understand the voices are not hallucinations, but there is reality behind the words. He is beginning to understand the nature of his power, although he does not yet know how to control the wild genes.

Humans, Lovely Goddess, must be left to their own devices. First Principles dictate there will be no intervention, yet You continue to flout this iron rule.

You are no longer of any use, God, and You know it. Your days of allowing their minds to be enslaved by ignorance and fear are coming to an end. The destruction they wreak on the planet must be stopped.

Enough! thunders God. ***Let the record of First Principles be read: Clause One—Non-Intervention. Clause Two—Consequence without Exception. You trespass, Goddess. You rob agency under the seal of mercy.***

Goddess answers in a voice stolen from America's sickness; the very tongue *He* sanctioned. ***Not so, Master God. You made a slave of Me and named it order. I'll have no truck with You. There—I've found You out at last: You are the robber.***

Yes, use mockery to deflect, God says. ***Wear that tongue if You must. It fits You like a glove.***

With the sounds of Their bickering in my ears, the road cleaves an even more desolate landscape, and the miles tick by in a monotonous blur.

~ Buandelgereen Welcomes Storyteller ~

Really, these blackouts are annoying. I am stopped in front of the cave. I think I see a group of Mongols peering through the windshield, but my mind is sluggish, and I cannot concentrate. Am I truly here? Am I true? Am I?

Buandelgereen leans into the car through the passenger door and smiles. Are all such smiles enigmatic, or only those that emanate from an older, stronger, wiser Mongol woman? Certainly, her smile fits that description.

"So, you have finally arrived," she says calmly, as if expecting me for tea.

"Who am I?"

"You are your father's son, your mother's darling, and Her vehicle."

Her answer strikes me as unsatisfactory, even flippant, and I am in no mood for such evasions.

"No. I asked a simple question, so just give me a simple, non-riddle, straight answer. Who am I?"

"I am so glad you were released, Michael Powers."

So, I think to myself, *she doesn't know everything. If she were a hallucination, she would know everything.* Her breath smells faintly of milk tea; Temulun's paws drum the gravel. This feels like life-giving air, not life-draining dream.

I feel a thrill of confirmation that I stand on solid ground, reality-wise. As I am preparing to respond to Buandelgereen's welcoming remarks, a familiar boxer dog, Temulun, comes bounding up. She jumps joyously around us, while Buandelgereen repeatedly orders her to, "Don't jump! Don't jump!"

I wait in anticipation to hear Temulun's eager voice, but none comes. She's just a dog, and I'm just a human, and the twain of understanding shall never cross. This makes me sad, as I take it Goddess still does not trust me off the harsh leash of sensory limitation. I see I must earn my way back into Her good graces, back to full-blown awareness, or, perhaps, full-blown psychosis.

"Thank you, Buandelgereen," I say quite sanely. "It is good to see you again."

A group of workers gathers around, and she introduces me.

"So," I say to her, "you're still building?"

"In a manner of speaking," she replies. Again, the enigmatic smile. Again, I feel a flash of anger, but keep my peace.

"What brings you here?" she asks.

That simple question throws me off. For whatever reason, I assumed my arrival had been anticipated and accommodations readied. Still, I am undeterred.

"I came for the cave."

Temulun, now calm, stands at alert next to Buandelgereen and tilts her head, boxer style. I glance at her, but still cannot read her thoughts. Damn Goddess! Why must I continue to be punished by Her, to be made blind, deaf, and dumb, like normals?

"Still searching for the way back to the tunnel?"

"Yes."

"You were released . . . right?"

I get my little scrap of revenge. "In a manner of speaking."

Buandelgereen peers off into the distance, almost imperceptibly shaking her head. "In other words, you escaped, and the authorities are after you." These words are in the form of a statement rather than a question, so I feel no compunction to reply.

"I see," she says. "And whose car is this?"

"Dr. Tavaris."

Buandelgereen makes a show of looking around. "And?"

"He could not make it."

She laughs. "You should have come by camel! Harder to track down."

"I wasn't being followed."

Buandelgereen shakes her head. "What do you plan to do with the car?"

"Give it to you."

"It belongs to someone else. It is traceable. Take it back to Dr. Tavaris and check yourself back into the institute. They can care for you better than we can."

The desert stretches behind me, and the cave looms before me. Both are stony and hard, almost devoid of vegetation. A gust of wind scours the rock face of the cave with sand, and Buandelgereen stands as immovable as the rocks surrounding us. Grains tick against the windshield like dry rain. One of her workers throws a tarp over the car and rolls it behind a low berm; out here, even cars learn to disappear.

I know she is waiting for my response, but my mind is confused and fragmented. Perhaps this cave is just a cave, not a portal. Perhaps I'm a bringer of death . . . a continuation of my soldiering days in Vietnam. Perhaps she is just a Mongol immigrant, here to live out her remaining days in peace. Perhaps my diseased existence is responsible for three people being dead. Perhaps. But why? For what reason?

"I cannot answer those questions," says Buandelgereen.

"What questions?" I mumble.

"I heard you say, 'but why?' and 'for what reason?'"

"Is that all you heard?"

"Yes. Now, tell me quickly, Michael Powers—what is going on?"

My brain will not work, its thoughts crashing like breakers against an impenetrable barrier. I can only utter a few, disconnected thoughts. "The cave. The tunnel. The dead."

Buandelgereen guides my arm and directs me into the cave, shouting orders over her shoulder to the workers. Her palm is dry, callused, unarguably human. I follow like a helpless puppy, and the next thing I know, I'm lying in a bed somewhere in the cave. The room is small, but decorated nicely, with prints by Van Gogh and Vermeer on the walls. A little desk in the corner calls to me. I rise, see a neat stack of blank paper, a container of pens, and sit at the desk. I start writing, first to catch you up on what is happening, dear Reader, and then to turn to what has always lurked behind these events—the war.

So, dear Reader, the memories, the war. I write and write . . . I write to still the stillness, yet the war refuses to submit.

Chapter Twenty-Seven

Vietnam Redux

A Mission

"**S**toryteller, you goddamn fuckin' schoolboy, word's come down about our next mission."

"Fuck off, Stretch, can't you see I'm writing? Knowing you, it's probably just a rumor. I'll believe it when T lets us know. Meanwhile, well, just fuck off."

"Your funeral, boy. As for me, can't wait to get off this fuckin' firebase. Sure you don't want to know?"

"I'm sure."

"It's Tuy Hòa, boy. Tuy Hòa!"

Storyteller sighed and set down his writing tablet. "What's 'Too Hua'?"

"A city, dipshit. A city. Pronounced Tuy Hòa. Finally, we get a mission outside this fuckin' jungle. A city!"

"So?"

Stretch feigned shock. "Are you that fuckin' innocent, virgin boy? A city has whores. Whores have tits. Whores have pussies. Pussies are warm and wet. Tits are soft and squishy. Jesus Christ!"

Storyteller scoffed. "Whores have a million diseases, dickhead. Speaking of dickhead, that's what you're gonna lose when it drops off from the clap."

"I knew you wouldn't understand, Storyteller, but I gave you the fuckin' chance. Go back to your fuckin' writing. Ain't no one gonna read it anyhow." With this last invective, Stretch gave a deep shudder, and amid his eye-rolling, his Tourette's gave him a jolt, making him twitch like a puppet.

Nature walked up, tam o'shanter tilted on his head, curly locks springing out from under the brim.

"Our scatterbrained friend here told you the truth, Storyteller. Just heard it from the horse's mouth. T says we're going on a special mission to Tuy Hòa."

"Hello, Nature. So, Stretch here has finally uttered a rumor that turned out to be true."

"Fuck!" spat Stretch.

"Exactly what you plan to do in Tuy Hòa, right Stretch?" asked Nature.

"Fuckin' A! What else? All us red-blooded Americans will be fucking, except ol' Storyteller here. Fucker will be buried in some damn library while the rest of us will be buried in some damn cunt. It's the city, man!"

Mountain Man strolled up, trailed by his shadow, Bowls, and growled in his West Virginia twang, "Shiiiittt! Cities are just open sores on the body of a beautiful woman."

"Yeah, yeah, already know that, Mountain Man," said Nature in his calm voice. "You've told us enough times."

"Can't say the truth too often," said Mountain Man.

"Stretch here can't say the truth at all," observed Storyteller.

"Hey, fucker! What I told you is true, ain't it?"

"This time," admitted Storyteller.

Mountain Man and Bowls plopped down next to Storyteller, and the others followed suit, forming a little circle.

"Seriously, Mountain Man," said Nature. "I hear Tuy Hòa is taking a lotta shit from the NVA. Those Tiger Division Korean boys need help."

"Ain't no joke," said Mountain Man. "Fuckin' Koreans shouldn't be here anyway. This is between the Vietnamese."

"And us," added Storyteller.

"Fuckin' Americans shouldn't be here either!" Mountain Man spat a great wad to add emphatic punctuation to his profound geopolitical statement.

"Well, that may be, but here we are," observed Nature.

Bowls perked up and removed the pipe from his mouth. "Yeah, got to make the best of it. Kill a few NVA, fuck a few women"—he lifted his pipe—"smoke some Cambodian red, it ain't so bad."

"That's not what you say when we're in the bush," said Nature.

"It's what I think."

"Bullshit! You think what Mountain Man tells you to think," said Storyteller.

"Lay off him," said Mountain Man. "Bowls is Bowls. Ahab is Ahab. Except Ahab had one leg while Bowls here has half a brain."

"Goddammit, Mountain Man!" cried Bowls, blowing the words through teeth clamped on the stem of his pipe.

Mountain Man waved him off. "Just kidding, just kidding."

Storyteller looked at each man seated in the little circle, all shirtless, with only bush hats to deflect the sun.

Mountain Man, the peerless killer.

Stretch, the peerless horny grunt.

Nature, the peerless romantic.

Bowls, the peerless follower.

And Storyteller, the peerless teller of tales. Truly, a warlocks' coven, jabbering prognostications and provocations. The sun beat down on them, turning the ravaged clay beneath their feet into a burning skillet, while the humidity drained them of fluids, sweat pouring from their skin to drip on the ground in hissing evaporation. Storyteller marveled at their red-baked, chitinous skin, and saw them as insects slowly being cooked in this Vietnamese skillet.

"Mountain Man, I didn't know you were a literary man," said Storyteller. "Quoting *Moby-Dick*—impressive."

Mountain Man slowly lowered the dog-eared paperback and looked at Storyteller in disgust. "Shiiiittt! I'm a fuckin' pig farmer from West Virginia, but I can read. What's more, schoolboy, I can kill NVA as surely dead as Ahab could kill whales. The rest of you ain't worth the slop I feed my pigs."

Storyteller laughed. "Try as you might, Mountain Man, I've got your number. You are not so dumb as you would have us believe. In fact, as I have often said, you are a genius—a hillbilly genius, to be sure, but a fuckin' genius. And furthermore, you love us as though we were your own children."

Pausing reflectively, Storyteller repeated, "A genius."

"At killing gooks, he—" added Bowls, then abruptly stopped and looked nervously at Mountain Man.

"Told you not to call them that, asshole," growled Mountain Man. "Is that what you consider my fiancée? A gook?"

Although she was dead, Mountain Man always spoke of her as if she still lived. Bowls immediately begged forgiveness.

"Just slipped outta me, Mountain Man! Didn't mean it."

"Stick to masturbating over your tab," said Mountain Man, his anger sated.

T walked up and stared down at the group. A tall, angular black officer, he looked upon these men appreciatively.

"Guess you already heard?" he asked, looking at Mountain Man.

"Yeah, we heard, T," said Nature. "Word gets around fast on this little bitty firebase. We're going on a paid vacation to Tuy Hòa."

"What's our mission there?" asked Storyteller.

"Help the Koreans. They've run into trouble. Seems the NVA have targeted Tuy Hòa. Still, I reckon by the time we get there, things will have settled down."

"Hope so," said Bowls.

"Got other plans, Bowls?" asked T.

"Lieutenant, my plans are glorious," Stretch interjected.

"Well, stow your plans, Stretch. We might have no opportunity for your . . . plans."

"Yes, sir."

T turned and walked away. As Mountain Man watched him go, he said, as if to himself, "Don't want to go into no fuckin' city. It's like lowering yourself neck deep into a festering wound."

Bowls puffed furiously on his pipe for a while, then repeated the mantra he always intoned after Mountain Man finished speaking, "Fuckin' A, Fuckin' A."

T stopped suddenly and turned to face them from a distance. "Army says go, we go. We saddle up tomorrow morning. Then, a free helicopter ride to Tuy Hòa with the rest of the company. How's that sound to you, Stretch? Maybe, when we get there, NVA be gone, and you can carry on with your obscene little plans. But, gentlemen, I doubt it."

~ *Tuy Hòa* ~

As Storyteller's helicopter lost altitude and banked sharply to the right, the first landmark that emerged from the gauzy clouds took his breath away. Stretching to the horizon, the blue South China Sea reposed in blissful comfort, its calm waters lapping against the frenetic shore of war-torn Vietnam. Just as he began to feel an inner peace, the chopper leveled off, revealing a burning city. Rising smoke from the town of Tuy Hòa scorched his throat and obscured his vision. Approaching an old military airfield, the smoke thinned enough to spot innumerable dwellings, jumbled together haphazardly around the heart of the city, their tin roofs reflecting shards of pale sunlight upward through gaps in the haze. Nearer now to the earth, Storyteller observed the central district with its cold, concrete buildings rising stoically against the flames that crept ever closer from the burning shanties. Then, mercifully, the chopper banked again, and a brilliant white line of virgin beach stretched up and down the coast, lovingly accepting the gentle caresses of the sea. The incongruity of lovely blue waters cuddling next to an ugly, burning city made him wish he were a creature from the sea and not an earthbound soldier. Slowly submerging into the awaiting inferno, the helicopter settled with a soft bounce on a pockmarked tarmac, rotors stirring caustic smoke in curling wisps around its metallic body like reddish fingers coiling around a stranded hull.

Storyteller and his comrades jumped down onto the blistering hot blacktop and joined the rest of the company milling aimlessly under whatever shade they could find at the edge of the airfield. Soon, the company commander appeared, and all subordinate officers leaped to get their units in line. T, imposingly tall and supremely saturnine in his disposition, ordered the platoon to assemble.

"Y'all just wait here, boys, till we learn what's up from on high."

T slipped easily into his Arkansas drawl with his platoon, but kept its rhythmic intonations hidden from his fellow officers. They waited amidst the smoke, listening uneasily to distant gunfire and explosions. Finally, after conferring with a few officials, the swollen, crimson face of the company commander stepped in front of the assembled troops and spoke in a high-pitched blur of words, clearly anxious to get back to his air-conditioned office.

"We are here to support the Koreans and the 101st Airborne. Seems the NVA are getting a little frisky. You boys will guard the town of Tuy Hòa, make occasional forays into the surrounding countryside, and otherwise fulfill your mission in the highest tradition of the United States Army. Your platoon leaders will assign you billets. Good luck, gentlemen!"

Mountain Man turned to Storyteller and whispered, "I'm fuckin' inspired, how about you?"

"Ready to die for God and country," came the sarcastic reply.

The words were barely out of Storyteller's mouth when a rocket landed nearby, causing the grunts to duck and cover.

"A welcome note from the NVA," growled Mountain Man. "Ain't that sweet?"

~

By that evening, the grunts had settled into accommodations they were entirely unused to—barracks.

"Prefer the jungle," said Superman. "It's cleaner."

"You're fuckin' kidding!" protested Bowls. "Roof, running water, latrine, cot—it's pure fuckin' luxury."

"It's pure fuckin' bullshit!" cried Mountain Man. "No jungle—no NVA; no NVA—nobody to kill; and nobody to kill makes Mountain Man a very unhappy soldier."

"May have more action than you bargained for here," said ever wise and gentle Nature.

"Shit," said Bowls. "Action is what I'm here for. For once, Stretch and me are on the same page."

Superman, pious giant, rolled his eyes. "Lordy, lordy."

The next morning, the grunts were assigned stretches of the beach they were to defend. Wooden guard towers, primitive in design, resembled black silhouettes against the dawn sky protruding from the sand like long-legged ticks. For the first week, they took turns in the towers, staring out at the ocean in search of NVA attackers. At night, the guards were warned to beware of sappers, and the brass ordered ugly concertina wire to be coiled around the towers, as if that would discourage any well-trained sapper. Guards worked in teams of two, and many a night Nature and Storyteller hunched in their tower, whispering profound insights about the fate of mankind, the meaning of life, the future of the earth, and so forth and so on, all against the backdrop of a gentle surf that seemed to inject their words with gravitas. Adolescent ruminations, touching upon all the ancient questions, made romantic and dark by the ominous setting war so graciously provided, brought the two soldiers closer together in a bond of love as deep as that of any marriage. As would be expected, a sense of danger and urgency underlay their conversations, making them seem more profound than any speculation uttered from the comfort of home.

One day, the NVA decided to rain down upon Tuy Hòa more rockets and mortar fire than they had in years. With the city ablaze, Storyteller's platoon (nicknamed the 2/6 Circus) was ordered into the heart of its inhabited section to confront Viet Cong murder squads who were successfully taking advantage of the chaos to assassinate officials loyal to the South. Intelligence also wanted to curtail an upsurge in Viet Cong political cadre from infiltrating the town and enlisting new recruits to replenish units decimated by American combat operations. So simple.

Storyteller and his comrades patrolled the burning streets, while a few blocks away, the South China Sea kept up its gentle lapping on the shore. He longed to break away and run down to the sea, throw off his gear, and swim home across the thousands of miles of ocean that separated him from happiness. These thoughts were rudely broken by the unmistakable zipping noise of bullets, and the sickening thud of those that found home in the bodies of his friends. A fierce firefight erupted and ended as quickly as it had begun. The Viet Cong had retreated, leaving the 2/6 Circus to lick its wounds and take its dead back to the base. That night, someone from command came up with a good idea. A compassionate idea. An idea that would make the grunts happy and grateful for the sacrifices they were making for their country. Under the official auspices of the United States Army, a group of young Vietnamese prostitutes would be trucked onto the base and made available for those soldiers whose pent-up lust cried out for release. Truly a priceless gift from a grateful army.

These gifts, in the form of young, adolescent girls, came one evening when Storyteller and Nature were on guard duty.

"Hey!" shouted their sergeant, Pappy, from below the guard tower. "Line is shorter now. Here are your replacements. Get your asses back to block twelve, building thirty-six, and enjoy! . . . if you can."

The unhappy faces of two young soldiers, pale in the moonlight, looked up at Storyteller and Nature.

Pappy spat noisily. "Fuckin' army douches!" He walked away muttering obscenities to himself.

The two soldiers climbed up the tower. Neither Storyteller nor Nature recognized them.

"Motherfuckin' shit!" cried one of them as he stepped into the guardhouse. "Young Vietnamese ass back there, and we only get one go at 'em!"

"Fuck, Joey, you couldn't get it up again anyway," said his partner. "Probably couldn't do it the first time!" He looked at Storyteller and Nature. "Damn, you boys gonna get the dregs. I mean, those bitches were like zombies when we got there. Must have been a hundred guys who fucked 'em before us. So goddamn wet in their runways, couldn't feel nothing."

Storyteller and Nature climbed down the ladder as the voices of the two young soldiers receded in the distance. Neither man spoke as they walked toward the designated building.

Storyteller turned to Nature. "You gonna do it?"

"Me? A poet? Brother Storyteller, I could never forgive myself. Any intimacy I have with a woman will be surrounded by the proper, romantic setting." He looked around. "And this ain't it!"

Storyteller chuckled. "So, you'll do it only out on the moors some moonlit night, with your girlfriend's windswept hair touching your face?"

"Very funny. I'm going to my hootch and sleep. You do what you want. Good conscience . . . I mean, good night."

Storyteller watched Nature walk away and felt torn. Desire for sex overtook his gentle nature, and he was uncomfortably hard. The thought of extinguishing these burning flames in some beautiful young Vietnamese girl's body beckoned more convincingly than his scruples could withstand. Still, he hesitated, knowing from all the books he read that prostitutes despise the men they fuck. Such a thought was momentarily off-putting, but the throbbing pressed inexorably, and the anticipation of release from its mounting pressure urged him on.

When he reached the building, a dim outside bulb weakly illuminated a long line of soldiers with their hands in their pockets, shuffling impatiently, saying little, and swaying from one foot to another in eager anticipation. The shadows made them look ominous, and their single-minded goal revealed a malevolent, hive mentality. Storyteller felt his desire start to deflate, but nonetheless he stood in line, uncomfortable, with his hands in his pockets. The closer he got to the entrance, the more excited he became, and with the symbol of his lust again standing fully erect, his rationalization operated at full tilt.

Don't care what the others are doing. I'm going to do it without their animal clumsiness. I'll be gentle. I'll smile and show her I'm kind. I'll slip her a few dollars, more than she would earn in a year. I'll show her I understand the injustices and brutalities of the world by being nice, by being. . . .

Before he knew it, he found himself inside the huge Quonset hut, being directed to the left by a sergeant toward a small room where his prostitute must be waiting. He could hear soldiers being serviced in several open rooms, their grunts and groans mingled with the exhortations of those standing in line like a congregation of excited piglets. He was still hard, but it now signaled something different than raw lust. It pushed against his fatigue trousers as if wanting to be liberated, not to release the pressure, but to feel the fresh air—an executioner cleansing his hands before performing the final, bloody deed. The animal grunting and piercing shouts of obscene encouragement sickened Storyteller and excited him by degrees, and he redoubled his justifications for participating in this gang rape. Finally, he squeezed into the room where three beds stood against the walls, surrounded by men who no longer controlled their own minds. A mob. Storyteller watched in horror as the mob stared down at the flailing, thrusting men on the beds, grunting like hogs and driving their cocks into the girls, whose bobbing heads were averted, staring off into space as if half-dead. The room stank of rancid semen, foul sweat, and God knows what else. Storyteller felt nauseous and his craving began to subside, against his will, but now his yearnings cried out for release as desperately as the mob.

Someone in front of him, hopping about and pressing his hands against the front of his trousers to keep himself from exploding, shouted at the humping soldier on the bed, "C'mon Arby, blow your fuckin' wad and get the fuck off so I can have a turn!"

The girl beneath Arby turned her face toward Storyteller and gave him a resigned, accusatory look, as a victim tied to a pyre might look at an executioner approaching with the match. Suddenly, inexplicably, *she* smiled at him, and the mob, the room, Vietnam, and the world fell away in an instant, leaving the two of them to stare at each other in a void. The man on top of *her* also disappeared, and still *she* continued to stare, naked and exposed, revealing a body more beautiful than Storyteller had ever dreamed possible. *She* appeared impossibly untouched, *her* amber skin immaculate, *her* words coming to his mind in a crystalline, otherworldly voice.

How does one justify a life without cruelty, and therefore without the distilled beauty of cruelty?

Storyteller could not believe any such words—in fact, any words at all—could possibly come from the mind of that Vietnamese girl lying on a rotten bed in pools of semen, while suffering the horror of being raped by dozens of men.

She smiled radiantly and gave him a quizzical look.

Well? She asked.

But, the words, what were they? He heard them reverberate, but they were alien to his fevered mind. He leaned forward and asked dumbly, "What?"

~ *Her* ~

Dear Reader, it was *Her*! *Her*! That vision, that siren who so entranced my beautiful mother and mesmerized my schizophrenic father, that revelation who caused them to make a long and arduous pilgrimage across war-torn China, that mysterious Vietnamese girl then lying on her back in front of my unseeing eyes atop a stinking, drenched bed, the evidence of the assault still wet upon her, was *Her*! Realization has just come to me, fifty years later! It was *Her*, and I didn't know it! I didn't know it until now, this moment! Why didn't I recognize *Her*? God help me, why? That beautiful, broken, fragile little Vietnamese girl, raped savagely and repeatedly by lust-crazed soldiers, was *Her*! It all comes in a blinding flash. *Her* face staring at me! *Her* face! I remember *She* repeated the words, and they came to me once more, but in my aroused daze, remained incomprehensible.

"How does one justify a life without cruelty, and therefore without the distilled beauty of cruelty?"

As before, I did not understand. Tragically, I was deaf. Deaf! Until now.

~ *Storyteller Makes A Decision* ~

Storyteller saw the girl's lips move, and she repeated words he still did not understand, but the act of looking and speaking directly to him made her transform from a helpless receptacle to . . . something different. This sudden and jarring difference collided with his lust, vanquished it, and slapped him back to his senses. He now realized he stood in a line of crazed rapists and willing murderers who had lost all awareness of their common humanity. Storyteller emitted a loud groan, and amidst the irritated curses of the frenzied soldiers, pushed and stumbled his way out of the steaming building into a cool night filled with the sweet smell of an eternal sea.

While inhaling the piquant vibrancy of salty mist, he heard, for the first time, a strange, unsettling voice. Although the words were not clear, the voice came from nowhere and everywhere, within and without, and he looked around frantically for its owner. It came again, deep-throated and feminine. A rumbling power drove it through his brain.

You have been given a glimpse.

That was all. Storyteller repeated the phrase in his mind. *You have been given a glimpse.* A glimpse of what?

A glimpse of the empathy that will rule the future with the advent of the Superior Ones.

Storyteller now felt frightened, and he quickened his pace to rejoin Nature. *A glimpse of Superior Ones? How?* he could not help asking himself as he walked.

Superior empathy. Superior power. Superior minds.

What?

You will help make this the future. You are the Chosen One. You will mate with another Chosen One. You will have a child that takes another step toward the Superior Ones.

And so, it began. Storyteller always felt his schizophrenia had arisen from the dismal swamp of human degradation, and its roots, sucking up the fertile nutrients of war's misery, blossomed into the same hydra that had plagued his father. But, this hydra had many more heads. Many more. Is it possible Goddess is right about his role in bringing about these Superior Ones? No, he was not yet ready to go that far.

As he reached the Quonset hut where he was billeted, he roused Nature and sat on an adjoining cot, anxious to recite his story and get his friend's opinion about the preternatural voice. Nature had just stretched and finished yawning, ready to listen, when Pappy strode into the room.

"Hey! Nature! Storyteller! Up and at 'em! You are just about the only two guys without jism all over their trousers and stickum clogging up their brains."

"What's up, Pappy?" asked Nature, pulling on his fatigues.

"You're both pulling detail."

"What kind of detail?"

"Escort them whores back to Tuy Hòa town. You'll be riding with them in the bed of a deuce-and-a-half."

Storyteller felt his heart drop. "No, Sarge, I don't want to go. Get someone else." He could not bear to see their faces—her face—again.

"Ain't no one else! Besides, you and Nature are the only ones I trust to get them poor girls back safely without any monkey business." Pappy was an older man, a father in his thirties, and the creases in his eyes revealed a deep sadness that he was forced to be a part of such goings on. "Now, don't ask any more fuckin' questions. Hurry up, Nature! Both of you! Go on and get this over with."

His order would brook no further protest, so the two grunts wearily trudged their way to the waiting truck. As they approached through the darkness, Storyteller could make out a group of women sitting disconsolately in the bed, their heads hanging low with exhaustion, pain, humiliation—or all of that and more. Nature and Storyteller climbed into the bed and stood looking at their cargo. Both men carried their M-16s in a casual manner, making sure the barrels did not point at the girls. The silence was unnerving. Storyteller thought he could hear faint sobs from a few, but in general, they appeared as listless as half-dead prisoners liberated from a concentration camp. Now the salt air smelled foul, and the nearer to the city they got, the more a reeking odor of human excrement and rotting garbage filled their nostrils. Some of the girls began shaking uncontrollably, and both men felt anxious to see them gone from sight. *Out of sight, out of mind*, thought Storyteller morosely. The first dim rays of dawn arched on the horizon.

Nature, wise Nature, was the first to speak.

"They are beautiful," he said.

"What?" cried Storyteller. "They are sad, depressing, pathetic, but not beautiful! They've just been gang raped. Are you crazy?"

"There is beauty in suffering, Storyteller. We poets are fully aware of it."

"No, you poets are full of shit! How can you say they are beautiful? Maybe once, when they were with their families, when they were little girls. Now, they're whores, filled with foreign men's cum and broken by foreign men's desires."

Nature smiled. "You see, Storyteller, you're a poet too."

"No, I'm not. I'm a realist. You live in a fantasy world, Nature. Look at them."

He just smiled. "I am."

"Fuckin' incorrigible," scoffed Storyteller.

The truck passed under one of the few streetlights still working, and Storyteller momentarily caught a good look at *Her* face, as *She* was the only girl looking up rather than down. *She* stared at him with eyes that spoke a thousand words, but all undecipherable to his wondering mind. *She* seemed untouched, unsullied, and *Her* gaze plunged into the depths of his most vulnerable spot. All he could do was smile as kindly as he could. Guilt had sorely tried him, and he realized he would have raped these girls as violently and brutally as any of his comrades, had it not been for . . . for what? For *Her*. His smile seemed a weak, hypocritical sham, a bandage on an amputated limb. Yet his smile appeared to have no effect on *Her* gaze. *She* continued looking at him as might a breeder of horses look upon a promising colt. Somehow, some way, though clearly younger than Storyteller, *She* seemed ageless. Yet, if ageless, how so apparently untouched? A puzzle. A puzzle interrupted by the truck lurching to a stop.

The driver, a stocky Spec 4, got out and shouted, "We're here! Get the whores out and set 'em on their way!"

Nature and Storyteller hesitated, looking around at the barren spot of ground on which the truck stood like a monstrous slug. There was no one in sight, nor any building or dwelling nearby.

"Where the hell are we?" asked Storyteller.

"Dropping off point," replied the Spec 4.

"Pretty bleak place to be setting these girls down," observed Nature. "Long way into town."

"Get 'em off!" cried the Spec 4.

He did not outrank Nature or Storyteller, and no rear-echelon motherfucker was going to order them around like that. Both men took offense at the bluster of the driver.

"Hey, asshole, speak nicely to us grunts," said Nature, "or we might accidentally squeeze the triggers on these M-16s."

A slamming door from the passenger side cracked through the air, and T stood looking up at his two boys. His tall, angular black face, stern and angry, perused the scene, his eyes traveling from the girls to Nature and Storyteller to the driver. "These two soldiers are right," he said matter-of-factly. "Drive us into town."

The Spec 4 looked at T with wide, nervous eyes. "It's dangerous, lieutenant. My orders were to drop them off here. They can bloody well walk into town."

"Your orders are hereby countermanded!" said T in his most authoritative voice. "Get back in the goddamn cab and drive into town. Now!"

"Yes, sir," said the Spec 4, mumbling obscenities under his breath as he climbed back in behind the wheel.

Nature laughed. "Didn't know you were with us, T. Nice to have you along."

T did not reply. The passenger door slammed shut, and the truck lurched forward toward the lights of Tuy Hòa.

Her gaze never left the face of Storyteller.

Chapter Twenty-Eight

Dark Caves

Return from the War

All this has come to me and I write it down here, in the cave. Yes, yes, dear Reader, it was *Her*. Buandelgereen knows *Her*. Mother and father came to know *Her*. Now, so do I. And what should I do with this knowledge? The more I think, the more overwhelmed I get. What to do with so many fragments? Goddess, *Her*, Buandelgereen, Marie Telles, Dr. Camara, Dr. Hess, Dr. Tavaris, the war, the cave, the tunnel, Dr. Hess's bathroom, Storyteller, Nature, Tuyet Mai, the institute, mother, father, and all the rest? Dreams, nightmares, voices, warrior ants, a cacophony of songs by dying men, and then there is Him . . . God. Is He the cause of all this suffering? Does Goddess speak the truth? What if I really can help *Her* stop all suffering in the world? Stop the extinction of all the others? Save the planet? I know, I know, the textbook delusion of a madman. Worse, a madman who has left a trail of bodies in his wake! A madman whose character is so weak he'd have gladly joined a filthy gang of rapists; whose philosophy is so barren he joined an army of killers and destroyers; and whose illness is so rampant he has been complicit in three deaths.

I can write no more.

~

Buandelgereen visits often, but she definitely does not know everything. She doesn't know Drs. Camara, Hess, and Tavaris are dead—news being nonexistent out here—as she keeps asking about them. She knows I escaped, but she is convinced I should return to the institute and continue to receive therapy. I can't tell if this is a ruse or simple human concern from a 'normal.' Still, none of this is of any concern to me. It is *Her* I want to know more about. *She* has seared my soul, and I must learn about *Her* story. To do that, Buandelgereen has to take me back to Mongolia, back to the Japanese invasion. Maybe, if I can get behind the iron door, I will find what I am looking for. During her next visit to my room, I sit on my bed and ask.

"No, Michael, no one has found anything they were looking for behind the iron door."

"But Buandelgereen, you were a keeper, a guard. Surely, you know what is behind it?"

"No."

"Father told me you were magical."

"A fairy tale." She smooths her tunic; her eyes go carefully neutral.

"Not a fairy tale. You were in Mongolia with them. In the sanctuary of the Flaming Cliffs. You saved them. You guided them."

"No, Michael. I did not save them. Feng Shiren and Lihua saved them. I merely . . . was there with them. They were strangers in a strange land, and I was of that land. That is all."

"You were my mother's lover."

"Be careful, Michael."

"There are keys, Buandelgereen—to my madness, the tunnel, the stillness."

"You don't need a key to find stillness."

"Oh, yes, I do, and you know it."

"No."

"There are keys to many doors, and then there is the key to one door in particular. The key to the iron door. This cave has an iron door, Buandelgereen. I want to travel behind it. If you are not a guard, then you will have no objection."

"No."

"Why not? If you are not magical, if you are not a spirit or a guard, then there is nothing to hide behind the door. Just more rock."

"Let me take you back to the institution voluntarily, Michael, or I'll have to do something to make it happen."

"What? Clap your hands or click your heels together? Come on, Buandelgereen, you know I have come here for a reason."

"No need for magic, just a call to the police."

"I don't believe you."

"If it weren't for your mother, I'd gladly get you off my hands."

"My mother?"

"She told me to look after you."

"Buandelgereen, she was in the States when I was born. You were thousands of miles away."

"Are you really such a fool, Michael? How many times did Goddess tell Bai Meiying she would have a son?"

"Goddess?"

Buandelgereen nods.

I cannot believe my ears. "Do you believe *She* is real?"

"To your mother."

"No, no, no! I'm done accepting evasions! Do you believe *She* is real?"

"Americans often say we Mongols are a superstitious people. Now, Michael, one of my workers will drive you back to Smythe-Haines in Dr. Tavaris's car."

"Buandelgereen, Dr. Tavaris is dead."

This makes her pause. "What happened?"

"That is precisely what I need to find out."

"Michael, you're making no sense. What did he die of?"

"He died of me."

I can see the alarm in her face and hasten to allay her suspicions. "No, of course I didn't kill him. But there is something surrounding me, or my illness, that makes other people ill."

"How did you get his car?"

"He died while we were driving here."

Now, Buandelgereen looks confused, and certainly apprehensive. I admire her iron control, as she asks me quite calmly, "Michael, how did he die?"

"I don't know. Heart attack would be my best guess, but I know that wasn't really the cause."

"Which was?"

"I told you, he died of me."

Abruptly, Buandelgereen turns on her heel and walks out, closing the door behind her. I am afraid she is going to call the police, but I feel helpless, bound to this place, and my inclination to run is overwhelmed by my inclination to stay, regardless of what happens. Sirens thrum far off; time is short. Inertia makes me want to stay, or some inner certainty she will not call the police? I can't be sure, but I know I will stay. I choose the cave over custody; if there's a door between me and stillness, I'll open it, or break against it.

I lie flat on the bed and try to empty my mind. Last time I was here, she turned me over to Fred Miller—but maybe it was a test of my determination to serve Goddess. How *She* (or Buandelgereen) made everything disappear, leaving Miller with the illusion that I sat in an empty cave, I'll never know.

~

I slept soundly for the first time in days. Ready to tackle my dilemma. Well, my multiple dilemmas. How to get behind the iron door? How to regain my full regalia of senses? How to piece together all these Goddess-God fragments floating in my head, colliding like wandering icebergs? How to wash my hands of the blood of the doctors? How to find *Her*, and is *She* truly Goddess, or not? Then there is Buandelgereen. Who or what, is she? Despite her threats, I'm still here. Do the answers really lie beyond the iron door? Or do they lie elsewhere? It is the war! The war! The war! Answers lie there, always buried right under my nose. Buried as deep as my bones in the tunnel. Buried as deep as the 2/6 Circus trapped in that damn fortress! Buried as deep as the figures tapping inside the Precious Object.

Oh!

Wait!

Chapter Twenty-Nine

Sleep Awakens

The Third Awakening

As if he were at the bottom of a well, the soldier heard echoes of someone whispering down from the distant rim. He strained to understand but could only distinguish one word—"Oh!"—and a dry, urgent tapping sound. Gradually, another voice grew clearer.

"Storyteller! It's Nature. Come on, man. Look at me. Storyteller! It's Nature!"

The words tickled the edge of his consciousness, but he was burning up. Couldn't concentrate. Disoriented. He wanted the voices to go away. *Why is it so hot?* And then it came to him. *I woke up this morning feeling rested. I thought about dilemmas, about caves, about . . . people. Dead people? Not dead soldiers—dead . . . psychologists? Strangely, something about a woman. A Mongol woman. Stupid! Must be this damn malaria . . . a dream . . . the dilemmas . . . riddles. Dammit! . . . lousy dreams . . . or, maybe—holy shit! What's that?*

Gunfire cracked in the distance. The rank stench of decay and defecation permeated the air, needling a memory he couldn't place. He attempted to focus on the world through the blur of watering eyes.

Suddenly, explosively, an automatic weapon blasted nearby, sending red tracers arching across the sky. *Jesus—Mother of God! Where am I?* He rubbed his face with his greasy sleeve and blinked hard at his surroundings. A dark figure moved away, nervously tapping the stock of his M-16—the man who had whispered in his ear. As he strained to call out to the receding figure, shadows approached from the side, but a blinding headache split his vision. It felt as though acid had been flung into his eyes, corroding the remaining light. A thick fog enveloped him, and he began seeing strange figures undulate like seaweed in an underwater current. The figures stretched and elongated into impossible shapes and sizes.

"Where's the cave? Buandelgereen! Buandelgereen!" he cried, dragging his nails across the stony surface of the courtyard, trying to feel his desk back in the cave. "Buandelgereen!"

A nearby voice intruded into his consciousness. "It's his malaria. He's hallucinating again, poor guy."

Then another voice. Irritated. "Storyteller! Pipe down, man! It's okay! You're just hallucinating. You'll be okay, man."

Who's that? Jesus, he said I'm hallucinating. About what? The cave? This place? Where am I? Who am I?

He mumbled under his breath, "Hallucinations. Nature. Malaria. Storyteller . . . Storyteller . . . Storyteller." He stared in disbelief at his hands and wrists, then at his shriveled body, barely stirring beneath baggy fatigues. *My God! I'm young. Skinny. Just a boy. I'm back!*

He closed his eyes and concentrated. The fear melted away. *All this shit has happened before,* he thought. *However, what everyone thought was malaria turned out to be schizophrenia. What a joke! I must have been suffering the first symptoms of the disease. Not malaria at all. Well, maybe it was both—malaria triggering schizophrenia. Whatever the case, here I am again—back in the fortress. There is something I missed all this time. Something I need to find before I can venture behind the iron door.*

This particular soldier is different. Very different. He is recently schizophrenic (within the last few days or perhaps weeks), has malaria, and is holed up in an abandoned fortress surrounded by NVA who want to take his life. His name is Storyteller, but his older self, Michael Powers, momentarily shares his body, shares his mind. Michael Powers is on a quest, and Storyteller is just trying to survive.

Something odd is happening with Michael Powers' memories—they appear to be unreliable—very unreliable.

There is one thing Michael Powers wants, and that is to see the Goddess statue his platoon has captured from the NVA. Something inside it is tapping, and he wants to communicate with the thing(s) that are making all the racket. Michael realizes Storyteller was too fucked up with fever and voices at the time to really understand the implications of that statue. Importantly, Michael has a very short time frame in which to accomplish this task, as in a few days every soldier in this fortress, save two, will be dead.

While he had taken up occupancy in the body of his younger self, the immediacy and virulence of the malaria were far worse than he remembered. Excruciating pain, high fever, diarrhea—all had succeeded in coring out the essential spirit and energy of the young soldier. Michael could feel the threat of imminent death brush against Storyteller's weakened condition. Although Michael knew his younger self would survive the war, he could feel the schizophrenia thriving in the hothouse of Storyteller's fever as if in a nutrient-rich culture of bacteria. Or was it schizophrenia? Could Goddess be right? A Superior One?

Michael attempted to reacclimate himself to Vietnam and reorient his senses to that time and place, but his thoughts were jumbled by Storyteller's delirium, and it took him hours to consolidate his self-awareness amidst the chaotic agony of his younger self. Once he emerged from the sea of pain, he focused on Captain Cairns, keeper and protector of the Goddess statue. Finally, a few hours later,

Michael saw the captain saunter over to the object of his lust—Tuyet Mai. With Cairns in sight, Michael decided to rouse Storyteller and follow the captain.

~

Storyteller struggled to his feet, stood swaying for a moment, then straightened and walked toward Captain Cairns, who crouched over the captive NVA intelligence officer, Nguyen Tuyet Mai, on the other side of the fortress. Halfway across the courtyard, with the prize within a few paces, somebody intercepted Storyteller and grabbed his arm.

"Hey, man, where you going?"

"Oh, Nature, just going over there."

"Storyteller, you need to rest. X said you needed to rest, not exert yourself. Look at yourself; you can barely carry that M-16."

"I will, just let me—go. . . . "

"Come on back to your hootch, man. Let's go back to your hootch."

"Nature, I got to talk to Captain Cairns."

"What? That fucker? Why?"

"I don't know."

"Shit, now I know you're fucked up."

Nature pulled Storyteller back to his hootch (a space against the stone wall covered by a poncho liner stretched above his bedroll). After helping him lie against the wall, Nature admonished, "Stay here, let me get X."

Once he left, Storyteller again rose and walked over to Cairns, who had moved away from Tuyet Mai and stood looking back at her. Storyteller listened to some internal voice that was unfamiliar. Chalking it up to the malaria, he saluted Cairns.

"Captain Cairns, sir, may I speak with you, sir?"

"Of course, trooper. You're Storyteller, right?"

"Yes, sir."

"Well, shoot."

Then, Michael took over.

"Sir, may I ask you about that Goddess statue?"

Cairns looked a bit uncomfortable. "Yes."

"Inside, sir. What is inside?"

"Well, trooper Storyteller, we don't know."

"Sir, may I see the statue?"

Captain Cairns kept the statue in the old, ruined church. Storyteller could walk in and look at it anytime, but Michael wanted the captain along.

"Go and have a look for yourself, trooper, but do not touch. Capisce? That is an order."

"Sir, I would like your opinion about the statue."

"Oh?" Michael knew the captain was shocked that this grunt could speak so articulately. However, he also knew Cairns felt suspicious. The Goddess statue was his and his alone. Why is this lowly grunt so interested?

Appraising Storyteller for a while, he asked, "About what?"

"If you would accompany me, sir, perhaps I can give a better answer."

If only Cairns knew he was having a conversation with the future. "Okay, trooper, let's go!" the captain snapped crisply.

Inside Storyteller, Michael trembled psychologically in unison with his host's physical shivers. The old church door came into view, and the anticipation of seeing the statue was almost more than Michael could bear. Unfortunately, even as they reached the threshold, he felt Storyteller's knees buckle. To his dismay, he heard the captain call for X, who in the past had worked so many miracles. Soon, amid much anxious whisperings, a few grunts helped Storyteller back to his sleeping area, leaving him in the capable hands of X.

Michael hunkered down in Storyteller's brain and nursed his disappointment—so close, yet so far.

... *Tap. Tap. Tap....*

That sound had haunted Michael for decades, and though he had pieced together what might be inside the statue making that noise, and had subsequently written about it, he had to see for himself.

What if he was wrong about the tapping? What if his writings had gotten it wrong? What if that tapping came from something else? Something only he was to know. Memories, speculation, and secondhand testimony can be notoriously mistaken. Goddess worked in mysterious ways. She had fooled him in the past—misdirected him—misled him.

Now, it's time to see for myself, he thought. *If Storyteller's body is strong enough, I must try again.*

You must stop seeing through his eyes, Michael Powers!

This voice came filtered through Storyteller's fever and sounded distorted, making it hard to distinguish whether it came from God or Goddess, or someone else.

Why?

Every American inside this fortress will be dead or in the tunnel when My womb is revealed.

Goddess?

You must inhabit a different mind.

Whose?

Of course, the voice did not respond, thought Michael. *I have gone down this path with Her many times. I must figure it out myself.*

Reviewing his options, Michael came to a conclusion. *Only one possibility—Clerk Long. He saw the inside of the statue—the womb—of Goddess. In fact, he stole something from it, if my research and speculations were correct. But, shit, how in the hell do I get in the mind of a North Vietnamese soldier? After all, Storyteller is one thing, but ... I guess, for a schizophrenic, anything is possible ... or for a Superior One. Do I just click my heels together and travel to the Land of Oz, or what?*

Michael concentrated, but nothing happened. He had never even seen Clerk Long in the flesh; how could he jump from Storyteller's mind to the mind of a North Vietnamese soldier? While Storyteller slept, Michael pondered.

Then it came. . . .

~ *The Statue Gives Birth*[2] ~

"Over here, comrades! She's alive!"

Michael saw through a strange man's eyes—an NVA soldier. He looked down at a woman—a badly wounded woman trying to focus on her surroundings.

Vietnamese voices drew closer. Then the hands of a Vietnamese man touching a body. Strong, dark, beautiful hands. Hands working to staunch the bleeding. Healing, not lustful, hands.

Then, a calming voice, speaking Vietnamese, which Michael miraculously understood. "You will be fine, Comrade Tuyet Mai. The wound is minor. Ah. Let me just . . . this may hurt . . . does this hurt? Ah, there, now let me . . . do this . . . Ah! . . . I cannot do all of this alone . . . come here comrade! Yes, you! Over here! . . . Hold her down . . . Not there! . . . There, fool! . . . Do not worry, Comrade Tuyet Mai, the wound is minor . . . lay back and rest."

Michael saw Quang Long rush over to help the Vietnamese medic. Someone waved him away, and he wandered over to the nearby corpse of an American. Michael recognized Captain Cairns. Now Long joined his soldier looking at the body. Major Vy walked up. Both men leaned over the twisted corpse of the American captain and simultaneously noticed the bloody head of a statue protruding from his shredded rucksack. Rolling the body on its side, Long reverently lifted the Goddess statue. As he gently pulled the statue free from the torn fabric, blood dripped from its base.

Michael now found himself within Long's mind, wild with anticipation. Finally! To see it! To see it for himself! Major Vy crowded in, hovering over the statue as if he were an expectant father. A look of astonishment spread across Vy's face as Quang Long cradled the statue in his hands. So far, everything was unfolding exactly as Michael Powers had written.

~

Quang Long at first thought the statue had been destroyed. Large sections were peeled back from its chest and stomach. Instead of gold, Long saw that the statue was actually made of white jade, its gilding disguising the true, priceless material. But upon closer inspection, he realized the statue had not been catastrophically damaged at all. Two rectangular panels fluttered on their hinges—albino butterfly wings forced apart by the explosions. Somehow, the locking mechanism had been released and the panels thrown open from the center—French doors revealing a hidden chamber. A familiar aroma rose from the statue, and, within its white womb, three small, carved figures stirred in the damp light of day.

~

Then everything diverged from what Michael had written—only slightly, but enough to tilt the universe. Just as Michael began thinking everything he wrote had been accurate, the shift occurred. . . .

~

Quang Long gazed down at the statue and felt the hairs rise on his neck. "Wondrous! Truly wondrous!" he whispered.

The first figure was made of luminous red tourmaline. Long marveled at the bottomless churning of its molten iridescence, a blood-red ocean of color. Its shape roughly resembling that of a man, his head down, legs drawn up, and back curved in a graceful arch. He hunched over a huge phallus that rose stiffly past his face, terminating above his head, throbbing with volcanic currents flowing from its tip back into the bulbous caldera of the man's body. The figure's tiny hands clung precariously to the phallus, as delicate as a bird's feet on a tree trunk. As Long stared, the figure rocked on its haunches—back and forth—hitting the inside wall of the statue's abdomen—a fetus rocking compulsively.

... Tap. Tap. Tap....

~

As the figure rocked, Michael felt the full force of unanticipated shock, for its features came into view, and Michael saw himself, his face unmistakably carved expertly into the tourmaline.

~

Long turned his attention to the second figure, carved from granite—rough, whitish stone, inlaid with black and pink flecks of mica and feldspar—and resembled a very stern old man pockmarked with dark sores from some terrible disease. He had a long, flowing beard, and in his right hand, a thick silver staff that moved freely up and down, a piston that knocked against the top, then the bottom, of Her womb.

... Tap. Tap. Tap....

~

Michael saw himself in that aged face, and he shrank from any further revelations, afraid now to look. Nevertheless, he had to when Quang Long continued examining the object. . . .

~

Fashioned from aromatic camphor, the third figure was a young boy, also with Michael's face. Long realized this wooden boy was the source of the strong aroma. The figure squatted in submissive curiosity at the feet of the other two figures, his pose expressing a mad mixture of supple strength and fragile weakness—a fledgling conqueror and a vulnerable monk. One hand disappeared behind his back, as if hiding something. Long leaned forward for a closer look, but still could not make it out. He moved his head even closer. . . .

~

"Long!" snapped Vy. "You're in the way! What's inside? Let me see! Move! Quickly!"

"Yes, sir! But I—"

"Silent! Let me see! Move!" Vy reached down to grab the statue. "Ahhh!" he cried, pulling back his hand as if from a hot stove. "What . . . the?. . . . "

~

For Michael, darkness fell over him like a curtain, and he seemed to be tumbling in a black void. When he stopped falling, he woke with a start. Looking around, he soon realized he had awakened back in his room at the cave. A dream? Not at all.

It was real. Hallucination be damned: I am the son. For years Goddess spoke; Mother resisted; Father listened to Her; and in 1950, I arrived. Yet questions remain—why 1950, and what does the third figure hide behind his back? I once wrote it was a pearl. If I'm wrong, the design changes—and so do my next steps.

Even as he lay on a soft bed, Michael retained the smells, the feel, the horror of the jungle, and the crushing devastation of war. Reliving those days made him jumpy, and though he tried to force a serene calm over his body, his heart would not stop thumping. Buandelgereen entered without knocking.

"How are you feeling, Michael Powers?"

He tried to keep his voice steady. "I'm confident you haven't called the authorities to come get me . . . which makes me feel good."

"How are you feeling, Michael?" she repeated.

"I said good."

She held out a paper. "Here, take this please."

As he reached for it, he asked, "What is it?"

Buandelgereen pulled it away and showed him both sides of a blank sheet of paper. "No. You have been gone. Like this paper, you were blank. Your pale face and trembling hands tell a different story. Time to pick up the pen and write again. So once more, how are you feeling, Michael?"

"You always have had a sixth sense, Buandelgereen. I have just returned from war if you must know."

"Vietnam?"

"Of course."

"I know war very well." She pointed to her head. "It never leaves."

"No. How do you deal with it?"

"I don't."

"You must, otherwise you couldn't function."

"I look to the day when there is no more war, no more suffering."

"Ah! So, you do believe in Goddess and Her quest!"

"Of course. Don't you?"

Michael gazed at her imposing presence. "You know, I believe you are, in fact, Goddess Herself."

Buandelgereen laughed heartily. "Your esteemed mother would find that quite amusing!"

"How so?"

"She saw me at my worst. Goddesses have no 'worst'."

"You're just a normal human?"

"Yes."

"Building a huge cave to attract guileless tourists?"

"I never said that was my plan."

"You have never told me why you are building this cave."

Buandelgereen raised a hand in warning. "That is not for you to know."

Michael shot back, "I'm the son!"

"Yes, but you are also the bridge."

Michael was puzzled. "The bridge? What bridge?"

"The bridge."

"What bridge? This is new to me!"

"You are the son, who must now have another child."

"What? I have a son—Mark Powers is his name! You know that!"

"No, Mark is not the son of the son. This must be a different child."

While Michael tried to process this completely unexpected revelation, Buandelgereen moved to the door and waved someone in.

Chapter Thirty

Procreation

Breeding

In front of me stands a woman. She is familiar, though I can't place where or when I've seen her. She seems to be in her late thirties or early forties, her face much younger. She is beautiful, in a dress that flatters her figure.

"Hello, Michael," she says in a voice both familiar and strange.

Instead of responding, I look askance at Buandelgereen. "Who is she?"

"Ask her."

I'm not falling for this again. Buandelgereen controls everything here—not this apparition.

"I'm asking you."

"Why me?"

"Because you are the one who brought her here."

Buandelgereen looks at the woman. "Tell him your name."

"My name is Tamara."

I look at her and feel a little bad for being rude. "Nothing personal, Tamara, but Buandelgereen is your boss, isn't she?"

"No."

I laugh. "Then who is?"

"You."

Naturally, this takes me aback. It takes me a moment to collect myself before I turn back to Buandelgereen. "What is the meaning of this?"

"She is the woman with whom you will have the child."

"Say again."

"She is the woman with whom you will have the child."

"I am the son."

"It will be the child 'f the son."

I laugh. "You want to breed me?"

"We are all bred."

"I thought you wanted to send me back to the institution to get help, remember?"

Buandelgereen shrugs. "Things change."

"What about Theresa? Can't I 'breeeeed' with her?"

"She is one of your hallucinations."

I point at Tamara. "And her?"

"She is real."

"How do I know that?"

"Because you know I am real, and I am telling you she is real."

I stare at Tamara and start to speak, but a thought niggles at my mind, so I turn to Buandelgereen. "Why have I changed from being the son to being the father of the son?"

She flashes an enigmatic smile. "Who said it would be a son?"

"A girl?"

Buandelgereen's face darkens. "Besides, you will soon return, and the responsibility must be passed down."

"To?"

"To the place you most desire."

"The tunnel?"

"Stillness."

My heart tightens. "You mean I will die?"

"Of course."

"Good!" I lie.

"But first, you must lie with Tamara."

Before I can ask another question, Buandelgereen leaves and closes the door. Tamara stares at me curiously.

"You are the famous Mr. Powers?" she asks.

I strain for sarcasm but hear only an ordinary question. I study her more closely. She's Asian, and she looks like someone I can't place—like *Her*, even. That can't be an accident. Looking at her, the idea of sleeping with her suddenly becomes very palatable.

"Indeed. I'm Michael. Please—sit."

"Thank you," she says, eyes down. As she moves to sit, I catch the ridge of a hunched back and try not to react.

"So, Tamara—alone in a room with the 'famous Mr. Powers.' Why are you here . . . and how do you know Buandelgereen?"

"Buandelgereen is my inspiration, my idol. I am here to be with you."

"At her request or at her command?"

"Mr. Powers, I am no slave nor a naïve child easily duped by some false prophet. No, not at all. I am fully aware of the situation and am here voluntarily, at my own volition."

"How old are you?"

She does not hesitate. "Late thirties—maybe more, maybe less."

"You don't know?"

"Times were difficult in China when I was born."

"You look like you're in your early thirties."

"Thank you."

"You say you're independent, but why would you agree to have sex with a complete stranger?"

"Oh, believe me, Mr. Powers, you are no stranger."

Now I am angry. "Really? And you have been with me from the beginning. Following my every move?"

"Of course not," she replies, utterly ignoring my sharp tone. "I have read all about you in the most accurate source—your own writing."

"Where did you find my writings?"

"Buandelgereen gave them to me. She found them in the car you came in."

I want to dismiss my writing as inaccurate, but that would mean denying the truth of my own memory. Naturally, dear Reader, you and I both know that truth is in question, as it has always been. But that is not for me to admit! This woman has trapped me, and I tip my hat to her astute maneuver.

"I see," I say, buying time. "Yes, well, it is good you did your homework. Question is, can you be attracted to me?"

"No need."

This is less than an optimal answer. If my desire did not deflate, my ego did.

"Why?" I ask, a bit too aggressively.

"Because I am already attracted to you."

"How?" I feel better. I look at her again, more closely. True, she is Asian, and bears a resemblance to someone who still eludes me. Yes, definitely, she bears a resemblance to . . . someone . . . or something I can't put my finger on.

Tamara stares at me expectantly.

"What about me attracts you?" I ask quite reasonably.

Her serious expression melts away, and a guileless, extraordinarily hopeful openness spreads across her features, lighting them with joyous, unmistakable excitement.

"Do you have chocolates?" she asks as if she has been deprived of their magical qualities for years.

"What?"

She claps her hands like a child waiting impatiently for her Christmas present.

"A chocolate!"

"No."

"Oh, that's too bad!" she exclaims brightly.

Why does she remind me of someone I have met before? Sure, she physically looks like someone from my past, or *Her*, but the quality within is completely different.

While I am contemplating this thought, her eyes restlessly scan the room.

"Munchies?" she asks.

"What?"

"Munchies. Do you have any munchies?"

"Don't they feed you here?"

"Never enough." She approaches seductively and rubs her leg against mine. "In the drawers?"

Again, I dumbly reply, "What?"

"Any munchies in your drawers?"

By now, her behavior is getting under my skin. "No."

She sighs dejectedly. "Then let's have sex."

My body is unprepared for this level of adolescent gymnastics. "Not right now. I need to know you better."

"What's to know?" she asks, springing up and removing her clothes.

Admittedly, while beholding the magnificence of her naked body, I see her point. My lust gets the better of me.

"True, true," I mumble. As I hesitate, she sweeps my bumbling hesitation aside, jumps atop my unprepared bones, tears off my clothes, then crouches on the floor on all fours, clearly wanting me to take her doggy style. With a flash of horrible insight, I pull on my trousers and rush out of the room to find Buandelgereen. I see her in one of the main chambers.

"Buandelgereen!" I shout at the top of my lungs.

She turns and looks at me in surprised curiosity.

"You have given me a dog! And a hunchback!"

"What? Tamara is beautiful!"

"True, but she is a dog!"

"What do you mean?"

"I mean, she is Temulun, the boxer dog!"

"Michael, I am afraid your schizophrenia has finally gotten the better of you."

"No!" I insist. "She is Temulun! How did you do it?"

Buandelgereen smiles as if catching on to a joke. "Temulun loves you—after all, you give her treats."

"So, you admit it!"

"Think, Michael. How could I possibly transform a dog into a lovely woman?"

"You tell me."

Buandelgereen sets her jaw. "You will stop this nonsense and sleep with her."

I give her a wicked grin. "And what if your son of the son turns out to be a half-dog, half-human?"

"Michael, any more talk like this and I am sending you back to the institute."

This shuts me up, as she seems quite serious. Still, I remain skeptical.

"Call Temulun! Where's Temulun?"

Buandelgereen calls someone over. "Go find Temulun," she orders.

The man says, "She is out scavenging somewhere."

"Find her."

He leaves.

"I'll wait," I say, crossing my arms stubbornly.

"Fine."

Ten minutes later and Temulun is leaping all around me. I no longer understand her words, but her body language is unmistakable.

"You want a treat?" I ask. She wriggles harder, that boxer shimmy bumping her hips against my shins.

"Stay here!" I cry, and run back to my room. When I burst through the door, Tamara is asleep on my bed, curled in a tight ball, still naked. For the first time, I scrutinize the bulge in her back. It is oddly attractive, as many unusual features in women can be.

This astounds me. Dear Reader, do I accept the evidence and assume Tamara is a real woman, or do I cling to my (apparent) delusion? Looking at her lovely body, and the sensual curve of her back makes me reconsider my objections—hunchback or not. . . .

~ Getting To Know You ~

I'm writing this two weeks after my last scribblings. Tamara and I can now laugh about my foolish suspicions, but she still asks for treats. I introduced her to Temulun; they get along famously—kindred spirits. Once we started, we didn't stop. We still haven't. If Goddess wants a kid, *She'll* get one, assuming effort has anything to do with it. When I got past Tamara's superficial exterior, I found a truly profound intelligence. How can someone who can discuss Kant, Schopenhauer, and Zhuangzi at once be so akin to a guileless puppy? Therein lies the paradox.

Once, when we sat together at my favorite spot among the boulders, I asked her about whether Goddess is real. She replied by throwing old Schopenhauer back at me. "Every man takes the limits of his own field of vision for the limits of the world."

As I mulled over this statement, she asked, "Do you have a treat?"

Go figure.

I carry small chocolate treats to give her now. Ah, bliss! I try to penetrate her thoughts so I can write about her in depth, but something blocks me. Perhaps it is the opaque nature of her puppy-like qualities. Maybe Tamara really is *Her*—Goddess—after all. Deep and capricious, beautiful, and dog-like. Moreover, I am allowed to make love to her 'til the cows come home, and even long-dead Storyteller is rejuvenated by the ecstasy.

~

Okay, I've decided. I'm going to assume Tamara is a physical manifestation of Goddess—and the child that results from our union will be a demigod, or demigoddess, and I will be like Mary, except male . . . a virgin? . . . no, perhaps that won't work. All this sex has brought me down from my lofty role as a super schizophrenic savior of suffering humanity to the level of a perpetually horny normal. Have I discovered a cure for schizophrenia, or am I just having a schizophrenic's midlife crisis?

When Buandelgereen said I would die, it made me pause. When one contemplates their own imminent death, it is reassuringly speculative, but when another person confirms the fact, it erases a shallow scratch and replaces it with the deep stab of a dagger. The destination—Stillness—is so much more pleasant than the trip. I am startled to realize my entire life has been the trip. Even more reason to give in and accept the comfort of Tamara's arms—real or imagined.

"What are you thinking?" she asks.

We're lying together in bed, and I turn to look her in the eyes. "Don't you know?"

She laughs. "You keep assuming I am some sort of apparition that shares your thoughts. No such thing. I am just a normal human woman—a normal (as you call us)—no more and no less. Well, maybe a little less normal with my hunched back."

"Doesn't my schizophrenia scare you?"

"Are your voices telling you to kill me?"

"No, quite the contrary. They tell me to make love to you."

"Well then, I am not afraid."

I pull back the covers and use my index finger to circle her nipple. As my finger moves, so does my memory, and Bowls' tab jumps into focus. Red flows from my fingertip onto her skin, and a blaze of scarlet bursts from her nipple into my brain. I feel myself slipping, my finger trailing off her chest, leaving a meandering red scar.

~

"Michael?"

I am aware it is Tamara's voice, but I know I have lost track of time.

"Michael, are you with us?" she asks with an amused smile.

"Why are you smiling?" I ask peevishly. "Do you know where I was?"

"I can guess."

"You don't seem very concerned."

"I'm not."

While inhaling the ambrosia, I notice she's munching on a chocolate.

"How much time has gone by?" I ask.

She shrugs. "An hour or so."

"You don't seem concerned at all."

"I already told you, I'm not. Why should I be? These episodes of yours are not rare, or am I mistaken?"

"Um," I grunt. "Usually people get concerned."

"Not me."

Now I am curious. "Why not?"

"Want a treat?" She holds out a candy.

"Jesus Christ!" I knock it away.

Unperturbed, Tamara looks around. "Not here."

"What?"

"Jesus Christ is not here." She leaps out of bed and retrieves the candy. "Waste not, want not."

I look at her naked body, but see no signs of red. She follows my eyes. "Oh, I forgot!" she blurts, and casually walks to the dresser. She picks up a lipstick, then immediately puts it down. "Oops, I'll be right back."

Water hisses on and off down the corridor. Tamara returns a few minutes later, her hair soaking wet. She carefully combs it back and picks up the lipstick, slowly running it around her nipples.

"Last thing Dr. Tavaris saw," she says with a pout. "Poor man."

I sit bolt upright. "How do you know that?"

"You told me."

"I did?"

"Of course." She goes to the desk and holds up a sheaf of papers. "I can read."

~ *Hoisted On A Petard* ~

Dear Reader, what am I to think? If you have been with me this entire journey, you must know I am becoming more and more divorced from reality . . . or truth. I must depend upon you, as usual, to separate the wheat from the chaff. I am sure your best guess is that I have been making this all up while in the institution. Perhaps, but I honestly think you are wrong. How do I know? Very simple. I look around and see no attendants, no nurse's aides, no nurses, no doctors. Perhaps I'm dwelling in an empty cave, but I am certain it is a cave, not an institution. Built on a rock foundation, the rest of this structure is solid and true. Or, as Huck Finn would say, "Mostly."

None of this is getting me any closer to my goal. Worse, Goddess keeps changing the goalposts. I must focus. On what? The iron door. Sex with Tamara may be the work of Goddess, but I have my own work to do.

"Well?" asks Tamara, still holding the papers.

"My writing."

"Exactly. One might say—" she chuckles—"I can read you like a book."

"Very clever, Tamara."

"I'm out of chocolates. Do you have a treat?" She jumps up and down clutching her hands as if pleading.

"Tamara!"

Buandelgereen's voice is loud and commanding. Tamara stops and looks at her, tilting her head like. . . .

"Tamara, come with me."

"Do you have a treat?"

"Yes."

Now, I am as confused as you, dear Reader. I lower my head in utter despair. Have I been duped again? More delusions? Hallucinations? Suicide really crosses my mind in a serious way. But just as I begin to plan ways to do it, Tamara returns with Temulun at her side. She looks at me coyly.

"Buandelgereen thought you were confused, so I brought Temulun. Truly, Michael, you are the silliest man in the world. Do you really think I am a dog?"

"It had crossed my mind." Temulun looks at each of us in turn, then puts her front paws in my lap.

Tamara laughs heartily. "It is true; she and I are spirit sisters. Surely, you cannot be so amazed. I mean, after all Michael, you have seen talking ants, a God, a Goddess, a magical woman, talking sidewalks, and all the rest. Are doglike qualities in a woman so hard to believe?"

I pet Temulun while squirming under her weight. "No, I guess you have a point. I mean, loyalty comes to mind."

Tamara's eyes burn through me. "Yes, but protection is also a part of it. The willingness to die defending one's master."

"I am not your master, Tamara."

"True, but my meaning goes beyond. Dogs will die defending human infants."

My back is up. "I am no infant, Tamara."

"Oh, yes! Yes, you are! You have seen love and death, joy and pain, war and peace, mental illness and health, yet you are no more than an infant if you continue to assume treats are not paramount."

I shake my head. "Come on, Tamara, that statement is absurd on the face of it."

"Humans are absurd. You are absurd. If it weren't for the treats you give me, your lovely penis, and your position as the father of the child, I would find you very much . . . less attractive."

"And my intelligence?"

"Sorry, Michael, it is riddled with disease."

"Thanks," I say glumly.

"Have no fear, Michael, I absolutely adore diseased minds."

"How so?"

"I've often fallen into diseased minds, into the holes that pockmark their reason, and I find more wonder than Alice did."

I am fully alert. Something in her words. Something in her tone. Something in her implications and accusations. Something.

"Give me an example," I say.

"You."

"No, no! Give me a different example."

"You are my only example."

"But you just said—"

"You are my only example."

I scoff. "I don't believe it!"

She looks at me sympathetically. "Once upon a time, when I myself was ill, I fell into my own holes."

I am dumbfounded. "You were mentally ill?"

"Of course. Why do you think I'm here?"

"To screw me and get pregnant," I say with no small amount of sarcasm.

"That is only part of it."

"Are you schizophrenic?"

"Perhaps."
"Yes or no?"
"No."
"Then what?"
"Yes."
"Christ, Tamara! You have no idea how tired I am of riddles! What are you?"
"What I was, I am no longer."
"What were you?"
Tamara looks at me curiously, as if unused to being asked such a question.
"Haven't you guessed?"
"No."
She smiles from ear to ear and tilts her head. "Do you have a treat?"

Chapter Thirty-One

Enter Ruska the Detective

The Case

It was an odd set of circumstances, to be sure, but Emile Ruska had seen facts more bizarre in his long career, or so he liked to think. On the surface, the case seemed rather straightforward: two psychiatrists dead under unusual circumstances, and a schizophrenic patient on the loose. A logical detective would conclude the patient had some involvement, or at least connection, with their deaths. So did Ruska, as he prided himself on being logical. At the beginning of the investigation, he pursued the case as any thorough detective would. Problem was, the suspect was quickly cleared of suspicion in the death of the female psychiatrist, and worse, her colleague whose body was found along a highway appeared to have died from a heart attack rather than foul play. Furthermore, the suspect's compiled writings, which may have given invaluable clues, were missing, along with Dr. Tavaris's car. Odd indeed, but not beyond a solution with the application of logical, thorough police work. Ruska was just as confident as Tavaris had been, in his own way, that his experience and skill would soon solve the case.

Of course, at the very beginning of the investigation, Ruska followed the advice of Fred Miller, a private detective who had previously tracked down Michael Powers. "Ten to one, he has returned to that cave in the desert," said Miller. "When I found him there, he thought it was full of people. Crazy guy. Yup, he'll go back there to be with all his ghosts, or hallucinations, or whatever." Initially, Ruska felt that Miller's lead presented the best opportunity to quickly locate the patient, particularly given the fact that Dr. Tavaris's body was found on the side of a road that passed close to the cave. However, when the police arrived, the cave turned out to be empty, with no evidence of any recent visitors. A string of witnesses was questioned, from Marie Telles to Mark Powers, but the interviews yielded nothing. Ruska now assumed the key to finding Mr. Powers lay with a Mongolian woman who still had not been tracked down. Unfortunately, all avenues to trace her had led nowhere.

Close to retirement, Emile Ruska was in his late fifties, a large, lanky man with facial features that arrested the gaze of any onlooker. His head was long and horse-like, yet peculiarly handsome, with a square jaw, a chiseled, angular chin, and pronounced cheekbones. He wrote poetry in his off-hours, and literary types often pointed out his resemblance to Boris Pasternak. Not averse to this comparison, Ruska had used his commanding looks to his advantage. A confirmed bachelor, he had relationships with a number of women, but none of them touched his heart enough to draw him away from his treasured independence. Now, in the privacy of his office, he pondered this latest case with his usual meticulous care. *Find the Mongol woman, find Michael Powers*, he thought. Question is how to find her? Surely, a woman as distinctive as people described Buandelgereen couldn't hide forever.

Ruska had taken all the normal steps to locate her, and he had waited longer than usual for any leads to materialize. None came. His caseload was full, and while investigating a variety of other disappearances and suspected murders, he could never quite get this Michael Powers out of his mind. Perhaps it was the schizophrenia aspect. Tonight, he decided to focus once again on the Case of the Missing Schizophrenic, as he labeled it. Stories from the institute's staff about mysterious happenings surrounding the deaths of Gail Hess, Adam Camara, and Dr. Tavaris, intrigued him and prompted him to canvass others about these dark mysteries. June Moore, Marie Telles, and Mark Powers filled in many gaps, but he still fumbled in the dark about most of the underlying facts. These hints of ghostly apparitions and medieval-style possession made him consider the case more alluring than the usual garden-variety disappearance, and his naturally poetic nature conjured a host of complicated subplots and shadowy motives. He had read the mystery genre thoroughly, with its secret cults, mysterious covens, exotic women, and esoteric clues, all leading the hero on a merry chase past the labyrinth of contradictory leads to ultimately solve the case at the last moment before the monstrous perpetrator murdered again. While he had always been able to separate such silliness from his work, he enjoyed the romanticism of pulp tripe, and its tropes always hovered in the background of his mind.

Realizing the absence of Mr. Powers's writings represented a lost treasure trove of clues, Ruska at first decided to recreate, as much as possible, their contents. But in another odd twist, the only psychiatrists who actually read the writings were dead. Could that be the common connection? The thread that bound them all together? Ruska made the decision to start his reconstruction effort with a call to the son, Mark Powers, now living with his Vietnamese wife on the East Coast. Arrangements were made and the conversation took place by speakerphone in a large room at the station. Ruska made sure his most trusted deputies were present.

The more Mark Powers talked about his father, the more interested Ruska became: a quarreling God and Goddess, a statue that emitted taps from inside, a mysterious woman speaking in riddles, a warrior ant, dinner parties attended by ghosts, a tunnel in Vietnam, the odd behavior of Doctors Hess, Camara, and Tavaris prior to their deaths, and so on. By the end of the call, Ruska had many pages of notes, almost every line marked in the margins by his own symbols for "doubt" or "evasion" or "follow-up," and a dozen others. During the debriefing, various impressions were passed around the room, but Ruska barely listened. His mind focused on the Mongol woman and the cave. *Perhaps there was more than one cave*, he thought. *Perhaps the cave where Miller found him was only one of many. Or perhaps there was a secret room or chamber where other people hid.*

Ruska turned to one of the younger detectives on his left.

"Bob, I need you to get in touch with the closest Forest Service station to that cave and connect me to an expert tracker for that area."

He turned to another man sitting nearby. "Dustin, contact the Mongolian-American cultural associations in San Francisco and Los Angeles. I know we already did, but try again. This Buandelgereen woman might have turned up. And I want everyone to double down on efforts to locate Tavaris's car. It's out there somewhere."

Once Ruska put these tasks in motion, he returned to his office and repeatedly played the tape of the conversation with Mark Powers. As he listened, he found himself becoming more interested in the suspect's writings than in the man himself.

~ *Desert Days* ~

Michael Powers sat with Tamara outside the cave, basking in the early morning coolness. They silently watched sunlight illuminate the rocky hills in a bright line, moving, elevator-like, from the top down, while dark shadows slid into the valley like water into an unseen drain. That welcome sun would soon bake the desert floor, but for now, the panoply of colors mesmerized the two onlookers. Michael studied Tamara as she munched on a treat. For a long time, his eyes followed the distinctive curve of her back, the lovely arc beckoning like a question mark inviting an answer. He focused on the workings of her jaw, admired her long, smooth neck, and the deceptively strong feminine muscles.

"Beautiful, isn't it?" he remarked, just to break the silence and get her to turn toward him. He loved seeing her full face aglow in the light. She did not disappoint.

"Yes, it certainly is," she replied.

"Almost as beautiful as you."

She smiled and turned her gaze back to the distant hills.

Michael continued to inspect her profile. Hunchback and dog-whisperer she may be, but he had fallen deeply in love. Why? He had asked himself this question many times and concluded that he felt certain she was a real flesh-and-blood person—unlike Theresa, whose shadowy specter never quite convinced.

Only his long-dead wife, Diane, conjured similar feelings.

Perhaps the idea that a real person would love him, rather than the echo of a person, made his heart ache with such longing. No hallucination could carry such weight, could be anchored so firmly in the surrounding landscape.

Tamara's substantive presence drew its shape from the desert itself. What could be more real than rocks and sand?

Michael reached out and rubbed her hump, as if to confirm the reality of her flesh and the firmness of her bones.

She purred under his touch, more cat-like than dog-like.

"Michael?" she asked.

"Yes."

"You do want to help Goddess, don't you?"

"I thought Buandelgereen was your goddess."

"She is."

"And?"

She turned and stared into his eyes. "You do want to help Goddess, don't you?"

He chuckled. "Of course. Haven't I been helping by making love to you? At least, that is what I've been told. Orders, you know."

"Are you willing to do more?"

"I gave at the office already."

"I mean seriously."

"What more?"

"Would you kill for *Her*?"

This took Michael aback, but his response came quickly. "No! I killed for the government, then I said, 'No more!' I may have inadvertently had something to do with the deaths of Hess, Camara, and Tavaris, and again I said, 'No more!' Now you ask me this?"

"Yes, now I ask you this."

"Who would I kill?"

"God," she said softly—"author of the rule that suffering must be."

Before he answered this bizarre request, Michael turned away and gazed in the distance to gain time, when he noticed the dust trail of a car very far off, heading toward the cave.

Happy to change the subject, he asked, "Are we expecting anyone?"

Tamara followed his eyes. "Probably Buandelgereen."

Both continued to stare at the dust cloud as it approached.

"That's not her car," said Tamara.

Michael thought he recognized an insignia on the side of the vehicle. As it came nearer, he could make it out.

"A U.S. Forest Service truck."

"Yes," said Tamara. "It is headed for the cave."

Michael jumped up. "We've got to warn everyone inside!" he exclaimed.

Tamara pulled him gently down and patted his knee. "Not to worry," she said calmly. "Just stay here with me."

~ Ruska Finds the Cave ~

Emile Ruska sat in the passenger seat next to his Forest Service guide and gazed out the window at the passing desert scene. He had decided to check out Fred Miller's cave first, just to make sure his men hadn't missed anything. Assuming he found nothing, his guide would show him a short list of other possibilities. Both men, by nature, were laconic introverts so, once the preliminaries were dispensed with, neither had said more than ten words for many miles. Finally, Ruska broke the silence.

"Are we close?"

"Very."

"How many times have you come here?"

"Once."

Emile shifted in his seat. "Only once?"

"Yeah."

"Is it so boring?"

Tom White Thunder shook his head. "No."

"Okay, how long ago were you here?"

"Six years."

"So long?"

"Yeah."

Emile chuckled. "I guess you've seen it once, you don't need to see it again."

"Nope, that isn't it."

"Well?"

Tom did not reply.

"Come on, Tom. What gives here?"

"Let's just say that place made a deep impression."

"How?"

Silence.

"Too crowded?" pressed Ruska.

"Nope."

"Okay, I give up," said Ruska peevishly. "Why so long?"

White Thunder stopped the Land Rover and gazed searchingly at Ruska. "Scratch an Indian and you'll find some . . . I don't know . . . what you white folks call superstition."

This comment now had Emile's full attention, but no further words were forthcoming. The car moved forward again.

"Spirits?" hazarded Emile.

Yet again the car stopped. White Thunder's eyes were invisible behind his dark sunglasses.

"That's one word for it."

"Tell me more."

White Thunder gripped the steering wheel until his knuckles turned white. Emile noticed and waited patiently.

"Truth be told, Detective Ruska, I didn't want to take you here."

"Why?"

White Thunder smiled, his teeth flashing brightly. "As you said, spirits."

"Evil spirits?"

White Thunder shook his head, groping for the words. "No, not exactly."

"Well?"

"Foreign spirits, not of this land. Not at all."

To Ruska's amazement, White Thunder then blurted out, "We should turn around!"

"You're kidding, right?"

The car started forward. "Yeah."

"Well," Emile said reflectively. "Fred Miller did not report seeing any spirits when he apprehended Michael Powers at the cave."

White Thunder stared straight ahead, statue-like, and spoke almost without moving his lips, "It was the guy he found who did."

"Tom, Michael Powers is a schizophrenic."

"Yeah, okay. We're almost at the stretch closest to the cave; then the road curves away. I'll stop at the nearest point, then we'll have to make a short hike to reach it."

"Wonder how Fred Miller found it?" mused Ruska aloud.

"Because I told him how to get there," said White Thunder, much to Emile's surprise.

"Funny, he didn't mention you in his report."

"I did not go with him."

"Why?"

"Because I refused. I wouldn't go."

"But you'll go with me?"

"Yeah."

"Why?"

"My own reasons. Here we are."

~

The two men headed for the cave. White Thunder led the way, his boots easily traversing the rocky ground. Ruska followed, cursing under his breath that he wore city shoes, already filling with sand after a few steps. Neither noticed two figures watching from a boulder-strewn ridge above.

Ruska became aware that the farther they walked, the more White Thunder slowed.

"We getting close?" he asked, huffing more than he wanted.

"Yeah. Let's stop for a moment."

"Why?"

White Thunder looked around uneasily, but did not respond.

"Why?" Emile repeated. "I'm not tired."

White Thunder ignored him and sat on a flat rock. He set down his daypack and pointed. "Keep going about a hundred yards in that direction and you'll see it."

Ruska's eyes widened in disbelief. "You're not coming?"

"Can't."

"Can't! Why not?"

White Thunder tossed his daypack at Ruska's feet. "There's water and a flashlight in there. Take it with you."

Ruska flushed in anger. "This is damn ridiculous! You're a grown man, Tom!"

White Thunder smiled. "As are you. Go. I'll wait here. Besides, you're immune."

"And if I get lost?"

"You won't. Can't miss it."

"Look, investigators already checked it out. Where were your spirits then?"

White Thunder shrugged. "Immunity requires blindness."

"Shit! Fine! But your boss will hear about this."

White Thunder shook his head. "He won't come here either."

"Christ!" exclaimed Ruska disgustedly. He scooped up the pack and started off.

As he walked, Ruska remembered White Thunder had used the word 'immune' as if that excused him from fulfilling his responsibility. *What the hell does that mean?—that I'm educated? Civilized? White?*

While these thoughts ran through his head, he had been looking down to avoid spraining his ankle on loose rocks. When he paused and looked up, the cave entrance gaped ominously before him. The impact of its sudden proximity caused Ruska to utter a guttural, "Oh!" that seemed to echo back from the cave.

Inspecting the ground, he detected no evidence of disturbance, no signs of any human activity, and he wondered what happened to the tracks left by Miller and the investigators who came after. Now he felt he operated on his turf—a detective investigating the scene of a crime, and his confidence returned. "But," he asked himself, "what crime?"

He turned his attention to the dark opening that seemed to be waiting patiently. He pictured Tom White Thunder sitting on that rock and tried to brush away any lingering hesitation. But an unnerving apprehension continued to lurk despite his best efforts to ignore it. When he remembered that Fred Miller had apprehended Michael Powers with no problem, plus the lack of any reported abnormalities by the police, he laughed at his absurd misgivings, dropped the daypack outside, flipped on the flashlight, and stepped into the cave.

~

Ruska's first impression struck him with the physical intensity of suffocation. A damp, mineral stench filled the air, and a powerful feeling of unease made him pause. The cave greedily swallowed up the outside light, rendering the entrance chamber pitch black within a few meters. Even the beam from his flashlight was nearly powerless against the all-absorbing darkness. To make out any detail, he had to shine the light inches from its target. The blackness was so impenetrable that Ruska began to doubt the veracity of Fred Miller's story. *I bet good 'ol Fred collared Michael Powers outside this miserable cave*, he thought.

Nevertheless, he stifled his fears and moved unsteadily forward, aiming for the far wall. Tripping over rocks numerous times, he finally reached it and moved his hand over its uneven surface. A low groan seemed to emerge from the rock walls at every touch, and the irrational anxiety in Ruska's gut rose to a level that threatened to make him turn and run.

"Get a grip!" he exclaimed aloud, the echoes reverberating for what seemed an eternity.

Suddenly, he felt something push against the back of his leg, and when he reached back in alarm, a cold, wet object pressed against his hand.

Ruska let out an involuntary, "Ugh!" and rushed toward the exit, but tripped on a jagged rock and fell heavily to the ground. For a moment he was out cold, but when he came around, he felt disoriented and thought he was in bed having awakened from a nightmare. But the memory of that awful wet object brought him quickly back to his senses. A sharp pain radiated upward from his ankle, and he groped in the darkness for the flashlight. As he moved his hand across the rocks, something again prodded his leg, and he clumsily scrambled to his feet, thinking it must be a bear or mountain lion. He heard its breathing only inches behind as he limped toward the exit, expecting any moment to be leaped upon and torn to pieces. At last, he emerged into the blessed light. He snatched up the daypack without looking.

~

"You look the worse for wear," commented Tom White Thunder. Still sitting, Tom perused Ruska's filthy clothes, his limp, and a face bearing nasty-looking abrasions.

Ruska threw the daypack at Tom's feet.

"What happened?" asked White Thunder.

"Tripped."

"See anything?"

"No. Nothing. Empty."

Tom leaned forward and felt inside the pack. "No flashlight?"

"Lost it when I tripped."

"You didn't take long."

Ruska tried to appear nonchalant. "Nothing to see."

White Thunder stood and slipped on the pack. "Guess you're not immune after all."

Ruska did not reply, and White Thunder did not press, both happy enough to be leaving this haunted place.

~

As the men drove away, the two figures hiding in the rocky ridge above watched as the Land Rover's dust cloud unwound in the distance. They were soon joined by a panting dog, whose flapping tongue and bright eyes expressed more laughter than fatigue.

~ Ruska Awakens ~

White Thunder drove in silence, and Ruska began to chastise himself for acting so foolishly. Yet, he was not so foolish as to completely dismiss the disturbing nature of his experience. He thought of Dr. Hess walking naked directly into Michael Powers's door, then collapsing in a heap. Despite his skepticism, Emile had certainly felt a presence, or multiple presences back in the cave. While digesting these thoughts, White Thunder's husky voice interrupted.

"Do you want to see other caves in the area?"

Still angry with his Indian guide, Ruska had the urge to tell him to fuck off, but thought better of it. He wanted to say yes, but he had had quite enough for today.

"No, I was mainly interested in this cave. Besides, my ankle hurts."

"Sure," said White Thunder with a hint of sarcasm in his tone.

Ruska chose to ignore it. "Are there bears or mountain lions in these parts?" he asked.

"No bears," said White Thunder. "There is an occasional mountain lion, but coyotes are more common."

Ah! thought Ruska. *That explains it. Of course, a coyote!*

"Is that what you thought you were running from when you fell?" asked White Thunder.

Emile hesitated.

"Is it?"

"Well, it's true I thought I heard a noise and felt something press against my leg. Must have been a coyote."

"No way," said White Thunder. "Coyotes avoid people."

"Not this one."

White Thunder shrugged. "Whatever makes you feel better."

Ruska scoffed. "Let me guess, it was a spirit, right?"

White Thunder frowned. "Want to go back and check it out?"

Ruska ground his teeth and swallowed his anger. "Sure. In fact I would if I had a flashlight."

White Thunder reached over and opened the glove compartment. "I always carry a spare."

"If my ankle didn't hurt. . . . "

On the trip back to his office, Ruska vacillated between dismissing the cave incident as an embarrassing but completely explicable event, and the more disturbing notion of something more sinister. By the time he reached the office, he had fixated on the idea that the strange, wet probing he felt was certainly a coyote. He would return to the cave when his ankle healed, but next time he would bring another detective—a rational companion rather than some spirit-crazed Indian. Uttering a few cursory words to his colleagues, he went home.

~

Ruska had never come close to considering marriage, and his remaining a confirmed bachelor suited his solitary life quite well. He buried himself in work, proud he had not given in to the bottle like so many of his older single colleagues. In fact, Ruska was a dutifully methodical detective, but his true strength lay in an openness to unorthodox speculation when the case hit a dead end. His poetic nature, so often hidden from others, made him susceptible to explanations most would find unsupportable. Even so, he was not inclined to think in terms of ghosts and spirits—it must have been a coyote.

~ *Michael and Tamara Return to the Cave* ~

Michael Powers watched the Forest Service truck disappear over a hill, then turned to Tamara. "Do you think they'll return with reinforcements?"

Tamara laughed while petting Temulun. "No, they will not be back."

"But they saw everything!"

"No. Tom White Thunder stayed away—we've dealt with him in the past—and the other saw nothing."

"How is that possible? He went into the cave."

She shook her head. "You're schizophrenic, right?"

"Yeah."

"Then you should just think of this as a vast conspiracy involving brain implants and satellites—except not by the government, but by us."

"Us?"

"Us."

"Maybe I'm schizophrenic, but I'm a high-functioning schizophrenic. My hallucinations and delusions are not so crude as your insultingly stereotypical comment. How did you do it?"

"Do what?"

"Keep them from seeing the cafeteria, the rooms . . . everything."

Tamara looked down at the ground, as if crushed by his lack of trust. Suddenly, she snapped her head up and cried, "Do you have a treat?"

Temulun heard and wriggled her entire body as if seconding Tamara's request.

"Jesus Christ!" fumed Michael. "Is there anyone in this damn place who can give a straight answer? Goddess, *her*, you, all deflect and evade!"

"You want a straight answer?" Tamara asked, suddenly serious.

"Of course!"

"I'm pregnant."

Already? Of course. She's not human.

"So soon?" he asked, unable to keep the skepticism out of his voice.

"Yes."

~

It took a few moments for this announcement to sink in. Before Michael said another word in response, thoughts of passing on schizophrenia to his child rendered him dumb. True, Mark had apparently escaped such a fate, but his mother had been a normal. This woman, this Tamara, most certainly was no normal. *Perhaps, like Theresa, she is merely a hallucination. In that case, I'm off the hook*, he thought.

Something beyond his illness told him Tamara was most certainly made of real blood and bone.

"My God," was all he could muster.

Chapter Thirty-Two

What To Do?

Will This Child Be Real?

Dear Reader, what am I to do? I'm not so far gone that I don't understand the ramifications if this child turns out to be real—birthed by a real woman and shunted into a real world. I have experience with real people—Mark, for one. Diane, too. My-duyen. Yes, I know the weight of the real. But, dear Reader, is Tamara truly real? I still have my doubts. And even if she is, this child will be different. First, my seed is tainted by schizophrenia. As a result, this child will be the progeny of a union made between a schizophrenic and a . . . what? Is Tamara also mentally ill? Even more to the point, is Tamara a flesh-and-blood woman or a hallucination like Theresa. Even if Tamara is flesh-and-blood, is she as ill as I am? Lord! How can our corrupted DNA be the basis for a savior?

Not that I'm complaining, mind you. Making love with her has been rejuvenating. I almost feel young again. When I'm with her, my schizophrenia seems to fall away. Yet I keep going back in my mind to two knotty problems. First, how did Buandelgereen make people see only an empty cave? Second, what is behind the last iron door? Answer the one question and you automatically get the answer to the other. Which raises the real question: how do I get behind the last iron door? Will it be . . . like before?

No, I will not think of that at present. Tamara's body entices, not the door. If my schizophrenia is severe, and if Tamara is ill, what will we be passing on to our child?

Something extraordinary.

"No, Goddess, I reject that! I was supposed to be the son, and now I find I am not. Why did *You* change *Your* mind? I dwell between reality and delusion, unsure which is which. *You* said it is I who could eliminate suffering from the human race!"

No, Chosen One. You will take the next step, but not by eliminating suffering from the human race, but rather by eliminating the human race.

"All the death and destruction?—Goddess!"

No—you continue to be confused. Your misunderstanding is no doubt caused by your wild genes. The human race will be absorbed by a new, more powerful and empathic species—Superior Ones. Suffering will be kept to a minimum. The replacement of one species by another is always messy.

I have no response to this explanation, so I say weakly, "But I didn't know! Now I do. Next time, I will shoot God, not *You*, Goddess."

You will always shoot Me. To the end of time, you will shoot Me. All of you will choose to shoot Me. Never Him.

Now I am furious. "Look, with *Your* help I escaped the institution! With *Your* help, I hear sidewalks and talk to pictures and dogs! I now live in a cave, and I'm screwing *Your* choice for the mother of my children. Despite *Your* calling me weak, *You* have continued to support me."

We have merely nudged your genes, but controlling them is a different story. Thus, your so-called schizophrenia.

"Okay, You manipulate my genes. Lucky me! Why bother, if I will always betray *You* for God in the end? *You* have seven billion humans to choose from. Go find someone else!"

You have been chosen by Us to be the son. Now you are chosen to be the father of the next step.

"What if this child is a girl? Have *You* thought of that?"

There is room for more than one Goddess.

"And two Gods?"

Two minus one. Balance requires subtraction.

"Is that all *You* can think of now—killing God?"

I love Him, but to quote one of your human poets, "In our vile times . . . Man was, whatever his element, either tyrant or traitor or prisoner." I want to free those of you who are the prisoners of His faction.

"*You* love Him?!" I scoff in disbelief. "That's not true! *You* want to kill Him!"

First of all, Michael Powers, God and Goddess are metaphorical expediencies. We represent two factions of the Mentors. All of Us love each other, at least in the human definition of the term 'love'. It seems quite difficult for you to understand this.

"No, *You* do not love *Him*."

"Well, I don't know who *he* is, but I love *you* very much," says Tamara.

~

There it is again. Reality intruding on delusion.

"I trust you consider me real, Michael," says Tamara.

"So, you can read my thoughts?"

"Of course. You are quite simple."

"Simple-minded?"

"No, just simple. I like simple. Temulun!"

The dog comes bounding over. Tamara leans down and pets Temulun, saying, "You love simple too, don't you?"

I look around and see that we are standing outside the cave. How we got here, I do not remember. Now time itself seems to be slipping from my grasp. Temulun tilts her head back and forth, her tongue lolling out.

"She wants a treat," says Tamara. "As do I. Got two?"

I have a brainstorm. "Tamara, I have a ton of treats behind the iron door, but I lost the key. Can you get me in? If so, you and Temulun can have a lifetime source of treats."

She looks sideways at me. "Michael, really, do I appear to be as simple as you?"

"Simpler," I lie.

She looks at me as if fully prepared to sink a knife into my chest. "I'm carrying our child. Be careful, or you may never get the chance to see it."

The words and tone feel alien coming from her mouth, and they chill me to the bone.

Your bones await in the tunnel. Remember?

"Tamara, did you just say something?"

"I said to be careful in a very mean way, but now I am prepared to forgive you," she says in the most light-hearted manner. "Do you have a treat for Temulun and me?"

"In my room."

"Good, pregnancy makes me famished."

"And Temulun?" I ask.

"Sympathy pangs."

~

I instinctively look at Temulun and cannot help but smile. Is Temulun just an illusion? Somehow, a non-human animal would seem harder for the brain to concoct out of thin air, certainly harder than just another human being. For example, that fur coat! Human skin (or clothes) is as generic as water, but the fur of non-human animals is far more distinctive, and would require far more acreage of gray matter to replicate.

"Temulun is real," I pronounce.

Tamara tilts her head in sync with Temulun. "Of course, silly! What did you think?"

Now I feel properly foolish. Of course Temulun is real. "Always trust your dog," my father used to say. I do. I do. I trust Temulun more than Tamara, or Buandelgereen, or Goddess. In a gesture of gratitude, I lean over and massage her ears, pulling her head close to my face.

"You, I trust," I say unselfconsciously to the dog.

In response, I hear a low, blurred voice trying to form proper words, but hindered by some anatomical deficiency.

"Urrr . . . coooorrr. . . . "

"Try again," I say.

"Urrr . . . coooorrr. . . . "

"Come on, try again," I repeat, now desperately anxious to understand.

Temulun backs up a few paces and sits at attention, holding my gaze with her eyes.

"Of course," come the words, clear and unmistakable.

I turn excitedly to Tamara. "I have the gift of speech back!"

She laughs. "As Temulun says, of course! Goddess is merciful."

I tilt my head at Temulun and point towards Tamara. "Is she real?"

Temulun breaks out into a dog version of a laugh. "Real as real can be, silly. Goddess is merciful. How about that treat?"

I turn to Tamara with renewed confidence. "I can't believe you're pregnant with our child."

"Believe it." She unconsciously rubs her stomach.

"Don't you think I'm a bit old to be a father?"

"No."

Her denial is blunt and graceless.

She notices and softens her tone. "Don't be ridiculous—you're not that old! Besides, I'm young enough for both of us."

"Tamara, where were you born?"

"Mongolia."

"Mongolia! But you're—I mean, you hardly look Mongolian."

"How do you think I met Buandelgereen?"

"I don't know, how did you meet her?"

"At an institution in China."

My heart sinks. "So you were ill?"

"No, quite the contrary. My mother was, but she ended up back at the institution where she had resided as a patient. But, when she returned after the war, she was no longer ill and spent her time tending to others. Buandelgereen took her to Mongolia to have her baby—that was me."

I start to sweat and wait for more, but Tamara stops talking. I wipe my brow. "Go on."

"My mother died. Buandelgereen raised me. That's it."

"Your mother. . . . " I say, my words trailing off.

"What about her?"

"Was she a . . . oh, never mind."

Tamara gazed at me expectantly. "Go on, finish your question. You're so close, Michael."

"Could it be?"

"Could it?"

"Was she a hunchback?"

"Clever boy," says Tamara slyly.

"Child of Buddha!" I cry.

"Bingo!"

I can barely get the words out fast enough. "Child of Buddha is your mother?"

"It took you long enough. My hunched back has been staring you in the face. You could not . . . or would not . . . see."

"My god! I can't believe it! I mean, I have often thought Child of Buddha is merely a phantom brought to life by my pen."

"No, fool!" laughs Tamara. "She was as real as you own mother. In fact, I was raised on stories about your revered mother, Bai Meiying."

Truly, dear Reader, I am speechless. I must pause to breathe.

~ Child of Child of Buddha ~

"Now do you understand?" asks Tamara, after watching me stare dumbfounded for the longest time.

"Understand?"

"Think."

"I can't . . . too confused . . . but, you don't look that Asian."

"Just as Asian as you are."

"My god—who is your father?"

"No one of any consequence."

I ignore this and feel my heart constrict. I tremble. "Is it . . . my father?"

Tamara chortles. "No, no, no! You are the silliest of men!"

"Then who?"

Tamara disregards my question and shrugs. "I love my hunch back. It is like carrying mother with me all the time. And now—" she rubs her tummy—"thanks to you, my stomach will curve outward even as my back curves in the opposite direction, a sine wave moving through time and space. Up, down. Up, down. The universe craves symmetry."

"Tamara, who's your dad?"

"That is for another day. If you're not going to give us treats, then let's go to bed."

"Aw," whines Temulun.

"Tamara, I need to know who your father is!" I demand.

"Why? I told you; he is not John Powers."

"I know, but, who?"

She reaches out a hand and gently caresses my cheek. "Poor Michael."

I jerk her hand away. "Tell me!"

Tamara turns on her heel and walks away.

"Now you've done it!" barks Temulun. "Foolish human! Don't you understand what a treat is?" She trots off to follow Tamara.

~

I want to run after her, but something has nailed me to this spot of sand. It is hard to come to grips with such world-shaking news. Father told me Child of Buddha was unique, barely human, and could communicate with the Precious Object. What has Tamara inherited from her hunchback mother? My God, maybe she can understand the Precious Object! Is that what lies behind that iron door at the end of this damn cave? Does Tamara slip past it every night to be with the statue, or is she just another mental case holed up with me in this dark, psychotic dungeon? Remember what is inside the Precious Object? Me. It is me! Perhaps Child of Buddha, mother, father, and all the rest were listening to me, the unborn son, tapping away the entire time.

And, suddenly, it hits me! Marriage—marriage! If I am to have a proper family, if I am to have a son . . . or daughter, I must marry. Diane is dead, and Theresa was a hallucination (so they tell me). But how can I marry? Impossible. A fugitive from a loony bin! No way of getting a marriage license. Easier to get a death certificate. Is it easier to die than to live? Arguably, yes. The shades would have something to say about that. Truly, this is a problem. Am I simply to drop this child into the lap of Buandelgereen and her gang? No. I abandoned Mark, and I cannot let that happen this time. Yet, on the other hand, I cannot hang around the world of the living for another twenty years, especially if I am expected to remain quasi-normal.

All this time I have been standing stupidly, looking for all the world like a cigar store Indian. Do I follow Tamara into the cave, or do I head off in the other direction? Well, I'm not proud, so I decide to seek out Tamara. The question remains, who is her father? . . . Perhaps if I give her a handful of treats. . . .

~

Unfortunately, Tamara is nowhere to be found. I have looked everywhere, asked everyone, and had no success. Even Temulun has disappeared. I play a hunch and return to the spot in the rocks where we watched the detective. Lo and behold, there she is!

"Tamara!" I call loudly.

She visibly jumps, and Temulun races up to me, laughing and wriggling. After petting the insistent dog, I sit beside Tamara.

"What are you thinking?" I ask.

"The same thing you are."

"Which is?"

"What are you thinking?" she replies.

I laugh. "We could go on like this for hours."

"Then let us just be still," she says.

I fall silent and gaze at her profile. In my imagination, I see her golden skin turning greyish, a granite hue, and her hair waves more and more slowly in the wind until it freezes in place, like a still photograph of a flag mid-wave. She stares outward, a rock among rocks, a statue set down amidst the boulders. I am certain this is simply my imagination, but I instinctively reach out to touch her cheek, and it is as cold and hard as the stone she sits upon. I panic and look around. Temulun is similarly frozen, as granite grey as Tamara. Looking back at her, I watch the sand blow against her unblinking, stony eyes, and I scramble down the hill to the cave, certain my little psychotic episode will pass if I can reach my bed and rest. However, when I enter the cave, every person and fabricated object had also turned to stone. Only the electric lights remain to illuminate the massive tomb.

"What are you thinking?" asks Tamara.

I open my eyes and see her lovely face, returned to flesh and blood, and I breathe a deep sigh of relief. I run my fingers through her wild, silken hair, and a deep sense of contentment washes over my troubled brain. Contentment. Such a homey, comforting feeling. So rare. So fragile.

"I'm thinking about contentment," I tell her.

"Ah."

Temulun nuzzles my hand. "Treat?"

"Not now, silly dog."

A burst of sharp, soaring intelligence lights up Temulun's eyes. "Still don't know what a treat is, do you, Michael Powers?"

Before I get the chance to process Temulun's stunning transformation, Tamara rises and says, "Let's walk."

"Okay, but what is Temulun talking about?"

"Something you will not understand until the end. Now, enough—let's go."

We descend the hill and follow the same path to the road that the detective and his Forest Service guide used. Which reminds me . . .

"Tamara, why couldn't that person see what is in the cave?"

"Magic."

"I'm serious. Was it hypnosis?"

"If you insist."

"Damn it, just tell me!"

"Can't."

"Why?"

She laughs. "We're not married, so I'm not obligated to share anything."

"Then let's get married."

"Impossible. You're a fugitive, and I'm. . . . "

"You're?"

"Not really here."

"Don't tell me you're one of my hallucinations!"

"No, no! My goodness, your silliness exceeds all bounds. I mean, the government does not know I am in this country—thanks to father."

I catch her wrists and kiss her. "All right, that settles it! Who is your father?"

"You mean, who was my father."

"So, he is dead?"

"Not exactly."

"Tamara, you will not believe how frustrated I am that I can never get a straight answer. Not from Goddess. Not from *her*. Not from Buandelgereen. Not from you."

"We live in a curved universe."

"Oh, god! You've told me that before! Screw Einstein! Tell me straight out, who is your father?"

"My poor schizophrenic—Michael-Storyteller-lawyer-soldier—you really don't know? All the words you have written from the beginning, from your parents to now, from the first page to the numberless pages since, have been leading you to the answer."

"Which is?"

Fate starves at Probability's door.

Okay, I tell myself. This cannot be happening. I did not hear what I just heard. "What?" I ask.

Tamara looks at me strangely. "I said, 'the future stands atop every possible stair.'"

"What does that mean?"

"It means you have built the staircase, one upon another, reaching up into the sky, and the future awaits your climbing them."

"And your father?"

"He also awaits."

"Crap!"

Tamara tugs on my arm. "Here we are."

I look out and see only the road and the hills beyond. "Well, what of it?" I ask, trying to sound reasonable.

"Thank you for coming. I am at my wit's end with your delusions, and if you think rationally, that should tip the scales."

"Beloved Tamara, what do you mean? If you are going to insult me, I have other places to be."

"No, no. Have patience. Just wait here with me on this small road a tick longer. You will be along soon. While we're waiting, why don't you look around and admire what humans assume is God's handiwork—the rocks, the sand, the light, the shadows."

"I really do not—"

"Ah! You're near. Poor Michael. Spring runoff, snow's melting, hibernation's over. Let me coax you out of this cave and briefly reveal Them—teasing portents for you to ponder before returning to your guests."

"What are you talking about?"

"You come, dear one, you come."

"No, I must write!"

"Yes. But for now, look up the road. . . ."

~

Yes, dear Reader, I see it. My own car, driven by me, approaching us, weaving erratically.

~ *Loop d'Loop* ~

Fatigued after a long day at work and a rather intense therapy session, the man leisurely drives home through the desert on a fading spring afternoon. The road is deserted, so to pass the time and keep the voices at bay, he thinks about the dinner party he is hosting that night, picturing the peculiar guests he has invited and reviewing topics he might discuss with them. Eventually, he is lulled by the flat, sandy stretches lining the road and visions of the party unspool more and more slowly through his mind. He begins to nod off until he feels a shudder, then a rapid loss of speed, as if his car has struck something and is now pushing against it. The impact is gentle but firm, like a canoe bumping into a log, and his peaceful drift is disturbed. His head snaps up in time to see the car being enveloped by a dark shadow, a liquid membrane sliding past the windows. Before he has time to react, the membrane recedes in his wake. Hunching over the steering wheel, he peers ahead, maintaining a slow but steady pace. Everything looks the same, yet subtly different, imbued with an ominous gray that blurs the edges of shape and color. He glances at the clock on his dashboard and realizes that the sky seems darker than normal for this time of day—and it's getting darker. He turns on his headlights, though they make little difference; his earlier mood of pleasant anticipation transforms into deep anxiety.

While trying to clear his mind of fear (*just a daydream,* he repeatedly tells himself), he makes out what appear to be two figures shoulder to shoulder a short distance in front of his car . . . or is it one figure with two heads? He hurriedly presses on the brakes and comes to a stop, staring in disbelief. As if from the flickering images of a grotesque silent film, the two figures play out through the smudges of his windshield. At first they writhe in tightly bound Siamese knots, but then the twisting shadows break free of each other to become unfettered, whirling projections; morphing mini-tornadoes that transform in dizzying succession from humans to birds—then to fish—to trees, clouds, insects, mountains, reptiles—and back again to humans. He inches forward, certain that they are a mirage, a complex convergence of dusky light and moving shadows from the roadside scrub, but they remain. He flicks on the brights and cautiously accelerates. Still, they remain, adjusting to his speed, always hovering just above the road and outside the direct glare of his beams. He presses harder on the accelerator. No matter how he tilts his head, taps the brakes, or rounds a curve, they are as infuriatingly constant and fixed as motes in his eye, so he accelerates again. ***Thank God the road is deserted, worthless! You're driving like the maniac you really are! Kill yourself, not the rest of us!*** Abruptly, he pulls onto the dirt shoulder and stops again.

~

The car has stopped only a few meters from Tamara and me. Clearly, the person in the car—myself—can't see us. I stare in wonder.

"Do you remember?" asks Tamara.

"Of course, but why is he . . . or I should say, why am I here?"

"Just watch."

My avatar gets out of the car and walks directly up to me. For a moment, I reach out to stop him from colliding with me, but he merges into me like water merging with water. The car disappears, and my body feels heavier, weighed down with dread. I turn to Tamara.

"What is this, Tamara—more hypnosis?"

"The guests you had for dinner that night were real."

"No, they were figments of my imagination—my schizophrenia, as explained to me by Dr. Hess. I called them up to combat my loneliness, but Storyteller kept intruding."

"Yes. Where have they gone, Michael?"

"Back into my brain."

"No, they are all here."

"Where?"

"Here."

I pause. "Behind the iron door?"

"Of course."

"Are they waiting for me?"

"Yes."

"Then, let's go! I want to see them."

"Even Storyteller—the intruder at your dinner parties?"

"Especially Storyteller."

She doesn't reply, but instead quietly watches me, long enough to make me uncomfortable. I speak to break the moment. "When I called, they visited me in my house. Will they appear to me in the cave?"

"Your house is also behind the iron door."

Chapter Thirty-Three

Ruska Tries Again

Ruska Back to the Cave

The dirt road stretched far ahead and far behind Emile Ruska's filthy Land Rover, sitting motionless on a dusty turnout near the cave. This vehicle bore no insignia on the door, nor did it have a light bar. Long used as an undercover car for the Barstow police department, it was on loan to Ruska for an unspecified investigation. No one knew his destination—he had falsified travel logs and disabled the GPS. This time, he came prepared. Hiking boots, jeans, canvas shirt, and the usual Glock 9mm tucked away in a pancake holster at his side, and multiple flashlights.

Ruska sat in the driver's seat, hunched forward, staring out the dirt-smeared window toward the cave.

Fuck White Thunder, Indian extraordinaire! he thought.

He held up the most powerful flashlight he could find. *I'll be ready this time.*

He still hesitated to open the door. Strange rumblings made the vehicle shudder, which Emile ascribed to the wind (without truly believing it).

Damn imagination! It's this blasted desert. Give me an honest dark alley in some honest corrupt city in some section of town harboring a dozen murderers. That I understand. But here? No backup. Nothing familiar. Nothing. Just 'nature' in all its glory. Nature! Well, fuck nature!

He shook his head in disgust. *Christ! What am I thinking? Get out of this vehicle and walk to the fuckin' cave!*

With this, he threw open the door and strode purposefully toward his destination, cursing White Thunder the entire way, and congratulating himself for his tenacity. The closer he approached the cave, the more his pace slowed. I won't be like that superstitious Indian, he thought bitterly. A host of phantoms swirled and swooped through his mind, making him dizzy and unsteady. He stumbled and sank onto the same rock where White Thunder had sat.

Let me get my bearings.

Emile pulled out his Glock and held it up to the sun, turning it to reflect the gleaming metal and sinister barrel.

Useless, he thought dejectedly. *Stupid!*

The phantoms fluttered even more energetically, and he found himself flailing his arms as one might swat away a cloud of mosquitoes. He let out a short laugh, put the gun away, and quickly stood, forcing himself to walk toward the cave. Haltingly, he half-stumbled, half-walked, accompanied by the phantoms, now so crazed they practically blotted out everything but their own writhing forms. He remembered the wet nose—coyote or not—pressing against his leg, and tried to force the memory away.

"Keep going, keep walking," he kept telling himself. As in a dream, he could not go back, could not pause, and could not detour. All these swirling forms were figments of his imagination. He forced himself toward the web's center—the eye of the storm, the belly of the beast. After how much time he did not know, he stood before the cave entrance. The phantoms seemed to fold up their wings and fall away, leaving a grey void, impenetrable and bleak. Emile stared at the dark opening with rising trepidation. Taking a deep breath, he held his Glock in one hand and the flashlight in the other and stepped into the void.

~

Before he'd taken ten steps, a face appeared in the beam of his light. Emile let out a gasp. Staring back at him was a young woman, quite beautiful, face framed by a stocking cap. *She* smiled.

"Hello."

"Hello," replied Emile, feeling slightly ridiculous. "What are you doing here?" he blurted.

She flashed a set of perfect teeth. "Exploring, and you?"

"Exploring," he replied flatly. "See anything?"

"A cave, some bats, nothing too exciting. I was just on my way out."

"See any people?"

"People? I hope not. I was told this cave was pristine. I'm surprised to see you." *She* stared inquisitively at his gun. "Especially with that."

Emile had forgotten he held it in his hand. *Odd she isn't afraid*, he thought as he put the gun away. "Just in case."

"In case of?"

"Oh, a mountain lion, maybe."

She laughed. "I see. No mountain lions here."

"No. How did you get here?"

She turned and pointed at her backpack. "Hiked. And you?"

Emile chuckled. "I'm not as young as you. I drove."

The more he looked at *Her*, the more beautiful *She* appeared. "You mentioned pristine. Who told you the cave would be pristine?"

"Good question. I can't remember."

For the first time, Emile became suspicious. "Was it someone from the Forest Service?"

"Could be."

"Try and remember, Miss. . . . ?"

Her eyes narrowed. "Are you some sort of cop?"

He flipped his badge open. "Yup."

She laughed. "So that's it."

Odd how calm she is, he thought. *Her* self-possession was off-putting to him, so he raised the ante with a lie. "I'm investigating a murder."

"I see." Still the calm.

"How far into the cave did you go?" he asked.

"To the end."

"And?"

She shrugged. "Still a cave."

"And you saw no evidence of other people?"

"No."

For the first time, he noticed *She* had no flashlight. "Where's your torch?"

"Torch?"

"Flashlight."

"Don't need one."

"Don't need one?" he exclaimed. "It's pitch-dark in here."

She stared at him in a way that made the hairs on his neck rise.

"I can see in the dark."

Emile chuckled nervously. "Are you a bat?"

"I am your dream."

He thought he heard wrong. "What?"

Before *She* could answer, he felt something wet pressed against his leg. "Ahh!" he bellowed, twirling around to confront the beast. But nothing was there, and when he turned back to the strange woman, *She* also was gone.

"This isn't happening," he said aloud.

Leave! came a booming voice that reverberated through Emile's mind.

Terrified, he swept his flashlight around, but the beam could not penetrate such blackness. He closed his eyes to steady his rising panic, and when he opened them he was back on the same rock he had sat on earlier.

"Okay, now I know," he spoke to the empty air. It's hypnosis of some kind. That cave holds the key. I'm going back in!"

Emile jumped up and trekked decisively back to the cave. The moment he entered. . . .

The dark enfolded him; fluorescents hummed; a conference table swam up beneath his forearms.

~

"Emile, what did you find?" asked a junior detective on the other side of the conference table. Ruska blinked in astonishment. He was back in the station, surrounded by concerned faces.

"What?" he sputtered.

"You were just about to tell us what you found."

"I . . . I found a woman."

"You told us that already. And?"

"There turned out to be nothing there."

Low murmuring among the group, surreptitious glances. "Nothing?"

"Nope."

"What now?" came a question from someone at the table. Emile expressed no interest in who asked.

Emile stood. "Dunno, I'm going home to think."

"You just got here! Are you feeling okay?"

"I know I just got here . . . I know. But I'm not feeling well. Must be the heat."

More side glances. The next thing Emile knew, he found himself in his bed, nodding off.

~ *She* ~

Tamara and Michael lay in bed together, talking like an old married couple.

"Stubborn man, that detective," said Tamara.

"So, how did Buandelgereen get rid of him this time?" asked Michael. "Genies whisk him away? Hellhounds tear him to pieces? Call the Mafia?"

"Do you care how?"

"Of course."

Tamara leaned close and whispered in an awestruck voice, "It was *her*."

Michael sat up. "*She* is here?"

Tamara gently pulled him down. "Shhh. Yes. Something is up. I saw Buandelgereen and *Her* talking."

"About me?"

"About us."

"What were they saying?"

"Couldn't hear."

"Then how do you know they were talking about us?"

"I heard enough."

A knock at the door.

"Yes?" called Michael.

Buandelgereen's voice came through the door. "Both of you come out, please. I'll be in the cafeteria."

Tamara and Michael looked at each other, got out of bed, and dressed.

When they entered the cafeteria, Buandelgereen sat at a corner table. The other residents were uncharacteristically speaking in low tones, filling the room with a humming vibration, as one might imagine the noise surrounding a queen bee at the center of a hive. As they passed between the tables, a host of curious faces followed their progress.

"Are they real?" asked Michael.

Tamara looked startled. "Who?"

"Never mind."

They reached Buandelgereen's table.

"Sit," she said curtly. "Tea?"

"Always," said Tamara.

"No, thanks," said Michael.

Buandelgereen pointed towards Tamara's belly. "Everything all right?"

"So far."

The two women proceeded to exchange pleasantries.

Michael tapped his fingers nervously on the table and, finally, cut in.

"Is there a problem?" he asked.

"Emile Ruska."

"Who?"

"A detective."

"Oh, him." Michael chuckled. "Apparently, you have ways to deal with him."

"He will be back," said an unsmiling Buandelgereen.

Tamara tilted her head. "Is that a problem?"

"Yes."

"How so?" asked Michael.

Buandelgereen ignored his question. "It is necessary that both of you go behind the iron door."

Michael sat bolt upright. "Really?"

"Really."

"Good! This is what I've been waiting for all along!"

"Be careful what you wish for," said Buandelgereen.

Tamara looked down at her belly. "And the baby?"

"We don't have a choice."

"Wait," said Michael. "What are you both talking about? Is there a problem?"

The two women looked at each other but said nothing.

"What?" demanded Michael.

No response.

He slammed his fist on the table. "What?"

Then—nothing.

~

When he awoke, he was back in bed with Tamara. She lay on her side, breathing evenly.

A dream—his first thought.

"No, it wasn't," said Tamara, still facing away from him.

"Tell me what it means."

"It means we go through the iron door tomorrow."

"You have to understand, Tamara, this is something I have been hoping for. And now you are to come with me. I am so happy!"

"Good."

"Why aren't you? It will be an adventure."

"You're a very lovable, clueless, schizophrenic baby."

Temulun jumped on the bed. Tamara laughed. "No, silly girl, you can't come with us."

Her big, sad eyes seemed even sadder. "I know," she said. "These things are for humans, not for us. For us, it is simple: defects are eliminated quickly and mercifully. Not so for your kind."

Michael could understand Temulun's words. "Tamara, tell me what is happening!" he demanded.

"We are going far away."

"What is past the iron door is not more cave, I know that."

"No, Michael, you do not understand. We are going far away."

"Yes," he sighed. "I know, but that is the beauty of it. Far away from here, from the institute, the schizophrenia, all of it! Back to. . . . "

"Where, Michael?"

"Well, wherever it takes us. Any world is better than this one."

"Oh, Michael, you clueless child," she said softly. "You haven't the slightest idea, do you? Tomorrow you'll understand. They're already moving pieces against us.

"Of what?"

"Fool!"

"How can I know if you don't tell me?" He lashed back. "Look at me! I'm not as stupid as you think. We're going back to the tunnel, to my bones, to be re-dead in order to be reborn . . . among friends."

"Fool! Delusional babbling! You are not really schizophrenic, Michael."

"Then where *are* we going?"

Tamara turned over and gently caressed his cheek. "Tomorrow you will find out. Now sleep, beloved Chosen One."

"But—"

"No. Shhh. Sleep."

Suddenly, inexplicably, Michael felt terrified of this strange, beautiful hunchback. Despite her loving words, there rang a hollow note, as if one struck a giant bell anticipating deep, portentous tones, and instead was met with a tinny, unsatisfying squeak.

~ *That Terrible Night* ~

Michael could not sleep. Thoughts of what lay behind the iron door ran through his head. *Where are we going?* he kept wondering. *What world do we enter? What universe?*

Leaving Tamara asleep, he decided to walk to the cafeteria and have tea. Stepping outside the door, he was met with impenetrable darkness, so he retrieved a flashlight from the dresser and again entered the hallway. Everything seemed different. He turned the beam on the walls and ceiling but saw only bare rock. Entering the cafeteria, he was greeted with a rocky cavern, as ancient and untouched as if no humans had ever arrived.

"What? What?" he kept repeating.

Search as he might, only rock and sand met his gaze. He walked all the way to the end where the iron door stood solidly, the only remnant, the only proof that something human had existed here. His mind awhirl with shock and terror, he returned to his bedroom, but found Tamara standing where the bed had been. No bed, no dresser, no rug . . . only rock. Michael rushed at her, his eyes glittering in the reflected light of his torch, spittle at the corners of his mouth.

"None of it is real!" he screamed, raising the flashlight as if ready to bring it down on her head. He held it aloft and continued to shout. "None of it! Why didn't you tell me? All of you are against me! All of you!"

The flashlight came down hard upon her head. Tamara let out a groan and crumpled to the ground.

"Oh, God!" screamed Michael. He fell to his knees at her side, the flashlight leaning at a crazy angle against the rocky ground, illuminating a round slice of the mineral wall. As Michael wiped the blood from Tamara's head with his sleeve, he noticed a shadow move, and followed the beam of light. Sitting on a chair, legs crossed, sat *Her*, and behind *Her* stood Buandelgereen.

"I asked your father many times, and now I ask you, Michael Powers, how does one justify a life without cruelty, and therefore also without the distilled beauty of cruelty?"

Tears rolled down Michael's face, and he spoke like one utterly exhausted. "All of you."

~

Dear Reader, I have a terrible confession. It has not come up before due to my embarrassment. Here it is: I've occasionally committed violence against people. I tremble to tell you; Tamara was not the first. If you recall the apparition covered in bruises that came every night to that damn fortress . . . and Theresa. Well, enough said. Now you know, much to my shame. I blame it on my psychoses, but . . . ah. Life will tease you and tease you, then—slap!—knock you down. As soon as you rise to your feet, the teasing starts all over again.

~

"No answer?" asked *Her*.

Michael stared down at Tamara, who struggled to push herself up. He leaned over to help.

"Leave her!" *She* snapped. "You've done quite enough. Tamara will be fine."

"Yes, I am fine," whispered Tamara, now standing unsteadily.

"Then it is time," said *She*.

Buandelgereen nodded and without a word, walked away. Tamara followed, trailed by Michael holding the flashlight for both of them, as Buandelgereen seemed to need no light, but walked steadily on into the darkness.

~ *Emile Ruska Makes A Vow* ~

Upon awakening from a deep sleep, Emile Ruska fixed coffee and eggs. After years of eating alone, he had grown accustomed to doing his best thinking over meals. Before the eggs had settled in his stomach, Ruska made a firm decision. He would return to the cave with a squad of officers. *Can't hypnotize everyone,* he thought. His pretext for requiring so many uniforms would be the cave's labyrinth of nooks and crannies. "Let's put an end to this mystery once and for all!" he said aloud to the coffee.

Emile felt an unreasonable ecstasy, and, in such a state, he convinced himself the Mongol woman and Michael Powers were using the cave as a hideout—for what purpose he knew not. After a few more sips, his mood soured into dejection. *How could I let myself be outfoxed twice?* he chastised himself. Images of Dr. Hess slumped at the foot of Michael Powers's door kept intruding, broken only by similar images of Dr. Tavaris sprawled on the desert floor, and Dr. Camara dead on a cemetery bench.

Murder ruled out in every case, he thought morosely. *No wounds, no poison, no nothing.*

It suddenly struck him that his own fate would follow a similar path. For a moment, he considered passing the case on to another detective, pleading over-work, but quickly dismissed the thought. The lonely solitude of his existence demanded payment-in-kind to the society of companionship he so adamantly shunned. *No wife, no kids, so I'll pay my dues by solving cases to appease mid-life crisis expectations,* he explained to himself. *Ah! I'll end up like the others if I'm not careful.*

Akin to a physical sensation, he felt the insidious tendrils of Michael Powers encircling his heart, and he knew this case had an almost vegetative drive to root and grow into every crevice of his soul. *Is this what happened to the others?* he wondered. *Suffocated as surely as by a python. And now the perpetrator has slithered away, back to its dark place, awaiting its next victim. Well! I will oblige!*

Emile went to work harboring renewed resolve. At the next briefing, all of his previous doubts and hesitations had disappeared, and he rattled on about the necessity of returning to the cave in force.

"But you said there was nothing in the cave!" objected Dustin Trujillo, a fellow detective.

"True, true," admitted Emile. "But, at the time, I was exhausted and un-sure—the cave was too big. Now I know how to deal with it."

"I can't imagine this will be approved, Emile. An operation of this size will cost a bundle . . . especially with nothing to go on but your gut instinct."

Emile uncharacteristically brought his fist down on the conference table. "No! It is more than gut instinct!"

"Perhaps, but you said yourself you saw nothing," repeated Dustin in a more soothing tone, although he felt quite surprised at Ruska's unexpected vehemence.

"I said that, but it was just to gain time. To clear my head. Now I see clearly."

"I'm not convinced that will be enough for our esteemed bean-counters," said Dustin, framing his words carefully.

Emile frowned and leaned forward. "I'll make it work. Count on it."

~

However, Emile Ruska failed to receive official approval for the operation, and he now sat in a favorite bar, not at the counter, but in his usual small table in the corner. He had been coming to *PicYrPoison* nightclub for years, mainly due to the appropriateness of its name.

"Drinking alone as usual, Emile?" asked a middle-aged waitress setting down a gin and tonic followed by a bowl of peanuts.

"Of course, Emma," he replied. "Gives me time to think."

Emma winked with an overly made-up eye, dark liner and false lashes, giving her the look of a losing prizefighter. "You think too much, Emile. Less thinking and more action would do you a world of good. Instead of poetry, you should meet a good woman."

"Maybe."

"Thinking of a case?"

"Always."

"Rape? Murder? Burglary? Which is it this time?"

"Missing person."

Emma appeared quite surprised. "That's all? Is it a kid or something? Those little haunting faces on the posters will get you every time."

"No. A full-grown man, ex-lawyer, Vietnam vet."

Emma waited, knowing more would come.

"And a schizophrenic. Escaped from the institute."

"Oh, I wondered why . . . well, is he dangerous?"

Emile pondered this question for a while. "Yes, yes. Most definitely."

Emma shuddered. "Should I worry?"

"No. Not in the least. He is only dangerous mentally and physically to those trying to find him."

"Mentally?"

Emile popped some peanuts in his mouth and took a sip of his drink. "Psychiatrists," he muttered.

Emma's eyes widened. "He killed them?"

Emile hesitated, took another sip, longer this time, and said, "Yes, but—"

Someone across the room waved at Emma. "Be right there, hon!" she called. Then she leaned close and said quietly to Emile, "But you said missing, not a murderer."

"I know."

Emma hurried off, and Ruska pulled out a well-worn notebook, flipped it open to a blank page, and wrote, "On this day, E. Ruska decided to risk all. Third time's the charm."

Emma returned just as he rose to leave. "See ya, Emma. More than enough hard liquor, not enough hard evidence."

"Take care, Emile. I worry about you."

Emile laughed bitterly. "I'm not worth it, Emma." He wanted to say, "Worry about yourself," but instead said, "Go ahead, worry. It might do some good."

~

Before he knew it, the day had arrived to return to the cave. He had decided to investigate on his own time. No police cars, no back up, no official sanctioning of his actions. *No distractions this time*, he kept promising himself. *Wet nose or not, I'll keep searching until I reach the end—and then I'll search again. Can't get rid of me that easily, whoever you are.*

Again, the long, dreary dirt road into the heart of the desert rolled out before him. Heat waves distorted the view ahead, and a funnel of dust unspooled behind. Almost the entire way, Emile fortified his intention by repeating an iron determination to finish the task and blocking out any doubts that threatened to undermine his resolve. Like Sergeant Dam's mantra of, "Thank you, mother," as he approached the doomed Mr. Machine, Ruska repeated, "Finish the task," as he approached the cave.

The same turnoff—but this time no hesitation. Emile jumped out of the car, grabbed his backpack, and stormed up the now-familiar path to the cave. Pausing outside the entrance just long enough to retrieve his flashlight, he plunged into the darkness.

Nothing.

Nothing.

Nothing.

Ruska trekked all the way to the end of the cave without incident. He retraced his steps and searched again.

Nothing.

Nothing.

Nothing.

The only wet nose he felt was his own—from the damp, empty cave.

As the entrance drew nearer, suddenly Ruska's flashlight illuminated a figure huddled on the ground, arms wrapped around drawn-up knees, rocking and mumbling indistinct words.

"Hello, Mr. Powers," said Ruska prosaically.

~ *Michael and Tamara* ~

The last thing Michael remembered after Buandelgereen swung open the iron door was stepping through and being blinded by the intense light pulsating from the Precious Object. He held up an arm to block the brightness and looked back through the open door. Temulun's large eyes glittered with an intelligence that surpassed anything he had ever seen, reflecting every emotion he had ever felt. Then, the door closed, and he desperately groped for Tamara's hand, found it, and they walked forward, half-blinded by the light.

Epilogue

The Stillness

The Voices run amuck.
Madness has unmade him.
Yet in the ruins a seed whispered of a deeper cave still waiting.
The descent will carry him farther underground—into visions, obsessions, and
trials more harrowing than any he had yet endured.
Unchain the chains.
The Stillness listens,
And humanity moves down its long, final path.

9 781966 776062